WHISKED AWAY BY
HER MILLIONAIRE BOSS

NINA MILNE

HIS UNEXPECTED
TWINS

CARRIE NICHOLS

MILLS & BOON

First Published in Great Britain 2019
by Mills & Boon, an imprint of HarperCollinsPublishers,
1 London Bridge Street, London, SE1 9GF

Whisked Away By Her Millionaire Boss © 2019 Nina Milne
His Unexpected Twins © 2019 Carol Opalinski

ISBN: 978-0-263-27258-1

0819

MIX
Paper from
responsible sources
FSC™ C007454

This book is produced from independently certified FSC™
paper to ensure responsible forest management.

For more information visit: www.harpercollins.co.uk/green

Printed and bound in Spain
by CPI, Barcelona

WHISKED AWAY BY HER MILLIONAIRE BOSS

NINA MILNE

To my family for putting up with me
whilst I wrote this book!

CHAPTER ONE

BEN GARDINER, CEO and founder of Sahara Clothes, a global fashion house with retail outlets worldwide, stared across at his PA in horror. 'You want to take some time off next month?' he echoed. 'During Milan Fashion Week?'

'Yes.' Maree looked him directly in the eye. 'I know it's short notice but Edward wants to take me away on a romantic break.'

Ben opened his mouth and closed it again. 'And it didn't occur to Edward that you have a job?'

'Of course it did. But he won it—on a radio show. A two-week safari trip—it's the opportunity of a lifetime.' Maree took a deep breath. 'Actually, it's a bit more than that.'

'Oh?' Ben studied his PA. He could tell from her expression that she was working up to breaking bad news.

'We're getting married. The safari will be our honeymoon.' Once the words had spilled out, Maree smiled radiantly. 'And I know marriage is your idea of personal hell, but I am really, really happy and I want you to be happy for me.'

'I am happy for you.' And he was. Though a tiny bit of him was considering the impact on his work schedule. There was also the fact that... 'Isn't it a bit sudden? I mean, you haven't known Edward very long.'

'I know, but I'm sure this is what I want.'

Maree's whole face lit up, and obscurely Ben felt a sudden pang of near envy.

'I can't explain it, and of course I know there are no guarantees, but right here and now I am one hundred per cent sure that I want to spend my life with him and I know he feels the same.'

Any remaining tinge of green vanished as Ben manfully repressed a shudder and managed, 'Then I wish you every happiness.'

Which of course he did. He fully grasped that for some people it was possible to risk one's heart for love. It was just that personally he couldn't see the point.

Seeing Maree's sceptical look, he raised his hands. 'I am. Why wouldn't I be?'

'Because you know what I'm going to say next. My role will need to change a bit. Edward does understand how important my job is to me, and he realises that it is very hands-on, but I won't be able to work such insane hours any more.'

Ben knew he expected his PA to do way more than convention demanded—to go the extra mile. That was why he made sure he paid an excellent salary and chose the right person for the role.

'I thought you enjoyed this job.'

'I love it—and I've had a blast. But my circumstances have changed. I won't be able to travel at the drop of a hat, even if it *is* to a yacht party in Monaco, and I can't be on duty twenty-four-seven. Like the time last month when you called me at three in the morning to come to a business meeting.'

Ben gave a quick grin. 'OK. That *was* a bit much. But you have to admit it worked. That was an incredible deal we got signed—profitable and ethical. He even agreed to raise the rates he pays his workers to Fairtrade standards.'

'It was a fabulous deal, but I won't always be able to be part of that now.' Anxiety touched her grey eyes. 'You're not angry, are you? I'll understand if you want a new PA.'

'I'm not angry. At all. I'm happy for you and I would never do anything to jeopardise that happiness. If I start to expect too much or behave selfishly, make sure you tell me.'

He meant it; he would not be responsible for the destruction of another marriage. After all, he'd been responsible for the breakdown of his mother's—had been the catalyst and the unwitting cause of the rupture of a family.

His mother had had an affair and he was the result: a universally unwanted result. Unwanted by his unknown actual father, rejected by the man he had believed to be his father for the first five years of his life and loathed by his siblings, who blamed *him*.

In the bitterness of the divorce his half-brothers had elected to live with their dad and his mother had been stuck with him. She had also stuck *by* him, shown him care and love, and he would be grateful for ever for that. Even if in the deepest, darkest times of his childhood he'd wondered whether, if she could turn back the hands of time, she'd wish him away. And how could he blame her if she did?

Enough. He'd come to terms with all that. He had decided to live his life to the fullest and show them all— his birth father, his fake father, his siblings, the whole goddamn world. And he had. He had achieved a success attained by very few, and his mother would never want for anything—he'd made damn sure of that.

But right now he said, 'So what are we going to do about a replacement for you next month?'

'I'll advertise internally and see if there's anyone who wants to step in.'

It didn't take a genius to hear the doubt in her voice.

'I take it you don't think there will be many volunteers.'

'Nope.'

'Why not?' For Pete's sake… He was an excellent boss.

'It's difficult. I did talk to a couple of people I thought would suit, but… Well, one of them is recently married and doesn't want to go away. I asked Tom Oliver as well, but his wife has just had a baby and he doesn't want to travel to Milan.'

'There must be someone else.'

Maree shrugged. 'You're quite a hard taskmaster.' Before he could protest, she raised a hand. 'OK. A more diplomatic response might be to say you have high expectations.'

Ben sighed. 'I get the picture. You don't have a queue of qualified people who want to go to Milan with me. Fine. If need be I'll survive without a PA.'

He'd find someone else to go to Milan with him. Just in a different capacity.

Three weeks later

Sarah Fletcher stood in the ladies' restroom of Sahara Fashions' London headquarters, her trusty trolley of cleaning materials next to her, and ran through her mental checklist.

Floor mopped and polished: tick.
Toilets cleaned: try not to think about it, but tick.
Mirrors polished: tick.

Her gaze caught a glimpse of her reflection and she flinched. She still wasn't used to her natural hair colour—she'd dyed her hair for so long that the red now looked all wrong—and it jolted her memory neurons with grief.

Imogen. Her identical twin. If Imo was alive this was what she would look like too. But Imo *wasn't* alive. She'd lost her twin sister twelve years before. Diagnosed with leukaemia aged thirteen, she'd died after a two-year struggle against the illness. Snuffed out before she could experience very much of life. The unfairness of it all still burned.

Focus on something else. Before the still razor-sharp edge of grief and guilt cuts too deep.

A large notice hung up by the mirrors caught her eye.

Urgent Internal Vacancy
Wanted: Temporary PA to Ben Gardiner
Duration: Two weeks
Pay Grade: Excellent
For details contact Maree Whitaker

Sarah frowned, sure she'd seen other notices like it littered round the offices over the past three weeks—clearly there wasn't a queue of applicants. Which meant Ben Gardiner must be a difficult boss, despite being gorgeous, loaded and successful, as well as London's most wanted bachelor—at least according to the last article her mother had showed her.

For a moment Sarah allowed herself a daydream. She was a high-flying executive PA, rather than a mop-to-the-ground part-time cleaner-cum-sales-assistant in a clothing store... Though actually she wasn't even that. Worry twisted her tummy. The shop she worked for had closed down, so right now she was fully reliant on this job.

Keep calm. Somehow she would find another job. She had to—for Jodie's sake.

An image of her six-year-old daughter filled her mind—Jodie, with her vivid red hair and her gap-toothed smile.

The most important thing in the world was Jodie and she would give her daughter the best possible start in life. Guilt tugged at her again. She certainly hadn't given Jodie a good father. And her own stupidity in her teen years meant she was in no place to get herself a *good* job. Not with a criminal conviction, however unjustified, and no qualifications.

Steely determination filled her. She'd turn it around. She *would*. For Jodie.

But right now she'd better get on. She was on probation and she could not afford to lose this job as well. So it was time to go and empty Ben Gardiner's bins; it might not be high-flying but it would pay the bills.

Two minutes later Sarah raised her hand to push the office door open and halted as she heard voices from inside.

Ah...

In the past four weeks Ben Gardiner had never been in his office in the evening—most days Sarah was pretty sure he hadn't even been there. But someone was definitely in there now. A female, by the sound of it, and an angry one at that. Her higher-pitched tones were interspersed with the low, deeper rumble of a male voice.

Clearly not a good moment to empty the bins, then.

As Sarah stepped back the door burst open and a woman exited. Though 'exited' was an understatement. This woman swept out and anger radiated from each long-legged stride. Her dramatic swirl round to face the interior of the office was followed by, 'You will never know what you missed, Ben!'

Sarah blinked and realised the identity of the woman: short dark hair, endless legs, a classically beautiful face seen on billboards and fashion magazines. This was *Leila Durante*—supermodel and diva, who had the reputation of only dating the hottest, most famous bachelors in town.

Sarah stepped back into the shadows.

'When you change your mind let me know. But know this: I will not wait long.'

Ben Gardiner appeared in the doorway. 'I won't change my mind. So don't wait at all.'

The supermodel practically hissed and then marched off.

What now? In an ideal world Sarah would don a cloak of invisibility, but that wasn't going to happen. Perhaps she'd get lucky and Ben Gardiner would retreat into his office without spotting her. *Ha!* Since when did luck single *her* out?

Instead he turned to her. 'As first dates go, that wasn't great,' he observed. 'We didn't even make it to the restaurant.'

Sarah gulped. The man looked even better in the flesh than he did in his publicity photos and in magazines... He was tall and lithely muscular, clad in a dark grey suit that added to his aura of lazy power. His dark hair was rumpled, with a hint of curl, and he was tall and lithely muscular, with an aquiline nose, a six o' clock shadow— or perhaps better to say seven o'clock shadow—and dark blue eyes that added to his air of sheer sexiness.

'Um… No. But, just so you know, I wasn't eavesdropping. It's…' She gestured to the cleaning trolley. 'I was… um…about to…um…do your office and…'

For heaven's sake. This was ridiculous. Yes, the man was extremely gorgeous, hotter than hot coals, but that shouldn't render her incoherent.

He was a man, just like any other man—except somehow his genetics had conspired to give him the looks of a sex god. And genetics, as Sarah knew oh, so well, could hand out disaster—hence Imo had ended up with leukaemia and Sarah hadn't. Outwardly they had been identical, but inside Imogen had been doomed from birth. So she of all people should not judge anyone based on their genetic inheritance.

'Are you OK?' The deep voice held concern.

Pull yourself together.

She needed this job.

'I'm fine. Um…' If she said *um*… one more time, so help her, she'd kick herself around the building. 'I'll come back later to do your office.'

Ben frowned. 'Have you actually got any other offices to clean?'

'U— Not as such, but really it's not a problem.'

Now his expression held more than a slight hint of bemusement. Please, *please* don't let him notice that her legs seemed to have turned to mush. Along with her brain, clearly.

'I'll come back later,' she said firmly.

'Really—no need. I'm just finishing up; come in now. It's not a problem.'

Only it was. The wretched man seemed to have utterly messed with her hormonal balance. It was ridiculous, and she needed to get over it right now. He was the ultimate boss—a millionaire with a glittering lifestyle—and she was a cleaner on probation, a single mother who desperately needed to keep her job. So, time to lock down her hormones, get in, clean, then get out.

'OK. Thanks.'

Clutching the trolley, she followed him into the office.

Ben sighed. So much for his dinner date with Leila; perhaps he should care more, but in truth he didn't. Leila had completely overstepped the boundaries he'd clearly drawn out and thought she could get away with it. She'd had the temerity to arrange an interview with a celebrity gossip magazine for the two of them as a couple. Well, *she'd* misjudged her man and *he'd* had a lucky escape.

He glanced at the witness to the tail-end of their showdown; he hadn't really been able to see her in the dim light of the outer offices. Interest sparked as his fashion eye assessed her automatically. Medium height, long-legged, hair an arresting shade of red, scraped up into a ponytail, large brown eyes flecked with green.

Aware that his glance was on the verge of being overlong, he swiftly focused on his computer screen as she switched the vacuum cleaner on and started to push it around the floor.

Perhaps he should try to rustle up a replacement date for the evening? But the idea didn't appeal.

Leila's agent had contacted him to ask him if he wanted to take the supermodel out for dinner and he'd agreed. He'd believed that Leila was exactly his type of woman: a woman with the same expectations from a relationship as he had. Short-term and fun. As a bonus she already had fame and wealth, so he'd figured she wouldn't be after his.

Turned out he'd been wrong.

Yet, despite his annoyance, he could still smile. Who would have thought twenty years ago, when he'd lived in near poverty on a council estate, branded a failure, that one day a supermodel would seek him out?

The answer to that was no one. *Look at me now*, he thought. Literally. Sat here. For a moment he stared out of the immense glass windows of his office. Once his vista had been a run-down London tower block—now he overlooked some of London's most iconic attractions.

He returned his gaze to the computer screen, to the photos of the latest range of clothes about to hit the shops. *His* shops. *His* line. *His* brand.

A sound from behind him distracted him from his thoughts. There was a small intake of breath, the stalled whir of the vacuum, and he turned his head to see the red-haired woman hastily averting her gaze from the screen, a flush on her cheeks.

'Sorry. I didn't mean to look.'

'That's OK. Be my guest. It's our new range.'

'I...um...'

Stopping, she looked up at the ceiling in clear exasperation, though he wasn't sure why.

He pushed his chair backwards to afford her a better view of the screen and flicked through the pictures, talking as he went. 'The line is *über* ethical—Fairtrade plus—and the idea behind it is that the ordinary is extraordinary. That fashion should be aimed at everyone, and these are clothes and designs *for* everyone, because everyone can look good every day. Yes, people will have to pay a little more, but I want these to be clothes that people keep—not dispose of when another trend comes along.'

He looked up at her, struck anew by her exquisite bone structure, the high cheekbones, the set of those enormous eyes.

'What do you think?'

'I love it. The catwalk inspirational styles are still a bit out there, but they echo the idea of the ordinary being extraordinary. So that fringed dress is mad, but I guess a model could carry it off, and then you have that amazing fringed dress for the high street. And that asymmetric floral dress is fabulous. And those shoes...'

Her enthusiasm was palpable. It lit her face and a sudden frisson jolted through him. She was close enough that he could catch a whiff of berry shampoo and see the silken gloss of that glorious hair.

Get a grip, Ben.

This woman was an employee. Quickly, he moved his chair further away from her, to ensure she had space, and nodded. 'You sound like you know what you're talking about.'

'Not really. I used to work in a shop on the high street—just as a sales assistant...just part-time.'

'That's a lot of *just*s. It's an important job. I always say that our sales assistants are vital. They are the ones who interface with the customers—the ones who can feed back what the customer wants. They represent us—and they need to genuinely understand and love the merchandise.'

'Or at least be able to fake it if they don't.' As he

frowned, she gave an audible gulp. 'I only meant some-times people need the job because they need to pay the bills. In the real world a sales assistant may have to pre-tend.'

'Would *you* do that?'

Brown eyes met his directly. 'Yes. If it put food on my table, I would.'

Ben blinked and felt a sudden prod of discomfort. This woman was spot-on and how the hell had he forgotten that? A sudden memory flashed before him of his own mother, desperate for work, near-destitute because she'd been given short shrift in her divorce proceedings. She had applied for job after job, come home time and again after an unsuccessful interview. *Too many years out of the workplace. Not qualified enough.* She would have faked pretty much anything for a job.

That was the real world—exactly as this woman had said. The woman who was now looking at him with anx-iety in her eyes.

'But, for the record, I genuinely love what you've shown me. That wasn't faked. I hope I didn't overstep in any way?'

'No, you didn't.'

Ben realised that he must be glowering and that the woman must think it was because she had upset him. How was she to know that memories of his childhood still had the power to sear old wounds?

With an effort he forced a smile to his lips. 'Honestly. I'm pleased you like the new range.'

She ducked her head in a nod. 'I'd better get on, then.'

As the vacuum cleaner whirred back into life he re-turned his eyes to the screen and studied the outfit on display and the slogan above it. *The ordinary is extraor-*

dinary. Had he forgotten what that really meant? Was he so out of touch with the ordinary that he'd completely missed the mark with this new range of clothes?

Ben wasn't sure he liked the answer to either question.

Her voice distracted him. 'Well, goodnight. Thank you for showing me the new range.'

'Goodnight.'

He looked at her departing figure: straight back, long legs, medium height, slim but not skinny. Her words echoed in his head: *in the real world.*

'Actually. Hang on a second…'

CHAPTER TWO

SARAH HALTED MID-STRIDE. She'd clearly blown it. First she'd witnessed the whole Leila incident, then she'd been caught spying on his confidential designs, and after that she'd pretty much told him he didn't live in the real world.

Great! Clearly for some reason she'd forgotten that he was a multimillionaire CEO and her big boss. *Idiot.*

Slowly she turned. 'Did I miss something?'

'No.' His cobalt blue eyes held a thoughtful expression. 'Not at all. But I think *I* might have. I was wondering if we could continue our conversation over dinner.'

'Dinner?'

'Yup. I've got a table booked at Tatiana's. Seems a shame to waste it.'

'You want to take *me* to Tatiana's instead of Leila Durante?'

'Yes.'

'Why?'

Despite her best intentions, her hormones had registered that Ben Gardiner had ditched his jacket and was now sitting in rolled-up shirtsleeves that exposed his tanned forearms. Sarah wasn't sure what was so fascinating about the contrast between his pristine white shirt and the honey tone of his skin, but her gaze had snagged and stuck.

Perhaps she should just go along with this, but instead she said, 'It doesn't make sense. I am not exactly your usual type of dinner…*associate*. I'm not a model, or an actress, nor famous in any way whatsoever. Plus, you don't even know my name.'

To give him his due he had the grace to look a touch abashed, but not for long. 'You're right. What is your name?'

'Sarah Fletcher.'

Rising, he walked round the jut of his light wooden desk and headed towards her. 'Pleased to meet you, Sarah Fletcher.'

He held out a hand and for a few seconds she looked at it, reluctant to actually make contact. What was the matter with her? It wasn't as if they'd combust if they touched.

And of course they didn't. Yet as she placed her hand in his she registered strength and warmth. A tingle shivered over her skin and she stared down at their clasped hands.

She looked up as he smiled at her. 'I'm sorry. I should have explained this better, but now we're properly introduced would you come and have dinner with me? I'd really like to continue our conversation and get more of an insight into how sales assistants think and work. Maybe I've lost touch with what's going on at ground level, in the real world, and maybe you're the right person to set me straight.'

'So you want to go out for dinner with me to get my take, as a sales assistant, on the viewpoint of the ordinary woman on the street?'

'Exactly. No strings attached.'

Their gazes caught for a heartbeat and her brain scrambled. 'Strings? Um…yes. I mean, no. I'm good, thanks.'

Thanks? What was she thanking him for? And why was she still holding his hand?

Amusement glinted in his sapphire eyes now, but there was something else too—an awareness. And who could blame him? The signals she'd just sent out weren't hard to read; she'd practically drooled and this man was no doubt an expert in the art of body language. This was nuts. She had barely noticed a man in the past six years.

If she had any sense at all she'd refuse his offer, go home and have a nice cup of tea with her mum. Mind you, her mum would think she'd lost the plot; her hormones certainly knew she had. What possible harm could there be in having dinner with him? One meal. In a restaurant for the stars. With the man who headed up Sahara Fashions.

Whoa. Hang on.

The man headed up an entire retail corporation. It was time to get over her hormones and start using her brain. This was an opportunity. A chance to get herself a job. If Ben Gardiner recommended her to one of the Sahara stores, perhaps she could wangle an interview. But first she had to let go of his damn hand.

Doing exactly that, she stepped backwards. 'Um… Dinner sounds great. Though I do have a request.'

'Go ahead.'

'I told you I used to work in a clothes store. Unfortunately it closed and I lost my job. I would love to work in a Sahara outlet and I wonder if you could interview me over dinner to see if you think I'm a good fit. And if you do maybe you could recommend me for a sales assistant job.'

Sarah paused for breath, aware that she had dug her nails so deeply into the palms of her hand that it hurt. She forced herself to relax as he studied her expression.

'I leave recruitment to my managers—I don't tend to interfere. If you're interested in a vacancy, why haven't you applied online? With your experience you would have a good chance of an interview anyway.'

In theory he was spot-on. But there was the small matter of her criminal conviction. She almost never made it to interview stage. These days she didn't even bother applying.

For a stupid moment she was tempted to tell him the truth, explain the facts, but what was the point? Yes, she'd been completely innocent, but why should he believe that? No one else had, and she could still taste the hopelessness, the fear, as she'd told the truth only to have it rejected. She would never forget the moment she had realised that she'd been set up and that her boyfriend was leaving her to take the fall.

But she could not explain that to this man in the here and now.

'I understand that, but *your* recommendation would give me an edge.'

He hesitated, and then shrugged. 'If after dinner I think you're suitable, I'll recommend you for an interview. Not for a job. Because that is the store manager's call—he or she knows the existing team and requirements better than I do.'

'That's fabulous. Thank you. Really.' She couldn't help the smile that lifted her lips; this could be the break she'd been hoping for.

'Then let's go.'

'Yes. But…' She looked down. 'I can't go to Tatiana's in this. I'll need to meet you there after…' After she'd magicked up a suitable outfit from thin air.

'We'll stop at a Sahara store on the way and you can pick something out.'

Sarah hesitated. Logic dictated that for Ben Gardiner the gift of an outfit was the equivalent of a chocolate bar. Yet her scruples protested. 'That seems wrong.'

'We're going to a Michelin-starred restaurant; it's good publicity for Sahara if you're seen wearing the label. Look at it as an interview test. We expect our sales assistants to be able to help customers pick the right clothing—this will show me if you can do that.'

Panic fluttered inside her, but no way would she show it. This was her chance to land an interview, secure a job, pay her bills *and* afford ballet lessons for Jodie. The idea galvanised her.

'Sounds good,' she said, her mind already playing with ideas so she'd know what to look for. 'I just need to put my cleaning stuff away and sign out.'

'Go ahead. I'll close down in here.'

Pushing the trolley ahead of her, Sarah exited the office and headed to the room that housed the cleaning supplies. She put everything away and then dialled her mum's number. 'Hi, Mum. It's a long story but I've been asked out to dinner.'

'A date?' Her mum sounded thrilled—she was always telling Sarah she needed to get out more. But Sarah had no intention of doing that. Jodie came first, and she didn't want the complication of introducing a man into her daughter's life. It was hard enough to explain Jodie's actual father—or rather the conspicuous absence of said father.

Telling her, *Well, darling, last I heard Daddy was in prison, and long may he stay there*, wasn't ideal.

'No. Not a date. It's complicated.'

No need to tell her mum about the possibility of a job interview recommendation; she didn't want to get her hopes up. So maybe it would be best not to even mention Ben Gardiner until she got home.

'It's still a chance for you to go out for dinner. Take it. Jodie is fast asleep, and even if she does wake up I'm here.'

'I know you are, Mum. Thank you. I owe you.' More than she could say.

Again guilt piled onto her. After Imogen's death twelve years previously Sarah had behaved appallingly—gone so far off the rails she hadn't even been able to see the tracks. She'd messed up her education, and had sprinted, danced, whirled and run with the wrong crowd. All in a desperate attempt to *feel* something, to block out the horror of her guilt and grief over her sister's death.

God knew her parents had tried to help, but they had had their own grief to deal with. In the end, trying to cope with that as well as Sarah had driven her father to the bottle and led to the disintegration of their marriage.

Enough.

Her mother had forgiven her, taken her and Jodie in, and now the three of them were a happy family unit. As for her father... It was best not to go there; he was lost to her. His descent into alcoholism had changed him beyond all recognition and he wanted nothing to do with her.

'You don't owe me anything, sweetheart. Enjoy yourself. Really. I'll ask Georgia over and we'll have a good old catch-up.'

'OK, Mum. I shouldn't be too late. Give my love to Georgia.' Georgia was her mother's best friend and like a second grandmother to Jodie.

Right. Deep breath. The die was cast and she was going out to dinner with the head honcho.

As if on cue, the office door opened and Ben came out, jacket back on. Sarah gulped.

'Ready?' he asked.

'Sure.'

'Then let's go.'

She followed him to the lift, suddenly stupidly aware of his sheer *presence*. From the tips of his gelled hair to the handmade shoes on his feet, he exuded an aura of leashed, lazy power. Unfortunately he also exuded a gorgeous whiff of something her hormones identified as sheer *yum*—fresh, woodsy, with a hint of citrus.

Oh, God, was she actually leaning in for a smell?

The lift pinged to a stop and she practically leapt out through the doors and had to force herself to slow down as they crossed the marble lobby. The idea was to impress him with her poise and professionalism.

They exited the building as a sleek black car drove up to the entrance. A car with a driver—this was a true glimpse into a different world.

Ben opened the back door and she climbed in, slid all the way across the cream luxury leather and fervently hoped she hadn't left a smudge of dirt. She tried not to look across at the solid muscular bulk of his thigh, relieved at the space between them.

'The flagship store, please, Leo,' Ben said, and the car accelerated smoothly forward.

Sarah focused on the London streets—the hustle and bustle, the red splash of the double-decker buses, the throngs of people, the lit-up shopfronts that glittered and lured, the restaurants… The atmosphere of the city seemed more vibrant, brighter than usual. And all the while her thoughts raced, considering a suitable outfit.

Professional, as this was like an interview. Stylish. Fashionable, but to suit her body shape. Not sexy, but she did need to look good. Because that would give her confidence, and Lord knew she needed that. Not too expensive, but not too cheap.

'Here we are.'

They got out of the car and walked to the front of the store and Sarah scanned the carefully arranged mannequins in their autumnal garb. After all, if someone had already put together the perfect outfit in the window that would be helpful. But no such luck.

He entered a security code and within minutes they were inside the store.

'Take your pick,' he said. 'I'll be over there.' He pointed to an alcove that had been cleverly furnished as a waiting area, with plush seats and magazines and a water machine. 'You've got half an hour.'

'Right. See you in thirty.'

Already scanning the racks, Sarah turned and headed down the main aisle. Panic fluttered. The store was huge and she was unfamiliar with the layout and this was important. If she wanted Ben Gardiner to recommend her for an interview then she needed to show him that she appreciated clothes, loved the Sahara range and was able to choose the right outfit for the occasion.

Fifteen minutes later she'd made her selection, opting for something bolder than a little black dress, but not too over the top. The black and white dress was perfect. It had a bold black pattern on a white background, not too long, not too short, and it skimmed her tummy and accentuated her long legs. Scoop-necked, it avoided a showy plunge, and the short sleeves showed off her slender arms.

Black high heels had been easy to grab from the rows of shoes on offer, and a splash of colour from a small red clutch bag that matched a lipstick she happened to have in her own bag.

Sarah studied her reflection and knew her hair would look better loose. But she couldn't do it. Not yet.

Jodie's voice rang in her ears. *'Mummy, do you dye your hair because you don't like being ginger? Gemma told me that ginger people smell. Does that mean I smell because my hair is red? Cos my hair is really red. Do you not smell because you dye your hair? Can I dye my hair?'*

After that conversation, there had only been one way forward. Sarah had stopped dyeing her hair—but she hadn't been prepared for the effect it would have on her, the avoidance of mirrors, the sudden sharp bursts of grief and guilt.

Not now, Sarah. This dinner was too important.

Quickly she released her hair and then tied it back into a softer twist. It looked better now, but wouldn't distract her.

A glance at her watch and she exited the changing room and made her way back to the alcove, heels clicking lightly on the floor, heart thudding against her ribcage. Sudden realisation slowed her steps. This wasn't just the pinch of nerves because she wanted to pass an interview test—this was a desire to spark admiration in Ben Gardiner's eyes. She wanted him to be bowled over, wanted to see the spark of reciprocal attraction.

What the hell?

Reciprocal attraction would get them nowhere; it certainly wouldn't get her a job. Plus, why *would* he reciprocate? This was Ben Gardiner—he'd been splashed across the gossip mags with supermodels and actresses on a regular basis.

So it was imperative she kept this professional. Yet *still* her heartbeat continued to accelerate as she headed through the racks of Sahara merchandise, the billboards and empty tills towards him.

CHAPTER THREE

BEN LOOKED UP from his phone, where pieces of fruit whizzed across the screen, alerted by the faint sound of heels on the store floor. Curiosity and a sense of intrigue touched him as he watched her walk towards him—emotions that sparked into appreciation.

She'd got it spot-on. The outfit was perfect for dinner—a judicious mix of professional and fashionable. More than that, though, was the way she wore the clothes—as if they were made for her.

His only quibble would be that she should have left her glorious red hair loose; instead it was up, though she'd softened the style a little by looping it into a twist.

'Excellent choice.' He cleared his throat to try and excuse the strangled tones.

She did a quick twirl and, dammit, he nearly swallowed his tongue.

'So do I pass the first test?'

'Yes.'

Get with it. This woman was a prospective as well as a current employee. Not—repeat for emphasis, *not*—a date.

'Thank you.' There was a heartbeat of silence. 'Mind you, I do realise I was spoilt for choice. Perhaps a harder test would have been to take me to a random charity shop and see what I could pull together there.'

The words were breathless, wide brown eyes were still locked with his, and now awareness glittered in her gaze as she stepped close. He caught a tantalising hint of her grapefruit-tinged scent, and just like that he completely lost the thread of the conversation.

Silence lengthened, stretched and echoed round the dim interior of the store, until his brain finally kicked in with a staccato burst.

'Yes,' he said in the hope that that would encompass a correct response. 'Now we'd better go.'

'Yes,' she echoed.

It still took them a moment to actually move, but once they'd started both of them accelerated towards the door.

Back in the car he relaxed slightly. He had to douse this whole attraction thing and remember what was important here: to get a feel for how his workforce thought, to make sure he was still grounded; to assess whether Sarah Fletcher had what it took to be a Sahara Sales assistant. That was what this dinner was about.

Fifteen minutes later they pulled up in front of Tatiana's, located in one of London's most renowned hotels.

A doorman opened the door and they climbed out, and he sensed Sarah step a little closer to him, though she didn't falter as they made their way through the glass revolving door and towards the restaurant.

'Mr Gardiner. Welcome.' The maître d' glanced at Sarah and to his credit didn't give even the slightest indication that he had expected a supermodel. 'And your guest, of course. Please come this way.'

He led them through the opulent room and up a couple

of stairs to a central table, and handed them two leather-bound menus.

'Mario will be over shortly to take your order.'

'Thank you.'

Sarah smiled up at the maître d' before he glided away and Ben was struck afresh at the classical slant of her face: a face that would age with beauty and class.

'This is incredible.' Her smile was tentative. 'Though if I'd known I'd be sitting on a mustard-yellow armchair, I might have picked a slightly different outfit.'

'I'm glad you like it.'

'I do! Those chandeliers alone are awe-inspiring. I mean, where did they get them from? And how can something so immense also be so delicate? Each one is so pretty and yet magnificent.'

'They redecorated a year ago; it was pretty luxurious before, but now it's…' He glanced round at the powder-blue walls, lined with Greek-style moulding and *objets d'art*.

'Imposingly rich, yet somehow it feels a bit like a private dining room rather than a restaurant. Maybe it's because they've spaced the tables really well.' She looked down at the menu and exuded a sigh. 'I may need a little time.'

She wasn't kidding, and yet he didn't mind the wait as she read the menu carefully, clearly weighing her choices. In truth he welcomed the opportunity to study her. Light from the chandeliers tinted her hair with auburn, and her face was creased into an endearing frown of concentration.

An elusive idea niggled at the back of his brain, but he couldn't quite grasp it. The latest Sahara slogan rang in his mind. *The ordinary is extraordinary.* His new range was for people who lived in the real world, and yet he himself no longer did. So—dammit—had he got it wrong?

He stole another glance at Sarah as she looked up from the menu. 'Right. I think I've decided. Though it wasn't easy. I'm not sure I even know what some of these things are, but I think I'll go for the stone bass—unless you think that's a mistake? It comes with rock oyster sauce and pickled mushrooms.'

'If you don't like it we'll swap,' he said. 'I'm going for the duck, with mandarin butternut puree. Does that sound OK?'

'That sounds wonderful—in fact maybe I should have that—but...'

It was impossible not to smile at her frown of indecision. 'We can go halves.'

'Thank you. This certainly makes a difference from pizza!'

She gave a sudden smile when she looked at his expression and he blinked.

'I'm guessing it's been a while since you had pizza?'

'Yes.' Her smile seemed to have rendered him tongue-tied. All suave sophistication had exited the restaurant and the appearance of the waiter was a relief.

'Champagne and a selection of canapés,' Mario announced. 'And then if you are ready to order?'

Once he'd taken their choices and left, Ben lifted his glass. 'To the real world,' he said.

'Yours or mine?' she asked.

'Both. Because they are both real.'

'Even if never the twain shall meet?'

'They are meeting now. You're here.'

'Sure. But…' She pressed her lips together, studied the canapés, chose a tiny blini topped with smoked salmon.

Ben shook his head, realising that whatever she had been about to say she'd deemed it inadvisable. 'If this is going to work we need to agree something upfront. I want your honest opinion. No faking. Agreed?'

A hesitation. Another canapé—this time a thin wafer disc, topped with a delicately flavoured cheese concoction. Then, 'You're sure? You want my unvarnished opinion on everything? No faking at all?'

'Precisely. I promise you there will be no adverse effects on your job interview. I will tell you here and now that I'll arrange an interview with the manager at my Mayfair store. No matter what.'

Yet her eyes were still flecked with doubt, so in response he pulled his phone out and wrote an email, then turned the screen so she could see the words—a request for an interview to be set up. As she watched he hit 'send'.

'Done. So now we are agreed? No faking.'

Her smile illuminated her whole face. 'Agreed.'

'OK. So what were you about to say?'

'That, yes, we *are* both here, but this is just a blip. I'm not meant to be here. You can afford to come back next week, or tomorrow, or whenever you like and you'll most likely bring a celebrity or actor with you. Someone from *your* world.'

'I…' He opened his mouth and then closed it again. There had been no censure in her voice, her tone had been observational, and yet he sensed defensiveness creeping into his stance and he shook his head to repudiate it.

Yes, he liked to eat in the best restaurants, and enjoyed the knowledge that he could afford it. Tangible proof that he'd made it. A way to show the world and his family that he was worth something. And, yes, he loved being successful, revelled in the power that wealth and status gave him. The power to lavish money on his mother, to show her that her choice to keep him had been the right one, to make up for all those years she'd struggled.

Who said money couldn't buy happiness?

'Ben?'

Sarah's concerned voice penetrated his sudden lapse into a trip down the tarnished road of memory lane.

'I didn't mean it as a criticism. You're entitled to your world—I only meant it's very different to most people's. Most people have to worry about bills and rising food prices and whether they can afford ballet lessons for their kids. Ninety-nine per cent of the population can't afford to eat here because the cost of a meal is probably more than their monthly food budget.'

She was right.

'Which is why I want to hear your take on things,' he said. 'I'm hoping that our new range of clothes isn't out of touch with what the customer on the high street wants. The idea is for these clothes to be everyday, normal clothes that you feel good in all the time.'

'The type of clothes I'd wear to have a pizza?'

'Yes.'

As she considered her response Mario returned with their starters and Sarah beamed up at him. 'This looks amazing. They both do,' she added as she looked across at his plate.

Once the waiter had disappeared as unobtrusively as he'd appeared, she gestured to his. 'But what *is* it?'

'Cauliflower,' he explained. 'Infused with lemon curry oil and topped with parmesan. You want to try some?'

'Sure. And you can have a bit of mine. Scallops with

artichoke puree and some sort of sauce—a truffle *jus*, I think.'

As she tasted a sample of his she closed her eyes, and he was tempted to do the same, to block the effect she was having on him. Instead he asked, 'Well?'

'It's delicious. I had no idea cauliflower could taste like this—it's like magic.'

He grinned. 'I'm not sure the chef has an actual wand, but perhaps that's his secret.'

'Anyway—sorry. I'm here to give you my opinion on clothes, not vegetables. Right… Well, I'd have to see the clothes in more detail, but going for a pizza could be different, depending on the occasion. A family dinner might get messy—globs of tomato sauce, drips of ice cream. So you'd want clothes that are easy to wash and that also won't show up grubby stains too much. Or you may go out and eat pizza on a date—and you may travel there by bus. In that case you'd want a more layered look—something pretty under something practical. Or you may be going after work—in which case you'd need something light and sparkly that you can put in your bag and use to transform your work clothes. Anyway, you get the picture.'

He did, and what he liked—alongside her spot-on observations—was the animation that lit her face, the way she waved her hands around to emphasise a point.

'So that's what you'd want to wear and what you would want to sell?'

'That goes back to the point I made earlier. I don't necessarily have to buy in to the whole range of clothes to be able to sell it. What's right for me isn't what's right for everyone. I don't have to love it to promote it.'

'So I should be looking for a good sales technique over genuine love for the product?'

'In an ideal world you'd need both. But sometimes loving a product isn't enough; there's a whole lot more to it than that.'

'I get that. My business model is based on giving customers what they want, and for that I rely on feedback from the sales floor. I expect my sales force to listen to what the customer wants rather than push them into buying the wrong clothes just to get a sale. Happy customers come back.'

'I agree with all that—but again, with respect, all that is manager-speak.'

'Meaning...?'

'OK... Imagine that you are a sales assistant, you love the product, and you know company policy is to listen to the customer and deliver "excellent service", et cetera, et cetera. I am the customer. I've come in and I've tried on an outfit—a pair of jeans that are clearly a size too small for me and a tie top. The same outfit that is on one of your billboards, only the model happens to have super-skinny legs and a toned, flat stomach.' She glanced down at her own midriff. 'Trust me—I have neither attribute. So, are you picturing it?'

Oh, God. It had all been going so well.

Ben reached for his wine glass, changed his mind and opted for water instead. He told himself that the temperature in the room could not have gone up. 'Um... yes. Um...'

Pull it together Ben. This is a serious conversation.

'You want to know what I would say—would I give my honest advice or would I tell you that it looks great?'

'Exactly. Because there are so many questions here.

You don't want to damage someone's self-esteem. Women have enough issues with their body image as it is. But equally the truth is that different fashions suit different body shapes. So here I am, standing in front of you, an ordinary person in the changing room. I'm wearing a tie top that emphasises assets I don't have and exposes a midriff that is less toned than it could be. What would you do?'

'I'd tell you that as long as you're happy with the outfit that is the most important thing.'

She raised her eyebrows. 'But surely that would imply that you don't like it?'

He had to get a grip. Unfortunately that was proving hard, because right now he liked it a whole lot—he was sure the outfit would look pretty damn good on her. But that wasn't the point and he knew it.

Focus. And as he considered her words he realised exactly how difficult the question was. What *would* he say?

'OK. The point of Sahara clothes is to make the customer feel good in themselves. So, personally, I believe that it doesn't matter if your tummy is toned or not. The important thing is that you feel happy and comfortable showing off your shape or size. If you feel good about yourself you can carry off any fashion.'

It was his turn to trail off as he spotted her raised eyebrows.

'That's all very well, and I completely agree with you, but...'

'But it doesn't answer your question. What should I say to the customer?'

Disbelief touched Ben—*why* couldn't he work out an answer? Instead he was sat here spouting manager-talk. *Blah-blah-blah.*

'OK. I give in. What's the answer? What would you say?'

Sarah speared a final scallop as she considered the answer. 'I'm not sure there *is* a standard answer, because you have to consider each situation individually. You'd say something different to a teenager than you would to a middle-aged woman. But you could compliment her choice of outfit. So maybe, *That's a great combination—one of our best sellers, in fact.* And then I'd ask questions—ask if she has any reservations, or what she wants the outfit for. Create an opportunity to offer a different choice. I might say, *If you want, I can get you another of our most popular combinations*, and I'd get her something more suited to her body type. Then I'd leave the choice to her.'

Ben studied her for a moment. Sarah Fletcher knew her stuff. She was intelligent, had a good grasp of fashion and customer service and could forge an excellent career in retail. At a guess he'd put her in her mid-twenties. So why on earth was she working as a cleaner when her interests were clearly elsewhere?

Not his business.

'OK. I like that,' he said. 'I think it would be useful if we ran a few seminars for our sales assistants and put them through a few hypothetical scenarios like that.'

'Another idea would be to have more ordinary-shaped mannequins in store. That way you can actually show that your new designs are really made for ordinary people.'

If they really are...

The words were unspoken, yet they echoed across the table and Ben stared at her. Had he really thought about that? Yes, he did agree in principle that the ordinary was extraordinary, that clothes should be designed for all shapes and sizes, and that had been his vision. But had he made sure that vision had been translated into the real world, where people came in very different shapes and sizes compared to the models he paid to advertise his products?

There were too many questions, and he certainly couldn't get all the answers here and now.

Pushing his empty plate away, he looked up at the ceiling and then back at Sarah. She was a woman who made him think, and right now he needed that.

The idea that had niggled at the back of his brain suddenly came together. 'I've got a proposal for you,' he said.

CHAPTER FOUR

SARAH STARED ACROSS at Ben. 'A proposal?' she echoed. 'What sort of proposal?'

For a completely mad moment she wondered if he wanted to turn this into a real date. Perhaps he'd actually meant proposition.

Daft.

Yet her hormones told her it wasn't, and they informed her that inexplicably, against all the odds, Ben Gardiner was attracted to her. And now they were waving pompoms and telling her to do something about it.

Clearly her hormones weren't linked to her brain. Her brain told her that, lowering though it was, the chances of Ben being attracted to her were minimal. Yes, occasionally she'd had a vibe, but that was no more than wishful thinking—on her hormones' part anyway. In truth, Ben Gardiner had been completely professional; if anything *she* had been guilty of sending out the occasional wrong signal. Well, no more. Because right now, hopefully— *please, please, please*—Ben was about to tell her that his proposal was to give her a job and allow her to bypass the interview.

Before he could answer, their main courses arrived, covered with silver cloches which the waiter removed with a flourish. Knowing how important it was to be appreciated, she reined in her impatience and smiled up at him, inhaling the delicate, tantalising aroma of her stone bass. 'It looks and smells divine, thank you.'

The waiter smiled back, melted discreetly away, and she turned her gaze to Ben, waiting, trying not to appear overeager.

His cobalt blue eyes assessed her and she'd swear she could almost hear the whir of his brain.

'I really want to continue this conversation,' he said at last. 'You've given me a good insight into the real world and I need that right now. I think you can help me make this new range work.'

'Anyone off the street could do that.'

'Maybe. But I don't want anyone off the street. Because I've found you.'

Sarah wasn't sure where this was headed, but she had to focus on her endgame: a job; she needed a job. 'So what exactly is your proposal?'

'I'm going to Milan Fashion Week and I'd like you to come with me. As a consultant.'

Sarah stared at him, heard a clatter as her fork dropped onto her plate. For a foolish second she allowed her imagination to grasp the idea and run, let a fantasy form pictures in the air. *Milan.* The city of fashion and culture. The cathedral, the gallery that housed the world's oldest shopping mall, the catwalks, her and Ben walking the Italian streets...

Whoa. Stop.

The images lingered in the air and then dispersed in the chandelier-lit illumination of reality.

'There you go again. Life doesn't work like that. I can't just drop everything and go to Milan for a week.'

'Why not?' His expression was serious. 'You said you'd been made redundant from your sales job. I'm sure we can manage to get you time off from the cleaning job. You're looking for work; I'll pay you well. So, unless you're moonlighting as a surgeon or a teacher, why not?'

Sarah told herself that there quite simply hadn't been any reason to mention Jodie up to now, but guilt nipped her. Had she not wanted to tell him? Not wanted him to know, to judge? *Yuck!* And no way. Jodie was the very best thing that had ever happened to her. Jodie had given her the strength to turn her life around, to reverse her downward spiral towards apathy and despair. She had been determined not to take her daughter down with her.

'Because I have a daughter. And I can't and won't up sticks and leave her.'

There was a silence.

'Could your husband or partner look after her?' he asked.

'No husband or partner. Jodie's father isn't on the scene.'

More silence, and now his cobalt blue eyes held something else. Something she couldn't identify, though it didn't feel like judgement or censure. More like shock.

Meeting his gaze full on, she said, 'Which is fine by me.' No way did she want him to see her as someone to pity. 'But the point is I can't take off to Milan at the drop of a hat.'

'How old is Jodie? Could you bring her?'

Sarah blinked. 'No, I couldn't. She's six, and she's at school…and I can't leave her for a week. I've never even left her for a whole night.'

The idea was impossible, and yet for a treacherous second regret panged at the lost opportunity.

Enough. The whole idea was nuts.

'So I really appreciate the offer but I can't do it. I'd be happy to chat by email?'

He shook his head. 'Thank you for that, but I need more. I want your opinion on the fashion shows, on the catwalk. The new range is due out soon. I want your opinion on if I've got it right. If it reflects the catwalk… if you have any ideas I can use to tweak it if need be.'

'But that's insane. You've got designers, PR people—experts. Why do you want *my* opinion? I'm *one* person.'

'Call it gut instinct. I believe you'll bring something unique to the table.'

He pushed his plate away and she sensed his energy, knew that he'd like to be up and pacing as he thought.

'And you could model the clothes—wear them in Milan, give me your personal opinion. Which will also be a great form of advertising. This is a *good* idea. I know it.'

'It's not even a real job,' she pointed out. 'You're making it up on the spot.'

He grinned an audacious grin and her toes curled.

'That doesn't mean it's not valid. I trust my instinct. You would be my promotional consultant. I'd pay you a one-off fee for your opinions on my range, and in Milan you'd represent the whole idea of the ordinary as extraordinary.'

His enthusiasm was contagious, and his almost Pre-Raphaelite sculpted features expressed such belief in himself. A self-belief she could only envy even as she recognised that the scenario he described was no more than a fairy-tale fantasy. Things like this didn't happen to her. This was *his* world. Ben Gardiner was a man with a vision—a man who made things happen and lived a life larger than hers. That scared her. The risk of it all was almost a taunt to the universe. Better to keep her head down, behind the parapet, so the universe didn't notice her. Didn't drop any more hammer-blows.

It was time to pop the bubble.

'It may be a great idea but you'll have to find someone else. Which really shouldn't be too hard. Isn't that the whole point? The ordinary is extraordinary? If you go into one of your stores tomorrow you can find someone just as ordinary as me who will jump at the chance of going to Milan. I have responsibilities here.'

He picked up his glass of wine, swirling it contemplatively. 'I get that. But I'd like to see if there's a way to figure out a way round them.'

'There is no way round a flesh-and-blood six-year-old.'

And no way she could or would leave Jodie for a week. The idea twisted her gut with its sheer impossibility. What if something happened to Jodie in her absence? Some horrible twist of fate that took her daughter from her. The risk could not be taken.

'And I don't want there to be. Jodie is my priority.' A small sigh escaped her lips as the last lingering wisps of the 'Sarah in Milan' scenario misted away. 'But, truly, thank you for the offer.' She took a deep breath. 'I hope this doesn't mean you've changed your mind about the interview.'

Annoyance tightened his lips. 'Of course I haven't.' He reached into his pocket, pulled out a business card and scribbled a number on the back. 'That's my mobile. I'm leaving on Sunday afternoon. If you change your mind let me know. Otherwise, good luck at the interview.'

'Thank you.'

An hour later, after Ben had dropped her home, Sarah tiptoed into Jodie's room, looked at her daughter's much-loved face as she sprawled on the bed, her teddy clutched under her chin. Sarah's heart turned over. The emotion confirmed the decision she'd taken—it was unimaginable to leave Jodie.

Tiptoeing out, she entered the lounge, where her mother and Georgia awaited her, impatience etched on both faces.

'So—spill,' her mother said, handing her a steaming cup of cocoa. 'Who did you go to dinner with and where did you get that dress?'

'You really won't believe it.'

'Try us.'

'Half an hour later both older women stared at her, jaws to knees.

Her mum picked up her mug and then put it back down. 'Ben Gardiner wants you to go to Milan Fashion Week with him? He wants your input on his latest range and he wants you to wear the new Sahara line of clothes?'

'Yes.'

'And you turned him down?' Georgia emitted a groan. 'Are you mad?'

'I explained that I can't leave Jodie.'

The two women exchanged glances and her mum leant forward. 'Yes, you *can*, sweetheart. This is a marvellous opportunity for you—the chance of a lifetime.'

Sarah shook her head, looking at her mother in disbelief. 'You can't *possibly* think I should go?'

Mary Fletcher knew how precious Jodie was to Sarah—knew too how life could destroy you without warning. And yet, there was no doubt on her mother's face at all.

'Darling, I do think you should go. You're my daughter

and I love you. I also love my granddaughter, and I am more than capable of looking after her for a few days.'

Sarah bit her lip. It wasn't that she didn't trust her mother—she totally did. But panic sloughed off her skin at the enormity of the whole idea of Milan, told her it would be wrong to leave her daughter.

'But what about your work?'

'I'll help as well,' Georgia said. 'I'm your godmother and Jodie loves me too. Your mum and I will sort it out. Of course Jodie will miss you, but you should do this.'

Guilt flicked her nerves. How could she even think about it? Jodie was only six. What if something happened at school? Happened because she wasn't there to prevent it? An accident…a quirk of fate?

After all, accidents did happen, and fate had a habit of dropping the axe with no warning at all. All those years of believing Imogen was a healthy double of herself and then—*wham*—the doctor's serious face, her mother's tears, her father headed for the whisky bottle.

Perhaps her mother read her expression, because she leant forward. 'I swear I'll look after her, sweetheart.'

But even her mother hadn't been able to save Imogen. Nobody could have done that—not Sarah, not anyone. Yet, logical or not, the idea of leaving Jodie made her clammy with panic,

'I can't do this.'

'Yes, you can.' Georgia stepped in again. 'Because it would be for Jodie. The consultancy fee would be enough to pay for ballet lessons and a birthday party. But, more than that, I think she would be proud of you for getting the job. It will be good for her to see how talented and wonderful you are. And if you impress Ben Gardiner, who knows where it could lead?'

'Georgia is right, sweetheart. This is too big a chance to miss,' her mother intervened. 'Take it. I promise I will call you if Jodie gets so much as a cold.'

'But…'

'Do it for Jodie.'

Sarah's head whirled and panic danced in her tummy. She wondered if her mother would still advocate a week away if she knew that a factor in this equation was the hum of attraction that bloomed at the mere idea of being in Ben Gardiner's presence. But that shouldn't stop her, because her mum and Georgia were right. This truly was an opportunity, a chance to turn her life around, and she did have to take it.

'You're right. Thank you both. I'll talk to Jodie tomorrow.'

And so the next day, as she made Jodie's favourite weekend breakfast of pancakes, she broached the subject. 'Guess what, sweetheart?'

'What?'

'I got offered a job yesterday. And part of that job means I would need to go away for a few days. To Milan. In Italy.'

'Can I come?'

'No. One day maybe we could go on holiday to Italy, but this time I'll take lots of photos and videos for you and I'll talk to you every day. And Grandma and Grannie Georgia will look after you.'

Jodie thought about it for a minute. 'Is it a *good* job, Mummy?'

'Yes.'

'Then you should do it.' Jodie grinned suddenly. 'I can tell everyone at school that my mummy has gone to Milan for work.'

It was clear that the prospect gave her a great deal of pleasure, and in truth Sarah couldn't blame her. God knew it wasn't often that Jodie had anything to boast about, and she knew it was sometimes hard for her without a dad. There were lots of kids whose parents had split up, but the utter absence of a father was difficult.

'You do that, sweetheart.'

Jodie thought for a minute. 'And I'll tell everyone that redheads are winners!'

Sarah managed a smile. 'That's what Aunty Imogen always said.'

Jodie beamed at her, ate the last mouthful of pancake and wiggled of her chair. 'Can I watch some cartoons now?'

'Of course—for a little while. Then we'll head to the park, and you have Holly's birthday party this afternoon.'

Once Jodie was settled in front of the TV, Sarah hauled in a breath and went into the bedroom she shared with her daughter. She stood by the window and stared at the azure-blue sky, the scud of clouds, the people walking the London streets. Tried to calm her breathing and the pound of her heart before punching Ben Gardiner's number into her phone.

One buzz, two, three…and then a deep voice. 'Gardiner speaking.'

'Hi. It's…um…Sarah. Sarah Fletcher. We met…'

'I know who you are.'

Amusement vibrated across the line and the molten chocolate of his voice shivered over her skin.

'I wondered if…if the offer to come to Milan is still open? My mum and her best friend have said they will look after Jodie and I have decided I'd like to do it.'

A heartbeat of silence and she braced herself for rejection. Then, 'Fantastic. We fly out tomorrow afternoon. But we'll need to sort some details today and go to the warehouse, so you can choose some clothes from the new range.'

'Shall I meet you there?'

'It's easier if I pick you up. About an hour?'

'I'll see you then. Thank you.'

And the only reason her pulse-rate had upped a few notches was in anticipation of the clothes, not the man.

Perhaps if she told herself that enough she'd believe it.

CHAPTER FIVE

BEN DROPPED HIS phone into his pocket, surprised by the level of jubilation he felt. On a *business* level. Because he knew that he was right. Taking Sarah Fletcher to Milan was a sound choice. Instinct told him that—the instinct he'd relied on plenty of times in order to pull off the most outlandish of deals, or to take a quirky fashion risk that the pundits had told him he wouldn't work in a million years.

But it was more than that. From the moment she'd told him she had a daughter, that she was a single mum, he'd wanted to give her a chance in a way no one had given his own mother a chance years before. And, dammit, he was glad she'd decided to take it.

The downside being that now he and Sarah would need to spend a lot of time together, which meant he'd have to erase the attraction angle, somehow school his libido to block the insidious physical pull, to counteract it with professionalism.

Because Sarah Fletcher was an employee, and whether that was as an office cleaner or on a freelance consultant contract was a technicality.

It didn't matter anyway, because Sarah Fletcher was a single mother and he did not ever get involved with those. The capacity for complications, angst and hurt was too large. The possibility of impacting on a child's life unacceptable.

So he'd ice the attraction. How hard could it be?

An hour later the question was answered as his car pulled up outside Sarah's house. She stood outside, dressed in a simple floral sundress with a cream jacket over the top, and she looked ridiculously pretty.

He climbed out to open the car door for her.

'Hi.' There it was again, the catch in his throat, the slight breathlessness.

Sunlight glinted on her hair, tingeing the tied-back tresses with chestnut, brown eyes met his and he'd swear she rocked back slightly, before ducking her gaze away and sliding into the luxurious interior of the car.

Be professional. Block the attraction. Remember?

How hard could it be?

Extremely hard, when he could almost *see* the sparks zip across the car, singeing the leather of the seats.

'I'm glad you changed your mind about accepting the role—that you managed to sort out childcare.' His mention of her daughter was a deliberate reminder to himself of her off-limits status.

'Yes. My mum and my godmother are happy to look after Jodie—they all seem pretty excited by the arrangement.'

'And you? Are you excited?'

'I'm excited about Milan, and I'm excited about the work, although I will miss Jodie. But they persuaded me this is too good an opportunity to miss.' She turned to face him now. 'So, are we headed for the warehouse?'

'Yup.'

'That's pretty exciting in itself. All those clothes and products. I'll feel like a kid in a candy store.'

He shrugged. 'I'm not sure you'll get that much of a buzz from it; it's basically a big building with lots of clothes in it.' At her expression he raised his eyebrows. 'You look surprised.'

'I'm not surprised. I'm shocked.' Her expression was half serious, half doubtful. 'You're kidding, right? You're head of a retail empire you built from scratch—the clothes *must* give you a buzz?'

'Nope. They're a product. A means to an end.'

'You're telling me you're not interested in fashion?'

'Not on a personal level. My personal tastes are irrelevant, and they would skew the dynamic. The key to Sahara is providing the customer with what they want, and running a fair and happy workplace. That is the way to make money.'

'But something must have drawn you towards clothes and fashion?' She had turned towards him and genuine interest sparked in her brown eyes.

Ben hesitated, and then thought, *What the hell?* This, at least, was a conversation—better than sitting awkwardly in silence, trying to ignore the attraction.

'I set up a business of sorts when I was fourteen,' he said.

He'd vowed that he would get them off that bleak, graffiti-strewn estate and return his mother to leafy suburbia. He'd vowed he'd make money so that his mother would want for nothing—so that never again would their lives be snatched away or turned upside down.

Because he'd figured it out. Money talked. It also sang and laughed. Gave you power. Love gave you nothing but misery. Lesson learnt.

'I picked stuff up cheap—from the internet, from locals, wherever I could—and sold it on at a profit. I noticed that clothes always did well. I got my hands on a job lot of white T-shirts…figured I could find a better way to sell them. I came up with some pretty good slogans and I paid someone a bit to paint them on. They sold like hotcakes and it made me think. People like fashion—and, more than that, people want to express their individuality. Fashion gives me so many different ways to provide what people want. When I got a bit older I set up a market stall. I loved the buzz from the sales—that feeling at the end of the day when I'd sold it all.'

He came to a halt and shook his head.

'Sorry—you didn't ask for an autobiography.' And he didn't usually feel the inclination to give one.

'No need to apologise. I'm fascinated. Genuinely.'

She reached out and touched his arm, as if to back up her sincerity. The sensation was fleeting, and yet ridiculously intense, and he'd swear he heard her intake of breath as she moved back towards the window.

'It's a bit hard to picture you at a market stall,' she said, and her voice was a touch higher than usual.

'I was pretty good at it. Actually, I was *very* good at it.' Seeing the doubt in her expression, he grinned. 'You want a demonstration?'

'Here?'

'Why not? OK. Here goes… Roll up, roll up!' His voice slipped automatically into the cadence and rhythm of the marketplace, instantly transporting him years back, to the crisp London air of the market, the clang and bustle of setting up his pitch, eyeing potential customers. 'Come and see the show. How about this? A pound for whatever I sell next—can't go wrong, really. Who'll bid a pound? You will? OK, here you go, sir. One paper bag—good for the environment. But that doesn't seem fair, does it? So how about I put in this T-shirt and—you know what?—as I'm feeling generous I'll throw this one in as well. One for you and one for your missus. Look at this—excellent quality. Just the feel of it against your skin will bring a smile to your face. And that's what I want, ladies and gents! I want to bring a smile to your faces. So come and have a look at what I'm offering next... And so on and so forth.'

He leant back and saw Sarah's lips curve up in a smile that snagged his gaze on her mouth.

'I can picture it now,' she said. 'You standing in front of your stall... I bet you cleaned up. But you were selling clothes—that must have inspired your sales pitch.'

'Nope. It's not the product—it's how you sell it.'

Her eyebrows rose. 'So you're saying you could sell anything?'

Hearing the dare in her voice, he let his gaze meet hers, and underneath the challenge he sensed awareness swirl and solidify into a pull of attraction, a frisson he could almost see shimmering between them. Her eyes dropped, her cheeks flushed slightly and he knew she could feel it too.

Focus. 'Yup. Try me. Pick something—first thing that comes to your head.'

'Um... Ki—' Her eyes widened, her expression stricken as she broke off. 'Lips—' Now her eyes closed, then flashed open as she continued with hardly a skipped beat. 'Stick. Lipstick. How would you sell that?' Delving into her bag she pulled out a tube and handed it to him.

Kudos to her for the recovery, but he couldn't help his feeling of deep satisfaction at the confirmation that she too was aware of the attraction, that the idea of a kiss was at the forefront of her mind.

'Roll up, roll up! You've seen me sell the big stuff, and

now I have some small stuff. But we all know size isn't everything. Isn't that right, ladies? So today I am selling this here.' He held up the lipstick. 'But if it's not about size, what *is* it about? Well, I think it's about colour—and this is a colour that delivers a subtle *wow*. And, yes, I did just make that phrase up—but I think this lipstick does have subtle *wow*. If you want someone to notice your lips, to focus on them, notice the contour and the shape, then this is for you.'

And heaven help him. Because now his eyes zoned in on Sarah's lips and for a second he nearly faltered. But then he pulled it together.

'And it's not just about other people—it's how it makes you feel, how it makes your lips feel. This is good quality—excellent quality—and that means it will make your lips feel good, glossy, smooth… This lipstick delivers happy lips and that's what we all want.'

There was a silence as Sarah lifted a hand to her lips and ran a finger over them. His eyes followed the movement and he pushed his hands under his thighs to counter the urge of his fingers to follow hers. He imagined the feel of her lips under his touch. *Hell*.

Closing his eyes, he made an attempt to regroup. 'So, am I an ace salesman or am I not?' he managed.

A second of silence and then she nodded. 'You win. You're a natural salesman. That is my lipstick and I was about to buy it from you anyway.' A pause. 'I accept that it's your business that is most important to you, not your product. But do you really think you would be equally happy running a business that manufactures…cleaning products?'

'Absolutely.'

Sarah gave a sudden chuckle, then shook her head.

'Sorry. I just don't believe you. I'm trying to picture you in the market selling loo rolls. I mean, what could even *you* possibly do with that. *Roll up, roll up! See what I have here...* Then what?'

'I'd play it as a guessing game. Roll up, roll up! Guess what I have to sell today. It's not glam, ladies and gents, but it's definitely one of life's essentials—and, believe you me, the texture and the quality is of gravest importance. You wouldn't want to miss *this* off your shopping list.'

'Hang on!'

Sarah reached out and put her hand on his arm again, and this time there was no point in denial; her touch stopped him in his tracks.

'I've got it. How about this? Ladies and gents, forget the paddle—this is a product you *definitely* don't want to go up the proverbial creek without.'

Her tone was gleefully full of pride as she awaited his response and he laughed.

'Perfect. I vote we go and find a crate of loo roll and head to the nearest market and pitch a stall.'

Now her chuckle morphed into a laugh. 'Can you imagine the tabloid headlines? *Sahara CEO loo-ses the plot!*'

The silliness and her sheer delight at it caused his laughter to deepen and she joined in. Eventually they both subsided. And then, as remembered laughter echoed, actual silence reigned.

Hell.

The idea behind this conversation had been to lock the attraction down, but as a strategy it had failed entirely—because as he looked at her laughter-flushed face and the sparkle in her eyes he was grateful for his seat belt. Otherwise he was pretty damned sure he'd slide across the cream leather and gather her into his arms.

All in all, it was a relief when the car glided to a stop.

'We're at my office. I need to pick up the paperwork. Back in five.'

Sarah watched Ben head towards the revolving glass door that led into his headquarters and let out her breath in a whoosh. No point ducking the issue—she wanted to kiss him. With a yearning that almost scared her.

Before she could bang her head against the window in sheer frustration he returned, slid back onto the seat and handed her a piece of paper.

'Your contract and a schedule for the next few days.'

'You move fast.'

'It has been said.'

Another silence descended as, unbidden, an image of him moving across the sleek leather seat filled her mind and her tummy tightened, her muscles clenching in an effort not to start the move herself. The image of her hand cupping his cheek stuck, and she could almost feel the light stubble against her fingers. Her lips tingled in wishful anticipation...

Enough.

She reached out and nearly snatched the paper from him, forcing herself to look down at words that seemed to waver and jumble before her gaze.

The timetable was concise, packed with catwalk shows and drinks parties, and as the information permeated through the scrambled filters of her brain she tried to focus her mind, to concentrate on putting outfits together in her head as she planned a capsule wardrobe for all occasions.

But even as she did so the realisation dawned on her that, according to this schedule, they would be together for nearly every waking minute. *Bad, bad idea.* Did she have a crush on him? Just because of his chiselled visage, his sculpted body—was she *that* shallow?

Looking up, she studied his face, the lithe muscles of his arm, the breadth of his chest, and realised that, yes, she was as shallow as a puddle on a sunny day. Worse than that—in the past twenty minutes she'd figured she might actually *like* him.

'Do I need to attend the social stuff?'

'Yes—to see what people are wearing. And it'll be a good opportunity to make contacts and network. People are the key to any organisation, so I like to hear what people are saying officially as well as unofficially. Expert opinions, rumours… It's all important stuff. And the parties and events are usually fun.'

'Fun' did not sound like a good option. Did she want to party with Ben Gardiner? Absolutely not. In fact, this wasn't about fun full stop.

'I'm not here to have fun,' she said. It would make her feel guilty—as if she were enjoying being away from Jodie. 'This is a job.'

'Are you saying a job can't be fun?' He shook his head. 'I think the whole point of work is that it *should* be fun. I hope all my employees derive enjoyment from what they do. That's why I pay everyone well—from the factory staff upwards. Happy staff make a better company. I'd prefer it if you attend the parties, but I'll leave it to you. I'm paying you a fee for your opinions—it's up to you how you garner them.'

Fee. She hadn't even looked at the contract, so distracted was she by his presence, by her foolish reaction to him. *Idiot.*

She scanned the document, saw the figure and blinked in disbelief. 'Ten thousand pounds? For a week's work. You can't pay me that much.'

Guilt slammed into her as she realised exactly why she had avoided looking at the contract. Because it felt fake—wrong. Because, like it or not, this was a contract made under false pretences. Ben Gardiner didn't know he was taking on someone with no qualifications and a criminal conviction. Would he have hired her if he knew that? Accepting the sales assistant interview on false pretences had made her feel bad enough, but she had justified it for Jodie's sake. But this…? Even for Jodie, suddenly seemed too much.

Ben frowned and studied her expression with eyes that seemed way too full of discernment, and she flicked her gaze away.

'I believe that to be a fair fee,' he said. 'I appreciate that you're turning your life—and Jodie's—upside down. It includes a reasonable amount for childcare and compensates you for the five days and nights that you will be away.'

Days and nights. Sarah knew that he simply meant the time she would be away from home, but all she could think of was the fact that she would be with Ben for an overwhelming amount of that time. Under false pretences. Sure, she hadn't actually lied, but there was an assumption, a presumption, that she was a qualified non-criminal.

'It's too much.'

Ben frowned. 'It's a fair fee.'

For a second she hovered on the brink of confession,

and then she pressed her lips together. It was too risky. If she told him, he might pull the job interview. All she could do now was give the job her all—do it to the best of her ability and more.

'Thank you. I will do my best.'

For a moment his frown deepened, as if he were still trying to read her very soul, but this time she held his gaze.

It was a relief when the car stopped and she realised they were at the warehouse. And an even bigger relief when they walked in and she could immerse herself in a sensory experience that had nothing to do with Ben Gardiner and everything to do with the incredible display of fashion and its components.

The building was filled with the hustle and bustle of operatives picking out and sorting orders, while the very air seemed clothed in fabrics, textures, materials and designs.

'This is incredible. I can practically taste the fabrics. This is a shopper's paradise.'

'It's also hopefully a well-oiled machine. Our stock processes have to work efficiently or the whole system would collapse.' He gestured across the floor. 'The new range is securely locked away in a different part of the warehouse.'

They walked up to the next level, down a corridor, and he stopped outside a door, tapped in a passcode and they entered.

'Wow, wow and *wow*,' Sarah said.

She turned to him and saw no mirror of her own feelings. His stance reflected an attitude approaching indifference.

'It really doesn't do it for you, does it? The place could be full of toilet rolls. I still don't get it.'

Ben looked round. 'I *am* proud of this—I'm proud of what I've built up, proud of the company's success. But my buzz comes from making Sahara even more successful, generating growth and new lines, expanding into new countries. Taking the Sahara brand global. At the end of the day, whether it's detergent or fashion, it's money that talks the sweetest talk. It's the profit that matters.'

'That's a bit cynical.'

'That's life.' His tone was absolute. 'Money makes the world go round. I don't have a problem with that. At all. It makes everything simple. You give, you take, you deal. Life as a market stall.'

'Emotions don't work like that.' This she knew. No amount of money could have compensated for Imogen's death. No amount of money could have defined her joy at Jodie's birth. 'There are some things that transcend money. Life, death, happiness, grief.'

Ben shook his head. 'Money still helps. It can pay for private treatments, assuage grief by providing counselling. It can allow you to take time off from work. If your grief is connected to a relationship breakdown it can definitely ease the path of moving forward. As for happiness—my money has purchased plenty.'

Yet his cobalt eyes were shadowed, and she felt a mad urge to step forward and put her arms around him. But that way lay madness indeed.

'You mean your lifestyle? The accessories, the fast cars, a driver, parties on yachts?'

'Yes.'

He met her gaze coolly, and yet somehow she didn't fully believe him, sensed there was more to it than that.

'My money allows me a lifestyle that brings me happiness. Isn't that what everyone wants?'

'Sure, but I just want…*enough*. I want enough to give Jodie a good start in life, enough to pay for ballet lessons, enough to keep her healthy and happy.'

'But why stop at "enough"?'

It was a good question, and it jolted her even as she considered the answer. 'Because you don't need to have the most expensive toys or designer shoes to be happy.'

'You don't need them, but sometimes it's nice to have them. So why not go for it?'

'Because then it becomes meaningless. Surely limitless wealth gets boring?'

'Not so I've noticed. Because there's always something more to aspire to.'

'Even when you have everything? If you can afford it all—a fleet of Ferraris, a string of houses—then doesn't it lose the sparkle, the sense of achievement?'

'No, because you can always up the ante. Buy a castle, get a yacht, start a whole new business… Go into real estate, or hotels, or even on a quest for a new and improved cleaning product. The sky is the limit. There are always new challenges.'

For a moment she envied him that drive and ambition, but she knew it wasn't for her. In truth it scared her, unsettled her, took her way out of her comfort zone.

'I think I'll settle for giving Jodie a good start, and securing a steady job is the best way to achieve that.'

Ben frowned. 'What about what *you* want? For you. Not for Jodie.'

'I want what is best for Jodie. The two are interlinked.'

'OK. So do you want her to try to be good *enough*? Or the best?'

She could feel her eyes narrow. 'That's sneaky,' she said. And way too close to the bone. 'I want her to be the best she can be.'

'Exactly. The *best* she can be—not just as good as she can be. There's a difference. I'm just saying, whatever your goal, make it a big one and go for it.'

Only it wasn't always that easy—not when she'd messed up as badly as she had. That made any possible goals smaller and the road a whole lot narrower. Once again regret touched her.

But now Ben frowned, stepped forward and studied her face. 'Sorry. I've upset you and I didn't mean to. I get carried away sometimes; I didn't mean to criticise you.'

The apology touched her. 'It's OK,' she said, and then, seeing the frown that still creased his forehead, she smiled. 'Honestly. Now, I'd better get started on these clothes.'

'Go ahead—knock yourself out. I'll go and do a walk-about, have a chat to some of the operatives. I'll be back in about half an hour.'

True to his word, half an hour later he returned—just as she was checking through her selection of clothes.

'I got us some food from the canteen,' he said. 'I hope this is OK.'

He handed over a packaged sandwich and she smiled her thanks.

'I've made a choice based on what you said yesterday,' she told him. 'You want some clothes that are keepers, so I'll make sure I wear items for more than one occasion, because that's what you do in ordinary life. I'll mix and match and I'll use accessories to jazz it all up.'

She took one last glance at her choices and frowned. 'I wonder if you should get someone else as well—

someone with a different body shape and colouring to me. I keep forgetting there are some colours I really can't wear.'

'Keep forgetting?' he asked, his voice tinged with curiosity.

Damn—she wished she could take those words back. She kept her tone of voice factual. 'I spent quite a few years dyeing my hair.'

'Why? Your hair is an incredible colour. It's stunning.'

His voice had deepened, was edged with awareness, and suddenly she wanted to let her hair loose, shake it free so he could appreciate its full glory.

'If I could bottle it as a dye I'd sell it,' he said.

'At a market stall?' Her voice was shaky.

'Roll up, roll up! Ladies and gents, do you want hair that looks like this? Vibrant, softer than silk, with gloss and verve?'

His voice sent a tremor down to her nerve endings, fizzed the blood in her veins, and her scalp tingled as if craving the feel of his fingers gloriously tangled in her hair.

'A colour so beautiful it will make you smile whenever you catch a glimpse of yourself in the mirror...'

The words jolted into her as a vision of Imogen flashed before her eyes—almost as if her twin were here in the warehouse.

How Imo would have loved this—revelled in the idea of modelling clothes. Imo had been a born performer, an extrovert, a drama student. As a girl she'd loved their hair colour—would have used it now to be noticed. Imo would have been a poster girl for the extraordinary, but it was Sarah standing there, talking, laughing, living, feeling, fantasising. Imogen was gone, her vitality no more…dust to dust and ashes to ashes.

Pain gripped her, and a sense of wrongness. Followed by another wave of dark, deep pain…an ache that seared and burned.

'Sarah? What's wrong?'

Pull yourself together.

'Nothing. Nothing's wrong.'

Except her behaviour. This was a job—it was not an opportunity to flirt. It was all about a chance that she was taking for Jodie's sake.

'I'm fine. Just had a sudden dizzy spell. Probably hungry.' She held up the sandwich. 'I'll eat this and I'll be fine. But if it's OK with you I need to get back soon. I want to spend some time with Jodie before we leave tomorrow.'

'No problem. I'll get your choices packed up and sent to Milan with us. I'll pick you up tomorrow at three to take you to the airport.'

CHAPTER SIX

BY SUNDAY AFTERNOON Sarah wondered if it was all a dream, even as she zipped up her suitcase. How was it possible that she was going to Milan as a 'promotional consultant'?

Jodie bounced on the bed and then came and sat on the suitcase, her green eyes bright from excitement and, Sarah suspected, from worry.

'How many days till you come back?'

'Five sleeps, sweetheart. But I'll call every day to say goodnight and I'll blow you a kiss all the way from Milan.'

'And it will go through France and across the Channel and land on my cheek?'

'That's right.'

'OK.'

Jodie jumped up and gave her a hug and Sarah felt love well up inside her. Love and a sudden question as to whether this really was a good idea.

Too late. This opportunity was too good to miss—and the fee alone would make a huge difference to Jodie's future.

One last hug for Jodie and her mum and then, heading for the door, she could see Ben's car waiting by the kerb.

She turned for a last look at her daughter and a sudden zigzag of panic nearly skewered her to the spot. How could she leave her daughter? What if something awful happened? What if...?

As if reading her expression, her mum waved and made a shooing motion with her hands, and Sarah forced her legs to keep moving. Once in the car she scrunched herself into a corner and focused on breathing, grateful that Ben didn't try to initiate conversation during their journey to the airport or their walk from a strangely sparse car park to...

A private jet.

Sarah's footsteps came to a halt. 'I...I assumed we'd be flying on a normal plane...a commercial flight.'

'I part-own this with a few other businessmen.'

Of course he did.

Eyes wide, Sarah followed him aboard, showed her passport and looked round the luxurious interior. The whole place was more reminiscent of a hotel than a plane.

She sat down opposite him in a ridiculously comfortable chair and knew that this should be making her feel better, safer. But it didn't. Anxiety churned her tummy as the roar of the engines indicated that the jet was about to take off and she wrapped her hands together in a death grip.

Ben's deep voice rose above the vibrations. 'Have you flown before?'

'Not for years.'

Images began to stream through her mind as the jet took off, ascended up and up and then levelled off. Fourteen years before, when life had been normal. A family holiday. She'd been en route to Spain, sitting next to Imo, who had gazed with avid appreciation out of the window. Sarah, a little more cautious, had wondered what exactly kept the plane in the sky. Nerves aflutter, she'd stared straight ahead, trying to tell herself that the laws of physics meant it all worked and that there was nothing to worry about. Imo—her other half, the other part of her—had held her hand and chattered away about how much fun they would have.

But now Imo was gone, and without her normal life had disintegrated. Sarah had spiralled into a disastrous relationship, her parents' marriage had fallen apart, and her dad now saw life through the bottom of a whisky bottle. The memory of the last time she'd seen him burned in her soul, and the vitriolic words he'd thrown at her still brought a bitter taste to her mouth. That was what loss did: it pounded normality and happiness into a gross distortion.

Panic and fear coalesced inside her, writhed and shuddered together, and she unclicked her seat belt, not sure what she would do next. Race to the cockpit and make the pilot reverse?

'Sarah? You need to tell me what's wrong.'

Ben's voice was calm and now *he* clicked his seat belt undone, rose to his feet and moved towards her.

'Whoa.'

He crouched in front of her seat, took her hands in his, and somehow the firmness of his grasp, his cool authority, his sheer aura penetrated the fog.

'Are you scared of flying?'

She shook her head. 'I don't know. I was always a nervous flyer, but back then...' Back then she'd had Imo and now she didn't. Back then she hadn't had Jodie. 'I'm terrified. I can't take the risk.' Her voice was too high, the words staccato as they tumbled out. 'I can't die. I can't leave Jodie.'

Because she knew the agony of being left, and the idea of Jodie abandoned to grow up without a mother was all too much. It was foolish of her to be here on this private jet with a gorgeous millionaire on her way to a dream job in Milan; foolish of her to tempt fate.

'Hey. Listen to me.' Ben's calm voice penetrated the panic. 'I want you to focus and I want you to tell me five fruits beginning with the letter *B*.'

What? The request was so unexpected she blinked. 'Why on earth would I do that?'

'Humour me. It helps stop panic or anger. It helps regulate emotion. I understand you're scared, and we'll figure out what to do about that. But first think of five different fruits beginning with the letter *B*.'

He was insane—though somehow his voice, the feel of his hands on hers, steadied her, and almost against her will her brain started to consider the question.

'Banana.'

'Good. Four to go.'

'Breadfruit.' She was nearly sure that existed. 'Blueberries…blackberries.'

Now she started to go through the alphabet Ba… Be… Bi… She looked up at him. 'Don't tell me the answer. Just tell me that there *is* a fifth.'

'There is,' he confirmed, his cobalt blue eyes studying her calmly, and she felt the panic recede a little more as she focused and the minutes ticked by.

'Are you feeling better?' he asked.

'Yes. A part of me still wants to run screaming into the cockpit and tell the pilot to turn around, but I'm guessing that would be complicated.'

'It would. Would it help if I gave you some safety facts and statistics?'

'No!'

It was hard to keep the bitterness from that syllable as panic threatened again. Statistics meant *squat*. What were the statistics that had meant Imo died while Sarah lived. Fifty-fifty? What were the odds of Imo getting leukaemia? They hadn't changed the fact that the disease had clutched her sister in its grip and hadn't let go. Despite the sixty-five per cent survival rate.

Anger at the unfairness of it all wrestled with her guilt.

'Then what can I do to help?'

'Distraction worked,' she said, and suddenly there was another emotion in the adrenalin-fuelled mix.

She'd been granted life—a life she'd nearly wasted and thrown away. But here she was, just inches away from Ben, her hands still entwined in his. Gently she freed one, and almost as if in a dream she reached out, pressed her hand against his chest, heard his slight intake of breath.

So alive, so big, so strong, so...*there*.

Another flash of Imogen: her twin's face, the same face she saw every day in the mirror. *Go for it, Sarah. Don't waste time. Live.*

The beat of his heart was strong under her fingers— proof of his vitality. Raising her eyes, she met the vibrant blue of his, saw awareness in his gaze, the darkened cobalt, the flare of unmistakeable desire. And the bone-deep knowledge of how life could be snuffed out—how fate could take a swipe—urged her to live in this moment and this one alone.

So she leant forward and pressed her lips tentatively against the firmness of his mouth.

She heard his slight intake of breath, as if her movement had freed him. Then his hands cupped her face with infinite gentleness and he deepened the kiss. Her lips parted with a small sigh and her whole body suddenly felt boneless as sensations rocketed through her, tingled every nerve end, made her feel gloriously, immensely alive.

Moving as one, they both rose and she pressed closer to him, her entire being focused on this dizzying, intoxicating stream of pleasure.

Until the plane hit a pocket of turbulence and reality broke in.

His hands dropped to her waist to steady her as she pulled back and stared up at him. Shock widened her eyes and she could hear the pounding of her heart, the raggedness of her breath.

Oh, God. What had she done?

'I'm sorry,' she whispered.

'Stop. There is no need for you to apologise. None at all. There were two of us involved.'

But she had instigated it, and right now, if they hadn't been however many thousands of feet in the air, she would have welcomed a hole appearing to swallow her up. But there was nowhere to go, nowhere to run.

'I panicked. I...I truly don't know what came over me.'

Apart from a bad case of lust. But it had been more than that—it had been an affirmation, a confirmation, a reaction to his warmth, his strength and his unexpected understanding.

Enough. There was no need for analysis.

'I guess I needed distraction and the panic kind of made me lose the plot. I'd appreciate it if we can forget this, or at the very least put it behind us as a moment of insanity.'

'Agreed.' He ran a hand through his hair and grimaced. 'I guess we should have stuck to the names of fruit.'

She gave a shaky laugh, relieved at his effort to turn the clock back to pre-kiss time. 'OK. I cave. Tell me the fifth.'

'Actually, there are plenty to choose from. Bayberries… and I'd have given you blackcurrant as well. Then there's a bear berry and of course the betel nut.'

'It was a great distraction technique—but what made you think of it?'

A moment's silence and then he shrugged. 'It's a tactic I've used myself in the past. Not so much for panic as to regulate other emotions. I do understand how it feels to be gripped by an emotion, to feel out of control.'

Sarah shifted to face him. She'd heard the sincerity in his voice, but it surprised her. 'It's hard to imagine you not in control.'

'I can name you three fruits beginning with the letter *W*. Trust me, I've worked through the alphabet a few times. Anyway, I'm glad it helped.'

His tone unmistakably drew a line under the subject, and in truth she didn't dare ask him to elaborate— it wasn't as if she wanted to discuss the reasons for her panic. It would be best to regain the professional footing that had been so disastrously lost in the past hour.

In unison, they snapped open their laptops and settled down to work.

Half an hour later, having breezed through Customs with ease, they emerged from Milan's airport. Next to him, Sarah paused and looked around, her shoulders relaxed for the first time since that disastrous kiss.

Ben uttered yet another mental curse. What had he been *thinking*? The answer to that was obvious. He hadn't been thinking at all. He had simply reacted. And it had been…magical, incredible, glorious. And against every principle he had. Sarah was a single mother, a colleague and soon to be an employee.

Yet he'd kissed her. In part to allay her anguish, her fear, her terror. Not for herself, but for her child. Her love for Jodie was so intense it touched him, whilst also reminding him that there would be no one to mourn *him* if the plane tumbled from the sky. No one he would regret leaving behind.

Which was exactly as he liked it—he could live his life as he pleased, safe in the knowledge that he was hurting no one. But he shouldn't have kissed her, and now it was impossible to erase that kiss from his memory bank.

But he could try.

He saw the chauffeur holding a card with his name on it, raised his hand in salute and headed towards the sleek black car that would take them on the short journey to the hotel. In the car, he watched Sarah's face as she looked out of the window, snapped pictures and looked anywhere but at him.

Even as they pulled up outside the hotel and she alighted she kept her gaze averted, and he couldn't blame her.

'Here we are,' he said.

As always, the façade and location of the hotel triggered in him a sense of satisfaction, representing for him how far he had come. The marble-clad building was set in acres of tranquillity, an oasis of greenery, trees and stately plants, a botanical garden that provided a bubble of quiet and peace amidst the bustle of central Milan.

As they trekked across the black marble lobby a woman walked towards them, a welcoming smile on her face.

'Eloise,' he greeted the manager.

'Ben. Good to see you again.' She glanced discreetly at Sarah.

'This is Sarah Fletcher. A colleague of mine. Maree is on her honeymoon this year.'

'Ah. Please wish her well from me. I will get someone to show you up to your suite. Your baggage has already been taken up.'

Next to him Sarah shifted, glanced at him in question, and he realised he hadn't mentioned the suite to her.

'Not necessary, Eloise. I know the way and we're travelling light.'

Once in the glass lift he explained.

'The suite is enormous. Two separate en-suite double rooms with an immense living area in between. Maree used to have a separate room when we started out, but after a while it seemed easier for work purposes for us to share a suite. Especially given its size.'

Could he emphasise its measurements any more?

'It's fine. There's no reason why it shouldn't be.'

The attempted breeziness of her tone blew hollow, and he had not a doubt that they were both reliving that toe-tingling kiss. Sarah raised a hand to her lips in a jerky movement, and he forced himself not to let his gaze rest on her mouth.

It was hard to say who was more relieved when the lift eased to a halt and the door opened to give them sole access to the top floor.

'Here we go.' He opened the door, then stepped back

to allow her entry, hearing her intake of breath as she stepped in.

'This is…' Her eyes widened as she walked across the living area to the floor-to-ceiling windows that overlooked the garden. 'I have no words.'

The first time he'd stayed there he'd felt exactly the same—overwhelmed by the enormity of the teak-walled room, the granite fireplace, the shelves of books of all genres and sizes, the terrace that wrapped round the whole room, providing an awe-inspiring view of the gardens and Milan itself.

'Later, when we come back, we can sit and look at Milan by night.'

'I could sit there for the whole trip—but that's not what you're paying me for. We need to leave in half an hour and I'm nowhere near ready. Pre-catwalk party hosted by one of the fashion houses, right?'

'Right.'

'OK. I'll be quick. But I need to call Jodie first.'

Tugging her phone from her pocket, she turned from the window and headed for her bedroom. Fighting the urge to watch her departure, Ben headed for his.

He changed quickly into a white shirt, light trousers and grey jacket, no tie. Moments later he exited into the vast lounge area, where Sarah was already waiting, standing by the window.

'I don't think I'd ever get tired of this view,' she said. Turning, she gestured downward. 'Does this look OK?'

'Perfect.'

The elegant off-the-shoulder black dress, simple yet individual, had a band of ruffled flowers across the top. The material curved and flowed, falling to mid-calf. The strappy high heels were fun and sassy, as were the statement long black earrings. Though once again his fingers itched to let her hair down, to see it loose in all its glory.

Why, he wondered, did she always keep it up? Why grow her hair at all if she never let it loose? Perhaps it was metaphorical. Perhaps Sarah Fletcher *never* let her hair down.

'Any advice? Obviously my ordinary world doesn't include star-studded parties.

'Be yourself. All those stars are only people—catapulted to fame due to a mixture of luck, graft and talent. Some of them were just in the right place at the right time. For some it's luck that genetics gave them a look that is fashionable today. But they're all still people.'

'OK. Be myself. And I'll do my best not to make an absolute muppet of myself.'

Yet she didn't exhibit any undue signs of nerves as they made their way to the venue, a bar and restaurant in one of Milan's top places to be seen—a converted sawmill that was the talk of the town.

Once there, he could see why. The brick and raw cement structure was imposing, yet still industrial, and inside the impression of cavernous space almost overwhelmed the viewer. Antique chandeliers lit up the bare walls and exposed beams, shining on the art deco tableware and chairs. Two long tables formed a cross in the middle of the stone floor, their surfaces littered with a medley of teapots, silverware and pitchers. The overall result combined minimalist functionality with glamour.

'It's like something out of a kids' book. I'm almost expecting talking rabbits and giant chess pieces to appear,' Sarah said. 'It's surreal and I cannot believe I am here.'

'I sometimes still feel the same way.'

Even now it did feel unbelievable to him that he'd

clawed his way up, proved the worth of his existence. Now he fitted right in with these guests, who came from all echelons of immense wealth and fame. He talked and walked and chatted and charmed and… And she matched him.

She didn't put herself forward, but neither did she seem overawed, and he couldn't help but be impressed by her poise, and by her ability to manoeuvre her way through the canapés, careful only to choose those that could be eaten with dignity.

Belatedly it dawned on him that he was focusing most of his attention on Sarah, but it was hard not to be aware of her when she was so close that he could smell the tang of her shampoo, sense the warmth of her body.

It was time to focus on someone else—anyone else. So when he was approached by a woman he recognised as a top fashion buyer he did his best to enter into the type of business conversation he excelled at: a networking opportunity to ensure that should she ever look to move jobs she'd approach Sahara first.

Yet even as they spoke he was *still* aware of Sarah, who had discreetly gravitated away from him. Now she was in animated conversation with a famous Hollywood actor and heartthrob—tall, blond-haired with twinkling brown eyes—who had charmed many a woman.

On autopilot, Ben drew his conversation to a polished close and headed straight to Sarah's side, uncomfortably aware of the unfamiliar emotions in his gut. Jealousy? Protectiveness? He wasn't sure.

Sarah looked up at him, her smile illuminating her face. 'I was just telling Sam here that Jodie will not *believe* I've met him. So now I have a selfie and an autographed napkin!'

Holding out his hand to shake the actor's, Ben managed a smile, reminding himself that he *liked* Sam, that he was nice man. Maybe he had a bit of a reputation as a ladies' man but, hell...glass houses, pots and kettles and so on.

'You two going to Marina's party after this?' Sam asked. He nodded towards the fashion buyer. 'Joanna's gonna be there.'

'Not for me,' Sarah said. 'It's a big day tomorrow and I want to be able to focus on all those catwalk designs. Plus, nothing could top this.' She waved the napkin in the air before looking up at Ben. 'But you should go.'

'Nope. I'm good—ready to call it a day. Catch you later, Sam.'

He saw Sarah's small frown, but she remained silent as they exited the party, found a taxi, arrived at the hotel, entered the lift, and then their suite.

Then she turned towards him, her expression a combination of hesitation and determination, as if she'd spent the journey back steeling herself. 'Can we talk?'

'Of course. Shall we sit? May as well be comfortable.'

She hesitated, and then walked over to one of the cushioned wicker chairs and perched at the end, whilst he headed to the minibar.

'Drink?' he offered. 'Neither of us partook at the party.'

She nodded. 'A glass of red would be nice.'

Once he'd handed her a glass, he sank down onto the seat opposite her.

'What would you like to talk about?' he asked.

CHAPTER SEVEN

SARAH WASN'T SURE she wanted to talk about anything, and already regretted starting this conversation. Worse, she had a nasty suspicion that her reason for starting it was less than stellar.

Throughout the entire party she'd been so madly, horribly aware of Ben—the accidental brush of their hands, the solid warmth of his body, the deep timbre of his voice. And then, when she had seen him with Joanna, she'd been...*angry*. Because for one terrible, bunny-boiling moment she'd watched the fashion buyer smile at Ben and the word *mine* had flashed into her brain.

Which was ridiculous. One kiss—which she was desperately trying to regret and forget—and she had morphed into an idiot.

Which was why she'd decided they needed to talk—have a proper conversation that would hopefully cure her of this stupid attraction.

So she took a sip of wine, savouring the spicy, full-bodied taste, glanced out at the panorama of night-time Milan and then looked at him. His body language was relaxed, his large hand cradling his glass of wine as he waited.

'I don't want you to feel as though you have to baby-sit me.'

His expression was unruffled. 'I don't. I saw and was thoroughly impressed by how you held your own at the party.'

She couldn't help the small smile and the glow of warmth his words brought, even if she wasn't now sure how to take the conversation further. She knew she was skirting the real issue.

'Thank you. But you know you didn't need to come back here; you could have gone on to the next party.' She took a deep breath and forced herself not to clench her nails into the palm of her hand. 'With Joanna.'

His calm expression was replaced by sheer bafflement, followed by the dawning of anger as his lips set in a grim line. 'Joanna Michaels is a fashion buyer for Bramley Trussel. She's extremely good at her job. I like her, and if she ever wanted to move jobs I'd welcome her at Sahara. *As an employee*. I was networking. I kissed *you* a few hours ago—do you really think I am now looking for a woman to "party" with?'

'I don't know. I mean… That kiss… I know it didn't mean anything. You kissed me because it would have been rude not to and you wanted to distract me. It's not like you *wanted* to kiss me…'

Her voice trailed off as his jaw dropped and he stared at her for a full ten seconds before he shook his head. 'Do you genuinely believe I didn't want to kiss you?'

'I don't know,' she said again. It wasn't as though her experience was extensive.

His lips turned up in a sudden smile. 'Sarah Fletcher, rest assured that I wanted to kiss you. To be brutally honest, I've wanted to kiss you since I first set eyes on you.'

'You have?' Perhaps it was politically incorrect or unprofessional, and perhaps it was daft, but she couldn't help the goofy smile or the ridiculous glow of sheer satisfaction. 'Then why haven't you?'

Argh! Not what she had meant to say at all.

Closing her eyes, she said, 'Please forget I said that.'

A chuckle greeted this. 'Actually, I'll answer the question. For a start there is the whole boss-employee situation. Plus, as a general rule of thumb, I don't go around kissing anyone unless I'm one hundred per cent sure they're on board with the idea.' He paused, and then his tone became serious. 'But there is a lot more to it than that. I have some pretty specific relationship rules as well.'

'They have to be women like Leila Durante? Women with beauty, fame, wealth?'

'No.' Ben shook his head. 'I do sometimes date models or celebrities, but not because of their status. Leila and I didn't even make it to the restaurant, remember? And that's because she broke one of my absolute rules in a relationship. She agreed to an article with a celebrity magazine, featuring the two of us as a couple.'

'Before you'd even been on a *date*? Why would she do that?'

'Who knows?' His tone implied that he didn't care. 'Perhaps it was for publicity—perhaps because she hoped to be the first woman to get me to "commit". Any which way—it wasn't going to happen. Because I have no intention of committing.'

'At all?'

Ben wasn't even thirty yet—why would he rule out marriage?

'At *all*. My relationships are strictly time-limited. That

is the rule—the box that must be ticked—and my partner must feel the same, be on the same page as me with her expectations. I only date a woman when I'm sure what I have to offer and what she wants to receive are the same.'

'You're making it sound like a trade agreement.'

'That's exactly what it is. And when I make a trade agreement I make damn sure it's watertight.'

There was a silence as Sarah pondered his words. She knew that she should leave it and change the topic of conversation. Instead she swirled the wine in her glass, watching the red liquid eddy, and tried to keep her voice light. 'Just out of interest, what *do* you have to offer—and what do you expect to receive? Obviously I'm asking for a friend...'

He gave a quick smile. 'For a limited period of time I offer fun, in bed and out, and I offer the chance to do anything you want to do.'

In bed and out.

The words echoed between them and her face flushed as images streamed in her imagination: tangled silken sheets, her hands on the hard muscles of his body, the feel of his skin against hers... *Whoa.* Carefully she placed her glass down, worried she'd miss her mouth if she tried to drink. His dark gaze met hers, and now there was a wicked glint in their depths. As if he could read her mind. As if he matched her thought for thought.

She cleared her throat. 'And what do you expect in return?'

'Pretty much the same. I'm a great believer in mutual benefits.'

Now he was undoubtedly teasing her and her eyes narrowed. 'You expect a fair return on your investment? Someone who gives good...*dividends*?'

It was with satisfaction that she saw him splutter on a mouthful of wine. He just about recovered enough to nod.

'On a serious note, though, when you say "limited period of time", what do you mean?'

'A month—tops.'

'But…how does that *work*? Is it a lunar month? So that on day twenty-seven you—what?—have one final moment of fun, then get dressed and say goodbye?'

'Yes. The whole point of our time together is that it is enjoyable, and both of us can enjoy it without anyone getting hurt or having any regrets.'

'So it really *is* a business deal?'

'Yes. No… It's a mutual agreement—an equal partnership, if you like. It means the relationship doesn't have to be deep or meaningful or complicated or messy. And the most important thing is that no one gets hurt.'

'But what if you actually *like* each other?'

'We do like each other. I wouldn't want to spend that long with someone I didn't like or enjoy spending time with. And I'm not indiscriminate—I only tend to date a couple of times a year.'

'I don't get how you can so categorically rule out a long-term relationship?'

'Because I really can't see the point.'

'Why not?'

'Because it opens you up to a lifetime of worry and angst and the potential to hurt or be hurt.'

Sarah blinked. 'But it also opens you up to the possibility of a lifetime of love and happiness.'

'My way of life brings a lifetime of guaranteed happiness.'

'What about love?'

'Too much risk of mess and complications and misery. Seems to me that love can end up being one-sided, and then any benefits stop being mutual.'

'OK, then. What about family? Don't you want kids?'

'Nope. The whole idea leaves me cold—refrigerated, in fact. The idea of that sort of responsibility—someone dependent on me—isn't for me.'

'But you're missing out. I guess it's not logical, but from the moment I held Jodie in my arms I knew she was the most important person in my universe.'

Her daughter had rescued her from herself, given her a reason to exist. But even without that Sarah knew she would have felt that same overwhelming love.

'Call me selfish, but I'll give the whole thing a miss. Being a husband, a father—it's too much of a commitment. I'm OK with being by myself.'

But he *wasn't* selfish—she wasn't sure what made her so certain, but she was. Perhaps it was because he'd given her a chance…perhaps it was because she sensed his relationship rules were based around his own moral code of not wanting anyone to get hurt.

'Maybe you're just being realistic. In your world it *is* harder to remain faithful, and the divorce rate is higher—that's partly why so many Hollywood romances break up.'

She realised immediately that had been the wrong thing to say. Anger thinned his mouth to a grim line and his cobalt eyes hardened.

'Fidelity is not the issue,' he said.

But along with the anger there was truth, and an underlying shadow of hurt.

Hurriedly she waved her hands. 'I'm not accusing you of being unfaithful. Truly. I only meant that maybe you limit the time period because you're worried you might be—or worried *she* might be… After all, temptation is all around you, and I guess the fact that you are a young, hot millionaire doesn't hurt. Women must throw themselves at you. What I meant was kudos to you—you've recognised that a relationship would be hard so you aren't risking it.'

The grim line remained thin, and there was a definite suggestion of gritted teeth as he spoke. 'I did not say a relationship would be hard for me. I said I am *choosing* not to have one. And it is *not* because I doubt my ability to be faithful—I simply cannot see the point of commitment. Taking the risk of being hurt or inflicting hurt when there is no benefit to the risk.' He took a deep breath and suddenly his lips relaxed into a smile. 'But it's good to know you think I'm young and hot.'

She opened her mouth, either to deny or at least protest, but no words came. 'Yes, well…don't let it go to your head,' she muttered. 'Because this is one woman who is *not* throwing herself at you.'

And if he mentioned their kiss she'd kill him.

'So who *would* you throw yourself at? What's your take on relationships? Your criteria? Do you want the happily-ever-after, fairy-tale ending?'

'Nope.' Though even as she shook her head she wondered if her denial was strictly true.

In reality it wasn't exactly that she didn't *want* it, more that she couldn't picture it at all. Any attempt and the picture went fuzzy—she couldn't bring it into focus, couldn't envisage the chain of events that might lead her to the altar. She couldn't see even the possibility of a happily-ever-after.

'There is no way I'd complicate Jodie's life, or take

the risk of introducing a man into her life who might not stay the course. That's the risk *I* wouldn't take.'

She'd messed up badly enough with her choice of Jodie's father—she'd not add another mistake to the mix.

He frowned. 'But what about what *you* want? Do you want a relationship?'

'Maybe one day, when Jodie is much older and has left home, I would consider it. I do like the idea of companionship—someone to watch a movie with tucked under a fluffy blanket on the sofa with a cup of cocoa.'

Ben stared at her and she couldn't hold back her laugh—a laugh that dragged a reluctant grin from him.

'Your face! I guess that's anathema to you?' she asked.

'Actually, no, it's not. I just can't imagine it.'

For a treacherous moment, though, she *could* imagine it—curled up under a blanket with Ben... For a heartbeat the image solidified, and then it dissolved into the illusion it was.

'I guess you need to be together longer than a month to get to that level of cosy. Or maybe it's just too ordinary. Another example of how different our lifestyles are.'

'But it does show that that is what you want. Cosiness... intimacy.'

She'd swear his lips twisted, as if the words tasted sour.

'So why wait?'

'Same reasons you won't commit. The benefit doesn't outweigh the risk.'

'So you won't even date for the next twelve years?'

'What's the point if I'm not willing to take things further?'

'You may meet someone who will change your mind.

Why not try a few dates, see a guy for a while, make sure he's a good guy and then involve Jodie?'

'I don't *want* to meet anyone who will change my mind.'

Because it wasn't that easy. How the hell was she supposed to know if he was a good guy or not?

Plus 'Finding a good guy does not guarantee a permanent relationship. To quote you, it could be complicated, messy, and someone may get hurt. If that someone is Jodie, it's not happening on my watch. In fact—' she picked up her wine again '—in one way we're on the same page. Neither of us is looking for commitment.'

'But *I'm* still having…fun.' He wiggled his eyebrows. 'Receiving "dividends". I don't want commitment, but that doesn't mean I've given up on *some* type of relationship. You've chosen a life of celibacy and to eschew *any* relationships.'

'I'm fine with that. I will not introduce someone into Jodie's life just to have him snatched away when she's learnt to love him. Jodie comes first.'

'That's admirable.'

Now his voice had softened, and a shadow flashed across his eyes, reawakening her stupid urge to reach out to him.

'I mean that. But you can take that principle too far. *You* are important too.'

'I know. But temporary relationships like yours wouldn't work for me.'

'Why not?'

Sarah stared down into her wine, considered her answer and tried to imagine what it would be like to be one of Ben's temporary women. 'The way you describe it sounds fantastic. Carefree, glamorous…sparkling conversation, fine food and wines—a one-month fantasy.'

'Don't forget the great sex too.'

'I hadn't forgotten.'

Her turn for gritted teeth now. God knew she was trying not to think about the great sex. She didn't need her already overheated imagination to be stoked further.

'I was including that in the fantasy bit.'

'As long as you weren't missing it out. So what's wrong with the scenario?'

'Maybe it's a scenario that only plays out well in *your* world—a world of wealth and glamour as its backdrop. Imagine it in the setting of my more mundane world. I live with my mum and Jodie; my mum would be babysitting. I'd need to get home before Jodie woke up in the morning. We could maybe afford to go out for a pizza, or a drink and a game of pool. But that's not the real problem. I think no matter what the backdrop it would still feel cheap and I'd lose my self-respect. And I can't do that.'

Because in those dark years with Kevin—those fuzzy, horrible years that she wished she could scrub from her skin and her soul—she'd had no self-respect at all. She'd never go back there again; she needed to be able to look Jodie in the eye every day.

Ben leant forward, his cobalt eyes steady and sincere in the moonlight. 'All I can say is that I don't feel any loss of respect for the women I have been involved with, and I genuinely don't think I lose any respect for myself. I don't see my dates as cheap—I see them as equals: women who know what they want and can put those expectations into words. I would never want anyone to lose their self-respect over me.'

His broad shoulders lifted in a shrug and he shifted so his face was in shadow.

'I'm not worth it.'

The words were said lightly, yet they didn't *feel* light.

Sarah studied his face and wondered whether he was truly questioning his self-worth. She sensed a strand of vulnerability in his aura of power and it touched her, tugged at her chest.

But before she could say anything he continued. 'Hence my rules,' he said. 'A woman has to be on the same page as me.'

Silence.

'She has to want the same type of arrangement as me, and the most important criteria is that no one gets hurt. That's also why I wouldn't get involved with a parent. I'd never risk a child getting hurt.'

'And that's why I won't get involved with anyone—I won't risk Jodie getting hurt. So I guess we both have our own moral codes and rules that work for each of us.'

'And never the twain shall meet?'

Sarah nodded and tried to ignore the regret that looped inside her. 'So no more kisses.'

'No more kisses.' There was both regret and finality in his tone. 'But, for the record, that one kiss we shared was a humdinger.'

She nodded, quelling the urge to ask for one last glorious sample. They had both laid down their rules and there was no way to breach them.

One last sip of wine and she placed her empty glass down. 'I'm glad we had this conversation.'

And she was—because mixed with regret was also the slow burn of satisfaction that the attraction was mutual, that he wanted her too. And also relief that the elephant in the room could now be acknowledged.

Rising, she tried to smile. 'I think I'll call it a night.'

'Agreed—on both counts.'

He rose to his feet and she was oh, so aware of his gaze as she turned and headed to her bedroom.

She tried not to wish she wasn't walking there alone.

CHAPTER EIGHT

THE NEXT MORNING she awoke with butterflies in her tummy that even the opulent magnificence of the bathroom couldn't alleviate. Once dressed in a carefully chosen poppy print lacy dress, demurely high-necked, but eye-catching in its vivid colour, she exited her room, drawn by the tantalising waft of coffee.

She stopped on the spot at the sight of Ben, newspaper spread open, laptop on, sitting at the huge table. If only he wasn't so gorgeous…if only a sudden shyness hadn't rendered her frozen. She felt a shyness cast in worry that there would be a lingering awkwardness after the previous night. Had she *really* called him hot?

But his expression as he looked up held nothing but warmth and his tone was matter-of-fact. 'I ordered room service,' he said. 'But if you'd rather eat in the restaurant I can have it all moved down.'

'Nope. This is perfect.'

'The calm before the storm,' he said.

'I think the storm may be going on in my stomach,' she said. 'Nerves.'

'What are you nervous about? Last night you weren't daunted by all those people.'

'It's not the people. I want to do a good job.'

'You will. Again, all you have to do is be yourself. That's what I want—your opinion, your observations, your take. Then, in a couple of days, give me a rundown.'

His words did calm her—they made it sound easy, or at least doable—and she helped herself to scrambled eggs and smoked salmon. She smiled her thanks as he poured her a cup of coffee, then waved her hand and said, 'You don't need to entertain me. Go back to work. I want to run over the day's itinerary.'

Even though she knew it by heart, it still seemed surreal. Two shows. One a tried-and-tested designer followed by an up-and-coming brand. Sudden excitement replaced her nerves as she realised that the challenge was a welcome one. That this really was a chance to show what she was made of. A step towards a better life for her daughter.

But even Jodie was forgotten once they arrived at the first show, which was being held in a former *panettone* bakery. The whole floor was exotic with flowering shrubs to act as a backdrop to the minimalistic designs—clothes that somehow combined geometry with fluidity, the exaggeratedly bizarre with the normal.

This was like nothing she had ever experienced before. The buzz, the atmosphere, the sheer extravagant feel of it all… Disbelief threatened again as they took their places in the front row, and after that the day became a blur of activity.

From the old bakery to a top designer's show—in a basement which been converted into the equivalent of a medical operating theatre, complete with tables, surgical sheets and operating theatre spotlights to illuminate the catwalk. As they sat down a soundtrack of heart monitors and emergency calls mixed with opera added to the mood.

'Is this normal?' Sarah murmured to Ben. 'I mean, how are we supposed to appreciate fashion against all this?'

Yet somehow, as the show started and the models sashayed or swaggered down the catwalk, it all worked. The models in their capes and scarves…the stark drama of it all.

Sarah wrote and wrote until her hands ached, praying she'd be able to read her notes later on.

She was utterly mesmerised by it all—by the colours and the buzz, the beauty and the professionalism of the models. By the intakes of breath, the smells, the hum, the silence, the applause, the sheer *excitement*. By the clothes—the bold cuts, the lavish quirks—and the sashay and sway of the models. The attire of the audience, their avid faces, the emotions of the room… All of it captured and fired her imagination and captivated her interest.

But throughout it all she was still aware of Ben— because whilst the rest of the room was avid, he wasn't. His expression was one of cool interest, and at no point did she sense any genuine emotion or reaction.

She remembered what he'd said the previous day, that it was the ideas that led to the bottom line that floated his boat. For him this was simply a means to more money, more power, more success. Why did he still crave it so badly? What made him tick?

Studying his face, she had a sudden urge to shift closer to him, to tell him it was OK—that he had nothing left to prove. *But that was absurd.* So she turned her attention back to the next model, studied the outfit, jotted down more notes…

* * *

The next two days spun by in a frenzy of activity and colour and noise and parties. But at the end of each day there were no more glasses of wine sipped on the terrace overlooking the moonlit Milanese streets. Instead they both headed straight for their respective bedrooms.

Today Ben sat at the desk in the suite, waiting for Sarah to appear. A morning show and an early lunch party done, they'd returned to the hotel. She'd gone to get her notes for the presentation of her ideas so she'd be ready for a discussion on her observations and opinions.

He was looking forward to what she had to say. Because over the past few days he'd been blown away by her—had found himself sneaking little glances at her face, fascinated by her concentration, her sheer enjoyment, her genuine interest as she worked. Her focus was absolute, her energy unflagging. Every so often she would disappear, and he suspected she was speaking with her daughter, but she maintained a professional aspect at all times.

As the days had gone by he'd found himself thinking about her more and more, wondering about her life and how she had ended up as a single mother. At a guess he imagined a university relationship that had ended in pregnancy. But that didn't make sense. Her daughter was six now—why wouldn't Sarah have resumed her studies, or at least opted for a different, better job?

He looked up as she came in, sensing her nerves. It was strange that she had fitted into this setting with such poise and yet anything work-orientated caused her aplomb to waver slightly. As always, her beautiful hair was pulled away from her face—another mystery, another unasked question—and she had chosen a monochrome outfit. A long-sleeved black top tucked into an asymmetrically cut long white skirt, simply adorned with two black buttons. The overall effect was simple and arresting—truly the ordinary made extraordinary.

She placed her laptop on the table and then handed him a report, beautifully bound. As he opened it he saw from the layout that she'd made it look both professional and appealing.

'It's a summary of my ideas,' she explained.

At first her voice betrayed her nerves. Her presentation was slightly breathless, her pitch a little high, the words a little fast. But then she got into her rhythm as her enthusiasm for the subject overtook her nerves. Her expression radiated her belief in her opinions and admiration touched him in recognition of the hard work and effort she'd put in.

'I thought the shows we saw all had one thing in common—they were less vibrant than in previous years, less "out there", and also less…overtly sexy. So your "ordinary is extraordinary" theme is right on target. Hemlines were lower…less cleavage was on show. But I do think you have a chance to add something here. I love the muted look—I think it's classic and elegant—but I think there are times when people do actually want to look sexy. Not necessarily when they're out partying, but perhaps for a wedding anniversary or a big date. So perhaps you should offer a few items like that and develop some occasion-based advertising. A wedding anniversary is an ordinary yet extraordinary occasion, and even if you're celebrating at home with a takeaway it's OK to dress up… I also loved some of the frivolous extras out there—like exaggerated sleeves to add a bit of drama, an exposed zip to brighten up an outfit. So how about doing some fun accessories like the ones the models used? That flamingo umbrella was fantastic—though I was less sure about the pink body stocking.'

At the end of half an hour, as she concluded, he rose to his feet and clapped. 'Sarah Fletcher. The best thing I ever did was bring you here. That was amazing and I'm going to send this straight to the design team. There are some excellent points.'

'Really?'

Her face lit up, causing his breath to catch in his lungs, and all common sense exited. For days it had reigned and now its time was over.

'Really. Hand on heart. So now we celebrate.'

Sarah frowned. 'We've got a show we should attend, and...' She hesitated. 'And after that I wondered if I could have a couple of hours off. Just so I can nip out to get some souvenirs.'

'I can do better than that. Let's call it a day for work. We'll go see Milan and souvenir-shop. What do you think?'

Indecision etched her features as she caught her lip between her teeth. 'I...I told you...I didn't come here to have fun. I came here to work—not to jaunt about Milan.'

'I get that, but your job is done. We have a day and a night before we go, so let's make the most of it. There's no point working for the sake of working, and we've earnt the right to enjoy ourselves a little. Not as boss and consultant—just as two people.'

'Yes, but... I mean, you don't have to come with me. I'm sure you have better ways to spend a day off.'

'Nope.'

A small alarm bell rang in the recesses of his brain when he realised that in fact he didn't. That he wanted to spend the day with Sarah. The need to justify this provided an explanation.

'You've done a fantastic job and I'd like to show my appreciation of that. So let's go. Unless… Is it me?'

Wouldn't that be an eye-opener? If in fact Sarah was looking for a diplomatic way to avoid his company?

'Would you prefer to go by yourself?'

'No.' Her eyes closed in rueful acknowledgement. 'That's the problem.'

'Ah. I've thought about that…'

'You have?'

'Yes and I've decided—screw it. We're both adults, and we're attracted to each other, but we've decided not to act on that attraction. It doesn't mean we can't enjoy each other's company. Right?'

That inner voice tried to point out that there were flaws to this logic, but Ben was having none of it.

Doubt and desire warred in her brown eyes and then she nodded. 'Great. I'll just change quickly and then I'm all yours.' She stared at him in almost comical dismay, then managed, 'So to speak…' before turning and practically fleeing from the room.

Nice one, Sarah.

Annoyed at herself, she quickly shed the skirt and top and opted for a red lacy dress. It was not what she would have chosen if she were going alone, and she almost decided to change into jeans and a top. But the dress was pretty and…

Admit it, Sarah.

It was a touch sexy as well. Sure, it had a demure collar at the neckline and it hit mid-calf, but that was combated by the mesh underlay and peek-a-boo lace. But, sensible or not, she was wearing it.

After all, none of this was sensible. Because whilst her brain told her it wasn't a date, her emotions felt it was exactly that. It was as if by presenting her report she had cut the employer-consultant connection.

Instinct told her she was playing with fire, tempting fate, that this was a mistake, but once ready she flicked a glance in the mirror and headed for the lounge, determined to make sure to play this down.

It was a resolution that dissolved the second she set eyes on him when, as always, the sight of him flipped her tummy and tingled her toes.

'I'm ready to go,' she managed. 'Let's do Milan.'

As they exited the hotel it felt good to walk along tourist-thronged streets, through narrow alleys redolent with the tantalising smell of pizza. Part of that pleasure came from walking close to Ben, feeling the warmth and strength of his body, the awareness and an added edge as she moved slightly closer to him.

You're playing with fire, warned her inner voice.

Just one round, her body argued back. *Not enough time to get burnt...the flames are under control.*

'Cathedral first?' he suggested. 'Il Duomo is an absolutely incredible place. I visit every year.'

'With Maree?'

'No.' He grinned. 'Maree isn't big on culture or sight-seeing. This is something I usually do by myself.'

'Oh...' Doubt flickered. 'If you'd prefer to split up...?'

'Nope. I'd like to go with you. I think you'll appreciate it and...'

'And?'

'It'll be nice to witness your enthusiasm. Your face literally lights up.'

Sarah wasn't sure how to respond to that, so she settled for annoyance. 'So you like my lack of sophistication?'

'No.' He shook his head, refusing to rise to the bait. 'I like your enthusiasm. I like that you are enjoying yourself. Your sophistication and poise has been completely evident these past days.'

There was that all too familiar shiver of guilt—because she *was* enjoying herself. Of course she missed Jodie—she really did. But, having spoken to her twice a day, she knew her daughter was perfectly happy, having fun with her grandmother, and secure in the knowledge that Sarah would be home soon.

So she knew her guilt to be misplaced—and yet it persisted. Guilt that she was here under false pretences, and a generalised guilt that had seemed to be part of her very soul since Imo had died. A guilt she managed to push away whilst she was working, but now... This was sheer indulgence.

For a moment she considered the option of turning tail and heading back to the hotel. But that would be downright rude—plus she suspected that Ben would demand and be entitled to an explanation.

'In that case, lead on,' she said instead.

'They say all roads in Milan lead to Il Duomo,' he said.

Indeed, she could see its looming majesty as they walked. But nothing could have prepared her for the up-close reality, the sheer vastness of the light marble façade with its fairy-tale undertones of pink, orange and blue.

'How can a building be so colossal and yet so delicate? The spires are like a forest, reaching for the sky.'

'Apparently Mark Twain described it as "So grand, so

solemn, so vast! And yet so delicate, so airy, so grace-ful!"'

'Well, he got that spot-on.'

'Rooftop first, and then we can look inside?'

'That works for me. I can't believe you can actually walk on the roof.'

Once they'd ridden the elevator up she really did feel as though she needed to suspend belief. She felt the mag-nitude of being atop the magnificent building, walking between the lacy spires of delicate marble and the pleth-ora of rich carvings, sculptures and gargoyles on view.

'Look.'

Ben was pointing upwards, and for a moment instead of following his instruction she focused instead on the sculpted length of his arm, the outline of muscle, and imagined that given a chance the Renaissance sculptors would have loved to use this man as a model.

She gulped and then caught sight of the statue atop the cathedral's main spire.

'The Golden Madonna, symbol of the city. She's watched over its people for centuries.'

Turning to look down at the streets below, Sarah felt almost dizzy as she gazed at the surroundings and tried to imagine all the work that had gone into building it.

'All those people all those centuries ago were just as real as all the people down there now. Different clothes, different outlooks, but essentially the same as us—all part of humanity.'

'Yes, it's humbling to realise how ephemeral our lives are in the context of time, but it doesn't make an indi-vidual life any less vital and important just because it's one of billions. Every life is important and worthwhile.'

His voice was quiet, but ringing with vibrant sincerity, and she nodded.

'Each of those people down there has their own problems, and it doesn't matter if they're rich and powerful or poor and without any influence.'

She gave him a sideways glance. 'Do you really believe they're equally important? Doesn't that become harder when you're rich and powerful yourself? Surrounded by successful people? Isn't it a bit like standing up here and thinking everyone else looks like ants?'

'No. It won't happen to me.'

'I bet that's what they all say. It must be difficult to maintain perspective—after all, that's why you hired me, isn't it? Because you were worried you'd lost touch with the ordinary world?'

Doubt touched his face and then he shook his head. 'I will always believe that everyone is equal. Because I know what it's like to be seen as an ant—insignificant, invisible.'

She sensed that up here, amidst the glory that had endured for so many hundreds of years, it was easier for him to share, and quietly she said, 'Tell me.'

There was a slight hesitation and then he shrugged. 'When my mother got divorced she ended up losing her lifestyle. Her middle class, affluent life crumbled and I saw her become invisible. Unimportant. Her friends looked through her; it was as if she wasn't even there. I won't treat *anyone* like that. *Ever.*'

'I'm sorry.'

And she was—not just for his mother, but for the young Ben, who would have watched his mother's humiliation. For a moment she could see that younger version of himself in the shadows in his eyes. She wondered what ramifications the divorce had had on him.

Without thinking, she shifted closer to him so they were side by side. 'Divorce sucks.' It was messy and complicated—maybe that was why Ben was so anti-commitment.

'It does. But I vowed that I'd make it up to her, and I did. She will never want for anything again.'

Sarah frowned. *Make it up to her?* That almost implied he felt it was his fault.

'She must be very proud of you,' she said. And now she wondered if his drive to succeed and make money had been in part at least for his mother. To give her back the lifestyle she'd lost.

'Yes. I hope so anyway...' But there was doubt in his voice, a hint of vulnerability that tugged at her heart.

'I can guarantee she is. And not because you're rich. But because she's your mum. I bet she was just as proud of you when you made your first sale in the market stall as she was when you made your first million. Am I right?'

'Yes.'

But he sounded as if he were humouring her in order to end the conversation, and she knew there must be a shoal of messy complications behind the story. But right now she regretted that she'd made him sad, and without thinking she reached up to smooth the crease from his brow.

Once started, she couldn't stop. Her hand trailed down his cheek over the jut of his jaw and she felt the small shudder than ran through his body. Oh, God, how she wanted to stand on tiptoe and press her lips against his. But she couldn't—she mustn't. No more kisses. That was the rule.

So she let her hand drop to her side and they stood for

a long moment, their gazes locked, his cobalt eyes dark with desire. She saw his hands clench against his thighs and knew the movement was to stop himself from pulling her into his arms.

'Let's go down,' he said, his voice rough with frustration and edged with desire.

'Good idea.'

Once in the interior of the cathedral she lost herself in its beauty. She counted the pillars carved in dark stone, studied the marble floor with its stunning black, pink and white design, and gazed in awe at the stained-glass windows.

Once her sanity was restored, she suggested, 'Time to shop?'

It looked as though he too had found a way back to friendship mode, and he turned himself into the equivalent of a tour guide, giving her a running commentary as they headed to a shopping mall.

It was the oldest in history, with an impressive glass-covered arcade. He helped her find the perfect store for silk scarves for her mum and Georgia, and guided her to a more touristy place to pick up souvenirs for Jodie.

'What do you think?' she asked, holding up a snow globe with a miniature model of the cathedral inside and shaking it.

'It's cute.'

'We collect them,' she explained. 'Any time we go out for the day, this is the souvenir we buy. This or a keyring. It's a tradition.'

'I was wondering…'

His voice trailed off and she looked at him in question, hearing the uncharacteristic diffidence in his tone.

'I'd like to get Jodie something too,' he said. 'A thank-you for lending you to me.'

The words were imbued with too much meaning and they sent a shiver down her spine.

'Maybe this?' He'd picked up a medium-sized teddy bear wearing a T-shirt saying *I love Milan* on it.

'That's perfect.' As she looked at him holding the bear there went her heart again, hip-hopping and pulling its strings at the same time. 'She'll love it.'

A sudden memory hit her of a similar teddy bear, a different slogan. Imo holding it in the hospital, clutching it like a talisman.

Sarah shook her head to displace the memory, aware of Ben's sudden sharp glance at her.

'All done with the shopping?' he asked. 'Then I have the perfect place to eat.'

CHAPTER NINE

'WHERE ARE WE GOING?' she asked.

He smiled. 'Pizza,' he said. 'The best pizza in Milan, apparently.'

'That's perfect.'

Carefully she folded away the wave of sadness, sensing he was aware of it, and she smiled up at him, touched by his innate understanding that she didn't want another fancy meal, that she craved something more ordinary.

Arriving at the restaurant, he stood back to allow her to enter first. She could feel the nape of her neck tingle at his closeness, and the small of her back craved his touch.

Once inside, she drew in a breath. The interior was basic, raw and rough, with high ceilings and tables of unvarnished wood. High bar stools stood at the entrance and the walls were almost empty of decoration. The whole look was a kind of post-industrial chic, with low lighting.

'I love it,' she said.

'Pizza and cocktails,' he replied. 'I've never been here before but it seemed right.'

For a second she paused. 'Right because I'm not one of your highfalutin dates?'

His face fell for a second, and she grinned at him and instinctively put a hand out to cover his arm. 'I'm teasing you. I love it. It's perfect—and, remember, I'm *not* one of your highfalutin dates.'

'Good.'

His smile warmed her, as did the feel of muscle under her fingertips.

They were soon seated and she stared at the cocktail list, eventually making a selection, and then turned her attention to the pizza menu. Finally she looked across at him and saw an amused look on his face.

'I have never seen anyone take so long to come to a decision.'

'This is *important*.' Hearing the vehemence in her own voice, she smiled. 'There is nothing worse than picking something and then wishing you'd chosen something else.'

The waiter, who must have been discreetly watching, approached and took their order. She turned back to Ben and once again felt a sense of wonder that she was here, with this man, this man who, despite the fact they had agreed to forego attraction, still wanted to spend time with her. The idea dizzied her.

'I want to say thank you.'

'What for?'

'All of this. We're headed back tomorrow and…and I've had the most incredible time. I've enjoyed every minute.'

The cathedral, the glasses of wine staring into the moonlight, the kiss, the hum of desire… *Stop!* That was *not* why she had come to Milan.

'The fashion shows, the opportunity to witness the catwalk first-hand, to taste it, hear it, be within touching distance.' That too was the truth—she *had* revelled in the work. 'It's hard to believe I've also garnered a lucrative fee.'

'You've *earned* it.'

The waiter returned with their drinks and she accepted hers with a smile. 'I never realised a cocktail could be so beautiful.'

Yet this one was, in its curved glass, an orange concoction topped with a white flower and a mini-skewer of tiny strawberries.

Holding it up, she said, 'To you.'

He shook his head. 'To us.' The words resonated between them and he added. 'We made a great team.'

Sarah noted his use of the past tense. She felt regret, followed by a pinch of guilt. There was no regret or sadness to be going back to real life—her life at home with Jodie. Yet as she clinked her glass against his a small whisper at the back of her brain reminded her that it wasn't over yet.

There is still the night ahead.

To drown it out, she said with determination, 'And I've got my Sahara interview next week.'

'I know you'll ace it.' Ben hesitated, sipped his cocktail. 'There is something I don't understand, though.'

'What's that?' Wariness flared.

'I don't get why you're working as a cleaner and a part-time sales assistant. There's nothing wrong with either job, per se, but you've shown me this week that you're capable of achieving a far more lucrative and, I suspect, fulfilling career. PR... Management... A different role in the fashion industry.'

Careful here.

Sarah put her cocktail down on the table, untasted.

'Right now I don't want to pursue a high-flying career; I want to be there for Jodie, so I need a job that allows me flexibility for school drop-offs.'

Ben shook his head. 'That doesn't make sense. Plenty of women in PR and management keep working when they have children.'

'Yes... But...' She picked up her drink again. 'It's just not a good fit for me right now.' She took a sip of her cocktail in the illogical hope that it would mask the lameness of her answer.

'Why not? You want to give Jodie the best start in life so surely you want to earn more money? And what about *you*? You deserve job satisfaction—a challenge, a career path.'

He leant across the table and touched the back of her hand lightly, as if to make sure he had her attention, and the contact zinged through her.

'I've seen your talents—you're articulate, good with people, observant, smart, not afraid to come up with ideas—and you have the confidence to hold your own in a room of celebrities.'

The warmth in his eyes and in his voice suffused her with a glowing pride in her achievement. But the flush was short-lived, as the past cast its cold shadow. This was all built on a lie. Ben Gardiner didn't know the truth about her—didn't know the depths to which she'd sunk.

'Thank you, but right now I am happy where I am.'

'I don't believe that. I recognise talent when I see it and you are definitely hiding yours under a bushel. Why not apply for a job at the Sahara head office?' He pulled out his phone. 'I can check the vacancies right now.'

'No!' From somewhere she forced a laugh. 'Slow down! And listen. That is *not* the route I want to go. It's my choice—my decision.'

Though how she wished it could be different. No qualifications and a criminal conviction… Even with Ben's recommendation that would come to light in the vetting process for a head office job, or somewhere else along the line. The humiliation of exposure, the idea of the disappointment in Ben's eyes—her skin flushed at the very thought.

'Please, just leave it.'

As he opened his mouth to reply the waiter approached again.

'Oh, look. The pizza!' she exclaimed.

Hopefully it would be a conversation-stopper.

Ben waited as the pizzas were placed in front of them and Sarah chatted to the waiter, then raised his eyebrows when the conversation finally ceased and the young man left their table.

'You're probably eligible for the record for the longest time spent discussing green olives.'

'Ha-ha! Actually, I was genuinely interested.'

Her lofty tone brought a smile to his lips—one that widened as he saw the answering reluctant smile on hers. 'So it's nothing to do with you wanting to change the topic of conversation?'

'Nope. This is delicious,' she added. 'Why don't you try yours? Then we can discuss black olives as well.'

'Actually, I'd rather go back to our previous discussion.'

'Well, I wouldn't. Just leave it.'

'I can't.'

He could see that something was tearing into her pride in the job she'd done, and he sensed that whatever it was had prevented her from pursuing a life of her own. He hoped it wasn't the belief that she couldn't be a good single mum *and* have a career.

'You can. Really you can. For example, did you know that black olives are just riper green olives? See, that is way more interesting than talking about me.'

'Nope. It really isn't. Come on. Humour me. Let's just look at the vacancies at head office.'

She gusted out a sigh. 'Why are you doing this?'

'Because I hate to see all your potential wasted.' *As his mother's had been.* 'Because I don't want you to look back and regret lost opportunities.' *As he worried his mother had.*

'I won't. If I miss out, I'll accept that it's my own choice.'

'That doesn't stop regret.'

She placed her slice of pizza down and studied his expression. 'This really matters to you,' she said. 'Why?'

'I told you about my parents' divorce—how my mum didn't do so well in the settlement. No house, no money... just me.'

It was hard to keep the bitterness from his voice. His mother loved him, he knew that, but he also knew she'd had no choice but to take him. There had been no one else.

'After the divorce she tried to get a job—any job—but no one would employ her because she had no experience, and because she wanted hours that fitted around me. She tried everything. She ended up cleaning the houses of her so-called old friends for a pittance. One even employed her to serve at her dinner parties, to kowtow to the people with whom she'd once eaten. But that wasn't enough to pay the rent. We ended up in hostels, and once nearly on the streets, until we managed to get a council house.'

And he'd hated every minute. He'd known that some-how it was all *his* fault. But he'd made up for it. Now his mother lived in the lap of luxury.

'So that's why it's important to me that you fulfil your potential and consider a job that is right for you. My mother was and is bright and capable—she deserved a chance. Shouldn't have been penalised because of me.'

'No, she shouldn't have been. But you know it wasn't your fault, right?'

Dammit.

'Of course I know that.'

But the words sounded hollow, even to himself, and he could see both understanding and compassion in her brown eyes. For a second he wanted to lose himself in that, and then panic jolted through him—he'd shared what he'd shared for a reason.

'But this isn't about me. It's about you.'

'And I really appreciate you telling me. But I promise you my reason for not searching for a better job isn't be-cause of Jodie, and I'm sorry if I misled you.'

Sarah sipped her cocktail as if for courage and he could see her shoulders suddenly slump, her eyes fade, and he almost wished the compassion back.

'I won't accept the job or the chance because I'm not qualified for it. Not qualified for anything. I dropped out of school…hung out with the wrong crowd of peo-ple for years. I don't have a single GCSE—didn't pass a single exam.'

Ben blinked. He truly hadn't seen that coming. It was almost impossible to imagine the woman sitting opposite him as a school dropout, let alone spending years with the 'wrong crowd'. But he could see the truth in the way she looked away from him, wriggled on her chair, picked up her pizza and put it back down again.

And all he wanted to do was reassure her. 'Hey. Look at me.'

With palpable reluctance she lifted her eyes and met his gaze with a dullness in them he hadn't seen before.

'You've clearly turned your life around. And I'd put good money on the fact that if you hadn't dropped out of school you'd have passed the lot. I'm also sure there were extenuating circumstances.'

She shook her head, and he'd swear he saw the glimmer of tears.

'Why would you be so sympathetic? Why think that?'

'Because I trust my instincts and you've proved that you're talented and professional.'

'But I still wouldn't qualify for the type of job you're thinking about at head office. I know that. Every employer wants at least an English or a Maths GCSE, if not a university degree. And it wouldn't be fair for me to leapfrog someone else with only the CV I have. I wouldn't ask for nor want you to use your influence to get me a job. I messed up. I made bad choices. I won't take an opportunity from someone who didn't. And I understand if you want to pull the interview.'

As he studied her expression questions abounded in his brain—why hadn't she got some qualifications in more recent years? Maybe enrolled on an evening course? Done it online? Perhaps he should ask—but he could sense her sadness and knew she must have her reasons.

'Thank you for your honesty. And I definitely don't want to pull the interview. You will be an asset to Sahara in any capacity.'

'Thank you. That means a lot to me. And, Ben...?'

She reached across the table and laid a hand on his arm. 'I'm sorry that your mum had such a hard time, but I also know that no job or career would have been more important than you. She would never have blamed you.'

And she hadn't. But he'd known it was his fault—and the knowledge had been a hard, solid weight in his gut. After all, everything else was his fault.

A memory flashed and seared—his brothers, whom he'd looked up to, loved, and who no longer loved him. He saw their faces pinched with misery and anger as they told him that it was all *his* fault, that he was a bastard, that the man he'd believed to be his dad wasn't, that he wasn't a 'real' child.

No wonder he'd been confused. He hadn't even known what a bastard was. But he had known that he was the cause of the implosion of his family. The devastation of his mother. He could still hear the sound of her crying herself to sleep after his half-brothers had decided to end their visits. Even then he'd figured that parenthood really wasn't all it was cracked up to be.

And this was why he didn't revisit the past—it simply brought back a wave of memories of things that he couldn't change. It was the here and now that was important, and these days his mother had a lifestyle of luxury and was back in contact with his brothers.

And he was sitting here in a restaurant with Sarah and he didn't want this memory to be tainted in any way for her—he wanted to see her smile again.

He covered her hand with his. 'Thank you,' he said. 'And I have an idea. We seem to have lost our celebratory mood, so how about we go and stroll along the streets and eat gelato for dessert?'

Her face lit up with a smile. 'I'd like that.'

CHAPTER TEN

AS THEY EXITED the restaurant into the moonlit night it felt to Sarah as though the darkness held motes of magic. Emotions swept through her. Her heart twisted in sympathy for the child Ben had once been, because he must have been thrown into confusion and turmoil by his parents' divorce. But she felt a deep warmth that he had shared his pain with her, even if she sensed he hadn't told her the whole story.

She moved closer to him, wanting so badly to take his hand, but instead she shoved her fingers into the folds of her dress. And as they walked Sarah could feel anticipation, nerves and a whole flotilla of impulses fizz in her veins.

Don't be an idiot.

Nothing was going to happen. It would be foolish, stupid and wrong and she knew that. Knew it with every fibre of her being. But just for now she wanted to pretend, to suspend reality and indulge in illusion.

A fantasy that she and Ben Gardiner were in a relationship, the parameters of which she refused to consider. Whatever boundaries had been laid down, they were together, heading back to the hotel for a night of...

'Sarah?'

Ben's voice interrupted her and she gave a sudden little jump. 'Yes?'

'You're power-walking.'

'Oh. Sorry...' *For heaven's sake—this is ridiculous.* 'I must be looking forward to my gelato.'

'Then let's try the *gelateria* over there.'

A few minutes later she was looking down at the selection and eventually she settled for one scoop of lemon and another of chocolate.

'Delicious,' she said. 'Thank you. The perfect end to the evening.'

Only she didn't want it to end.

It doesn't have to...

The night was still ahead and it held the promise of possibility. One last night. And then, once they went home, they wouldn't meet again. Simple as that.

You only live once, whispered that insidious voice. *Fate can bash you on the head at any time. Grasp this opportunity... Because a night with Ben will be an experience worth having.*

Daft.

Yet as he finished his ice cream and smiled down at her, her tummy flipped, and she knew, regardless of common sense, that if she wasn't careful she was about to mess up big time.

'Shall we head back to the hotel?'

'Sure.'

She continued the lecture to herself as they crossed the marble lobby, rode the elevator and entered the suite.

'Nightcap?' he offered.

'That would be lovely.'

Huh? screamed the voice of caution.

It would be fine. There was no harm in sitting in an

armchair and having a conversation. Then going to bed. Alone.

Accepting a glass of red wine, she smiled up at him. She saw the serious look on his face and her smile was swapped for a question.

'Is there something you want to talk to me about?'

'Yes.'

Her heart pitter-pattered. Perhaps his thoughts had lined up with hers? Perhaps he was going to suggest… suggest what? A one-night stand? No, he wouldn't do that. His principles would hold out better than hers. After all, he could have a wild night with the likes of Leila any time.

Exactly.

And how would she feel if in a few weeks' time she saw a celebrity article showing Ben's next partner?

'Go ahead.'

'I want to offer you a job. At head office.'

Ah. OK. Whilst she had been in the world of fantasy Ben had been thinking of practicalities.

'I want to offer you an internship that you'll do alongside a study programme. A programme that we'll factor in to your contract. I believe you have a future in fashion, and I'd like it to be with us.'

Sarah stared at him, and now warmth of a different kind flooded over her. Tears threatened the backs of her eyelids. He hadn't just been thinking about practicalities, he'd been figuring out a way for her to have a chance—despite the mistakes she'd made in the past. The chance his mother hadn't been given.

'I…I don't know what to say.'

'Say yes.'

'I can't.'

'Why not? If you're worried about favouritism, don't be. I wouldn't offer this if it wasn't a good deal for me as well. I truly believe you'd be an asset.'

His belief meant more to her than she could have realised, and for a moment she revelled in it—before the moment she'd been dreading came. The decision was oddly easy now. Of *course* she wanted this job, but she'd be building a career on a foundation of mistrust and she couldn't do that.

'I appreciate this more than you will ever know,' she said. 'But I genuinely can't accept.' She took a deep breath and a sip of wine. 'I know I owe you an explanation, so here it is. I've told you that I've got no qualifications, that I dropped out of school and ran with the wrong crowd. Part of that wrong crowd was my boyfriend—Kevin. He was a few years older than me, and on the outside he looked cool…rebellious. I got sucked in.'

She'd been so mixed up, with her grief and her guilt, the injustice of Imo's death tearing at her insides. So she'd told herself that it was OK for her to do it—anything to get out of the house where her parents' marriage had been disintegrating.

All she'd wanted was to escape the deep-down suspicion that Imo had been her dad's favourite—the daughter he'd been closer to. Avoid the knowledge that her own face had become a constant reminder both of what he'd lost and the guilt he felt at his favouritism.

But no excuses. She would not use Imogen's death to excuse her own horrendous choices.

'Anyway, long story short…I ended up with a criminal conviction for possession of drugs.'

No point in a protestation of innocence. Why should he believe her? No one else had.

He stilled, studied her face, and then he spoke. 'I'd like to hear the long story.'

'Why?'

'Because it matters. My instinct tells me that no matter what or who you were back then you would never have had anything to do with drugs. That it would never be in your nature.'

Again tears threatened.

'And I also believe in second chances. Even if you were guilty I do not believe that one mistake should blight the rest of your life. A life you seem to have turned around. So tell me the long story. The full truth.'

Oh, God. What to do? It sounded as if he'd give her the job regardless, so why relive the past? Why take the risk of adding him to the ranks of people who didn't believe her? Because that would hurt way more than it should.

Sarah bit her lip, looked into the deep, dark blue of his eyes and realised that she owed him the truth. If he didn't believe her, so be it. Yet she realised too, how badly she wanted him to have faith in her.

'Try me,' he said again, his voice deep but gentle.

Imperceptibly she shifted closer to him, wanting the warmth and solid bulk of his body near her. No. That wasn't fair. Instead she shifted away but turned to face him so he could read her body language. The man was an expert, after all.

'Kevin was a loser, but I wouldn't admit that at the time. I believed in loyalty, trust and the power of love.'

It was hard to believe she could have thought that what she'd had with Kevin—that dependent, illusory state—was love.

'I'd left home by then and was living in a hostel. Kevin was in a gang. I managed to convince myself that it was only to be cool, for street cred, and that it didn't mean anything. He got into a fight with a rival gang and they planted the drugs in my room—they thought Kevin lived there too. They tipped the police off, my room got raided and the police arrested me.'

Her skin became clammy at the memory. At first it had all seemed so preposterous. Surely the police wouldn't believe she'd had anything to do with it? But they had.

'It turned out that Kevin was involved in things I genuinely had no idea about.' Her eyes met Ben's. 'I realise how stupid that sounds, but I believed everything he told me. I had my head so deep in the sand it's amazing I could see anything.'

'Surely they believed you? You had no record and they had no proof the drugs were yours.'

'But they did. Kev was so scared he'd go to prison that he tried to persuade me to take the fall for him. But I said I wouldn't.' She'd retained *some* small shred of common sense. 'So he set me up. He persuaded a number of his mates to come forward and testify against me. They claimed they saw me buy the drugs.'

The memory was enough to make her shudder, and her skin crawled with remembered fear.

'And no one believed me. I couldn't prove I was anywhere else on those dates, so I was convicted. As it was my first "offence" I got a very short sentence and community service. But it's on my record for ever.' Her lips twisted. Perhaps I deserved it—a conviction for my own stupidity.'

'No.' Now Ben had shifted closer to her, and his hand covered hers in a grasp of reassurance. 'You didn't deserve that. *Any* of it.'

Hope beat a tattoo on her soul. 'You believe me?'

'Yes, I believe you. I don't think you would ever get involved in any way with drugs. It wouldn't be in you. I also suspect a good lawyer would have proved your innocence at the time.'

Sarah gave a shaky laugh. 'I didn't know any good lawyers. I was too dazed, too in shock to think straight. I should have contacted my parents, but I felt so ashamed, and it felt so hypocritical to run to them for help. I kept thinking that it was all a mistake, that of course Kevin couldn't have done that to me.' She took another look at him. 'You really believe me?'

He reached out and tilted her chin upwards, so she had to look directly into his eyes, where he could see sincerity blazing forth. 'I really do.'

Then, as if to seal the declaration, and as if he couldn't help himself, he shifted forward and brushed his lips against hers.

He pulled back and she couldn't help her small gasp of protest. So she leant forward, cupped his cheek in her hand and felt rough stubble under her fingers. She pulled him towards her—and then he was kissing her again.

The world tipped into slow motion, the dusk seemed to blanket them, and she closed her eyes to lose herself in sensation: in the firmness of his mouth, the taste of his lips, the shifting of the sofa as he moved closer to her and angled their bodies to a perfect fit. Then he deepened the kiss and her lips parted on a small gasp of pleasure. Her body shivered as a ripple shuddered through his broad frame.

It was like floating on a cloud of cotton. Nothing else mattered…nothing at all…

Until he pulled back and she saw regret fighting the desire in his eyes.

'I'm sorry.'

'I'm not.' To her own surprise, she wasn't. 'I wanted to kiss you.'

New-found optimism, a bubble of joy, and the relief of telling him the secret she'd buried for so long replayed again and again in her head, turning her lips upward in a smile.

'And I enjoyed every second.'

Now his own lips turned up. 'That's good to hear. But…'

'But it can't go any further. I know that.'

A part of her wanted it to, but she knew he was right. A one-night stand wouldn't work for her. She wasn't wired like that. She didn't want to sleep with someone who had already factored in the goodbye. Because whilst she had no doubt the night would bring a physical satisfaction she couldn't imagine, she sensed it would also bring emotional hurt. She wouldn't be able to read the headlines about Ben with his next woman. It was as simple as that.

And so she slid away from him and rose to her feet. 'But now would be a good time for *this*. Wait here a second.'

Ben tried to focus, tried to think, but his brain had been frazzled by that kiss, by its intensity, its sweetness…all underlain with the knowledge that it could go no further. However much his body wanted more, yearned for more, he knew it couldn't happen. They'd already crossed a line and, foolish though it sounded, that kiss had transcended the physical.

It had been a kiss that had stemmed from an emotional connection.

And that was disastrous on so many levels he wasn't even going to analyse it.

What Sarah had shared with him had made that even more absolute. Kevin had been a loser, an idiot and lower than scum. Sarah knew that, but still felt she'd deserved everything she'd got, and her fear of losing her self-respect made more sense than ever. He would not be the person responsible for that loss.

Sarah deserved a real, long-term relationship with a man who would love and cherish her and look after her. In other words, not him.

The realisation was strangely bleak but absolute.

'Here.'

Refocusing, he saw that Sarah was standing in front of him, her face flushed, partly with the after-effects of their kiss but also, he sensed, with a touch of embarrassment.

She held out a package—a wrapped package. 'What is it?'

'It's a gift. I was going to give it to you on the plane on our way back, but now seems better.'

'You didn't have to get me a gift.'

'I wanted to. To say thank you. This has been magic. You've made a real difference to my life with this opportunity. The money will make a huge difference to Jodie's future, but it's more than that. You've shown me what I'm capable of. So this… I mean, I know it can't really show you, but I wanted you to have it… If you don't like it…'

Taking the gift from her, he realised that he had no idea what to say or how to react. When was the last time anyone had given him a gift?

He unwrapped it carefully as emotion tightened his chest. It was a picture—a quirky black and white shot of the cathedral.

'Thank you.' The words were a little hoarse.

'If you don't like it, that's fine. I just thought…because you said how much you love the cathedral…'

'I love it. I really do. Thank you.'

He wanted to say more—hell, he wanted to stand up and pull her back into his arms. He wanted to—

Instead he cleared his throat. 'When did you get it? I had no idea.'

'When I said I needed the loo after we left the cathedral. I—'

Before she could complete the sentence her phone rang, and she frowned as she rummaged in her bag. For an instant he could see panic etched on her face and an echoing alarm pinched his nerves.

'Mum? What's wrong?'

He couldn't make out the answer but he saw her relax. Her expression morphed from terror to surprise—a frowning surprise. He watched as she paced, asking the odd question, but nothing added to his understanding of events.

Then a few final sentences. 'Mum, we'll sort it out one way or the other when I come back. And it does sound positive. It's fine. I love you too. See you tomorrow.'

Dropping the phone, she turned to face him.

'Is everything OK?'

'I'm not sure.' She ran a hand over her face, almost as if to wipe away the worry and concern, and he felt a shimmer of need, a desire to walk over and pull her into a hug. Instead he compromised by moving a bit closer. Reminded himself that if Sarah needed help it would be better to offer it on a practical level. Money. Cold, hard cash. Because that was the help he was best equipped to give.

'Is Jodie OK?'

'Yes, she's fine. It's…' She began to pace.

'If it'll help to talk, I'm happy to listen.' Because he wanted to help, but couldn't figure out how if he didn't know the problem.

This drew a half-laugh as she paused mid-stride. 'I've told you so much this evening I might as well keep on going. My parents divorced eight years ago.'

Her tone was factual but Ben knew that she felt responsible. He recognised the shadowed, stricken look in her eyes.

'Whilst you were with Kevin?'

'Yes. My father became a functioning alcoholic who gradually morphed into a dysfunctional one. He lost his job—lost everything. Mum tried to help, to hold their marriage together, but she couldn't. They ended up divorcing. After Jodie was born I tried to reach out to him, but he didn't want to be reached out to. Didn't want anything to do with me *or* Jodie.'

Her pain was so palpable that he had to do something. He moved into her path so she had to come to a halt, and put his hands on her shoulders.

'I'm sorry. Divorce is hard, regardless of the circumstances. But alcoholism adds a whole new dimension; it changes a person. I imagine that makes the loss greater?'

'Yes. The dad I remember was gone. He was a good dad when w—' She stopped. 'When I was growing up. A happy, loving dad, who carried me around on his shoulders, did embarrassing dad dances at birthday parties… But that man is gone; the last time I saw him he ranted and raved…said Jodie was tainted.'

He could hear the hurt and bewilderment, the anger and sadness in her voice. And he too knew the pain of losing a father—not to death but to change. He had lost the man he'd believed to be his dad for the first five years of his life—the man he'd loved and who had loved him. That love had stopped—been switched off as easily as a faucet.

'I'm sorry… I wish I could take that hurt away, but I can't.' Somehow, almost without realising it, he had taken her hands in his.

'Anyway, Mum just called because he has been in touch. Dad has joined Alcoholics Anonymous—he's trying to turn his life around. He wants to make amends.'

The scepticism in her voice was clear, alongside more than a hint of bitterness.

'That's a lot for your mum and you to take on.'

'Yes… Mum is going to see him tomorrow—after we get back. He's in a hostel now, but he's been living on the streets in Newcastle.'

'It's good that he's trying. It's positive that he wants to turn his life around.'

'Yes.' But the dull flatness of the syllable sounded forced. 'I just don't want Mum to get hurt, and I don't want Jodie to know about any of this. It all feels a bit…' she managed the ghost of a smile '…complicated.'

The word was a reminder of exactly why he didn't want relationships—why he had refused to be part of his mother's attempt at reconciliation with his half-brothers. He had fully supported his mum's desire to be part of their lives again and would do all within his power to make that happen. He would fly them and their families over from Australia, where they now lived—anything his money could buy he would provide. But no more.

'Would it help if you got home earlier? Would it make you feel better to see your mum? To allow her to go and see your dad sooner? I should be able to move our flight.'

'Are you sure?'

'Consider it done.'

'Thank you. *Really*.'

And as she looked up at him there it was again—the urge to hold her, to try and take the burden from her shoulders.

Instead he gently released her hands. 'You're very welcome. Now, why don't you try and get some sleep and I'll let you know how soon we can fly.'

CHAPTER ELEVEN

SCANT HOURS LATER, ensconced once more in the luxurious interior of the private jet, its engines roaring in preparation for take-off, Sarah looked across at Ben, full of gratitude for his willingness and ability to make this happen purely to allow her to get home earlier. For his innate understanding of her need to be with Jodie and her mum at this time.

So much had changed since their flight out; she'd learnt so much more about this man who, even now, amidst her emotional turmoil, still raised her pulse-rate as he smiled across at her.

'How are you doing?' he asked. 'Nerves under control?'

'Yes.' And in truth they were—although there was still a flutter of fear in her tummy which she was only just able to quell. Helped by the knowledge that this was the quickest way to get home. And also helped by the reassuring warmth of his presence.

Another emotion swirled into the mix: a whirl of sadness. Because after this flight she wouldn't see him again.

As if his thoughts had followed her own he said, 'When we get back would you like me to start the paperwork for your job in head office? I meant what I said last night about the intern's job.'

'And I truly appreciate the offer, but I can't take you up on it. Or at least not yet. You see, I'm not sure how things will pan out with my dad, but I do know I can't rely on my mother as much for childcare. There are school holidays to think about. I'd be working and studying and looking after Jodie—I'm worried Jodie will suffer.'

Ben considered her words, a slight crease on his forehead. 'There are answers to that—after-school clubs, other types of childcare, flexible hours. I can't help thinking there's something else—some other reason. Is it because of what happened between us?'

His frown deepened and she could see the concern on his face. She hastened to speak, to reassure him. 'No. Truly it isn't. We agreed not to regret that kiss and I don't. It's not you. It's…'

It was all the reasons she'd stated, but Ben was right—there was more. Alongside the practicalities was an innate, illogical knowledge that it was somehow *wrong* to take the chance on offer.

'It's just that the time isn't right. I've also been thinking that Jodie and I may need to move out of my mum's for a bit.'

'Why?'

'Because I know my mum. She won't be able to abandon my dad in Newcastle. Dollars to doughnuts she'll bring him back to London. In which case she'll want him to be able to come to the flat. I don't want to be there and I certainly don't want Jodie to be there.'

She could hear the bitter undertone in her own voice but it was impossible to erase the last time she'd seen her father. The squalor, the empty bottles and a man she'd barely recognised. A father who had ranted at her, his words slurred, accusing her of breaking her mother's heart with her behaviour, of letting the memory of her sister down. And worst of all had been his repudiation of his granddaughter.

'She'll be tainted by that waste of space who fathered her. Blood will out, m'girl. And hers is tainted.'

There'd been a pause as he'd taken a hit from the bottle in his hand.

'Just like my Imo's was. My poor precious Imo.'

Then he'd cried—loud, unabashed sobs—but when she'd approached him he'd pushed her away.

'Get out, get out, get out! Your face! It's a reminder of all I've lost. Get out.'

It was a scene she'd shared with no one—not even her mother. The hurt was too deep.

Aware that Ben was watching her closely, she summoned a brisk note to her voice. 'So I think it makes sense for Jodie and me to move out. For a while, anyway.'

'Where will you go?'

'I'm not sure yet. I need to talk to Mum first; it could be I've got this all wrong. But I can find a flat on a short-term let. Thanks to you I'll be able to afford it.'

'With the money you wanted to put aside for Jodie?'

'Plans change. It's Jodie I need to think about. I don't want to move far from her school, and I need to be near Mum. She'll need support. But, like I said, it could be I'm jumping the gun. My dad may not want to come back to London, or Mum may decide it's best to leave him in Newcastle.'

Ben thought for a moment, rubbing the back of his neck. 'If you do need to move at short notice, why don't you and Jodie come and stay with me for a bit?'

Huh? 'Stay with *you*? We couldn't do that.'

'Why not? I have an enormous house in London. It's got five bedrooms, four bathrooms. It makes sense. If you need somewhere to stay temporarily, use my house. It would save you money—and hassle.'

'But it's your *home.*'

'No matter. I'm not in it that much. It's big enough that we'd all have plenty of space. We'd barely even notice each other.'

As if...

Her hormones could sniff him out at fifty paces. And why was she even *thinking* about this? Because it might make practical sense—nothing more.

'That's really kind of you and I will consider it if we need to move out.'

'Just let me know. I can have a car or a van at your door to pick you and Jodie up whenever you need it.'

'That's really kind…' she repeated, and as she spoke the pilot's voice boomed out, announcing that landing was imminent.

Once home, Sarah let herself in and tiptoed into the lounge. Seeing her mum was still awake, she felt her heart turn over with love.

'You didn't need to wait up. It's the early hours of the morning.'

'I got some sleep. I just got up early,' Mary said. 'Welcome back, sweetheart.'

She hugged her mum, saw the worry lines around her eyes and said, 'I'll quickly go and look at Jodie and then you need to tell me about Dad.'

A couple of minutes later they sat together, as they had so many times before, cocoa in hand, and Mary sighed.

'He sounds like he means it. I spoke with his doctor. He's been sober for two weeks now. But he's not finding it easy. It's hard for him to face up to where he is without the bottle to make reality a bit blurry.' Tears glistened in her brown eyes. 'I don't know how it's come to this, Sarah. He's been homeless—on the streets. But he says he wants to turn things around, and when I offered to go and see him he sounded so grateful I could have cried. I did cry, in fact. We talked for hours. He's thinking about coming back to London. He thinks it might help him.'

'Did...?' Sarah had to clear her throat to get rid of the hitch. 'Did Dad mention me?'

'Yes. I think he's deeply ashamed. He didn't tell me the full story. I'm not sure he can even remember exactly what he said when he last saw you, but whatever he can recall I think he regrets very much.'

The words were a balm—though not enough to erase the raw truth of that last meeting.

'I'm glad he mentioned me, and I hope that Dad does it—I hope he succeeds. And if it's easier for you both— if he is serious about coming back here—I can move out for a bit.'

Mary shook her head vehemently. 'Absolutely not. This is your home. Yours and Jodie's. I would never ask or want you to leave it. Not even for your dad.'

'I know that, Mum. I'm offering. Just to move out for a bit. That way if you want to you can bring him back here, or he can come and visit. Or even stay here for a bit whilst you sort out somewhere more permanent.' Sarah's gaze skittered away. 'In fact, Ben said we could stay with him.'

Her mother stared at her. 'Stay with Ben *Gardiner*?'

Sarah could feel the slight flush coating her cheekbones. 'Yup. It's a favour. He said he has a huge house and we'll barely even see each other. He'll probably be away on business anyway.'

'And you're happy to do that?'

'Yes.'

For the life of her she couldn't think of anything else to say.

Mary looked at her closely and then clearly decided not to pursue it further.

'OK. I'll bear it in mind as an option when I see him tomorrow. Thank you, sweetheart—but know this: your home is here.'

'I know that, and I appreciate everything you've done for me and Jodie, more than I can ever say.'

It was another hour before she and her mum finished talking and Sarah tiptoed into the room she shared with Jodie and fell into bed.

Thoughts swirled and chased through her tired mind, but her last thought before she fell into restless sleep was Ben. Along with the insidious realisation that a part of her *wanted* to go and stay with him.

Danger! Danger! Danger!

Her subconscious was a Klaxon…

Two days later Ben paced his house, then checked the rooms for the hundredth time and his watch for the millionth. He forced himself to go into his study and sit down. This was daft. This was no big deal. Sarah and her six-year-old daughter were coming to stay for a while. This was a favour for a…a colleague. There was no reason for his nerves to be twanging as though he'd drunk a vat of espresso.

Madness.

Once he'd welcomed his guests, he'd barely see them.

The chime of the doorbell broke into his thoughts and he headed for the door, pulling it open with a smile, very aware that Jodie would be feeling a little unsettled at being uprooted from home.

'Hey.'

'Hey…' Sarah's smile looked a little forced, a little tired, a little worried—he guessed the emotional turmoil of her father's return was taking its toll.

'You must be Jodie.'

He looked down at the little girl on the doorstep and held out a hand. She surveyed him for a long moment and he studied her back. The family resemblance was uncanny, though her eyes were green instead of brown, and the very seriousness of her expression tugged at his chest.

'I'm Ben.'

Solemnly she shook his proffered hand. 'Thank you for inviting us to stay. And thank you for my bear. I named her Benedetta.'

'You're very welcome and that's a perfect name.' He meant it. 'Now, let's bring your stuff in and then I can show you around.' Once the suitcases were deposited by the front door he said, 'Let's go.'

Jodie's eyes widened. 'It's like a…a palace,' she said as they walked along the wide, plushly carpeted hallway and up the stairs.

Smiling down at Jodie, he pushed a door open. 'I've put you and your mum in adjoining rooms, but if you prefer to share that's fine too. I've put an extra bed into one of the rooms.'

Ben tried not to hope too much that he'd got it right. He'd tried to prepare a welcoming room for a six-year-old without unduly flaunting his wealth, hearing Sarah's voice in his head telling him it was important to keep it 'ordinary'.

Jodie gave a little squeal of pleasure as she ran towards the bed.

'Your mum mentioned you like unicorns so I thought you might like one in your room.' The large, fluffy cuddly toy had seemed like a nice idea. 'And I picked up some books you might like. Your mum also mentioned you like pirates.' The book was filled with different pirate stories and activities.

He glanced quickly across to Sarah and the smile she gave him both warmed and embarrassed him.

'Thank you,' Jodie said as she picked up the unicorn.

'You're welcome.' He pointed. 'And through that door is your mum's room.'

All he'd done there was put some fresh flowers in as a welcome and a small box of expensive chocolates.

'You've gone to a lot of trouble. Thank you.'

Her smile was genuine and it lit up her tired expression, giving him a warm sense of satisfaction. He'd got it right—he'd lightened her load a little.

'No problem. I'll give you a hand moving your stuff and then I'll leave you to settle in.'

'We're going on a day out,' Jodie said. 'We're going to the cinema and to have some lunch.'

'That sounds like fun.'

'What are *you* doing today?' Jodie enquired, her little voice ultra-polite.

'Um… I…I haven't decided yet.'

'Would you like to come with us?'

Sarah blinked and he saw surprise cross her face.

'Jodie, I'm sure Ben has better things to do.'

'But he doesn't,' Jodie pointed out.

Ben couldn't help but smile. He caught Sarah's eye and his smile broadened at her look of embarrassment.

'And,' Jodie continued, 'it's mean to leave him out.'

'Well…'

'It's very kind of you to ask me, Jodie, but I think your mum might have planned a girls' day out.'

Jodie frowned. 'Don't you *want* to come?'

To his utter surprise Ben realised that he did. Perhaps it was the knowledge that his own flesh-and-blood niece and nephew had never met him, and would therefore never ask him to go to the cinema, or perhaps it was the fact that the day suddenly seemed to stretch emptily ahead. Who knew?

'I do want to come, but…' He glanced across at Sarah. 'I don't want to intrude.'

Bafflement switched to resignation in Sarah's brown eyes and he could almost see her forcing her lips to turn up in a smile. 'You wouldn't be intruding at all. But be warned: it's not the sort of entertainment you're used to.'

This last was said in a low voice as she walked towards the door.

She turned back to her daughter. 'Jodie, honey, why don't you go and get your suitcase, unpack, and get ready to go?'

The little girl nodded and skipped off. Once she was back and in her own room, Sarah gestured towards the stairs. Ben, assuming that she wanted to talk to him in private, led the way down and into the lounge.

'I'm sorry,' Sarah said softly. 'I never expected her to ask you. I'm sure this is the last way you want to spend your Sunday.'

'It's not a problem at all. Really. I'm touched that she even wants me to come.'

He saw the frown furrow her brow. 'What's wrong?'

'It's unusual for her to ask someone she doesn't know to come on a day out.'

'Maybe she likes me?' Ben suggested. Was that *so* out of the realms of possibility?

'She must do. Are you sure you want to come?' Doubt filled her voice. 'We're going to catch a bus and get ordinary cinema seats and… This isn't like it was in Milan. This is Jodie's world and…'

'I get it. Don't worry.' There it was again—a sudden desire to tug her into his arms and kiss away that worried crease on her forehead.

'And you have to let me pay. We're staying with you and it's important to me.'

He blinked, saw that she really meant it, and nodded.

'And thank you for Jodie's presents, and for making us feel so welcome—it's really kind of you.'

'No problem.'

'Also…' Now the worried crease returned in full. 'I haven't told Jodie that my dad is staying with Mum. I've just told her it's an old friend. I don't want to get her hopes up.'

'Got it.'

Another example of the level of complications that came with familial territory—a reminder that his own chosen path was the optimal one.

Twenty minutes later they were on the top level of a double decker bus, with Jodie chattering excitedly, Sarah laughing. He couldn't help but wonder what it must be like to have that sort of bond. Complicated. And terrifying, he decided as they alighted from the bus and Jodie slipped her hand into Sarah's. That level of responsibility, trust and love. The pain of losing that, as his mother had, would be horrific.

As they headed for the cinema Jodie asked, 'Mum, which friend is coming to stay with Grandma?'

Ben saw tension enter Sarah's neck and shoulders, but her voice was calm.

'An old friend, sweetheart.'

'Do you know him?'

'Yes.'

'Shall we visit him?'

'Maybe when he's feeling a bit better. But to start with it's best to see what Grandma thinks.'

'We could help him.' Jodie turned to face Ben. 'I've got a stethoscope and I think I may be a doctor when I grow up. I want to help people who are sick because of—'

'Oh, look. Here's the cinema! Popcorn for everyone?'

Sarah had practically leapt into the conversation and Ben wondered why. Perhaps to steer the conversation away from the sick 'friend'? And yet instinct told him it was something else...

They entered the foyer, and as Sarah purchased tickets and popcorn the novelty of someone paying for him struck him, causing an odd sensation of discomfort. One that deepened as they made their way into the darkened cinema and handed their tickets over.

It occurred to him that they must look like a family. A unit. A couple with their daughter on a weekend outing. This was *not* his milieu, and for a daft second panic threatened—until common sense came to his aid. This was a one-off. Best to focus on the film—a clever animated story that appealed to all ages and taught a good lesson without being preachy.

'Did you enjoy it?' Jodie asked as they exited.

'I really did,' Ben said.

'Who was your favourite character?'

'I liked the supposedly wicked witch because she turned out to be good.'

'*And* she had red hair,' Jodie said with evident satisfaction. *And* she was strong and clever. And it was pretty good that she could do ballet and karate. I'm going to start ballet, and Mummy said maybe next year I'll be able to do tae…'

'Taekwondo,' Sarah supplied. 'So, are you ready for pizza now?'

'Yes.'

Once seated in the high street pizzeria, redolent with the scent of simmering tomato sauce and pizza dough, and busy with families crammed round the tables, Jodie settled down with the supplied crayons and children's activity booklet. Ben turned to Sarah, jolted anew by her fresh beauty. Her hair was tied back, as always, but pulled up in a clip so that tendrils of red fell to frame her face.

'What did you think of the film?'

'I loved it. I'm a sucker for a good animated film. Jodie and I sometimes have a Disney afternoon—don't we, sweetheart?'

'Yup. But Mummy says I should only run off with a prince if I get to have a sword and rescue him and be equals. Like in that film there. Because the witch fell in love with the hero even though he wasn't tall, dark and handsome and he wasn't a prince.'

'But he was kind and strong and…'

'And he had red hair too. A girl at school called Gemma Carling says that people with red hair smell and are bad—but that's not true.'

'It's not true at all,' Ben said firmly. 'It doesn't matter

what colour your hair is. What matters are the choices you make.'

Jodie tipped her head to one side, a mirror image of her mum.

'Gemma says that you're *born* good or bad and it's all to do with your mum and dad.' Her face scrunched into a frown. 'She says I'm probably *half* bad, because my dad may have been bad, but I don't know anything about my dad because he and Mum broke up before I was born and we don't know where he is. I probably am half bad.'

'I don't believe that.'

Memory echoed inside him—memories of his fear that he would be like his unknown father, his frustration at the complete lack of information, the obsessive studying of his image in the mirror for any clue. Did he look like his father? What was his name? And why had he been rejected?

'I believe it's all down to the choices you make—and I bet you make good choices.'

'Sometimes…' Jodie said cautiously and Ben laughed.

'We all make some mistakes. Sometimes you can make the wrong choice, but that doesn't make you bad either. Because next time you can always make a better one. You are in control of your choices.'

Perhaps this was too much for a six-year-old, but he still wanted to say it. After all, even if she didn't fully get it now perhaps she'd remember his words later.

'Does that make a little bit of sense?'

'Yes.' Jodie looked down at her drawing and picked a different crayon. 'But I still wish I had a dad. All my friends have dads. Most of them live in the same house as them. Except Tom's. His parents are divorced, but he gets two Christmases and he sees his dad every week.

Oh, and Holly's dad died, which is really, really sad. But she has lots of photos and he was a *good* dad.'

It was clear that Jodie had given this a lot of thought and something tugged in Ben's chest—sympathy, empathy and a strong impulse to help. His reaction was reinforced by the shadow that crossed Sarah's face.

'Do you know what, Jodie? I don't know who my dad is either. He may be good—he may be bad. But I try to be good, because I believe that is *my* choice and nothing to do with him.'

He felt Sarah still next to him, but he was watching the effect of his words on Jodie.

She looked up at him. 'You don't know who your dad is?'

'Nope. And I've turned out just fine. So you can tell Gemma Carling that she's got it all wrong.' It was irrational to feel so cross with an unknown six-year-old but he did.

Jodie smiled. 'I will.' And then, 'Really? Do you *really* not know your dad?'

'Really.'

'It sucks,' she said. 'Doesn't it?'

'Yes,' he said softly. 'It does. But you know what? I think we're both really lucky. Because we've both got lovely mums.'

Jodie nodded. 'Yes! Does your mum have red hair?'

'No. I'm afraid not. She has blonde hair, but she's still a fantastic mum. A real heroine.'

The conversation turned to all sorts of topics after that, and by the end of lunch Ben knew all about Jodie's best friend, her favourite sport and how much she was looking forward to learning ballet.

The tussle over who paid the bill was eventually decided in his favour. 'You paid for the cinema. I pay for lunch. Then we're quits.'

Once back on the bus, Jodie asked, 'Can we go to the park on the way back?'

'Sure, honey. I'm happy to take you—but Ben may have other plans.'

Seeing Jodie's hopeful glance, Ben shook his head. 'Nope. No other plans. The park sounds great. We can get an ice cream.'

He remembered their gelato by moonlight, and found it hard to believe that had been mere days ago.

'Goodie!' Jodie beamed at him. 'I'll show you how high I can go on the swings.'

The rest of the day was a far cry from his usual weekend pursuits. He watched Jodie as she soared high into the air and then raced around the park chasing the autumnal leaves, he watched Sarah as she interacted with her daughter, and then they all had an ice cream before boarding another bus for home.

Home. His home, not theirs. Yet in an alternative universe this would be how life was: a family day the norm rather than a one-off novelty. There were people who did this all the time—every weekend.

The idea assaulted his brain and panic resurfaced. It was a panic he needed to hide. No way did he want either Jodie or Sarah to sense it and be made to feel unwelcome.

So he smiled, and laughed, but once they were home he said, 'Thank you for a lovely day. I need to catch up on emails now, but help yourself to whatever you want. I'll be in my study. If you need me just shout.'

CHAPTER TWELVE

SARAH DROPPED A kiss onto Jodie's head and whispered goodnight. Her daughter was already half asleep, her bear and the unicorn tucked in beside her.

As she tiptoed from the room she wondered what to do next. Her plan to keep their distance had been sabotaged by Jodie's intervention and now she wasn't sure what to do. Stay in her room? Find Ben? She'd sensed his withdrawal earlier, so maybe she shouldn't intrude on his evening. But she wanted to thank him for the day, for what he had done for Jodie…

Fifteen minutes later, after a check-in with her mother, she headed downstairs. As she passed the kitchen a delicious aroma of tomato sauce and herbs tinged the air. She hesitated, then tentatively knocked on the open door.

'Come in. There's no need to knock.'

Ben turned from the counter and she gulped. His hair was shower-damp, with a hint of unruly curl, and the sleeves of his checked shirt were rolled up to show his forearms, the top button undone to reveal a tantalising triangle of flesh. Her thoughts jumbled.

'It's your home,' she managed.

'Have you eaten dinner?'

'Um…no. I made Jodie some scrambled eggs but I wasn't hungry then.'

'Well, if you're hungry now I've put a lasagne in the oven and there's plenty for both of us.'

'Are you sure?'

'Positive.'

'Then thank you. And I want to thank you for today too. Jodie had a fantastic day.'

'I'm glad. She's a lovely girl. You should be very proud.'

'I am. But I also want to thank you for what you shared with her. You didn't have to do that. Knowing she isn't alone in not knowing her dad has made a huge difference to her. She told me just now that it's made her feel less alone.'

Sarah was sad that her daughter felt that way, but that sadness was caught up with a glow that this beautiful man had helped soothe her hurt—especially as she knew it couldn't have been easy for him to share something so personal.

'So, truly, thank you.'

Her voice caught and she realised she had moved closer to him. Without thinking she stood on tiptoe, reached up and brushed her lips against his cheek, closing her eyes at the ridiculous intimacy. She caught his rough evening stubble and a hint of bergamot.

Move away!

Stepping back hurriedly, she hoped he couldn't hear the pounding of her heart.

'You're welcome. I'm glad it helped.'

His voice was slightly rough and she knew he was as affected by her proximity as she was by his.

Another step backwards. 'What can I do to help?'

'Nothing. Just sit down and I'll get you a glass of wine.'

Perhaps he wished to establish some distance, and perhaps he was bang-on right.

Sarah retreated to a rustic wooden table and sat down, watching as he moved around the kitchen, enjoying the lithe deftness of his movement as he opened wine and assembled salad ingredients. The whole scene was surreal, but she figured she might as well enjoy the dreaminess.

As he handed her a glass of red wine he asked, 'How is it going with your dad?'

'Mum brought him back today and he's going to stay with her for a week, whilst they sort out somewhere for him to stay. She says he's still fragile, but they have talked and talked and it looks positive. Which is great.'

'I'm glad. Now, I know you have your interview with the store manager tomorrow...'

The words were a welcome and prosaic reminder of the fact that soon enough hopefully he would be her employer.

'I can help you prep, if you like?'

She bit her lip. 'Is that cheating? It's a bit of an unfair advantage being prepped by the boss, isn't it?'

'Nope. It's called maximising your assets. I'm here. You're here. Use me.'

There was a depth of silence and he closed his eyes. When he opened them, he looked at her ruefully.

'So to speak... I meant I'm happy to answer any questions about the store, about the job, about Sahara.'

'Then, thank you. I'll take you up on that.'

'Go ahead.'

Twenty minutes later she whooshed out a breath. 'Consider me well and truly prepped.'

'Thank you.'

The oven pinged and as he bent down to open the oven door, heaven help her, she couldn't tear her gaze from the way his muscles tautened. Finally she managed to look away, humming tunelessly under her breath to cover her discomfort.

Until he looked at her, one eyebrow raised. Almost as if he knew she'd been ogling, and she felt heat rise to her face.

Carefully, he carried the lasagne to the table, followed by the salad bowl, and it was a relief to busy herself with serving the food and focusing on the practicalities.

He sipped his wine. 'Remember the head office option is still on the table.'

'I know.'

Yet somehow it was impossible to imagine herself taking it. She couldn't envisage herself in that setting, in that life.

'One day…when Jodie is older…when I've sussed out childcare options and…'

Her voice trailed off. Was she making excuses? Of course not. For heaven's sake—she was simply happy to have the potential of a permanent sales assistant job. That was enough. More than enough.

Determinedly she forked up some lasagne. 'This is amazing.'

'It's one of my mum's signature dishes. She comes over every so often, cooks up a storm and freezes it. She may not have red hair but she's a wicked cook. Jodie would approve of her.'

'I think Jodie would approve of anything you approve of.'

He took a deep breath. 'About Jodie…'

'Yes?' Wariness touched her as he shifted on his seat, as if he was about to start a conversation he felt less than comfortable with.

'I'm aware that she may want to talk to me more about her dad. So it would help me to know how much you've told Jodie about Kevin.'

It was a fair point. 'The absolute minimum. That we were both very young, he didn't feel he was ready to be a parent and we lost touch. She doesn't need to know any more than that.'

'I'm not sure I agree with that—and I'm pretty sure Jodie won't. Any day now she'll ask why you don't trace him to see if he's changed his mind.'

His voice was tight, and she knew he spoke from personal experience—that he had done the same.

'With social media the way it is Jodie will know that shouldn't be hard.'

'I'm not going to do it. I'll just tell her it's not a good idea. I won't tell her his surname, so she won't be able to trace him either. End of.'

'What if he's changed? People do.'

His voice was edged with a frustration that she knew wasn't directed at her, but was more an echo of his own feelings.

'I did check a couple of years ago. He was in prison. Armed robbery. I don't need to know any more than that.' The thought of Kev anywhere near Jodie terrified her. 'My job is to keep my daughter safe.'

'I understand that, but perhaps you should tell Jodie *something* about him? Even if you don't name him.'

'I can't.' Her voice flat. 'I just *can't.*'

'It's important.' His voice was low. 'Because Jodie is right. Not knowing sucks. I was desperate to know who I was. My mother had an affair whilst she was married and I am the result. She would never tell me the identity of my real father. She wouldn't tell me anything about him.'

'She must have had her reasons,' Sarah said staunchly.

'I'm sure she did, but I don't think any reason can justify holding back that information. Nothing can be worse than not knowing—it's like a constant question, and your imagination goes into overdrive. Every film or TV programme Jodie watches, every man she sees, she will wonder—could it be him? She might imagine that he's a hero, who will turn up one day and explain everything, or that he's evil incarnate and she might be like him.'

Sarah could feel her insides twist.

'But at least she'd have hope. Jodie can *hope* her dad is a good person—can dream or fantasise. Maybe that's better than knowing for sure that he's a violent criminal.' Her hands reached out for Ben's as she willed him to understand. 'How can I tell her that her father was a gang member, a man who betrayed me, a man who is in prison? What good can come of her knowing that?'

'Because it's better to know the truth—then you can deal with it.'

'I can't. I won't make her hate me.'

'She won't hate you.' His voice was gentle now.

'Yes. She will. How can I explain to her that I left home, hooked up with a man like Kevin, stayed with him for years and messed up my whole life? That he told me to get rid of the baby. I found out I was pregnant when I was in prison.'

She had never felt so alone, so terrified, and yet so determined to turn her life around.

'I was three months pregnant when I got out and hoped that Kevin would have the same epiphany that I did. That he'd want to change for our child…that we could salvage something from our years together. He laughed. In my face. Told me he was done with me. He told me to "get rid of the filthy brat", that I'd make a terrible mother anyway.'

Ben's face darkened. 'What a—'

'Waste of space?'

'Yes.'

He was silent for a moment and she wondered if he was imagining the conversation his mother might have had with *his* father, telling him of the pregnancy.

'That's why I believe she's better off with no dad than a dad like Kev.'

'No dad *is* better than a dad like that, but surely Jodie should be allowed to come to that conclusion herself?'

'No.' Sarah shook her head. 'That part of my life is over and I want it to remain forgotten—it's not something I want Jodie to know about. It was bad enough that a social worker was involved in our lives for two years, making sure Jodie was "safe". The fear that Jodie would be taken from her had been all consuming; even now caused her skin to clammy with dread. 'I'm a different person now, thanks to Jodie. Becoming a mother turned my life around for the better.'

'Then tell her that. Tell her the truth, Sarah. Not all of it right now, but a little. I am truly sorry for what you went through because of Kevin, but it's better for her to know—because not knowing eats away at you inside, and in the long run it will affect your relationship with her because she won't understand why you won't tell her.'

'Did it affect your relationship with your mother?'

'Yes, it did. I was desperate to know. I raged at her, threatened her, tried every manipulative ploy I could conjure up. I tried charm and persuasion too, but in the end I had to accept that she won't tell me. I realised that I was simply making her life even more miserable than it already was, so I let it go. And maybe she has her reasons. But from what you've told me about Kevin, from a personal viewpoint, I would rather know for sure that my dad was a lowlife than not know anything at all.'

Sarah tried to think. Her whole mind was awhirl. Of course she had thought about how Jodie must feel about her dad, but hearing the raw emotion in Ben's voice made her question her decision not to tell her about him. It made her wonder whether, in a way, it had been a selfish one, or one born of cowardice. Yes, she wanted to forget that part of her life, to paint over the past, but that meant expecting Jodie not to want to know a part of her, even though it was a part of her past and not her future.

'I'll think about everything you've said. I promise.'

'I can't ask more than that. And, listen, please know that I think you're a fantastic parent. Jodie is lucky to have you. Now,' he said, 'let's enjoy the rest of dinner. There's a cheesecake for dessert.'

The following morning, Ben opened his eyes and immediately knew something was different. He lay in bed for a moment, staring at the ceiling as the events of the previous day came back to him. Sarah and Jodie were in the house. He couldn't hear them, and was pretty sure he had awoken naturally, yet there was a different feel to the air. As if the house was revelling in having visitors.

He was being ridiculous.

Quickly, he swung his legs out of bed and headed for the shower. Afterwards, at the entrance to the kitchen, he stopped and blinked. Jodie was sitting at the table, spooning up cereal. Sarah was at the counter buttering bread—presumably for a packed lunch. The counter was cluttered with items, and mother and daughter were discussing the day ahead. It was a domestic scene that was likely being played out all across the country, but here, in his own house, *he* was part of it.

'Good morning,' she said.

'Good morning. Have you got everything you need? I've asked my driver to take you to school, if that's easier.'

'Cool!' Jodie's face lit up.

Ben nodded at Sarah. 'Lots of luck at the interview. I'll look forward to hearing all about it later.'

'Thank you.'

Ben had spent a ridiculous proportion of the day wondering how Sarah's interview would go, was going and had gone. He arrived home that evening with a daft sense of anticipation, to find her and Jodie waiting in the kitchen.

'Well, how did it go?'

'It was brilliant. Ellen was so lovely and she offered me the job on the spot. Three days a week, Tuesday to Thursday, to start with. I loved it. I really did. And I start tomorrow.'

Her enthusiasm was palpable, and it could be seen in the way she swirled around the kitchen making coffee.

'I bought cake to celebrate. So sit down and enjoy. It's triple chocolate.'

Ben felt his lips curve up into a grin. 'I am really, really pleased.'

Without thought he walked towards her, spanned her slender waist and whirled her round, catching the scent of berry shampoo and joining in her gasp of laughter. He caught a glimpse of Jodie's expression, registered the hint of speculation in her gaze and placed the girl's mother down.

Whoa. Rein it in...dial it down.

'That's fantastic news, isn't it, Jodie? I am very lucky to have someone as talented as your mum working in my organisation.'

Emphasis on working.

He could not, would not want Jodie to get the wrong idea. His gaze met Sarah's and he knew her thoughts mirrored his. He could see it in her eyes.

'I'm sorry,' he mouthed, his back to Jodie now, and she gave her head a small shake to indicate that he shouldn't worry.'

But he did worry. He had no wish to awaken any false hopes in Jodie's mind, so over the next few days he took absolute care to keep everything low-key. Professional but friendly. He kept the conversation to work-related topics—which wasn't hard, as Sarah was more than happy to discuss her workdays.

Soon enough a calm routine was established, so when he arrived home on Thursday and entered the kitchen to a decidedly heated atmosphere he halted on the threshold.

'But *why* can't I go?' Jodie demanded, and if she didn't actually stamp her foot Ben would swear she wanted to.

This looked like distinctly rocky territory and Ben backed out. 'Sorry. I'll leave you to it.'

'No,' Jodie said. 'I think you should stay. For a second opinion.'

Ben swallowed the grin that came to his lips. 'Well, I'm happy to oblige, but please remember my opinion is just that. I have no influence or any vote in whatever's going down.'

Sarah huffed out a sigh and then shrugged.

'Gemma has asked Jodie to a sleepover tomorrow night and she wants to go.'

'Is that the same Gemma who has such decided views on red hair?'

Yes,' Jodie said. 'But we're friends now. She says she *likes* people with red hair. And she says her mum and dad say we can have a nine o'clock midnight feast. *Please*, Mum. You can talk to Gemma's mum when you drop me off tomorrow, and you do already know her a bit.'

'That's half the problem…' Sarah muttered.

'Please, Mum. It will be fun.'

'But, darling, I didn't think you and Gemma were friends.'

'We are now,' Jodie said sunnily as she turned to Ben. 'What do *you* think?'

'I think it's not up to me.'

Jodie's face fell. 'Mu-u-m… *Please*. Just think about it.'

'Maybe. Now, why don't you do your homework and then you can watch a film?'

'OK…' It was an exaggerated sigh, but she did as she was told.

Once she'd left, Ben turned to Sarah. 'This is nothing to do with me, but I'm wondering why you're so anti the idea?'

'Because I'm pretty sure Jodie has been telling everyone about you and living here and that's why Gemma suddenly sees her as a cool kid.'

'And that's a problem because…?'

'Because it's not right. And I don't want Jodie to get her hopes up and then have Gemma drop her the moment we move back home.'

'But maybe this sleepover will actually cement a real

friendship—surely that's worth a try, rather than assuming it will all go wrong?'

Sarah sighed. 'I can't believe I'm saying this, but you're right. And Jodie was right. Sometimes it *is* good to get a second opinion. I'll go and tell her now.'

Minutes later Jodie swirled into the kitchen, ran straight at Ben and threw her arms round his legs. '*Thank you!*'

Ben froze. A funny whirl of emotion almost dizzied him as he tried to figure out what to do. Gingerly he put his hands on her shoulders to return the hug, and a strange warmth trickled over his chest like warm liquid honey.

'You're very welcome—but, remember, your mum made the decision.'

'I know, but thank you. *Woo-hoo!*' Jodie released him and with a sunny smile exited the room.

Ben stared after her and told himself that it was OK to feel a little strange. After all, it wasn't usual for him to have a six-year-old in his life.

Before he could compose himself, Sarah returned. 'That is one very happy girl. And in other news my dad has found a place, so Jodie and I will be moving home next week.'

'That's great.'

It *was* great—so why did his voice sound a little bit hollow? Yet more emotions slam-dunked him: sadness, regret, disappointment... *No way.* Because that made no sense at all. It was definitely time for Sarah and Jodie to move out and then his life could get back to normal. In the meantime...

'I was thinking we should celebrate your first week at work. Maybe we could go out tomorrow night?'

'Actually, I'd like to cook you a thank-you meal.'

'That's a plan.'

Sarah had told herself that she shouldn't be looking forward to this evening, but she was—and there didn't seem to be a damn thing she could do about it. Ever since she'd woken up in the morning she'd been giddy with anticipation—just as bad as Jodie, in fact. The two of them had been fizzing with happiness.

And now she was standing in the state-of-the-art kitchen ready to prepare a meal that she hoped would convey her—

She stopped mid-thought. Convey her *what*, exactly? Her thanks for asking her and her daughter to stay. No more, no less.

Time flew as she chopped and prepared, steamed, simmered, caramelised and stirred, until the kitchen was filled with delicate and tantalising smells. Then she showered, changed into a simple fitted monochrome print dress and arranged her hair in a mass on top of her head. Returning to the kitchen, she heard his footsteps and her heart began to pound. The beat echoed in her ears as the door opened and Ben entered.

He was wearing a suit today, a dark grey jacket over a blue shirt that echoed his eyes.

Only now did she realise how effective a chaperone her daughter had been. In Jodie's presence she'd been able to dam the attraction, not wanting her daughter to pick up on any suggestion that Ben might play the role of the handsome prince. But now a swell of attraction surged and threatened that dam.

It took all her willpower not to run straight at him and rip the damned shirt off. Instead, she turned her atten-

tion to the champagne she'd bought. She popped it open
and poured frothing bubbles into two flutes.

'Cheers—and congratulations on your first week!'
said Ben.

'Thank you.'

Silence reigned.

So how was your day?' she asked, and then wished she
could swallow the words. They were way too domestic.

'Good. Yours?'

'Good as well.'

'I bet Jodie was happy all the way to school.'

'Ecstatic.'

They both sipped in further silence.

'The food smells amazing.'

'Thank you. I hope it tastes as good.'

This was ridiculous; it was as if they were strangers.

The ping of the oven broke the awkwardness and gave
them both something to do as they carried the food out to
the dining room, where she'd set the table, having bought
flowers for the centrepiece.

'This is beautiful,' he said. 'You must have spent ages
on it.'

'I wanted it to be special. It was so kind of you to let us
stay here, especially when I know it has made it easier for
Mum as well.' She gestured to the food. 'Help yourself.'

To her relief, the *en croute* dish was cooked to per-
fection, and for a moment they both savoured the perfect combination of pastry and tender flakes of salmon.

Ben glanced across at her. 'Speaking of which—now
Jodie isn't here I've got a chance to ask about your dad.
How is he doing? Did you go and see him today?'

'He's doing well but, no, I didn't.' Her guilt at not

going was so strong she could taste it, but she quite simply had not been able to go.

'Do you want to talk about it? Maybe I can help. Give you a second opinion?'

For a long moment she looked at him and wondered how it had come to this. How had he slipped under her guard...under her skin? Was it his obvious concern for Jodie? Was it the understanding she'd begun to glean of him and the demons that dogged his steps? Was it the fact that his proximity heated her blood?

Whatever it was, she *did* want his opinion, his advice; she *did* want to talk it over with him. God knew it was a dangerous path to follow, but the danger was surely limited. In two days she would be back home. This was the last time she would confide in him.

'My dad wants to see me and I don't want to see him. I can't go.'

'Why not?'

'Because I can't erase what he said to me—the way he rejected my daughter. I can't bear it that he blames me for his alcoholism, for the divorce.'

The image was seared in her mind—the way he'd screamed the accusation at her in that squalid, bottle-littered room.

'I'm still so angry. And that makes me feel awful because I know I *am* partly to blame. I feel so...so mixed up. Like I can't forgive him *or* myself.'

'It was not your fault at all. None of it. You were sixteen years old. He was an adult—your parent. Your dad made the choices he made and those are *his* responsibility, not yours.' Gently, he put his hand under her chin and tipped it up so she met his gaze. 'I know how hard it is to accept that. I understand the sense of responsibility, the if-onlys and the what-ifs, the black tar of guilt that clogs your throat and fogs your brain. I *know*.'

And he did—she could see it in the cobalt depths of his eyes. '*How* do you know?'

His gaze didn't falter as he spoke. 'I told you about the divorce—that I don't know who my dad is. But I didn't explain how it all happened. My mum got married when she was in her early twenties, had a couple of kids, settled down to an affluent middle-class life. Then she had an affair and fell pregnant with me. My real dad didn't want to know, so my mum pretended I was her husband's— that I was child number three. Then, when I was five, I fell off my bike and my "dad" took me to A&E. Some- where along the line he figured out that I couldn't be his because of my blood type.'

The candlelight dappled his features with shadows as he gave a small mirthless laugh.

'It sounds like some sort of soap plot,' he said bitterly.

Only it wasn't. It was real and it had happened to Ben, and all Sarah wanted to do was hold him.

'The family imploded, exploded, combusted in the throes of a messy divorce. And do you know how many times I played the *what-if* game? What if I hadn't fallen off my bike? What if I had been more loveable? What if I hadn't been born?'

Her brain whirred and clicked as she tried to figure it all out. 'You said your mum and you were left together. What about your siblings?'

'They decided to stay with their dad.'

'But surely he…he still loved you? He believed you were his son for years—a bond must have been forged.'

'Apparently not.' His voice was dry. 'Apparently looking at me made him feel sick. I was a reminder of my mum's betrayal.'

Now she flinched, because she knew exactly how it felt to be that person—a reminder of pain and loss and grief. Instinctively she moved closer to him.

'My brothers took his side. I think they believed that if I didn't exist or could be magicked away then everything could go back to normal.'

Red-hot anger raged through her, heating her very blood, and she clenched her fists. How could they have been so heartless? She knew the damage their behaviour had caused that young five-year-old. She knew that Ben too had believed that it would have been better if he'd never been born.

So much made sense now—why he eschewed relationships and love. He'd experienced the pain of the fallout of love and messy human emotions in upheaval and had decided to avoid them at all costs.

'It was *not* your fault.'

'I know that. But it felt like it was. After all, if I hadn't been born, or if I hadn't fallen off that damned bike, it would have been different.'

Sarah shook her head, and now she reached out to touch his cheek, guiding his face to meet her gaze. 'It's not your fault. Your mother made the choices she made, and I believe she made them with the best intentions, but the responsibility lies with her.'

'She knows that—but the price she paid was too high. The loss of her lifestyle she could accept, but the loss of my brothers half killed her—however much she loved me.'

'Did she not even get to *see* them?' Sarah tried to

imagine how she would feel if it were Jodie, and felt her heart rend in her chest.

'To begin with there were visits. But they didn't really work. I tried to make myself scarce, but their dad was so devastated and angry and bitter that he poisoned their minds against her. In the end they felt they had to make a choice and they told her they didn't want to see her any more.'

'That is terrible. But it's *not* on you.' She knew he still believed it was, however much his head told him otherwise.

'Just like your parents' divorce, your father's alcoholism, isn't on *you*.'

'It's more complicated than that,' she said slowly, knowing that she was finally going to tell Ben everything.

CHAPTER THIRTEEN

BEN SENSED THAT she was on the cusp of sharing something with him that would be the key to unlocking her. He had no idea how the conversation had evolved to this point, but he knew he regretted none of it.

'Tell me,' he said gently.

'I had a twin sister. Imogen—Imo. My other half… my double. We were identical. On the outside anyway. It turned out that the inside was a different matter.'

Her voice was so sad that his heart ached, even as his brain tried to take in the enormity of her words.

'She had leukaemia. We found out when she was fourteen. When we were fifteen she…she lost the fight. Passed away. Such stupid phrases. She *died*, dammit. Imo died. That's all I could think at the funeral—through all the lovely words, the eulogy, the hymns. Imo was dead. I'd never talk to her again, never see her. Instead all I would see, every time I looked in the mirror, was *me*. The spitting image of Imo. But I lived and she died. Ashes to ashes, dust to dust. My beautiful sister. And how the hell was *that* fair? What quirk of genetic inheritance left me healthy and well and sent her to her grave?'

She stopped, swiped a hand across her eyes and blinked. The anguish in her eyes tore at him and he rose from his chair, moved to her side and took her hands in his.

'I'm so sorry…' It was all he could think of to say on a repeat loop. 'So very sorry. It's OK to cry. Let it out. I'm so very sorry.'

And then she did cry—heaving sobs that racked her body even as he held her, stroking her back, murmuring words of comfort.

Finally, she gave a last hiccup and pulled away, covering her face in her hands. 'I'm sorry. I can't believe I've just sobbed all over you. I feel like an idiot.'

'You aren't an idiot. You're grieving. That grief will always be a part of you, like your sister was.' He took her hands in his. 'I am deeply sorry for your loss. I cannot imagine what it must have felt like then or what it still feels like now.'

It explained so much about her—about the choices she had made.

He took a deep breath. 'It's not surprising you went off the rails. Or that your parents' marriage suffered and your father turned to alcoholism. But your father's actions are still not your fault.'

'But he believes it is my fault,' she said dully. 'I saw the pain in his eyes every time he looked at me. I reminded him of what he'd lost and he couldn't bear it.'

Ben's heart broke. How she must have hated herself, knowing that every time anyone looked at her she would be a reminder of loss and grief. Every time she looked at herself she saw her sister. Just as when the man he had believed was his father had looked at him, he'd served as a reminder of his wife's betrayal.

'That is still not on you. You were hurting too—you'd lost your twin. His actions hurt you, and it's OK to be angry about that. But it sounds like your dad wants to make amends, to take responsibility. Maybe he deserves a chance of reconciliation.'

She looked up at that. 'Would *you* do it? Would you reconcile with your brothers?'

'No.' His voice was flat. 'Because I don't believe that would be productive. But I have facilitated a reconciliation between my mum and my brothers.'

'It's not a business deal,' she said softly.

'Sure it is.' That was how he always handled relationships. 'I traced them. Their dad had remarried and emigrated to Australia. I gave Mum the details and persuaded her to contact them via social media. They're in contact and I am really hoping Mum will fly out to Australia soon.'

'But what about you?'

'I want no part of it. I want my mum to forge a new relationship with them, to see her grandchildren, to have her family back. But I don't want in.'

'Why not? I get that it would be difficult, complicated, emotional, messy—all the things you loathe—but maybe it would be worth it?'

The earnestness of her expression and the compassion in her brown eyes touched him, even as the enormity of what she was suggesting terrified him. The whole idea was akin to throwing himself off a cliff into a vortex of messy, complicated emotions.

'That's not the way I roll. I'd rather stay out of it, live my life without complications.' He squeezed her hands, wanting her to understand, to believe that this was truly the right way for him. 'I don't want involvement and all that comes with it. But it's different for you. You live your life by different rules, you're braver than me, and

I believe you have the inner strength and the courage to face the difficulties and see your dad, to try and work it out. You have the generosity of heart to forgive and move on if you choose to do so. If it's the right choice for you.'

Sarah smiled at him, the sheen of tears in her eyes. 'Don't make me cry again. I'm already splotchy and pink and…'

'Beautiful.' Reaching out, he took a strand of her hair gently and lifted it so she could see it. 'And this is beautiful. Don't dye it, don't tie it up, don't hide it. Wear it loose and think of all your good memories of Imo.'

For a long moment she stared at him. Then she reached up and released her hair. And as he watched it cascade around her face, and catch the light so it glinted and sparkled with auburn tints, he drew in a breath.

Her glance at him held both shyness and doubt and he wanted to show her how beautiful she was.

The yearning to kiss her was so fierce he closed his eyes. When he opened them again he saw desire spark in the gold flecks of her eyes and he couldn't help himself. He leant across the table and covered her lips with his, burying his fingers in the glorious silken locks. Euphoria soared—a dizzying liberation of all the emotions they'd shared. She gave a small gasp and pulled him closer to her, deepening the kiss. Desire pulsed inside him as he kept the kiss deep, languorous, slow, whilst anticipation built and tugged and demanded more.

He let his hands sweep the straps from her shoulders, revelled in the feel of her silken skin. He groaned as her fingers tugged at the buttons of his shirt with greedy need.

A last vestige of reason forced him to pull away with a ragged groan. 'I…'

Sarah's eyes were wide, shell-shocked, and she shook her head. She put her finger on his lips. 'No words. I want this. I want *you*.'

'Are you sure?' His voice rasped, edged with iron control and rough with desire.

'I'm sure.'

He exhaled a sigh of relief. 'Then come on.'

And quickly, hand in hand, they half-walked, half-ran to his bedroom.

Sarah opened her eyes, unsure what had awoken her from the depths of sleep. Memories surged through her brain and body. Passion and joy, laughter and desperation, sweetness and satisfaction such as she had never imagined to be possible. She lay still, encapsulated in the moment, and felt the warmth of Ben's body next to hers...

And then she registered what had woken her up. It had been her phone—the beep of a text arriving.

Next to her Ben sat up, swung his legs out of bed and rose, walked towards the bathroom. For a second she was distracted by the absurd male beauty of his body. Then she reached for her phone, relieved that she had thought to retrieve it from the dining room at some point in the night.

She saw that the message was from Gemma's mum.

Hi Sarah. Slight change of plan. The sleepover went really well and the girls would like to spend the day together if that's OK? If so, Jodie would like to swing by to pick up some stuff. We are out and about so could be with you at about nine-thirty. Hope that's OK. Let me know if not. Bella x

Nine-thirty. That gave her all of thirty-five minutes.

Ben re-entered the bedroom and saw her expression. 'What's wrong? Is Jodie all right?'

'Yes. But she'll be here at nine-thirty.' Sarah pushed the duvet off her in a panic. 'She can't suspect—she can't know what's happened.'

Her thoughts swirled and tumbled and she forced herself to inhale a deep breath. There would be time for thinking later; now she needed to act.

'Agreed.' Ben's voice was grim, his face shadowed as he tugged on his jeans, and Sarah *knew* he regretted the previous night. Pain jabbed at her chest.

Not now. There would be time for taking stock later.

She fired off a quick reply text and then scrambled out of bed and into a fever of activity.

A glance at her reflection made her groan. Her hair was dishevelled and she had swollen, thoroughly kissed lips. After the fastest of showers, she emerged to find Ben had started operation clear-up.

For the next half an hour they worked together in silence—though she was oh, so aware of the grim set of his lips.

By the time the doorbell pealed the house was set to rights. The dining table had been cleared, the dishwasher loaded, and all evidence of Sarah's presence removed from Ben's bedroom. Sarah had even rumpled her bed a little to look as though she had slept in it.

At the front door, Sarah forced herself into mum mode. 'Hi, darling.'

'Hey, Mum. I've had a fabulous time. Can I bring Gemma in to show her my room? Her mum is waiting in the car, so I said I'd be quick. I just need my hoodie and my wellies 'cos we're going to a farm.' She looked round. 'Where's Ben? I want to show him the slime we made. Also, if the farm is good, I thought we could go there with Ben.'

The words smote Sarah as she saw the look of hero-worship in her daughter's eyes.

Jodie turned to Gemma. 'Ben is so *cool*. He's my mum's boss, and he is really funny and kind and—'

'Jodie, honey, you need to grab your stuff. You can show Ben the slime later.'

'OK.'

Jodie led the way past the stairs and detoured into the kitchen, supposedly for a glass of water. She made another detour on the way back from her bedroom, into the lounge via the dining room, and Sarah was pretty sure she was looking for Ben.

What had she done? What had she done?

Had Jodie forged a connection with Ben?

Calm down.

She was overreacting.

'Tell Ben I'll see him later.'

'I will, sweetheart. Have a lovely day.'

Sarah waved goodbye, then closed the door. The click sounded stupidly final—a ridiculously ominous marker that a showdown was imminent.

She made her way to the lounge, where Ben was standing, and desperately tried to tell her heart not to flip, whilst simultaneously wishing she could walk over and smooth the crease from his brow.

'Hey,' she said.

'Hey. We need to talk.'

'Yes. I'm not sure what to say.' Too many conflicted thoughts jumbled her brain. 'So you go first.'

'I'm sorry. Last night should never have happened. It broke every one of my relationship rules—and yours.'

True. Yet she didn't regret her choice, and knew that even if she could turn the clock back she would make the same decision again. Because it had felt right.

Before she could say anything, he started to pace, ending up in front of her, his eyes haunted. 'Look, Sarah, I never intended to cause you hurt, or diminish your self-respect in any way.'

The pain in his eyes was acute and she spoke quickly, hoping he would hear her sincerity. 'It's OK. There was nothing cheap about last night,' She placed a hand on his chest. 'My self-respect is intact. But you're right. It shouldn't have happened. You're my boss.'

Last night that fact hadn't even crossed her mind—hadn't once entered the equation. It didn't make sense that even now she couldn't seem to conjure up any sense of guilt.

Suddenly the penny dropped and a clamminess sheened her neck.

She'd slept with Ben because she loved him.

No! Dropping her hand from his chest, she stepped backwards—as if by not touching him she could deny the knowledge. She couldn't love him—that way lay madness of a whole new type. *What had she done?* The ramifications started to roll in, sucker-punching her one after the other. Because in her foolishness she'd enmeshed Jodie in this false illusion.

It was love that had persuaded her to stay here with Ben, to go on outings with him, to have cosy heart-to-hearts. And Jodie had picked up on the signals. She remembered the look in her daughter's eyes from only moments ago, the tone of her voice. Panic threatened to engulf her.

Think. What to do?

'Don't look so worried,' she managed to say. 'What's done is done. We both made a choice last night and, right or wrong, we can't change it. The important thing is what we do next.'

Breath held, she waited, forcing herself to keep still, knowing that despite everything, despite all the evidence, she wanted Ben to pull her into his arms and to say that he too had had an epiphany. That he loved her...wanted to try and make a go of it...be a family...

Get real.

Even in the unlikely event that he'd try, how could she take that risk for Jodie? How could she put her daughter on the line? How could she have done this? Slept with him? Fallen for him?

This madness had to stop. *Now.* Before she scaled the heights of utter stupidity.

His voice was tight, almost brittle, his lips twisted, his eyes shadowed. 'We need to figure out damage limitation—what is best for you, what is best for Jodie.'

'It's best if Jodie and I leave today.'

She had to get them out of there—away from his presence, away from the spell he had cast.

Forcing her tone to remain even, terrified that those piercing eyes would read her all too well, she said, 'I don't want Jodie to pick up any vibes. It's the weekend and she'll be hoping that we'll all go out. The whole thing will become awkward. Also, the employer-employee line is way too blurred now. If I'm going to stay in this job we need to redraw it.'

Hold it together.

He ran a hand through his hair. 'Where will you go?'

'I'll find a B&B. Make it an adventure for Jodie.' It was what she should have done in the first place.

'I'll pay. We could choose a five-star hotel, or a—'

'No! This isn't about money and that *would* take away my self-respect. I'll go and start packing.'

Turning, she headed for the door.

'Stop. Please.'

CHAPTER FOURTEEN

As she swivelled round to look at him Ben wondered where those words had come from. He only knew that they had been torn, wrenched from the very depths of him. Because he didn't want her to go.

Then what do you want?

He didn't have an answer. Ever since he'd woken up he'd felt as though he were in a deep freeze, all emotions wrestled into lockdown so that he could figure out the best way forward, how to negotiate a way out of an agreement he'd actually failed to make.

Because the previous night had been nothing to do with a 'trade agreement'. Panic flickered inside him. Last night had transcended the physical—holding her, laughing with her, desiring her, the way she'd fitted into the crook of his arm.

'I...I don't want you to go.'

Brown eyes stared at him, the golden flecks seeming to glint with an extra luminosity, a directness that turned the flicker of panic inside him to a full flame.

'Why not?'

The pounding of his heart bruised his ribcage, echoing in his ears as he struggled for an answer. Why didn't he want her to go? And why did this hurt? Why was pain searing his gut, squeezing his chest?

All these years he'd avoided hurt and pain—had never wanted to cause or receive it. And, dammit, he wouldn't—couldn't—change that now. The idea of causing Sarah even a moment of hurt was more than he could bear. But he didn't want her to go, and that was irrational, foolish and ultimately pointless. Because he had nothing more to offer her. And if she did stay, then what?

Think of the subsequent mess. He had no experience of relationships. They were messy, complicated, scary. And it wouldn't just be himself who'd be risking it, it would be Sarah. And it would be Jodie. It was a non-starter.

This only proved that his rules had been right to begin with. They still held. The mistake he'd made here was that he hadn't stuck to them. Now there needed to be damage limitation. Sarah and Jodie would leave, his life would return to normal and all these messy, emotional things would vanish too.

Sorted.

But still, all he wanted was to go and pull her into his arms, hug her close, take her hair out of its ponytail and, yes, give her everything she had ever dreamed of. Ironically, if it were money she wanted—jewels, clothes, holidays—he could. But Sarah wanted more than that, and he didn't have it in him. He wouldn't risk being the catalyst or the cause or the trigger of pain ever again.

And so he stepped back. 'I don't want you to go because it's not necessary. You stay here. I'll move out for now.'

'That's mad. This is your house.'

'I know, but it makes sense. I can easily go away for a few days.'

He'd go back to his normal life—he'd go out and party, eat in fancy restaurants, enjoy his expensive lifestyle and it would all be fine. Money bought happiness, right? God, he hoped so.

'This is better for Jodie—no need for any awkward explanations.'

She bit her lip and then she nodded. 'Thank you.'

'I'll go and pack. Is it better if I wait and say goodbye to Jodie or go before she's back?'

'I don't know. Better to say goodbye, I think.'

Sarah ran a hand over her face, as if to wipe away the expression of worry and pain, but he'd already seen it. Again, his chest constricted at the possibility that Jodie had been hurt, had become attached to him, had built up even the smallest hope that he was the handsome prince who would carry her and her mother to a happy-ever-after. The idea darkened his very soul.

'Right. I'll wait until she's back, say goodbye and go.'

Later that day he entered the kitchen, suitcase in hand, and saw the strain on Sarah's face and the confusion on Jodie's as she looked up at him.

It was another punch to the heart but he forced a smile to his face. 'Hey, Jodie. How was the farm?'

'It was really fun. But…I didn't know you were going. I wouldn't have gone if I'd known.'

'It's a last-minute thing. Business calls.'

'But when you come back will we see you again?'

'Jodie…' Sarah's voice was soft but firm. 'I explained it to you. Ben is my boss. He was kind enough to let us stay in his house but once we leave there will be no need to see him again.'

'But I thought we were friends.'

The words seared him; he saw Sarah wince. 'We *are*

friends, Jodie. But you're going to be busy—and I'm busy too.'

Such stupid words, and Jodie dealt with them as they deserved. 'Too busy for friends?'

The words were another hit, and one that jolted him into action. This mess was not of Jodie's making, so he'd have to figure out a way to ease out of her life more gently.

'Of course not. I'll talk to your mum and we'll work something out. Maybe I can take you out for a day?'

'That would be good. But what about Mum? Aren't you friends with her any more?'

'It's complicated.' Such a cop-out; how had this happened? 'But now I have a flight to catch.'

Jodie wrapped her arms around him and held on tight and something tugged at his heart. This was all too much.

'Goodbye, Jodie.' An effort of will kept his voice even.

But then he turned to Sarah, her brown eyes enormous in her pale face, her hair pulled loose from her ponytail now. He moved towards her, lifted a hand to touch that bright, shining mass and brush her cheek.

'Goodbye, Sarah,' he said, and now his voice trembled slightly, taut with regret, sadness and a bleak sense of despair.

'Goodbye, Ben. Thanks for everything.'

CHAPTER FIFTEEN

Two months later

SARAH RUBBED A hand over her face, looked in the mirror and forced herself to smile. After all, she was meant to be happy. She looked down at her phone, at the email that told her she'd been offered a new job with a retail company called Howard and Frintel—a renowned high street chain.

And she did feel happy—or if not happy, then at least satisfied…proud of herself. The problem was she wanted to tell Ben.

Not happening.

The whole point of getting a new job was to cut all ties with Ben in the hope that it would cure her, or at least make her stop missing him.

When, true to his word, he had got in touch with her and offered to take Jodie out, she had kept their contact to emails only, and asked her mum to drop Jodie off and pick her up. Yet she had hung on her daughter's every word on her return, desperate to glean any information she could.

Madness.

She looked up as her mother entered the lounge.

'Hello, darling. I was hoping to catch you. Your dad says hi and congratulations on the new job.'

'Fab. I'll drop round and see him later today or tomorrow.'

Slowly but surely she and her father were progressing—with lots of tears and sometimes some pain. But the more they spoke the easier it became, and she could almost see the bridges being built, a new relationship being forged. Enough so that she planned to take Jodie to see her grandfather very soon.

Mary hesitated. 'Can we talk?'

'Of course. Is everything OK?'

'It is with me, but I'm worried about you.' Her mother ran a hand down her skirt in an uncharacteristically nervous gesture. 'I'm just going to ask you something straight out. No shilly-shallying. Do you love Ben?'

'No. Of course not. Why would you think that?'

But she couldn't hold her mother's gaze, knew the game was up.

'Because I'm your mum and I know you. Plus, Jodie has told me enough that I'm pretty sure I'm right.'

Sarah sighed. She knew she could continue her denial but what would be the point? 'Yes,' she said simply.

'Does he know? Does he not feel the same way?'

'He doesn't know, but I know he doesn't feel the same way. Even if he did it wouldn't make any difference. I wouldn't take it further.'

'Why not?' Mary frowned.

'Because it wouldn't be fair to Jodie. If I get it wrong—if it goes wrong—I don't want her to lose another dad. I messed up enough the first time.'

'And you think Ben is like Kevin?'

'No! Absolutely not! There isn't a single similarity

between them. Ben is a kind, good, generous man. He stands for everything Kevin wasn't.' She let out a sigh. 'But I still wouldn't risk it.'

'That doesn't make sense.' Her mum's voice was gentle now. 'If you believe Ben is a good man, do you think that if he grew to love Jodie, and she him, he'd leave her in the lurch if you and he split up? He has taken Jodie out twice since you moved back here and you aren't even dating.'

The words slotted into Sarah's brain. Why hadn't she seen that? Ben knew what it felt like to have love taken away, to be left in the lurch. He'd never inflict that on another person.

Sarah stared at her mother. 'You're right. But…but I still don't think I can take the risk.'

'Yes, you can.' Mary walked forward. 'I think this is to do with losing Imo. Imo lost her chance at life, Sarah. Don't lose yours too. She wouldn't have wanted that, and I don't either.'

Her mum pulled her into a hug, a fierce, strong embrace full of love, and Sarah returned it, her brain fizzing as it took on board what her mother had said.

Ben stared unseeing at the screen, a scowl on his face. Not that there was anything to scowl at. Scowling just seemed to come naturally these days. In actual fact the screen showed sales going through the roof—the new range was a massive hit and the resultant bottom line should be making him very happy.

But he wasn't. Wasn't happy at all. And it was beginning to get to him.

Maree knocked and walked in, a look of uncharacteristic wariness on her face.

'Bad news?'

'Nope. Just seems rude to smile when you're looking so grumpy.'

He gusted out a sigh. 'I think I'm getting an ulcer.'

'I don't think that's the problem.'

'What do you think the problem is?'

'I think you're missing Sarah.'

'Don't be ridiculous.'

What was even more ridiculous was that he had never intended to mention Sarah to Maree. But he hadn't been able to help himself. Because sometimes saying her name made him feel better—who knew how *that* worked? And eventually he'd dropped her name enough that Maree had made her own deductions.

'Not admitting something doesn't make it any less true.'

After a long pause, he shrugged. 'Fine. I miss her.' More than he would have thought possible.

He didn't understand how she had infiltrated his life so completely. Sometimes he'd turn, convinced he'd glimpsed her—the world suddenly seemed full of redhaired women. Other times he'd catch a waft of her scent. Too many times his hand had hovered over his phone. He wanted to hear her voice. He wanted to share things with her—to tell her that he'd summoned up all the courage in the world and messaged his half-brothers. To tell her that the new clothing range was a hit. To tell her a joke just so he could hear her laugh. It had half killed him not to grill Jodie the two times he'd taken her out.

'But it will pass.'

Maree raised a sceptical eyebrow. 'Any sign of that happening?'

'Not yet, but it will.'

'And that's a good thing because…?'

Now he rose and paced the room. One fist thumped the palm of his other hand. 'Because it wouldn't work out.'

'Why not?'

'It's too risky. And it wouldn't be fair to Sarah or Jodie. I am not equipped for relationships. I will not bring hurt and chaos into their lives.'

'Has it ever occurred to you that you might actually bring them happiness and joy?'

'No.' His voice flat.

'Then consider it. Don't throw away something that has the potential to be incredible and true and wonderful.'

With that, Maree slid off the desk and left the room, but paused to put her head back round the door.

'Also, Sarah handed in her resignation today.'

'What? *Why?*'

'I don't know everything, Ben. Maybe you should ask her yourself.'

Sarah paced up and down the lounge, trying to figure out what to do. Part of her advocated going to find Ben to tell him that she loved him. After all, she'd be no worse off than she was now. Only she would be. Because now she still had the merest sliver of hope...now she could still weave rose-tinted fantasies.

The downside was that her imagination also created other tapestries of *what if?* What if he laughed in her face? Not possible. OK, so what if he let her down gently, with pity in his cobalt eyes? *Yuck*. But, then again, what if...?

It would be better to just know.

Which was the exact argument he'd used to persuade her to share more about Kevin with Jodie.

What to do? What to do?

The chime of the doorbell interrupted her thoughts and she walked over to the buzzer. 'Hello?'

'It's me. Ben.'

Sarah literally jumped back from the entry phone. Was she imagining things?

'Ben?'

'Yes. Ben. Ben Gardiner. Remember me?'

'Yes.' *Get a grip.* 'Of course I remember you. Do you want to come in?'

Stupid question. She buzzed him in, opened the front door and retreated, resisting the urge to run round like a headless chicken. It wasn't as if it would do any good. She obviously didn't have time to do a makeover or meditate, and hiding under her duvet seemed pretty pointless. Instead she moved behind the sofa, to stop herself running straight at him and throwing herself into his arms, and stared at the door.

Calm down.

Yet her heart skipped, cartwheeled and crashed as he walked in, and she had to will her feet to remain still, to prevent herself from vaulting over the sofa.

'Hi.'

'Hi,' she replied.

'So,' he said, and anger vibrated off him. 'Why did you hand your notice in? Is it because of me? Because of us?'

Of course he'd be angry. Of course he would blame himself.

'Partly, yes—but it's OK. Listen… I've got another job. With Howard and Frintel. At their head office.'

Here at least was her chance to tell him.

'I sat my Maths and English GCSEs.' She couldn't help the pride in her voice. 'I don't get the results until January, but the person who interviewed me still seemed impressed. I'll be on a long probation period, because of my conviction, but I think she believed that I might be innocent. I'm glad you're here so I can thank you. You gave me that belief in myself—by believing in me you made me see that maybe other people would too.'

Not everyone—she'd had a lot of rejections too—but she'd persevered.

Now all trace of anger was gone, and his cobalt eyes were filled with pride. 'That is wonderful news. You must have worked incredibly hard—and, more than that, it must have taken courage to go into an interview situation and explain your conviction.'

'You unlocked something in me. You made me see that maybe there is a way forward despite my bad choices.'

He smiled at that. 'I'm glad.'

'Me too.'

There was a moment of silence, then she took a deep breath, bracing herself for another goodbye.

'You could have just called,' she said, with an attempt at lightness. Part of her wished he had, and yet part of her wanted to prolong this time together as long as possible.

'I could.' There was a silence, as though he were considering how to go on. 'But...I've missed you.'

'You have?'

'Yes. More than I can say. I've thought about you every day—nearly called you, nearly come into the store.'

'Why didn't you?'

'Because I want you to be happy. And, ironically enough, I realised I couldn't buy happiness for you. I could offer you any material thing you want, and enough money to give Jodie a million starts. I could deck you out in diamonds and give you houses all over Europe.'

'But that wouldn't make me happy.'

'No. And I didn't believe I had anything else worth offering.'

'And now?' Breath held, she clutched the back of the sofa and tried not to allow a tendril of hope to grow.

'Now I *do* have something to offer you: my love. My unconditional, absolute love. If you want it.'

His voice was small and Sarah's heart turned over, clenched with deep love and understanding. There was a hint of fear in this strong man's voice. As if he were afraid his love wasn't worth having.

And no wonder. All his life he'd had so much love to offer and no one had wanted it. Apart from his mother, and even then he'd felt his love wasn't enough to compensate her for what she'd lost. His birth father hadn't wanted him, and his supposed father and his half-siblings had stopped loving him, had flipped the switch off.

Now she did vault the sofa, and then she ran straight into his arms, wrapping her own around him. 'I *do* want your love. Because I love you too—more than you could imagine.'

His eyes widened and his arms tightened around her. 'You *love* me?'

'Yes, I do. With all my heart. You've made me see that it *is* possible—you've made me come alive. Ever since Imo died I've felt such guilt… I've been scared to live. I felt I didn't deserve it. Why should I get all the chances she will never have? But you've made me see it doesn't work like that. You seized life, decided to make it worth something. I want to do that too. I don't want to stay under the radar, scared to tempt fate. I want to *live*—to show Jodie that life is fun and vibrant. I want to love you and be loved by you.'

'You *are* loved by me and you always will be. And I

swear to you, Sarah, I will be as good a dad to Jodie as it's possible to be. She's already in my heart.'

'And you're in hers. I know you would never let her down.'

'I understand that we'll need to take things slowly, for Jodie's sake, while she gets to know me better. We'll play it however you want.'

'Thank you.' She tugged him down onto the sofa; snuggled into him, let joy wash over her. 'What made you change your mind?' she asked.

'You. You changed me. Just by being you. Ever since you came into my office you've changed me for the better. You've shown me that money can't buy happiness, and you've shown me that emotions are a good thing. The more I got to know you, the more I wanted to confide in you, to share my emotions with you, to be there for you no matter what. I didn't just want to have fun—you showed me that there's way more to a relationship than that. You changed the rules…you made me realise that a relationship doesn't have to end in mess and chaos just because I am a part of it.'

He dropped a kiss on the top of her head.

'I even contacted my half-brothers because you made me see that it was worth the emotional risk.'

She stilled, knowing what courage that must have taken. 'What happened?'

'It's early days but we're talking. It's painful, but it's also life-affirming, and I think maybe, possibly, one day we'll have some sort of connection. Maybe more.'

'Your mum must be excited.'

'Very—and I'm hoping that my new communication with my brothers will help nurture her reconciliation with them too.' His arm still around her, he shifted slightly to study Sarah's face. 'How's it going with your dad? When I last saw Jodie she mentioned him, so I'm guessing you did go and see him.'

'I did, and I'm very glad I did. I'm seeing him regularly now, and each time we get a little further. We're talking honestly, and slowly we're making a new bond—a different bond but a strong one. I'm taking Jodie to meet him next week and I'm not sure who's more excited. Her or him. Or me,' she added.

'I'm glad,' he said softly.

'A lot of it is thanks to you. You made me face up to the past, forgive myself for my bad choices and not take responsibility for my dad's. You made me let my red hair down. Now when I look in the mirror I see *me* and I *remember* Imo. You've truly changed my life. You've made me want to live it to the full, not settle for barely enough.'

'And you've changed mine.' He grinned down at her. 'You've saved me from a life of lonely old age.'

'I don't recall that you were planning on being lonely!'

'No. But I would have been. Because I wouldn't have had you by my side. To cuddle up with on the sofa in front of a film and to wine and dine in luxurious restaurants. To support you in sickness and in health. My soul mate. The person who showed me that my love *is* worth something.'

Sarah's arms tightened round him. 'Your love is worth the world to me.' She sighed. 'I am so happy. So ridiculously happy.'

'So am I. You and me... The best choice we ever made.'

And then he was kissing her. And it was a kiss that filled her with rightness and joy and exhilaration.

EPILOGUE

Six months later

SARAH PULLED HER cardigan a little tighter around her in the spring breeze as she exited the tube station and set off towards the London market where she had arranged to meet Ben.

Ben. Even now, six months into their relationship, her heart still skipped and her tummy still looped in anticipation of seeing him.

A glance at her watch made her quicken her step. He wanted to show her the market where he'd begun his business; their plan was to browse the stalls and then have lunch. A lovely ordinary and yet extraordinary way to spend the day before picking Jodie up from Gemma's.

Jodie had taken Ben into her heart with an instinctive trust and Sarah had watched the love between them deepen and blossom with a happy heart. Telling Jodie a bit more about Kevin had been easier with Ben there to support her, and the knowledge that Ben would always be there for Jodie warmed her.

Arriving at the market, she looked around at the hustle and bustle, the laden tables, the calls and cries of the traders. She imagined a younger Ben in his element, desperate to make money for his mother—his lovely mother, who had welcomed both Sarah and Jodie with open arms.

Lost in thought, it took a few seconds for the sound of a familiar voice to penetrate her consciousness.

'Roll up, roll up, ladies and gents! Because today is a special day—a very, *very* special day—and I'd like to invite you all to see what I am offering. It's a one-off, ladies and gents. A never to be repeated offer.'

Sarah blinked, turned and studied the dark-haired man, dressed in a checked shirt and jeans, standing behind a table. The table was nearly empty and yet already people had drifted towards the show.

'Ah, the very woman I'm after! You with the glorious red hair!'

Sarah gave a half gasp, half laugh. It was undoubtedly Ben, though what he was doing she had no idea.

'That's it. Come over. Because without you the show's finished.'

And so she walked towards the table—towards the man she loved.

'Roll up, roll up! This is the moment you've been waiting for! It's certainly the moment *I've* been waiting for. Because today I have only one item on display and it's not for sale, ladies and gents. It's on offer. But only to this one woman. The woman I love.'

And then he picked up the sole item on the table—a blue velvet box—vaulted over the tabletop and went down on one knee in front of her, opening the box with a flourish.

'Sarah Fletcher, will you marry me?'

As she looked down at him her heart turned over with love. 'I will.'

He sprang to his feet as their audience burst into applause and slipped the ring onto her finger. It was a simple, exquisite cluster of diamonds.

'Not a solitaire,' he said. 'Because neither of us will ever be alone.'

And, to the delight of the spectators, Sarah threw her arms around him and kissed him as though her very life depended on it.

* * * * *

HIS UNEXPECTED TWINS

CARRIE NICHOLS

In loving memory of my cousin
Captain Donald "Chuck" Elliott
of the Springfield (MA) Fire Department.

Chapter One

"How about that new guy from—"

"No." Ellie Harding paused mid-slice in the sheet cake she was dividing into equal squares to scowl at her friend's attempts at matchmaking.

Meg McBride Cooper stood on the opposite side of the rectangular table, a stack of plain white dessert plates cradled against her chest. Ellie and Meg were volunteering at the payment-optional luncheon held weekly in the basement of the whitewashed clapboard church on the town square in Loon Lake, Vermont.

"I don't need or want help finding a date," Ellie said, and considering what she'd survived in her twenty-seven years, going solo to a friend's wedding shouldn't even be a blip on her radar. Did her friends think she couldn't find a date on her own? Memories surfaced of how she'd sometimes been treated after her cancer diagnosis. She knew her friends didn't pity her, but experiencing being pitied behind her back as well as to her face as a child had made her more sensitive as an adult.

Ellie pushed aside memories and went back to slicing the chocolate frosted cake with vigorous strokes. Heck, guys called her. Yep. They called all the time. *Slice.* They called when they needed a shortstop for a pickup softball game or a bowling partner. *Slice.* One even called last month, asking if she had a phone number for that new X-ray tech. *Slice.*

Meg plopped the plates onto the table with a *thunk* and gnawed on her bottom lip as she gazed at Ellie. Yeah, Meg was feeling guilty and wanted to confess something.

"Spill it," Ellie ordered.

"Now, don't get mad, but…" Meg sighed. "I asked Riley if he knew anyone who might be interested in being your date for the wedding."

"Uh-oh. Is Meg trying to set you up with arrestees… again?" A fellow volunteer, Mary Carter, came to stand shoulder to shoulder with Ellie, another sheet pan clutched in her hands. Mary was the future bride in question and a transplant to their close-knit central Vermont community, but she had jumped into town life and activities with enthusiasm. "Really, Meg, don't you think Ellie can do better than a felon? I'm sure if I asked, Brody could contact one of his old army buddies. I'll tell him to only choose ones that have never been arrested."

Meg rolled her eyes. "I'm sure asking Brody won't be necessary, Mary."

"Just in case…" Mary set the cake next to the stack of plates. "Ellie, what are your feelings on speeding tickets, because—"

"Oh, for heaven's sake," Meg interrupted and made an impatient sound with her tongue.

Ellie stifled a giggle at their antics but couldn't decide if she was grateful or annoyed. Now that her two besties had found happily-ever-afters, they seemed to think it their sworn duty to get her settled, too. So what if she hadn't found Mr. Right yet? Between long shifts as a nurse in the ER and studying for a more advanced degree, she led a full, busy life, thank you very much.

Mary winked at Ellie. "At least *I'm* not trying to set her up with someone who's been arrested."

"As I've told both of you already, that guy wasn't under arrest." Meg planted her hands on her hips. "He just happened to be in the building and Riley recruited him for a police lineup, that's all there was to it. No crime. No arrest."

Ellie continued to slice the cake. "If there was no crime, why was there a police lineup?"

"I meant *he* didn't commit a crime."

Mary slanted a look at Ellie. "Please correct me if I'm wrong, but didn't the witness identify him?"

"Mary," Meg huffed. "You're not helping."

"Sorry," Mary said, but her grin told a different story.

Ellie sucked on her cheeks to stifle a laugh, grateful to be off the hot seat, even temporarily. She appreciated her friends' concern but she wasn't a project. At times like this, Meg conveniently forgot she hadn't dated anyone for five years until Riley Cooper came back to town after serving in the marines in Afghanistan. Ellie decided not to point that out because her friends meant well. And she didn't want to turn their attention—and matchmaking attempts—back to her.

Meg blew her breath out noisily, disturbing the wisps

of curly red hair that had escaped her messy ponytail. "I've explained this to you guys like a thousand times already. It was a case of mistaken identity. I swear."

"Uh-huh, sure." Mary laughed and elbowed Ellie. "Ooh, maybe Riley can get the sheriff's department to start an eligible bachelor catch-and-release program."

"You guys are the worst," Meg grumbled, and began laying out the plates.

"Yup, the absolute worst, but you love us, anyway." Ellie grinned as she plated cake slices.

"Yeah, it's a good thing— Ooh, Ellie, how about that oh-my-God-he's-so-gorgeous guy coming down the stairs? If I wasn't hopelessly in love with Brody..." Mary bumped shoulders with Ellie and motioned with head.

Ellie's gaze followed Mary's and her heart stuttered. *Liam McBride.* What was he doing at the luncheon? She'd had a serious crush on Meg's brother since...well, since forever. At four years older, Liam had seen her as an annoying kid and had treated her accordingly. By the time she'd matured enough for him to notice, she'd been "his kid sister's friend" for so long she doubted it registered that she was a grown woman.

"What? Who? Where?" Meg whirled around and made a sound with her tongue against her teeth. "That's Liam."

"Liam?" Mary's eyes widened. "You mean that's—"

"Ellie's date for the wedding." Meg swiveled back, clapping her hands together, her mouth in a wide smile. "It's perfect."

"What? No." Ellie took a step back, shaking her head and holding up the knife as if warding off marauding zombies. She could accept matchmaking between friends. Even being relegated to Liam's friend zone would be acceptable, but begging for a pity date? *Nuh-uh*. Not gonna happen. No way. "Absolutely not."

"No… *No?*" Mary glanced at Liam again and snapped back to Ellie, looking at her as if she were insane for refusing. "I don't know why you wouldn't want—"

"Because he's Meg's brother." Ellie sneaked another glance at the sexy six-foot-two hunk of firefighter strutting toward them.

From his chronically disheveled dark brown hair and broad shoulders to his slim hips, long legs and that touch of confident swagger, Liam McBride oozed pheromones. And Ellie longed to answer their alluring call by throwing herself at his feet, but good sense, not to mention strong self-preservation instincts, prevailed. Thank God, because she didn't relish getting stepped on by those size 13 Oakley assault boots. To him, she was his little sister's friend. The girl who used to make moon eyes at him, the teen who blushed and stuttered every time he talked to her. When she'd been diagnosed with cancer in her teens, one of her first thoughts had been that she might never get to kiss Liam McBride.

"Be right back," Meg threw over her shoulder and rushed to meet her brother as he crossed the room.

"Oh, my. I mean, I had no idea," Mary whispered, leaning closer to Ellie. "Whenever she mentioned her brother, I was picturing a male version of Meg. You know…vertically challenged, wild red hair, freckles."

Ellie burst out laughing, but drew in a sharp breath when Liam's head snapped up. His gaze captured hers and his lips quirked into an irresistible half grin. The air she'd sucked in got caught in her chest. Why did he have to be so damn sexy? As if handsomeness had been handed out unchecked on the day he received his looks.

"Liam takes after their dad," she whispered to Mary. And not just in physical appearance.

Ellie knew Liam and his dad had buried themselves in work when Bridget McBride got sick. Firefighting was an admirable profession, but relationships needed care and feeding, too. All Ellie had to do was look at her parents to understand the cost when one partner checked out emotionally during a life-threatening situation. She might have survived the cancer that had plagued her childhood, but her parents' close relationship hadn't. As an adult she knew the guilt she'd carried throughout her teen years was irrational, but that didn't stop it from gnawing at her whenever she saw her parents together. What happened to them proved no relationship was immune to life's challenges.

So she'd admire the sexy firefighter, and if given the chance, she'd take that secret Make-A-Wish kiss, but she'd keep her heart and hopes for the future far, far away from Liam McBride.

"Heart? You listening?" she asked sotto voce before sneaking another longing glance at Liam.

Liam's footsteps had faltered at that distinctive laugh. *Ellie Harding*. Her laughter, like her honey-brown eyes, sparkled and drew him in whenever she was close. Today, her long, shiny dark hair was pulled back and secured with one of those rubber band thingies his sister and niece favored. He shook his head and tried to force his thoughts into safer territory. As his sister's friend, Ellie was off-limits, a permanent resident of the no-dating zone. It was a good thing they lived three hours apart so he wasn't faced with temptation on a regular basis. The last time he'd seen her was at his nephew's christening, nearly nine months ago.

The fact that she'd had cancer as a child and could have died had nothing to do with his resistance to her charms. Nothing at all. He'd hate to think he was that shallow, despite knowing the destruction illness left in its wake.

No. His reluctance was because messing with a sibling's friend could have nasty consequences. He and his best friend, Riley Cooper, were just patching up a huge rift in their friendship. Riley had broken the bro code and Liam's trust by getting Meg pregnant before deploying to Afghanistan and disappearing from her life. But all that was in the past. His sister was crazy in love with Riley, who'd come back, taken responsibility for his daughter and convinced Meg to marry him. Riley was also the reason for the glow of happiness in his sister's eyes these days.

So he'd buried the hatchet, and not in Riley's privates as he'd longed to do once upon a time. He was even spending saved vacation time in Loon Lake to help his brother-in-law renovate. Meg and Riley were outgrowing their modest cottage-style home after the birth of their second child, James.

His gaze met Ellie's and objections scattered like ashes. Damn, but off-limits would be a lot easier if she weren't so appealing. Why some guy hadn't scooped her up by now was a mystery. He almost wished one had and removed temptation. *Almost.* Something he kept buried deep and refused to explore railed against the picture of Ellie married to a random dude, forever out of reach. Except out of reach was where she needed to stay, because he'd filled his quota of losing people. From here on out, his heart belonged to his job. *Stay back three hundred feet, Ellie Harding.*

"Liam, what are you doing here?" Meg asked.

"I'm here to help Riley with your addition, remember?"

"I mean here…at the luncheon."

"When you weren't home, I remembered you volunteered here on Thursdays." He shrugged. "So, here I am."

She grinned and looped her arm through his. "You have no idea what perfect timing you have."

Then she began guiding—yeah, more like frog-marching—him across the church basement toward Ellie of the twinkling eyes and engaging laugh.

Liam's indrawn breath hissed through his teeth. "Uh-oh."

"You're the answer to our problem," Meg said in a too-bright tone, and squeezed his arm.

"Huh, that's new." He gave her a side-eye look. "Usually you're accusing me of being or causing the problem."

Meg's expression was calculating, as if sizing him up for something. *Crap.* He knew that look and nothing good ever came from it. Now that she was happily married, she seemed to think everyone should be. Living three hours away, he'd managed to avoid her less-than-subtle hints that it was time he settled down. He loved his sister and was happy to help with the interior finishing work on her new home addition, but he wasn't about to let her manipulate him into any sort of permanent relationship. Even if the intended target had the most beautiful golden eyes he'd ever seen.

He made a show of looking around. "Where's Riley? Why isn't your husband here solving your problems? Isn't that what he's for?"

"Nah, he can't help with this one, so enjoy being the solution for once, brother dear." Meg stopped at the table where Ellie and an attractive dark-haired woman about the same age were dishing out slices of chocolate cake.

"Meg tells me you need me to sample that cake." He winked at Ellie, who blushed. His breath quickened at her flushed features. *Friend zone*, he repeated to himself, but his mind kept conjuring up unique and enjoyable ways of keeping that pretty pink color on her face.

Meg tugged on his arm, acting like her seven-year-old daughter, Fiona. "First, agree to our proposition, then you can have cake."

Ellie was shaking her head and mouthing the word *no*. Obviously whatever Meg had in mind involved her. Despite his wariness, he was intrigued.

Meg was nodding her head as vigorously as Ellie was shaking hers. "Ellie needs a date for Mary's wedding."

"I do not. Don't listen to her. This was all your sister's harebrained idea." Ellie dumped a piece of cake onto a plate and it landed frosting side down. She cursed and he cleared his throat to disguise his laugh.

"But Liam is going to be in town, so it's perfect," Meg said.

He winced. Tenacious was Meg's middle name. Another reason to keep Ellie in that friend zone. He'd have to live with the fallout into eternity.

"Hi, I'm Mary. The bride." The raven-haired woman set aside the slice with the frosting side down and thrust out her hand. "And you're welcome to come to my wedding with—" she glanced at Ellie "—or without a date."

He untangled his arm from Meg's and shook hands. "Thanks, I—"

"Oh, look. They need help at the pay station," Meg said, and scooted away.

"Nice meeting you, Liam. I'd love to stay and chat, but I promised to help in the kitchen." Mary disappeared as quickly and efficiently as his sister.

"Cowards," Ellie muttered, and shook her head. "Look, I'm not hitting you up to be my date for the wedding. I'm fine going by myself."

He nodded. Ellie was smart and independent, but that didn't mean she wanted to go to a wedding alone if everyone else was paired up. They could go as friends. And if he happened to hold her close as they danced… He shook his head, but the image of Ellie in his arms wouldn't go away. Huh, Meg wasn't the only tenacious person today. And damn if Meg hadn't once again manipulated him. "Are you saying you don't want to go with me? I've been known to behave myself in public."

Ellie raised her eyebrows, but her eyes glinted with mischief. "That's not what I've heard."

"Lies and exaggerations. Don't believe a word you hear and only half of what you see." He pulled a face.

"Uh-huh, sure." She laughed and went back to dishing out cake.

Her laugh washed over him and he arranged the plates so the empty ones were closer to her. People had begun lining up at the other end of the string of tables, but no one had reached the dessert station yet. He took advantage and hurried to Ellie's side of the table. He could help hand out the cake. Yeah, he was a regular do-gooder and it had nothing to do with standing next to Ellie and breathing in her light, flowery scent. "Why don't you want to go to this wedding with me?"

Ellie shook her head. "I'm not looking for a pity date."

He sighed. If she knew where his thoughts had been, she wouldn't be saying that. Besides, it wasn't like a real date because they'd be friends hanging out together. As simple as that. "So how do I appeal to your better nature and get you to take pity on me?"

"What? No. I meant…" she sputtered, her face turning pink again. She made what sounded like an impatient noise and put the last slice of cake on a plate.

He shouldn't, but he enjoyed seeing her flustered and if he was the cause, all the better, because she certainly had that effect on him. "How did you do that?"

She looked up and frowned. "Do what?"

He could get lost in those eyes. *Focus, McBride.* He cleared his throat and pointed to the last cake square on the plate. "You made those come out even."

A smile spread across her face and she glanced around before leaning close. "It's my superpower."

"I'm intrigued," he whispered, but he wasn't referring to cake or plates.

She straightened and turned her attention to a woman who appeared in front of them. "Hello, Mrs. Canterbury. Cake?"

After the woman had taken her cake and left, he bumped his hip against Ellie's. "Whaddaya say, Harding, help a guy out. Do your good deed for the month and come to this wedding with me?"

She narrowed her eyes at him. "Why? So I can perform CPR on the women who faint at your feet?"

Liam threw his head back and laughed. He spotted

Meg watching them, a smug expression on her face. He'd deal with his sister later. Maybe he could interest Fiona in a drum set or buy James, who would be walking soon, a pair of those annoying sneakers that squeaked.

Except he was intrigued by the idea of going with Ellie, so he gave her what he hoped was his best puppy-dog face. "Please. I hear it's the social event of the season."

"Oh, brother," she muttered and rolled her eyes.

Why had it suddenly become so important for her to say yes? He should be running the other way. Ellie didn't strike him as the sort of woman who did casual, and that's all he was looking for—with Ellie or anyone. Keep it light. No more wrenching losses. But that damn image of holding her while dancing, their bodies in sync, sometimes touching, wouldn't go away.

"How long are you staying in Loon Lake?"

Her question dragged him away from his thoughts and he frowned. "Exactly when is this wedding?"

"You missed the point. That was my attempt at changing the subject," she said, and greeted an elderly woman shuffling past.

Liam smiled at the woman and tried to hand her a dessert.

The woman shook her head and held up a plate loaded with meat loaf, potatoes and green beans. "Gotta eat this first, son."

Liam nodded, put the dessert back on the table and turned his head to Ellie. "I'll be here for a month."

"Goodness gracious, son, it won't take me that long to eat," the woman said before meandering off to find a seat.

Ellie giggled, her eyes sparkling with amusement, and he couldn't look away. *She's Meg's friend. Are you forgetting about cancer and how much it hurts to lose someone?* Sure, she was in remission, but there was a reason that term was used instead of *cured.* In his mother's case, the remission didn't last. Ellie was off-limits for so many reasons. But that message was getting drowned out. "So, you'll go with me to this wedding?"

"Look, Liam, I appreciate the offer, but—"

He leaned closer, dragging in her scent, and tilted his head in the direction of his sister. "It might shut her up for a bit. Let her think she got her way."

"Hmm." Ellie sucked on her lower lip for a second, then shook her head. "Nah. It'll just encourage her."

"It'll throw her off the scent if we hang out for a bit. We'll know that's all we'd be doing, but she won't." He'd lost his ever-lovin' mind. Yup, that must be the explanation for pursuing such an idiotic suggestion.

Ellie smiled and continued to hand out the cake. Although she had fewer freckles than she had as a kid, she still had a sprinkling of them high on her cheekbones and the bridge of her nose. He wouldn't have thought freckles could be sexy, but on Ellie they were, and he had to fight the urge to count them by pressing his fingertips to each one. Or better yet, his tongue.

"But we won't really be dating?" she asked during a lull in the line of people.

"Did you want to date?" What the hell was he doing asking such a loaded question? He handed out the last piece of cake to an elderly man in a Red Sox baseball cap.

"Meg means well, but it might be nice to take a break

from her matchmaking efforts." She picked up the plate with the frosting-side-down slice and held it up. "Split?"

"Sure." He reached for the fork she offered. His fingers brushed hers as he took the utensil and their gazes met. "Thanks. Looks delicious."

Her cheeks turned pink, making the tiny freckles stand out even more. As if they were begging for someone—him—to run their tongue along them. He cleared his throat and jabbed his fork in the cake.

"So, whaddaya say, Harding, do we have a deal?"

She shrugged. "Sure, McBride, why not?" Someone called her name and she turned away to leave but said over her shoulder, "We'll talk."

He set the fork on the empty plate and watched her disappear into the kitchen. She never did answer his question about wanting to date. Not that it mattered, because they would be hanging out. No dating. No relationship. Nice and safe: the way he preferred it.

Chapter Two

"Check out the guy who just walked in." Stacy, the triage nurse on duty, elbowed Ellie.

Ellie looked up from the notes she'd been studying to glance out the large glass window into the emergency waiting area. Her heart sped at the sight of Liam dressed in jeans and a dark blue Red Sox championship T-shirt approaching them. She hadn't seen him since the community luncheon two days prior, but he hadn't been far from her thoughts. If Stacy hadn't spotted him first, Ellie might have wondered if he was figment of her overactive imagination.

Ignoring Stacy's obvious curiosity, Ellie opened the door to the triage area. "Hey, what are you doing here?"

"Hey, yourself." He gave her that sexy half grin that threatened to leave her in a puddle.

Janitorial, mop up triage, please.

She clutched the clipboard across her chest as if it could protect her vital organs like a lead apron during X-rays. "Everything okay?"

"Heard you'd be getting off soon." He shrugged. "Thought you might like to grab some supper with me."

In the little office, Stacy cleared her throat, but Ellie ignored her.

Was he asking her on a date? "And where did you hear my shift was ending?"

"I asked Meg." He put his hands into his front pockets and hunched his shoulders forward. "So, how about some supper?"

A pen dropped, followed by a sigh. Stacy was probably memorizing every word and detail of the encounter to pass along later in the cafeteria.

Ellie shuffled her feet. Was she going to do this? *Repeat after me: "not a real date."* "Sure. I've got some extra clothes in my locker. If you don't mind waiting while I change."

From the sound of it, Stacy was rearranging files on her desk, and evidently, they were fighting back.

Ellie grinned and turned around. "Stacy, have you met my friend Meg Cooper's brother, Liam?"

Stacy stepped forward and stuck out her hand. "Pleased to meet you, Liam."

"Let me get changed. I'll be right back," Ellie said while Stacy and Liam shook hands.

Stacy laughed. "Don't rush on my account."

Despite Stacy's comment, Ellie hurried to her locker. Had this been Liam's idea or was Meg somehow behind this? After changing into jeans and a short-sleeved cotton sweater, she undid her hair from the braid and brushed it out. Even if this wasn't an honest-to-goodness date, she wanted to look her best. She fluffed her hair around her shoulders and applied some cherry lip gloss and went in search of Liam.

Hands shoved in his back pockets, Liam stood in front of the muted television in the waiting area. He turned as she approached and smiled broadly. "I gotta say, Harding, you clean up nicely."

"Not so bad yourself, McBride." She put her purse strap over her shoulder and waved to Stacy through the window. The triage nurse was with a patient but glanced at Liam and back to Ellie with a grin and a thumbs-up.

"I thought we'd take my truck and I can bring you back here for your car," Liam said as the automatic doors slid open with an electronic *whoosh*.

A light breeze was blowing the leaves on the trees surrounding the parking lot. A thunderstorm earlier in the day had broken the heat and humidity, making the evening warm but comfortable.

"Sounds good." *Sounds like a date.*

Using his key fob to unlock his truck, he approached the passenger side and opened the door for her. "Riley says that new hard cider microbrewery on the town square has great food."

"They do. Best burgers in town, if you ask me." She sucked on her bottom lip as she climbed into his truck. Everyone in Loon Lake knew Hennen's Microbrewery was the place to hang out with friends, while Angelo's was the restaurant you brought your date to. So, not a date. *At least we cleared that up.*

Once she was in the passenger seat, he shut the door and strolled around the hood of the truck. He climbed in and settled himself behind the wheel.

"Yeah, Meg mentioned that Angelo's has added a

dining patio but—" He started the truck and music from the Dropkick Murphys blasted from the speakers. Leaning over, he adjusted the volume. "Sorry about that."

His movements filled the front seat with his signature scent. She was able to pick out notes of salty sea air, driftwood and sage. Thinking about his aftershave was better than trying to figure out what he'd been about to say about Angelo's. Okay, color her curious. "You were saying something about Angelo's new patio."

He checked the mirrors and the backup camera before leaving the parking spot. "Hmm…oh, yeah. Meg said during the winter you can see across the lake to their house from the patio."

Serves you right for asking. "That's cool."

He cleared his throat. "She was going on and on about how romantic the new patio was with something called fairy lights."

Not exactly subtle, Meg. Ellie fiddled with the strap of her purse. "Yeah, they've got small trees in ceramic pots scattered around with tiny LED lights strung around the trunks and branches. Very pretty, with lots of atmosphere."

The air in the confined space felt supercharged with something…awareness? Chemistry? She couldn't be sure, couldn't even be sure that he felt it, too. Maybe this was all in her head. All one-sided, like it had been in her childhood.

He glanced at her for a second before bringing his attention back to the road. "So, you've been to Angelo's patio?"

Was he trying to get information on her social life or lack thereof? "No, but Mary and Meg have both been."

She huffed out her breath. "Believe me, I've heard all about it."

He reached over and laid his hand over hers. "Sounds like I may have to take up the challenge to be sure you get to experience this patio, too."

Her heart did a little bump, but she laughed, hoping to brazen through. "You signing me up as their new janitor, McBride?"

He squeezed her hand and brought it to his chest. "You wound me, Harding. I was thinking more along the lines of the waitstaff. I can see you in a white blouse and a cute little black skirt."

"Glad we cleared that up." She laughed for real this time. Date or not, there was no reason she couldn't enjoy being with Liam. Even if anything that could happen with Liam had nowhere to go. They didn't live in the same town. And then there was the whole thing with Liam having used his job to avoid dealing with his emotions. Even his sister couldn't deny that truth. But that didn't mean she couldn't enjoy hanging out with him while he was here. Having a life-threatening illness like lymphoma had taught her she didn't want to die with regrets if she could help it. After enduring chemo coupled with radiation, she'd been in remission for almost nine years, a good chunk of time, and her oncologist was optimistic but the experience had changed her outlook on life.

"How are the renovations coming?" she asked.

He squeezed her hand and put it back on her lap. "Is this you changing the subject?"

"So you *can* take a hint."

He jokingly muttered something about respect for her elders but launched into an amusing story about framing out the new master bedroom closet at Meg and Riley's place.

"That house is going to be awesome once the addition is finished."

He made a hum of agreement. "Yeah, I guess she made the right choice moving here."

"She said you had tried to get her to move into one of your rentals." She hadn't seen Liam's place, but she knew he owned one of those iconic Boston three-family homes commonly referred to as "three-deckers" by the locals. He'd purchased it as a bank foreclosure and had been remodeling it ever since, according to Meg. Ellie knew it was Liam's pride and joy.

"I did, but she's always loved this town and that vacation home. Even all the repairs it needed didn't deter her. My sister can be stubborn."

Ellie laughed. "Yeah, so I noticed."

"But I gotta say, she made the right choice for her." He stopped for a red light.

"What about you?" The words were out before she could prevent them.

He turned his head to look at her. "Me? I'm exactly where I belong."

Yeah, that's what she thought. And like Meg, he was happy where he lived.

Swallowing, she pointed out the windshield. "Green light."

She glanced at Liam's strong profile. Could *she* be happy in Boston? "No regrets" included trying new things, new places.

Hey, Ellie, aren't you getting a little ahead of yourself? This wasn't even a real date.

The route along Main Street took them past a few rectangular, early-nineteenth-century gable-roofed houses gathered around the town green. Some of the stately homes had been repurposed as doctors' offices, an insurance agency and an attorney's office, but some were still single-family residences.

The manicured common space boasted a restored white gazebo that doubled as a bandstand for concerts and picnics in the summer. Homes soon gave way to brick-fronted businesses, and the white Greek Revival church where they held the weekly lunches. With its black shutters and steeple bell tower, the church anchored the green at one end.

No doubt the town was picturesque, but she recalled how, when she was sick, the women of Loon Lake had worked year-round to keep the Hardings' refrigerator full of casseroles and sandwich fixings. In the summer, the men had made sure their lawn was mowed. In the winter, the men plowing for the town had been careful to keep the end of their driveway relatively clear.

He pulled the truck into one of the angled parking spots in front of the pub-style restaurant. "I'm assuming you've been here before, since you said you liked the burgers."

"Yeah, I've been a few times with some of the people from work."

He turned the engine off and opened his door. Ellie opened hers and was getting out when he came around to her side. He put his hand under her elbow to steady her as she scrambled out. His touch sent sparks up her arm…straight to her core.

You'd better be listening, she cautioned her heart. *Liam and I are hanging out, nothing more.* Unlike Angelo's, this wasn't a romantic date place. Since this wasn't a date, she had no right to feel disappointed. And she certainly had no right to be using or thinking the word *romantic* in context with anything she and Liam did.

They strolled across the sidewalk to the entrance, his hand hovering over the small of her back, not quite touching. How was she supposed to read the mixed signals he was sending? Maybe it was all her fault for trying to read things into his actions and words that weren't there. *Your fault because you wanted this to be a date and it's a let's-hang-out night.* She swallowed the sigh that bubbled up.

He turned his head toward her as they made their way toward the restaurant. "Something wrong with Hennen's?"

Had he picked up on her confusion? She shook her head. "No. It's fine."

"Hey, I'm not such a guy that I don't know what 'fine' in that tone of voice means." He held the glass entry door open.

After stepping inside, she glanced up at him, her eyebrows raised. "And what does 'fine' mean?"

The outer door shut, leaving them alone in the restaurant's vestibule. A small table with a bowl of wrapped mints and stack of takeout menus stood off to one side. Muffled sounds—music, conversations and clinking of dishware—came from beyond the inner door.

"I'm thinking it means there's something wrong and I'm expected to figure it out." His light blue eyes darkened.

Lost in those eyes, she had to swallow before she could speak. "And have you figured it out?"

"No, but I have an idea how to fix it." He took a step toward her, his intense gaze on her lips.

"Oh? You can fix it without even knowing what it is?" All thoughts of why she was even upset flew out of her head. Liam's sexy and oh-so-kissable lips took up all available space.

"Uh-huh," he said, and lowered his head. "I was thinking of kissing it and making it all better."

She noisily sucked in her breath. Were they really going to do this? Here of all places?

"Are you in?" His voice was hoarse, his expression hopeful as his gaze searched hers.

She rose on her tiptoes, placed her hands on either side of his face, pulling him close enough she smelled breath mints. "Does this answer your question?"

He dipped his head until his lips latched onto hers. The kiss was gentle, probing but firm. Her sigh parted her lips and his tongue slipped inside. The kiss she'd been waiting for her entire life was even better than she'd thought possible. It was sexy enough to send heat to her most sensitive areas and yet sweet enough to bring tears to her eyes. *Make-A-Wish, eat your heart out.*

She wanted it to last forever, but cooled air and noise from the restaurant blasted them as the inner door opened. Someone cleared their throat and Liam pulled away so quickly she swayed. His hands darted out, coming to rest around each side of her waist and lingering for a moment before dropping away.

"Ellie?" a familiar voice inquired.

Liam stepped aside and she came face-to-face with Brody Wilson. She groaned inwardly. As if getting caught kissing in public wasn't embarrassing enough, it had to be by someone she knew, someone who would tell his fiancée, Mary, who would tell Meg. Trying to salvage the situation, Ellie plastered a smile on her face, which was probably as red as the ketchup on the tables inside.

"This is, uh…a surprise." She turned toward Liam. "Have you two met?"

Brody juggled a large white paper bag into the other hand, then reached out to shake. "We met very briefly at Meg and Riley's wedding."

"Speaking of weddings, you must be the groom." Liam shook hands. "I met the bride a couple days ago."

"Yes, Mary mentioned that." Brody nodded, his assessing gaze darting between them.

"Are Mary and Elliott with you tonight?" Ellie glanced through the glass door to the restaurant.

"No. They're at home." He held up the bag. "I stopped to grab burgers on my way back from checking in on Kevin Thompson."

"Checking on Kevin?" Ellie touched Brody's arm. "Did something happen?"

Kevin Thompson was a local youth who could have headed down the wrong path if not for Loon Lake's caring residents. Ellie knew Riley and Meg had encouraged Kevin to stay in school, and Brody and Mary had boosted his self-confidence by having him interact with the kids at their summer camp for children in foster care.

The camp had been Mary's dream. When she and Brody became a couple, they'd started a nonprofit and made her dream a reality. Their farm on the edge of town was the perfect spot.

Brody nodded. "Yeah, he sprained his wrist yesterday."

"Oh, no. Wasn't he your helper for the carnival preparations?"

Brody sighed. "With Riley working on their house and picking up overtime hours, I hate to ask him, but I may have to if we're going to be ready on time."

Liam quirked an eyebrow at her. "What's this about a carnival?"

"I help out with a childhood cancer survivor group," Ellie said. "We counsel survivors and those going through treatment. Plus, every year we put on a carnival as a fun activity for the kids." She enjoyed giving back to a group that had been so helpful when she'd needed it. "We have as much fun as the kids and it's important for them to see they can get through sometimes grueling treatments and enjoy life."

"What sort of help do you need?" Liam asked Brody.

Brody stroked his chin with his free hand. "Mostly muscle and someone to assemble wooden booths. You good with a hammer?"

Liam bobbed his head once. "Sure. I'd be happy to help out."

The inner door opened and Brody stepped aside to let a couple pass through. "Ellie, why don't I give you a call later and we can make arrangements."

"That sounds good. You might want to get home before those burgers get cold or you'll be in trouble with Mary."

"Yeah, we don't want that." Brody laughed and winked.

Liam's hand found the small of Ellie's back as if magnetized. He licked his lips at the cherry taste that lingered on them. What had he been thinking, kissing her like that in public? Yeah, no thinking involved. Ellie's presence tended to scramble his thought process.

A hostess inside the restaurant greeted them and led them to a booth.

"Thank you for offering to help out with the carnival," Ellie said as she slid into the seat. "You're here working with Riley and now spending off-time working some more. Hardly seems fair."

He sat across from her. "Are you going to be there?"

"Yeah. I always help out," she said, and picked up the colorful menu.

Normally he'd run a mile from reminders of the disease that claimed his ma. Just thinking about cancer made his skin crawl, but he could man up and do this. For Ellie. "Then I'm in."

She gave him a big smile and flipped open the menu. Yeah, that smile was worth giving up a few hours to help some kids. He should regret the kiss but he didn't, couldn't regret something that felt so damn good. With that kiss, tonight felt more like a date, despite him being careful not to turn it into one.

He'd decided to keep things casual with Ellie because being in remission was no guarantee the cancer couldn't return. Nothing like wanting his cake and eating it, too, or in this case, wanting his Ellie and none of the burdens of a real relationship. How the hell was he going to make this work?

"Do you want to?"

Ellie's question brought him back with a jolt. Had he said any of that aloud? "Huh?"

She *tsk*ed. "I asked if you wanted to split an appetizer."

Before he could answer, someone called her name. Two men in EMT uniforms approached their booth. Liam frowned at the way they strutted over to Ellie's side. The tall one appeared to be around Ellie's age, while the shorter, dark-skinned one was older.

"Sorry, Ellie, we didn't mean to interrupt your date," said the older one.

She glanced over at Liam. "Oh, we're just—"

"On a date but it's no problem." What the hell prompted him to say that? He was still striving for control, for keeping his feelings casual. If they'd run into two of Ellie's female friends, would he have made the same claim? If he were a better man he'd know the answer. Since he didn't, that put him in the "not a better man" category.

"We're not staying, just picking up our supper, and noticed you in here while we were waiting," said the younger guy.

"I'm glad you came to say hi," Ellie said. "This is my friend Liam. Liam, this is Mike and Colton. As you can plainly see by their uniforms, they're EMTs. It just so happens Liam is a firefighter."

Liam shook hands with both men, applying a bit of pressure with the younger one, Colton, whose intense gaze had been on Ellie since they'd come over to the table. Yeah, more juvenile than a better man would behave, that's for sure.

"We missed you at the softball game last weekend," Colton said to Ellie, but gave Liam the once-over as he said it, as if Liam had prevented Ellie from playing.

Ellie rested her elbows on the table, lightly clasping her hands together. "Sorry I missed it. Did you win?"

"No. We got clobbered." Colton shook his head and scowled. "That's why we need you."

Mike backhanded his partner on the arm. "Looks like our order's up."

Colton nodded but didn't take his eyes off Ellie. "The cops challenged us to another game to raise money for a K-9 unit. You in?"

"Sure." Ellie smiled and nodded. "Give me a call when you get a time and place."

Liam bit down on the urge to tell the guy to get lost already. If Colton was interested, why hadn't *he* taken her to the new patio at Angelo's? *Pot? Kettle. You brought her here instead of trying to get reservations at Angelo's.*

"Some of the guys were talking about getting a bowling night together." Colton mimed holding a phone. "I'll give you call."

"Hey, man, you can't pick her up while she's on a date with someone else," Mike said, and attempted to pull his partner away from the table.

"Sheesh, I wasn't picking her up, just asking if she was interested in bowling. It's for charity," he grumbled, but turned back and grinned at Ellie. "See ya, Els."

Els? What the…? Liam ground his back teeth as the two EMTs walked away. "He was definitely trying to pick you up."

Ellie rolled her eyes. "Yeah, right. Colton called a couple months ago asking if I had the number of the new X-ray tech."

So this Colton was a player? Well, he could go play in someone else's sandbox. He and Ellie were…what? Hanging out to get Meg off their case did not a relationship make.

"Believe me, he was hitting on you," Liam insisted.

She glanced over at the two men leaving the restaurant.

"Maybe it didn't work out with the X-ray tech," Liam muttered, and shook the menu open with a snap.

"Maybe." She shrugged and set her menu down.

Did she have feelings for this Colton? He pretended to be interested in the menu's offerings. "That Mike guy—"

"Stop right there. You're not going to try to tell me he was hitting on me." She heaved a deep sigh. "Mike's happily married. He has a beautiful wife and two sweet daughters, all of whom he adores."

Before he could say anything more about either EMT, a petite waitress with a short blond bob and an eyebrow piercing came over to the table.

"Hi, I'm Ashley, and I'll be your server tonight," she said, and rested her hand on the table near his.

"I'll have a bacon cheeseburger and onion rings," Ellie told the waitress.

Ashley nodded and scribbled on her pad without taking her eyes off him. He echoed Ellie's order because he'd been too busy fending off her would-be suitor to read the menu.

"*Now* who is getting hit on?" Ellie said in a dry tone as she watched the perky blonde sashay across the room.

"Who? The waitress? She looks barely old enough to be serving drinks." He sipped his water. "And we were talking about you. Colton was definitely hitting on you."

She made a derisive sound blowing her breath through her lips. "I find that hard to believe."

He shook his head. Did she not know the effect she had on guys? That megawatt smile that made her eyes sparkle created a pull, one he couldn't deny. So why wouldn't any other guy feel the same? "What? Why would you say that?"

"Because guys don't see me like that. All they see

is a shortstop for their softball team or a bowler for charity."

"I don't know who put that idea in your head, but it's simply not true. And I'm a guy, so I should know." Damn. Why did he say that? If she liked this Colton dude, saying things like that might give her ideas.

She snorted. "I don't see you putting the moves on me."

"What if I were to put a move on you?"

"Yeah, right," she sputtered, and shook her head.

He let it drop, but began calculating how many moves he could make in thirty days.

Chapter Three

Several times during the day on Friday, Liam considered excuses to get out of helping Ellie with her carnival. Last weekend had been the anniversary of his mother's death from stage 3 breast cancer that had spread. The years had muted the pain, but he wasn't looking forward to all the reminders because it also reminded him of his friend and mentor, Sean McMahan. During Liam's year as a probationary firefighter, Sean had taken him under his wing and they'd become close. Cancer had claimed Sean eighteen months after Bridget McBride. And yet he couldn't—wouldn't—let Ellie down, so that evening, he accompanied her to the church where they were setting up for the carnival. He'd insisted on giving her a ride when she mentioned meeting him there. Generosity didn't enter into his offer; ulterior motives did. He wanted to see if she'd planned on coming or going with that EMT Colton, but her eager acceptance of his offer reassured him.

Liam resisted reaching for Ellie's hand as they descended the stairs to the brightly lit basement. The place buzzed with the sounds of hammering, chatter and laughter. The scent of raw wood and paint permeated the air.

"I promised to paint some of the signs and to help Mary corral some of the younger kids. We're providing nursery services to our volunteers," Ellie said with a touch on his arm. "I'll talk to you later."

Brody waved Liam over and wasted no time putting him to work constructing a booth for one of the carnival games. Brody gave him a rough sketch of what it was supposed to look like. After helping with Meg and Riley's renovations, this would be a cinch.

As Liam got busy laying out the precut wood Brody had supplied, a towheaded boy of around ten came to stand next to him. The boy shuffled his feet but didn't speak.

Liam picked up the first pieces. "Hey, there, I'm Liam. What's your name?"

"Craig." The boy glanced at his paint-stained sneakers. "Are you Miss Ellie's fireman?"

The pencil in Liam's hand jumped and messed up the line he'd been marking. *Calm down. He's a kid asking a question, not making an observational statement.* "I'm a fireman."

The boy's gaze rested on Liam. "I always wanted to be one."

Liam's heart turned over at the look of wistfulness on the boy's face. Did this kid have cancer? Or was he one of the survivors? The boy's choice of words hadn't gone unnoticed. "Have you changed your mind about it?"

Craig shook his head. "Nah. But my mom gets a worried look on her face when I talk about becoming a fireman…like she wants me to pick something else. She's been like that ever since my cancer."

"You still have lots of time to decide what you want to be when you grow up." What the heck was he supposed to tell the kid? Liam glanced around but everyone was busy building or shooing young ones back into one of the side rooms being used as a nursery.

The boy shrugged. "Yeah, the doctors say I'm in remission, but my mom still worries."

Liam knew how the kid's mom felt. He worried about losing more people to cancer, including Ellie, but he couldn't say that to the boy. "Do you think you could help me get this put together? I could use the extra hands."

Craig's face lit up as he vigorously nodded his head. "I sure would."

"Okay." Liam handed him a peanut butter jar full of nails. "You can hand me the nails when I ask."

The kid looked disappointed so Liam rushed to explain. "That way, I don't have to stop and grab one each time. This will go a lot faster with your help. And I'll be happy to answer any questions you have about firefighting as we work."

Craig seemed to consider it. "I just wish my mom wouldn't get that scared look when I talk about being a fireman."

"Well, you're still a little young to join. Maybe by the time you're old enough, your mom will feel better about you becoming a firefighter."

"I hope so. Does your mom worry?"

Had Bridget McBride worried when he joined the fire department? If she had, she'd kept it hidden. Of course, following in his dad's footsteps may have made a difference. He honestly didn't know if she worried because she'd never said so. "She might have."

"My mom says it's dangerous." The boy pulled his mouth in on one side.

Liam put his hand out for a nail. "I won't lie and say it isn't, but that's why you attend the fire academy for rigorous training and learn all you can about the job before getting hired. Even after you get hired, you're on probation."

"Huh?"

Liam resisted the urge to ruffle Craig's hair. Chances are the kid would be insulted. "It means you're still learning from the older guys."

Craig carefully laid a nail on Liam's outstretched palm. "You gotta go to school to be a fireman?"

"You sure do. Lots to learn about fires and staying safe." He hammered the boards together. At least with firefighting you had training and were in control of the equipment. It wasn't as if you could train for cancer. And doctors and others were in charge of the equipment to fight it, leaving you helpless. "We do all that training so we know exactly what to do to make it less dangerous. I can talk to the crew here in Loon Lake and see about taking you on a tour of the fire station. Maybe see what it's like to sit in one of the rigs."

Craig pulled out another nail. "That would be awesome. Thanks."

Liam nodded. "Sure thing. I'll talk to some of the guys."

"Miss Ellie says you're in Boston." Craig scrunched up his face. "How come?"

Liam took the nail. "That where I live, and my dad and his dad before him were on the Boston Fire Department. That's why I joined up."

"My dad's a lawyer. Is your dad still a fireman?"

"No, he's retired." Even after several years, it still felt weird to say that. Liam always thought Mac would be one of those guys who stayed until they carried him out the door. Had his dad let Doris talk him into retirement? He liked his dad's new wife. It had been awkward at first, seeing him with someone other than his mom, but now he was glad they'd found happiness together.

"What about your mom? Can you ask her? Maybe she can talk to mine and tell her it's okay."

Liam shook his head and swallowed. "I'm afraid not, buddy. My mom died."

"Cancer?"

"Yeah."

The boy nodded, looking much older than he should have. "That's a—" He broke off and glanced around. "That sucks."

"It does." Liam bit back a laugh. What had the kid been about to say? He caught that because he'd had to watch his language around his niece, Fiona.

"But Miss Ellie says you can't live your life afraid because you had cancer or you wouldn't have a life."

Liam began cleaning up after Craig left. He'd have to track down some of the guys at the Loon Lake station and see if they could arrange something for Craig. Maybe even something for the boy's mom to set her mind at ease. Ellie had said how she'd had to fight her parents' need to smother and hover even after she'd been in remission for the golden five-year mark. Her words, as repeated by Craig, kept coming back to him. *You can't live your life afraid because you had cancer or you wouldn't have a life.*

"I wanted to thank you for pitching in." A deep voice behind him caught Liam's attention.

He turned to Brody Wilson. "Hey, man, no problem. Glad to help."

Brody chuckled. "And earning Ellie's gratitude probably doesn't hurt, either."

Liam couldn't deny he liked putting that light in Ellie's golden eyes. "Looks like you have your hands full." Liam tipped his chin toward the curly-haired toddler chasing another boy around under Mary's watchful eye. Earlier, Brody had been chasing after his active son.

"Yeah, Elliott's a handful. When he's not sleeping, he's full speed ahead. He has no neutral." Brody's love and pride were evident in his voice and the expression on his face as he watched his son.

Liam knew from Ellie that Brody had adopted Mary's young son from her previous relationship with his half brother, Roger, who had wanted nothing to do with the baby. Elliott may have been rejected by his biological father, but Brody's love for the boy was obvious. "He's got lots of space to work off that energy. Meg tells me you've got a lot going on out at your farm. Some sort of camp for foster kids to come and enjoy fresh air and animals."

Brody laughed. "Yeah, believe it or not, I had picked that particular place thinking I wanted quiet and isolation."

Liam didn't know much about Brody except what

he'd heard from Meg or Ellie. But the guy had been through some nasty stuff during his time in the army, so his wanting someplace to nurse wounds, even the unseen kind, was understandable. "Funny how that sometimes works. What happened?"

"Mary and Elliott happened." Brody's expression went all soft. "I know it sounds corny, but they made me want to do what I could to make this a better world."

Brody had that same look Riley got when he talked about Meg. Ha, maybe it was something in the Loon Lake water. "And so you started the camp?"

"Camp Life Launch started as Mary's idea, but I guess you could say I took it and ran with it. Some of the guys I served with in the army are pitching in and we've even talked about doing something for returning veterans who might want to help with the kids or simply be surrounded by nature. You'd be surprised how calming watching the night sky or a pair of alpacas snacking on carrots and enjoying the sunshine can be."

Liam nodded and an idea struck him. Something Craig had said. "Sounds like something these kids might benefit from, too. Ellie says it can be hard for them to just be children, even after the cancer is under control."

Brody wiped a hand over his mouth. "You might have something there. The older ones might even enjoy volunteering as counselors to younger ones, show 'em life-after-cancer stuff. Kevin and Danny, those two boys your sister and brother-in-law were helping out, have turned into a valuable resource helping with some of our youth campers. I'll definitely talk to Mary about it."

Just then, Brody's curly-haired boy toddled up to

Liam. "Alley-oop," he said, thrusting his arms up and balancing on his toes.

"Alley-oop?" Liam shook his head and looked to Brody for help.

Brody chuckled and ruffled his son's hair. "Sorry, big guy, I don't think Liam understands Elliott Speak."

The boy bounced on his toes. "Alley-oop, alley-oop."

Brody glanced at Liam and laughed. "He's saying 'Elliott, up.' He's asking you to pick him up."

"Oh, okay, that I can do." Liam bent down and picked up the smiling toddler. He settled Elliott on his hip. "Have you been trying to keep up with the other kids? I think James is more your speed since he's still new to this whole walking gig."

"Won't be long before James will be running around, too." Brody laughed as he leaned over and chucked his son's chin. "Mary and I have started discussing giving this guy a brother or sister. We've been immersed in getting Camp Life Launch going this past year but things are settling down."

"Alley Daddy." The boy bounced up and down in Liam's arms.

"Yeah, that's your dad." Liam hung on to the agile toddler. Warmth spread across his chest at the feel of the toddler's sturdy weight in his arms. Holding Elliott had him thinking of what it would be like to have his own family. "You want to go back to him now?"

Elliott gave Liam a grin and pointed. "Alley Daddy."

Liam handed him over to Brody and the toddler threw his arms around Brody's neck.

"Alley Daddy." The toddler rubbed his face on Brody's shirt.

"I sure am, big guy." Brody rubbed the boy's back and turned to Liam. "He hasn't mastered his name yet."

Liam laughed. "I just got Fiona to say Liam and now James is calling me Meem."

"Meg is practically glowing these days. I'm so glad to see her happily settled."

"Yeah, I guess Riley has been good for her."

"Well, I know Mary and Elliott are the best thing that's ever happened to me." Brody shook his head as if in wonderment. "And I have a feeling this camp will be, too. If you ever want to stop by, feel free. Although I can't promise we won't put you to work."

"I may just do that," Liam said. Brody had the same glow of happiness as Meg. Would he ever be so lucky as to find such contentment? An image of Ellie came to mind and even the specter of her cancer returning couldn't chase it away.

"Thanks again for all the help. You should come back on carnival night and see everyone enjoying all your hard work."

Brody strolled over to Mary, who waved to Liam. Brody said something to her and leaned down and gave her a kiss.

"Hey, I see you're fitting right in." Ellie came to stand next to him.

"Fitting in?"

"Talking to Craig. He's been wanting to meet you ever since I told him I knew a real live fireman." Ellie hooked her arm through his. "Of course I was referring to your dad, but I guess you'll do."

"Hey." He drew his brows together and scowled, but his lips twitched with the need to grin.

"Did he ask about the job?"

"Yeah. He said his mom was trying to talk him out of it, but he's kinda young for her to be worried already." Liam leaned down and filled his nose with her scent.

"Things change when kids get cancer, and his mom has had a tendency to hover since his diagnosis. Fire-fighting can be considered a dangerous job."

Sure, but unlike cancer, *he* was in charge. "Yeah, I told him about all the training and safety equipment. I'd love to try to set something up locally if he wanted to visit the firehouse."

"That's really sweet of you. Thanks." She squeezed his arm. "What were you and Brody talking about?"

"He was telling me about the summer camp they've set up at their farm. When he said they had youths who'd turned their lives around act as counselors, I suggested kids like Craig might be interested in something like that, too. Maybe even act as advisers or counselors to children still going through that."

Her eyes widened. "You did that?"

"Yeah, why?" He tried to shrug it off, but the fact that she seemed pleased made his stomach swoop like it had on the day he'd shed his probie status with the department.

"I think that's a great idea. Thanks so much for sug-gesting it to Brody." She gave him a strangely amused smile.

Warmth rose in his face. How could he have been so oblivious? "You've already suggested it to him?"

She patted his chest. "Doesn't mean it's not a great idea, and I appreciate you taking an interest."

He grunted. "Are you patronizing me?"

She looked genuinely hurt and he regretted his ac-cusation.

"Absolutely not," she said before he could apologize. "Mary and Brody offered to give me a ride home so you won't have to go out of your way to take me back. Your sister's place is in the other direction."

"I brought you. I take you home," he said, and scowled.

"Okay." She checked her watch. "It's still early. How about if I make some popcorn and we watch a movie? That is, if…if you want to."

He draped an arm over her shoulder. "I'd love to."

Ellie tried to contain her excitement as Liam drove them to her place from the church. How was Liam supposed to see her as an adult if she acted and sounded like her teen self around him? She'd even been sitting on the steps to her place waiting for him when he picked her up. *Way to go*, she scolded herself. Except he'd said yes to popcorn and a movie. And now she probably had a big goofy grin on her face.

They pulled into her driveway and drove past a rambling log home more suited to *Architectural Digest* than Loon Lake. Although she hadn't been inside she knew the floor-to-ceiling windows in the back offered a breathtaking view of the lake. The motion-sensitive lights came on as Liam's truck approached the three-car garage where she rented the upstairs apartment. Despite living here for six months, she had yet to meet the absent owner of the impressive main house. Her rental was handled through a management company.

Liam pulled his truck next to her car. "Am I blocking anyone if I park here?"

"No. It's fine. The log home's owner is still absent."

He hopped out of his truck. "Who owns it?"

"That's the big Loon Lake mystery." She started up

the stairs to her apartment. Partway up, she turned to him. "There's a rumor it belongs to Thayer Jones, that ex-hockey player who grew up here. But no one really knows. Even Tavie Whatley doesn't know for sure."

Liam laughed. "Then it really is a mystery."

Warmth flowed through her at his laugh. "Yeah, I didn't think it was possible to do anything in this town without Tavie knowing all the details."

Seventysomething Tavie Whatley ran Loon Lake General Store and much of the town from her perch behind the cash register. She and her husband, Ogle, were not only fixtures in the community but the force behind many of its charitable endeavors. Brody jokingly called Tavie Loon Lake's benevolent dictator.

She unlocked her door and they entered her small but efficient kitchen. She loved the light gray bottom cabinets, porcelain farmhouse-style sink and open shelving above a wooden countertop. A breakfast bar divided the kitchen from the living area. Off the living room was a short hall leading to her bedroom and the bathroom.

"I'd give you a tour, but this is really it—other than the bedroom…" She cleared her throat. Why did showing Liam her bedroom feel so awkward? Her bed was made and there wasn't a stuffed animal in sight: an adult bedroom. Huh, did she want to avoid reminders she was an adult and old enough to be sexually active? "How about some popcorn?"

"Sounds good. Need help?"

"Thanks. I got it covered." She handed him the remote. "You pick something while I get it." She pulled out her glass microwave popcorn maker, glancing at him sprawled on her sofa. *Don't get any ideas*, she cautioned herself. They were hanging out, sitting together and watching a movie. She set the microwave timer and looked over at him again. She swallowed. When had her couch gotten so small?

Liam was flipping through the movies on her paid streaming subscription. "What do you feel like watching?"

"How about that new action movie with what's-his-name?"

He turned his head to give her one of his sexy half grins. "Are you psychic? That's the one I've been wanting to see."

She laughed. "Just another example of my super-powers."

The timer on the microwave dinged and she removed the glass popper. She poured the popcorn in the bowl and salted it. Handing Liam the bowl, she plopped down next to him.

"How about this one?" He clicked on a movie selection. "It's got what's-his-name in it."

She tossed a popped kernel at him, but he caught it in his mouth and grinned as he chewed. He set the bowl on the coffee table and leaned closer.

She couldn't be sure who moved first, but their lips found each other in a sweet kiss that held the promise of more. All thoughts of movies and actors flew out of her head. He angled his face closer and she—

The music for the movie startled her and she abruptly pulled away. "Sorry."

"I'm not," he said, brushing her hair off her cheek and tucking it behind her ear.

He leaned back on the couch and pulled her into his side. She cuddled next to him and tried to concentrate on the movie, but it wasn't easy with his body warm against hers and his luscious scent surrounding her.

As the credits rolled he set the empty popcorn bowl on the end table next to the couch and picked up a book that had been on the table.

"This looks like a textbook."

"Yeah, working on my advanced nursing degree."

He nodded. "So you can finally move away from Loon Lake?"

"What? Absolutely not." She wasn't about to abandon the people who'd been there for her and her family when they'd needed it. "I like living in Loon Lake."

He flipped through some of the pages. "Will you be able to use the new degree at the hospital?"

"I suppose I could, but they'll be breaking ground soon on a skilled nursing facility and I'm hoping to work as a nurse practitioner there. If I time it right, I will have my gerontology degree when they finish construction."

"Skilled nursing facility?"

Ellie grinned. "A nursing home."

"Is that nurse speak?" he asked and wiggled his eyebrows.

She rolled her eyes. "C'mon, you're not turned on by nurse speak, are you?"

"Only if you're the one speaking it." He put the book back and settled against the cushions. "Sounds like you have it planned out."

"I want to help the people I've grown up with. Give back to a community that gave so much to me. I haven't forgotten how everyone rallied around when I was sick." Damn. She hadn't meant to bring up the past like that. She glanced at him out of the corner of her eye.

When he didn't comment but put an arm around her shoulder, she relaxed against him. "What about you? I heard you're determined to follow in your dad's footsteps at the fire department."

He nodded. "That's the plan. I should hear if I made captain soon. My dad was one of the youngest captains and I'm hoping to follow suit."

"So we haven't convinced you yet that Loon Lake is a great place to live?" She tried to keep her tone light, but she needed to hear him say it so maybe her stupid heart would get the message.

"Are you kidding?" He shook his head as he toyed with her hair. "The Loon Lake firehouse is part time. If not for guys who are willing to work in the department on their days off from full-time jobs, Loon Lake FD would be an all-volunteer one."

"And that's bad why?" Her body tensed on behalf of the guys she knew who worked for the town.

"It's not bad. It's how most small towns are able to afford full-time protection," he said. "But it's not what I want."

She swallowed. Yeah, that's what she thought. Riley Cooper and Brody Wilson might have embraced small-town life, but Liam evidently didn't feel like he could do the same.

Chapter Four

Liam turned off his truck and grabbed a pizza box off the passenger seat before climbing out. It had been three days since he'd helped with her carnival. He glanced up at a curtain blowing in an open window in the upstairs apartment and inhaled a deep, satisfied breath. Ellie was in there.

Ellie had texted to thank him for arranging for Craig's visit to the firehouse in Loon Lake. When he replied, he'd suggested supper and she'd offered to cook for him. He'd responded that he knew she'd been on her feet all day in the ER and offered to bring pizza.

He was halfway up the stairs when her door opened and she stood silhouetted in the doorway. As if she'd been waiting for him, as if she'd been as eager to see him.

Don't make this more than it is, he cautioned himself. They were simply friends hanging out. Nothing more.

"Hey, there," she said, and grinned.

Dressed in a T-shirt and shorts that showcased her long, slender legs, she got his blood pumping.

He reached the small landing at the top of the stairs. She was barefoot and for some reason that had him struggling to drag in air. Who knew bare feet were sexy? To him, they'd previously only been necessary for walking. He stood mute in front of her, thinking about her purple-painted toenails until her welcoming smile slipped and her brows gathered into a frown.

Mentally kicking himself, he forced words past his dry lips. "Hey, yourself."

Yeah, a real smooth talker, McBride.

She held out her hands for the box. He passed it over but didn't let go of his end. Tugging the cardboard toward him brought her closer. He leaned over and gently brushed his lips against hers. After thinking about her all day, he couldn't resist and the kiss couldn't get out of hand with the box between them. He had this whole situation under control.

She sucked in air when they pulled apart. "Wha-what was that for?"

Yeah, what was that for? "It was meant as a greeting between two friends."

Something passed over her face, something he couldn't interpret and only noticed because he'd been staring at her.

"Well then, c'mon in…friend." She took the pizza and went inside.

He wiped his feet on her welcome mat before entering the kitchen. She set the pizza on the counter next to a bottle of wine and stood on her toes to reach up to grab plates from the open shelving. Her T-shirt rode up and revealed a swath of creamy skin above her butt. He picked up the bottle of wine to keep from reaching out and running his fingers along that exposed skin to see if it was as soft and smooth as it looked.

"I have beer in the fridge. If you prefer that over wine." She came down flat on her feet and tilted her head toward the stainless steel refrigerator.

"Thanks. I prefer beer." He forced himself to look away.

She set the plates on the counter and pulled her shirt back down. "A cheap date. Nice to know."

"Me, cheap?" He picked up the wine again. "Ellie, this is two-buck Chuck."

"But it was such a good month." She set napkins on the plates.

He bumped shoulders. "We talkin' last month?"

"Pfft. And you're such a connoisseur?" She pushed back.

"Hey, I've been down the wine aisle at Whole Foods."

When she rolled her eyes, he leaned down and gave her a quick kiss on the end of her nose.

"Wha-what was that one for?"

"For being so impertinent." He licked his lips before continuing. "Now that we've gotten that out of the way, let's eat. I'm starved."

To hide the color he was certain had blossomed on his cheeks, he buried his head in her refrigerator and pretended to look for the beer. He grabbed a longneck bottle.

"Yes, um…well…" She cleared her throat. "The breakfast bar or the couch? Your choice."

"Is this like Angelo's, where I can pick inside or patio dining?" What was that kiss all about? He twisted the cap off his beer and tossed the top into her recycling bin. This was Ellie and they were hanging out. He wasn't supposed to be thinking about her exposed skin or those tiny freckles or how shiny her hair looked. Or how he wanted to keep on kissing her until she was breathless.

"Exactly like Angelo's…if you don't count the lack of fairy lights, table service or cannoli." She nodded her head several times. "Couch or kitchen?"

"Couch sounds okay. That's what I do at home." He picked up the box and she trailed behind with the plates and napkins. "And what's this no-cannoli business?"

She set the stuff on the coffee table and snapped her fingers. "Actually, I do have some. Let me take them out of the freezer so they can defrost while we eat the pizza."

He set the box down next to the plates. "Frozen cannoli?"

She huffed out a breath. "Really? You gonna be a cannoli snob, too?"

He lifted his hands up as if surrendering, the beer dangling from his fingers. "I'll allow it since you haven't had Mike's."

"Mike's?" She went back to the kitchen area and took the cannoli out of the freezer, setting the package on the counter with a *clunk*.

"It's a bakery in the North End of Boston and totally worth fighting wicked traffic to get there." He took a sip of beer and set the bottle down. "I'll bring you some real cannoli the next time I come back."

"Thanks, but in the meantime we'll have to make do with Trader Joe's." She came back and sat on the couch.

He lowered himself onto the cushion next to her, close but not enough to crowd her. Or to tempt him into doing something he might regret. But she'd been into that vestibule kiss, his inner voice reminded him.

She flipped open the cover on the pizza, filling the room with the scent of fresh dough and pepperoni. Grabbing a plate, she set a slice on it and handed it to him.

"And you said there wouldn't be any table service," he said as he folded the piece in half and took a bite.

"I haven't had a chance to talk to Craig, but I hear he was on cloud nine after his visit to the fire station. Thank you again for arranging it."

"Happy to do it." Especially since it had given him another excuse to hang out with Ellie. He set his plate down. "Almost forgot. Craig made me promise to show this to you."

He pulled his phone out of a pocket and thumbed through his pictures until he came to the one of the youngster fitted out in bunker gear and handed it to her.

"Will you look at that. How did you manage this?"

He shrugged, but he loved making her eyes shine like a freshly polished fire engine. "I remembered the guys talking about another house getting their hands on reasonably authentic bunker gear in miniature for a Make-A-Wish recipient. I contacted the firehouse that arranged it and they put me in touch with the people they'd used."

She leaned over and kissed his cheek. "Thank you."

"Sure. My pleasure. He seemed like a nice kid." Damn but he wanted to turn his head so his lips were on hers.

She took another slice and put it on her plate but left it on the low table in front of them.

"Where'd the remote go? I always keep it here on the

coffee table." She pointed to the exact spot where it had been until he'd picked it up.

"Were you referring to this?" He held up the remote, trying not to laugh at her expression.

She tried to grab it, but he managed to keep it out of reach. Her shirt pulled up when she lifted her arm, exposing her stomach. Once again, his body tightened at the sight. He did his best to temper his reaction. If he wasn't careful, she'd know *exactly* what she was doing to him.

"I just want to see what's on your watch list," he told her, pointing the remote and chuckling, hoping to cool his rioting hormones. "Let's see what we've got here. Wait a sec, what's all this sappy romance— Oomfff."

She'd blindsided him by making a dive for the remote, but he reacted by pulling it farther out of reach, and she landed across his lap and chest. She struggled to sit up but he put his arm around her, trapping her where she was. Her honey eyes darkened as he lowered his head. He felt her tense, but then she melted against him once his lips touched hers. Her lips tasted like cherry. He kissed his way across her jawline, nipped her earlobe and touched his tongue to the spot where her neck and shoulder met.

Suddenly, "Bohemian Rhapsody" began blaring from the kitchen.

He lifted his head. "What the…?"

"My phone," she said in a breathless tone.

He pulled away, feeling equal measures of relief and annoyance. What was he doing messing with Ellie? She was Meg's friend…*his* friend. *Way to screw up friendships, dumbass.*

The air in the room suddenly felt thick. It was hard

to breathe, as if the oxygen had been vacuumed out. The phone continued to blast the unmistakable tune.

He managed to suck in some air. "Going with a classic?"

That was so not what he'd wanted to say, but the things he wanted to say were probably best left unsaid.

"It's a classic for a reason," she shot back, using her hands and elbow to scramble off his lap. Thankfully that elbow missed his important bits.

He shifted and adjusted his jeans. *That was a close call...*

Ellie went into the kitchen, arguing with herself whether the interruption was a good thing. It wasn't as if she'd ever aspired to be a booty call. And he'd pulled back in a hurry, so maybe it had been a good thing that he'd gotten freaked out. She grabbed her phone and checked the caller ID. Craig's mom. Was she calling to thank her for introducing her son to Liam? Talk about irony.

Ellie listened to the woman on the other end, but her gaze and her attention was on Liam, whose attention was on the television. Had he, like her, gotten caught up in the moment?

After accepting the gratitude and telling her she'd pass that on to Liam, Ellie disconnected the call. She tugged on the hem of her T-shirt and went back into the living area.

"That was Craig's mom. She said she can't thank you enough for arranging everything for him. The kid-sized bunker gear was the icing on the cake. She said she's having trouble getting him to take it off." She picked up her plate and sank back against the cushions. "We should finish the pizza before it gets cold."

He cleared his throat and picked up the remote again. "I see you've got *Seinfeld* on your list. Wanna watch some of those episodes?"

"Sounds like a plan. Have—have you ever seen the show?"

"No, but I've heard a lot about it. Another classic for a reason?"

"Probably." Were they going to ignore what happened? "Do we need to…uh, talk about…"

When he frowned, she waved her hand back and forth between them.

He sat forward a little, resting his elbows on his knees. "Do *you* need to?"

She shrugged. Did she want to discuss it or ignore it?

He straightened up and touched her shoulder. "This wasn't a booty call, if that's what you're worried about."

Worried or hoping? She huffed out a laugh. "If it was, it would've been a first."

"C'mere." He pulled her next to him and draped an arm over her shoulder. "Let's see what this show is all about."

"Sounds like a plan." She smiled and snuggled against him. "Catching up on our pop culture knowledge. There's talk about Hennen's starting a trivia night."

"We'll be an unstoppable force."

She liked the way he used "we" so casually. Tonight might be eating pizza and cannoli while watching classic television, but she would cherish this time spent with Liam. It wasn't what they were doing but being together that mattered.

When the episode ended, he turned his head. "Is there a path to the lake?"

"Yes, and not only a nice path, there's a small gazebo with a swing. I sometimes go down there in the evenings to unwind. Letting nature surround me is calming."

He rubbed his chin. "Yeah, that's what I was thinking... a nice night to be surrounded by...uh, nature."

She bumped his shoulder. "You are so full of it."

"Is it working?" He wiggled his eyebrows.

She heaved a sigh, but she loved that the awkwardness after the kiss had dissolved. "Let me get my shoes on and grab a sweater."

"A sweater? Ellie, it's August."

"For your information, I don't have the same amount of body mass that you do to keep me warm and sometimes it gets cool down by the water...even in August."

"Then go bundle up." He tilted his head toward the mess on the coffee table. "I'll pick this stuff up and put the leftovers in the refrigerator."

"A sweater is not bundling up," she muttered as she scooted off the couch but turned back. "Thanks for cleaning up."

In the bedroom, she pulled on her sneakers and grabbed a cardigan sweater from her bureau drawer.

"Do you have your key?" He touched her arm as she started to pull the door shut.

"We're only going down to the lake."

"But it's—"

"Loon Lake," she interrupted.

He gave her a look. "Please tell me you don't do this when you're alone."

"I don't usually go alone to the lake after dark. I love

listening to the loons, but if I open my windows I can hear them from the safety of my bedroom since those windows face the lake."

Landscape lights lit the crushed shell path and the dog-day cicadas serenaded them from the surrounding trees.

"Meg loves listening to the loons at night as they settle in and call for their mates to join them," Ellie said as they made their way toward the water.

"Yeah, my mom was the same. She used to drag us kids down to the water's edge in the evenings."

Ellie reached for his hand and squeezed. "I know you both miss her."

When she would have pulled her hand away, he held on.

"Yeah, as a kid I grumbled when she insisted on boring stuff like walks to the lake to stand around and listen. She said we were making memories and that someday I would understand. I would give anything now to tell her I understand." He sighed. "I never told her."

"I don't think your mother expected you to thank her, Liam. She probably didn't thank hers, either. But she passed on that experience by giving you a happy, secure childhood. Just as you'll do for your kids."

"Pfft. I know I disappointed her by choosing the fire academy over college."

"I'm sure she wanted you happy in your career." Her heart went out to him, reacting to the sadness in his tone. How could he not know this?

When he made a disparaging sound, she stopped and turned toward him. Most of his face was in the shadows but she didn't need to see his expression to feel his skepticism. "It's true. She told my mom how proud she was of how much you helped with Meg and Fiona."

He shrugged. "It isn't hard to love Fiona."

"But you put your life on hold to help out so Meg could finish her degree." She longed to make him understand, wipe away the self-reproach she heard in his voice.

"Put my life on hold?" He huffed out a mirthless laugh. "All I did was move out of a sparsely furnished apartment to move back home. Not exactly a big sacrifice."

"You did it to help. That meant a lot."

"When Meg finally confessed about the pregnancy, my mom had it all worked out that she'd babysit while Meg finished college. But then Ma got sick and Meg was ready to drop out. I couldn't let that happen. Mom had already been disappointed when I joined the department before completing my degree."

"So why can't you believe how proud she was of you for doing that for your sister?" Her hand still in his, she tugged on his arm.

He sighed. "It's not so much believing as wishing I had done more for her."

"As someone who has had cancer, take it from me— it eased her mind about Meg and Fiona. That means a lot."

"Yeah?"

"Yeah."

They came to the small gazebo and sat side by side on the wooden swing that hung from the rafters of the ceiling. He still had her hand in his. Using his feet, he set the swing in motion.

"You have a sweet deal here. How did you find out about the apartment?" he asked.

"I was on duty when an estate agent passed through the ER. He heard me talking with some of the other nurses about trying to find a rental apartment. He gave me his card and said to call him. At first I thought it might be a scam but Meg and Riley came with me to check it out. Other than being a bit farther out of town than I'd like, it's perfect."

He glanced around. "It's quiet. Has the owner ever shown up?"

"Not yet. They were still doing the interior work on the main house when I moved in. So it honestly hasn't been completed for all that long."

"Have you been inside?"

"Before they finished up, some of the workmen let me take a tour."

"Do you think you'll stay here for a while?"

"For now, yeah. When I was growing up we lived next door to my cousins and I loved it. Especially as an only child, it was nice to have playmates. My cousins and I are still very close today. If I ever get married and have kids, I'd love to live close to family, let our kids grow up together." She left out the part of dreaming about living with him and a couple of kids next door to Meg.

Jeez, live in your head much? No wonder you don't have an active dating life.

"If?" He turned to look at her. "What's this 'if' business? You planning to dedicate yourself to your career?"

"No. I'd love to get married, but first someone has to ask me, and I'm still not convinced I'll be able to get pregnant." She hated to admit it, but that fact alone sometimes held her back. What if she met a nice guy who wanted kids and she wasn't able to give him that?

"Because of the cancer?"

"Because of the treatments but yeah…because of the cancer. The doctors say it's possible, but possible and probable are two different things."

"Then I hope it happens if that's what you want."

"I've learned not to dwell on things out of my control." She shrugged. "Besides, there's other ways. Since becoming friends with Mary, I've given a lot of thought to fostering or at least helping out with their summer camp once they get the cancer survivors part going."

"Yeah, that seems like a worthwhile project. Whoever thought that up must be a genius."

She laughed. "I thought so, too."

Chapter Five

"Hey, Els, got any plans for tonight?"

The day after sharing pizza with Liam, Ellie had been on her way out of the hospital after her shift, but turned as Colton caught up to her. He and Mike had brought in a suspected heart attack just as her shift ended. Luckily, her replacement was already on duty for the night and she was able to leave.

She raised her brow. "Why? Did you lose the X-ray tech's phone number?"

"Aw, c'mon, you're not holding that against me, are you?" He stopped in front of her with a sheepish grin.

"No, but aren't you working?" she asked. Colton was a great-looking guy. One most women would be happy to date. But he had one big flaw. He wasn't Liam.

"My shift ends in an hour. Maybe we could—"

He was interrupted by "Bohemian Rhapsody." For

once, she didn't mind the interruption when she saw her caller was Liam.

"Sorry." Ellie pulled the phone from the front pocket of her purse. "Excuse me but I need to get this."

She had a pang of guilt but reminded herself that Colton had asked her for another woman's phone number. "Hey."

"Glad I caught you. Have you left the hospital yet?"

"No. Is there something wrong?"

"Nothing wrong. I simply hoped to catch you before you got all the way home. My dad and Doris arrived this afternoon and we're having an impromptu family cookout. Whaddaya say, Ellie, will you come?"

"But if it's family…" She was acutely aware of Colton watching her.

"You're family. Just say yes. You know you want to."

She clutched the phone tighter. Of course she wanted to say yes, but feared she was opening herself to more heartache. She glanced down at her scrubs. They were clean but they were still scrubs. "I'm not dressed for—"

"Did I mention it's a cookout?"

Could she pass up spending time with Liam? "Okay. What can I bring?"

"Just your cute self."

Colton's radio squawked and he held up his hands as if in surrender. "Gotta run. Catch you later."

Ellie waved as the EMT trotted away.

"Who's that with you?" Liam asked.

"Colton."

"The EMT?"

She nodded, then realized Liam couldn't see her. "Yeah, they brought in a patient as my shift was ending."

"So I'll see you in a bit?"

"I'm on my way."

* * *

Liam pocketed his phone and walked across the yard to his sister's place. He glanced at his watch. How long would it take for Ellie to get here from the hospital? What if Colton distracted her? He stumbled over a small exposed root in Meg's yard.

Meg glanced up from putting condiments, utensils and plates on the picnic table. "Is Ellie coming?"

"Yeah. She was just leaving the hospital." He shoved his hands in his jeans.

Inviting Ellie had been Meg's idea. That's right. All Meg's idea. He had this thing with Ellie under control. Although she didn't say anything, Meg had a smug smile on her face.

Yeah, the joke was on her because he and Ellie were just hanging out, throwing her off the scent. "Got any cold beer, sis?"

Meg tilted her head toward the house. "In the refrigerator. Get me one while you're at it and don't shake it."

He rolled his eyes. "I'm not twelve."

She rolled her eyes right back at him. "No, you just act like it."

"Yeah, yeah. Keep it up and you can fetch your own beer."

"And you can get in your truck and drive to the store and get your own." She planted her hands on her hips.

A screen door banged shut.

Mac McBride stood on the porch, arms folded over his chest. "Exactly how old are you two?"

"She started it."

"He started it."

Doris emerged from the house and stopped beside Mac, who put his arm around her.

The looks they gave each other seemed to say broken hearts did mend. Liam shook his head at the thought. Avoiding all that pain in the first place sounded like a better course of action.

His dad's new wife—he had trouble thinking of Doris as a stepmother—had been a widow who'd lost both her husband and only child to a drunk driver. And yet she'd found happiness again with his dad, and showered Fiona and James with as much grandmotherly love as his own mother would have. For that, and for his sister's sake, he was glad his dad and Doris had taken another chance. Since Mac's retirement, they'd purchased a Class A motor home and spent months at a time traveling.

Doris handed James's baby monitor to Meg. "He's sound asleep. Since he had supper he may sleep through the night at this point."

"Thanks for helping." Meg hugged Doris.

"My pleasure. I need to finish my pasta salad. Want to help?" Doris turned to Mac.

"I'd love to help." Mac grinned. Turning to his kids, he scowled. "Can I count on you two to behave?"

"Tell him that."

"Tell her that."

Doris slipped her hand in Mac's. "Let's get while the getting is good."

After they'd gone into their motor home, which they had parked in the side yard, Meg set the baby monitor on the picnic table and sat down on the bench. "Whaddaya think? Don't come a-knockin' if this van's a-rockin'."

"Eww." Liam shuddered. That was one picture he didn't want in his head.

"You're welcome." Meg gave him a toothy grin. "Hey, I thought you were getting a beer."

"I—" He stopped as a Subaru pulled into the long driveway. "Ellie's here."

Instead of going into the house, he swerved and headed toward where Ellie was parking her car. Meg snorted a laugh and Liam slowed his steps. He was greeting a friend, that's all, like he might greet Nick Morretti, the engineer driver on his shift, or any one of the other guys. *And when was the last time you wanted to plant a kiss on Nick?*

He opened Ellie's car door. "Hey. Glad you could come."

"Thanks." She swung her legs out and stood.

Reaching down, he took Ellie's hand as she stepped out. He looked up in time to see Meg's smirk. Canting his head to one side, he crossed his eyes at her. Meg responded by sticking out her tongue.

"That your dad's?" Ellie pointed to the motor home parked off to the side.

"Yeah, that's Matilda."

"He named it?" She laughed. "I love it."

He could listen to that laugh for the rest of his life. He took a step back and cleared his throat. Where did that come from? They were hanging out while he was in Loon Lake. Friends. Period.

Meg wandered over. "Ellie, glad you could come. My brother was just getting us beers. Would you like one?"

He winked at Ellie. "Or how about some cheap wine?"

"Hey." Meg shook her head. "Have you no manners?"

Ellie laughed. "It's okay. It's an inside joke."

Liam frowned. *Inside joke.* Isn't that what couples shared?

Friends could share them, too, he assured himself.

* * *

Ellie turned around as tires crunched on the gravel. A county sheriff's vehicle drove up and parked behind her Subaru. She waved to Riley, who flashed the emergency vehicle lights in response.

"You didn't tell me the cops were hot on your tail." Liam draped an arm over her shoulder as they walked toward the picnic table. "You led them right to us."

Ellie grinned. "Hmm…maybe Riley came up with a few more felons for me to date."

"Am I ever going to live that down?" Meg groaned and walked past them, heading toward Riley.

"What have I missed here?" Liam demanded, his gaze bouncing between Ellie and Meg.

Meg turned back, shaking her head. "It's nothing. All a misunderstanding."

"Just before you showed up at the church luncheon, Meg was trying to fix me up with some guy Riley arrested," Ellie told him. "She seemed to think he'd make a great date for Mary's wedding."

Liam scowled. "What? Why would—"

"Like she said, a misunderstanding," Ellie said, and explained what they were talking about.

Riley had gotten out of the car and Meg threw her arms around his neck and kissed him.

"Guys. Could you save that, please? You have company." Liam waved his arms as if directing airliners to the gate.

Ellie shook her head. The man had no clue how fortunate he was to have a family so openly affectionate. Even her aunts, uncles and cousins were more subdued in her parents' company, perhaps because they remembered how much things had changed during the cancer treatments, especially when her future had been uncertain.

Riley glanced around. "Where is everyone? I was led to believe we were having a big family get-together."

Riley kept his arm around Meg's waist as they strolled over to stand next to the picnic table. Riley grabbed some chips out of the bag Meg had brought out earlier.

"James is napping after having a meltdown and your daughter has another—" Meg checked her watch "—five minutes of house arrest."

"Uh-oh." Riley grimaced. "Would I be wrong if I assumed those two things are related?"

"And now for the *Reader's Digest* version." Meg grabbed the last chip in Riley's hand. "Fiona yelled at James because he threw her brand-new Barbie into the toilet when she left the lid up. James lost his balance and fell on his butt, but I think the tears were because his beloved big sister was mad at him."

Riley winced as he reached into the bag for another handful of chips. "Please tell me he didn't flush."

"Thankfully, no. We sent in G.I. Joe to do a water rescue." Meg giggled and turned to Liam and Ellie. "See all the fun you guys are missing out on?"

Liam took a seat on the picnic bench. "I'm sure if Ellie and I were in charge, we'd have it all under control, sis."

Meg rolled her eyes. "You are so clueless, brother dear. Right, Ellie?"

Ellie smiled and nodded. What would it be like to be a permanent member of this affectionate family? She sat on the bench next to Liam. She had to keep reminding herself they were hanging out so Meg wouldn't continue her matchmaking.

"Hey, two against one." Liam gently squeezed Ellie's shoulder. "Riley, some help here."

"Don't look at me." Riley held his hands up in surrender and leaned over to kiss Meg again.

"Jeez, guys, please." Liam brought his open palm toward his face and turned his head.

Riley laughed, giving Meg a noisy, smacking kiss. "Where are Mac and Doris?"

"They're in the motor home. Preparing the pasta salad." Meg made air quotes as she said it.

Liam groaned and buried his head in his hands, his elbows on the picnic table. Riley snorted with laughter.

"What's so funny?" Ellie asked.

"Ever since catching his dad doing the morning-after walk of shame, Liam doesn't like thinking about what his dad and Doris might really be doing." Riley clapped Liam on his shoulder.

Liam lifted his head, giving Meg an accusing look. "You told him."

"Of course. He's my husband." Meg put her arm through Riley's.

"Well, no one's told me." Ellie tugged on Liam's arm.

Liam shot Meg a you're-so-gonna-pay-for-this look. "It was after I'd moved to my Dorchester place. Meg was still living with Dad and had asked to borrow something. I don't even remember now what she wanted— that's probably my attempt to block the whole incident from my memory. Anyway, I stopped by wicked early one morning before my shift to drop it off. I was in the kitchen when Dad was letting himself in the back door wearing the previous day's clothes and looking way too satisfied for my peace of mind."

Liam closed his eyes and shook his head. Ellie laughed, enjoying spending time with the McBrides and being reminded some families laughed and teased and loved openly. Her parents were still subdued, as if joking around and having fun was asking for trouble. They might not have always been as boisterous as some families, but enough that she missed the love and laughter when they disappeared.

Riley gave his shoulder a push. "Think of it this way, McBride—Mac's still got it at his age."

Liam looked appalled. "Why would I want to think about that?"

"Face it. We're gonna be that age someday." Riley leaned down and kissed Meg's forehead. "I need to change out of this uniform."

"Is Fiona allowed out of jail?" Riley asked on his way into the house.

"Yes, tell her she can come out but Mangy needs to stay in the house or he'll be pestering us while we eat."

"You left the dog with her?" Riley shook his head. "Not much of a punishment if she got to keep her dog with her."

Meg shrugged. "I felt bad about her new doll."

"Was it ruined?" Riley frowned.

"No, but now it's tainted. Forever destined to be Toilet Barbie."

Mac and Doris came out of the motor home and crossed the yard. Doris set a large covered Tupperware container on the picnic table.

"Ellie, I'm so glad you were able to join us," Doris said, and gave her a motherly hug.

Ellie returned the hug. "Thanks for including me."

"Of course, dear, why wouldn't we?"

Ellie caught Liam's frown in her peripheral vision. Had including her been Meg's doing? She needed to be careful, or she would find herself with a one-way ticket to Heartbreak Ridge.

Chapter Six

Ellie checked her watch. Liam would be arriving soon to pick her up for Brody and Mary's wedding. She'd spoken to him several times over the phone in the week since the family cookout, but they'd both been too busy working to get together. At least that was the excuse he'd used, and she'd accepted it.

A car door slammed and Ellie contorted herself into another unnatural position but still no luck. That damn zipper was unreachable, despite all her valiant efforts. Footsteps on the stairs signaled that Liam was getting closer. No getting around asking for his help. Sighing, she opened the door and stepped onto the landing.

Liam looked up and paused partway up the stairs, mouth open and feet on different steps. He wore a deep charcoal suit, white shirt and royal blue tie. She couldn't decide which was sexier—Liam in a suit and tie or

Liam in his red suspenders and turnout pants. *How about Liam in nothing at all?* a little voice asked, but she quickly pushed that away.

With all the excess saliva, Ellie had to swallow twice to keep from drooling. "Liam…" Was that breathless croak coming from her?

"Wow, look at you." He shook his head and continued up the stairs.

She'd splurged on a cream-colored dress with a scoop neck, gathered waist and sheer organza overlay from the waist down. The bright blue embroidered flowers on the dress made a bold statement, but the royal blue peep-toe platform high heels screamed *sexy.*

He came to a halt in front of her. "Are you sure we need to go to this wedding?"

"Why do you think I bought this dress and these shoes?"

"To impress me?" His tone was hopeful.

You better know it. "Ha! You wish. Come in."

"Oh, I wish for a lot of things. Want to hear some of them?" His mouth quirked up on one side.

"I'd love nothing better, but I don't want to be late for Mary's wedding." She did her best to keep her tone light and teasing as she stepped back inside. "However, I do need a favor from you."

Once they were inside her kitchen, she pulled her hair over her shoulder on one side and presented him with her back. "Can you zip this up the rest of the way?"

He made a noise that sounded like it was part groan, part growl.

She glanced over her shoulder. "Problem?"

He shook his head and swallowed, his Adam's apple

prominent. "I'm just not used to having wishes granted so quickly."

A low, pleasant hum warmed her blood. "Helping me zip up was on your list?"

He snapped his fingers and made a face. "That's right. You said 'up.' Every time you say 'up,' I hear 'down' in my head for some reason."

"And what is this? Opposite day?" Thinking about his easing her zipper down gave her sharp palpitations.

"A guy can hope." His fingers caressed the skin exposed by the gaping zipper.

She drew in her breath. Was she going to do this? "Of course, I will need help *after* the wedding."

His light blue eyes darkened and glinted. "Anytime you need help getting undressed I'm your man."

"Good to know." She cleared her throat. "Now could you zip me up? *U-P.* Up."

He complied and rearranged her hair, pressing a finger to a spot near her collarbone. "You have a freckle right there."

"I do?" She'd always disliked her freckles, but it didn't sound as if Liam felt the same.

She turned her head toward him as he leaned over her shoulder. He cupped her chin to angle her face closer and kissed her. The kiss was hot and yet sweet, full of unspoken promises, a combination that had her blinking back tears of happiness.

Though neither one mentioned the kiss during the ride to the church, Ellie couldn't help replaying it. After the simple wedding ceremony, they drove to the far end of the lake in Ellie's Subaru for the reception, so she wouldn't have to climb into his truck in her dress and heels.

"This place is gorgeous," Ellie remarked as she and Liam walked across the parking lot toward the covered outdoor pavilion overlooking the lake. Flickering chandeliers hung from the A-frame log ceiling, and the tables, draped in white cloths, had flower centerpieces surrounded by votive candles.

"Is this what you would call romantic?" Liam had his palm planted firmly on the small of her back as they entered the venue.

She laughed and looked up at him. "Yes. Brody said he wanted Mary to feel like a fairy princess on her wedding day."

He gave a low whistle. "You're telling me Brody planned all this?"

"What? You don't think guys can be romantic?" She enjoyed teasing him, especially when he took the bait. "That's like the ultimate aphrodisiac to a woman. She'll pick the romantic guy every time."

He scratched his scalp. "Huh…"

"Relax." She grinned. "Brody came to Meg and me, and we suggested trolling Pinterest for ideas and put him in touch with people who could make it happen."

"Who knew you could be such a tease?" His mouth crooked at the corner.

"It's the shoes." She angled her foot from one side to the other.

"Are they imbued with special powers?" His eyes glinted as he admired her heels.

"They must be because they're holding your interest."

"You've always held my interest, Ellie."

Ellie wanted to believe him, but thinking like that

was going to get her heart broken for sure. They were just joking around talking like that. Weren't they?

"Hey, wait up, you two," Meg called as she and Riley crossed the parking lot toward them.

Ellie let go of their conversation as they fell into step with the other couple and entered the wedding reception. During the meal, Ellie did her best to ignore Meg's calculating grin every time she looked at them.

When the music started, Liam held out his hand and invited her to dance. Having him hold her as they danced was even better than she imagined...and she'd done copious amounts of imagining over the years. Her current fantasies regarding Liam were very adult.

"What you said back at your place..." he began, and tightened his hold on her as they swayed to the music, "about needing help getting undressed..."

"Whoa." Even with the shoes he was taller and she had to look up to meet his gaze. "When did unzipping my dress turn into undressing me?"

He wiggled his eyebrows. "Huh, I guess my brain was connecting the dots."

"It was connecting something, all right," she said, but cuddled closer to him until they were barely moving.

"Ellie?" he whispered, his breath tickling her ear. "You need to know I'll only be here for another week, maybe less. Riley and I are almost finished with the reno."

"I always knew you weren't staying in Loon Lake." It hurt, but it was the truth and she'd accepted that.

"I wanted to be totally up-front about that."

"I'm a big girl. I'm not expecting this every time I get involved with someone." She waved her hand around at the wedding reception. And that was true, but she

hadn't exactly been involved with a lot of guys. "Sometimes I just want to have fun."

Ellie couldn't help thinking dancing with Liam at the
reception was like a prelude to what was coming next.
After seeing the happy couple off to their honeymoon,
she and Liam held hands as they walked to Ellie's car.

They didn't talk much on the way back to her place
but the sexual tension was palpable—at least on her
end. She threw a couple furtive glances at Liam, but
his concentration seemed to be on driving. What if he
didn't want this? She hated the thought of throwing
herself at him if—

"Ellie?" He reached for her hand and enclosed it in
his much larger one.

Oh, God. Was he going to tell her he changed his
mind? Was he thinking of a way to let her—

"I hear you all the way over here."

"But I didn't say anything."

"But you were busy thinking it."

"Guilty," she admitted.

He angled a glance at her. "Are you having second
thoughts?"

"Are you?"

"No, but I will respect your wishes."

"Then I'm wishing you'd drive a little faster. Pretend
you're on your way to a fire."

"Fire?" He lifted an eyebrow. "More like a confla-
gration." Liam pulled the car into her driveway and
glanced over at her as he parked the car. "Still with me?"

"Absolutely."

He took her hand as they climbed the stairs. Once
inside her apartment, he kicked the door shut and took

her into his arms. He brushed the hair off her cheeks with his thumbs. "Sweet, sweet Ellie, I'm praying you want this as much as I do."

More than you could ever imagine. "Yes."

He rained kisses along her jaw and neck; when he got to her collarbone, he paused.

"I've been thinking about these freckles all damn day," he said, and pressed his lips along her skin, followed by his tongue.

She shivered, and with a low growl he swept her up into his arms and carried her into the bedroom, where he pulled her dress up and over her head, dropping it to the floor at his feet. Laying her gently on the white comforter, he spread her hair around her head.

Easing over her, he caressed the exposed skin on her hip. "Look at what we have here."

She lifted her head. "My surgery scar?"

"Nope. More freckles, but these were hiding from me all this time," he said, and bent down to kiss above her hip.

Her nipples hardened as his hand neared her breasts, making her shiver. She sucked her breath in when his fingers found her breast and kneaded the flesh. He rubbed his palm over her hardened nipple through the lace.

Wanting more, wanting his mouth where his hand was, she arched her back to press closer to him.

He ran his fingertips along the top of her bra and sent shivers along her nerve endings. She pressed closer and he pushed the bra down, freeing her breasts.

"Finally," she moaned.

He chuckled. "Is that what you wanted?"

"I was ready to do it myself."

He made a tutting noise with his tongue. "I never knew you were so impatient."

"Only with you."

"Then maybe you'll like this," he said, and lowered his head and covered her nipple with his mouth. His tongue made twirling motions around the bud. At her sharp intake of breath, he began to suck gently. The moist heat of his mouth made her tremble with need.

When he lifted his mouth and blew lightly on the wet nipple, she nearly shattered right then and there. With clumsy fingers, she unbuttoned his shirt, needing to touch his bare skin.

He lifted his gaze to hers, his eyes glittering with something raw and primitive. Something she'd never seen in him before, and it thrilled her. She hadn't finished unbuttoning his shirt, but he simply pulled it over his head and tossed it on the floor. Standing up, he shed his pants and boxer briefs, then slowly lowered himself back down on the bed.

She pressed her lips against the warm, smooth skin on his chest; he tasted tart and salty.

His mouth brushed over hers in a light, caressing kiss that had her wanting to plead for more. He slid a hand under her nape and drew her closer.

She closed her eyes as his lips moved in gentle urgency over hers. Her blood felt like high-octane fuel racing through her body. Every thudding beat of her heart had her wanting him more and more, until her desire rose to a feverish pitch. She could feel a tension building within her in a push-pull sensation, leaving her hot and moist in a need for the full possession of her body by his.

His tongue demanded entry to her mouth and she

opened with a moan of pleasure as it danced with hers, cavorting back and forth, sliding and caressing.

His hand covered one of her breasts and sent shock waves down to her toes. With his other hand behind her he unclasped her bra and tugged it aside. Once again his mouth claimed her breast, his mouth sucking the nipple and teasing it with his teeth. Her other breast begged for the same attention and she ground her hips against him.

When his mouth touched the other nipple she thought she would explode from the pleasure and the longing. He gave that one the same attention, licking, sucking and nipping at the rigid nipple. As he lifted his mouth and blew on the nipple again, her hips twitched and bucked toward his erection.

All her nerve endings humming and sizzling, she reached up and twined her arms around his neck. She pulled him down, reveling in the way his weight felt on top of her. He kissed her with a searing hunger, as if he'd been waiting for her all his life. He feasted on her mouth like a starving man.

His mouth left hers and he trailed sweet, tantalizing kisses over her shoulders, stopping to kiss the freckles on her collarbone, then moved again to her breasts. He drew his tongue lightly across the underside of her breasts and toward her belly button. He kissed a spot on her hip and let his tongue drift over the elastic waist of her cream lace bikinis. She arched her hips up and buried her hands in his disheveled hair.

His breath flowing over her created goose bumps on her flesh and a mind-numbing sensation in her pleasure-fogged brain. Just when she felt she couldn't stand it a moment longer, he touched the spot that had been begging for attention and she exploded.

She'd barely come back to earth when a foil packet rustled and she reached up to take the condom, saying, "Let me."

He handed the packet to her, his eyes dark with desire and gleaming with anticipation.

His gaze locked on hers and held her in an erotic embrace before he thrust into her. He withdrew and thrust again, more deeply this time, all the while watching her, his blue eyes blazing with a light that should have blinded her. The depth of their connection shocked her, heated her from the inside out each time he filled her.

The need began to spiral to life within her for a second time and all thought was lost; she could only feel, drowning in sensation. He increased the pace as she tried to reach for her release. They both fell into the abyss at the same time, their heavy breathing the only sound in the room.

Liam climbed back into bed after taking care of the condom and pulled Ellie into his arms. He was still processing what they'd just shared. Somehow it transcended mere sex. That fact should scare him, but he was feeling too boneless and satisfied to worry.

She sighed and snuggled closer, resting her head on his chest. "That was…"

"Yeah, it was." He kissed the top of her head and rubbed his hand up and down her arm.

"I never knew freckles could be sexy." She caressed his chest.

He twined his fingers through hers. "You better believe it."

"I always hated them."

"And now?"

She giggled. "I guess they aren't so bad."

"What was the scar from?"

"Surgery."

"For the cancer?"

"Indirectly. They moved my ovaries aside to decrease the chances of becoming infertile due to the treatments."

"I guess the treatments can be as destructive in their own way as the cancer." He squeezed her hand. "So did the operation work?"

"I won't know until I start trying, but like I said, it's possible. Why?" She moved her head back to look at him.

Her silky hair brushing against his chest wasn't helping his current condition. "I don't have any more condoms with me."

"And I don't have— Oh, wait!" She sat up. "Would glow-in-the-dark ones work?"

What was his Ellie doing with glow-in-the-dark condoms? Was there even such a thing? "Ellie, what the..."

She grinned. "Leftovers from Mary's bridal shower."

He shook his head. "Do I even want to know?"

She leaned over and kissed him. "Probably not."

His body won out over his good sense. "Where are these condoms?"

She reached into the nightstand and held up a foil-wrapped strand.

He rolled his eyes. "Ellie, this better not ever become a topic of conversation at a future family gathering, like my dad's morning-after walk of shame."

"I wouldn't dream of it," she told him as they came together again.

* * *

Liam awoke with Ellie pressed against him, her back to his front, his arm around her waist as if he'd been afraid of her escaping while he slept. Where the heck had such a crazy thought come from?

Glow-in-the-dark condoms aside, he couldn't remember the last time—if ever—he'd been this affected. He tried to tell himself it was because they had become friends. It wasn't as if he had developed deeper feelings.

He and Ellie were hanging out while he was here and if that involved some sex, so be it. They were adults. They'd acted responsibly. Yeah, okay, the condoms had been unique but they'd used them. Responsible. He could go back to Boston, to his regular life, with memories of their jaw-dropping sex. He—

His phone began to buzz. Not wanting to wake Ellie, he slipped out of bed and found it in his pants. Going into the kitchen area, he answered the call from Chief Harris.

Several minutes later, he ended the call. He puffed up his cheeks and slowly released the trapped air.

"Who was that?"

He turned to face Ellie. She wore a very unsexy fleece robe but knowing she was probably naked underneath threatened to send his blood pooling below his waist. He did his best to shove those thoughts aside. Unlike Ellie, he hadn't stopped to put anything on before answering the phone.

"Liam?"

"It was my chief. Some of the guys are out sick and he was asking if I could cut my vacation a few days short. Guys are reaching their max for working extra shifts."

She huddled deeper into her robe. "So you need to go back today?"

"Yeah." He rubbed his chest at the sudden restricting tightness from the thought of leaving Ellie behind. Of Ellie becoming involved with someone like Colton. A guy who had the temerity to call her asking for another woman's phone number. Surely Ellie was smarter than that. "I need to jump in the shower and collect my stuff and let my sister know."

She smiled but it didn't reach her honey-gold eyes. "While you're in the shower, I'll make some breakfast."

He went to her and kissed her forehead. "Thanks. I—"

She waved her hand and stepped back. "We both knew it was temporary."

Chapter Seven

Finishing his twenty-four-hour shift, Liam checked his watch as he headed out of the redbrick firehouse located in a densely populated area of South Boston.

"Got a hot date waiting for you at home?" Nick Morretti, the driver engineer on Liam's shift, caught up to him.

"I have last night's episode of *Around the Horn* waiting for me on my DVR." Liam stopped and turned to hold the door open. He hadn't had a date in the two months he'd been home from Loon Lake. Two months since he'd last seen Ellie. Last held Ellie. It wasn't as if they'd broken up, because there was nothing to break. They'd had fantastic sex after the wedding; that's all. No regrets. No recriminations. It all sounded very civilized. So why did it feel so shabby? *We both knew it was temporary.*

"Thanks." Nick grabbed the door and followed Liam outside. "When you gonna take that plunge and settle down? You ain't gettin' any younger."

Liam shook his head. "Have you been talking to my sister?"

Nick laughed and fell into step beside Liam as they went into the early-morning October sunshine of the parking lot. "Don't want you missing out on all the good stuff that comes with marriage and kids."

"Face it, Morretti, you're just jealous because I get to go home and watch sports highlights in my under-shorts." Yeah, the exciting life of a thirtysomething bachelor.

Nick laughed. "Is that what floats your boat these days, McBride?"

"It beats fishing a Barbie out of the toilet," he shot back. It did, didn't it?

Nick huffed out his breath. "Damn. When did Gina tell you about that?"

Liam barked out a laugh and tossed his gym bag into the bed of his pickup. "I was talking about my sister's kids, but do tell."

"And put you off marriage and kids? No way." Nick fished his keys out of his pocket. "Your sister, she's got what, two now?"

"And another on the way." Liam shook his head. "I swear all she and Riley have to do is look at each other and bam, I'm an uncle again. That's why I took all that vacation time up there in Vermont a couple months ago. I was helping Riley with an addition to their place. Only I didn't think they were going to need it quite this soon."

Nick opened the driver's door to a soccer mom–style SUV and climbed in. Sticking his head out the window, he wiggled his eyebrows. "And I suppose that attractive nurse I heard about was an entertaining perk."

Liam's fist tightened around his key fob and the truck's alarm beeped. Ellie wasn't a *perk*. She was... what? Some summer fun? Why did that have to sound so shabby? He wouldn't have thought that with anyone else.

He lifted his chin to acknowledge Nick's departing wave and climbed into his truck. He was bushed from taking extra shifts at a part-time station, but working had helped keep his mind off Ellie. That's the explanation he was going with. A decent few days of uninterrupted sleep and he'd be back to his old self, stop wondering what Ellie was doing. And he'd stop thinking about her honey-gold eyes, the way her hair smelled like flowers he didn't know the name of, and stop tasting the cherry flavor of her lip gloss on his tongue. Yeah, sports highlights, breakfast and stop mooning over Ellie sounded like a workable plan.

Ellie drew her knees up to her chest and bounced her feet on the concrete stoop of Liam's three-decker in the Dorchester section of Boston. A perfect example of the city's iconic multifamily housing units, the colorful home towered above her, looking like three small homes neatly stacked one on top of the other. The large bay windows curving around the right side of the building reminded her of a castle turret. No moat, but the roots from the lone tree in front of Liam's house had cracked and lifted the sidewalk as if trying to escape its concrete jungle. Poor tree.

God, first a car commercial last night and now a stupid tree. She swiped at a useless tear with the back of her hand. Damn her hormones for running amok and turning her into a crier. If this kept up much longer, she'd have to learn better coping skills. Not to mention perfecting those before Liam arrived home.

She inhaled and stretched her neck to glance up and down the quiet street. Why hadn't she called or texted first? Just because he was completing a twenty-four-hour shift this morning didn't mean he'd come straight home. He might stop off somewhere to eat or… She hugged her knees tighter. Or he might be with another woman at her place. She closed her eyes and swallowed against a fresh wave of nausea. What if he was bringing a woman home? After all, it had been eight weeks since their— Her chest tightened painfully as she searched for the right word to describe what they'd had. What had it been? A fling? An affair? Friendship with benefits?

Sighing deeply, she turned her head toward the glossy chestnut-stained front door behind her. What if there was a woman in there right now also waiting for Liam to come home? She made a choking sound before turning to face the street again.

No, there couldn't be, because if *she* saw a strange woman on her front porch for thirty minutes, she'd open the door and demand to know what was going on. However, it would serve her right for not calling ahead if there was another woman. She'd have to laugh it off and say something like, "I was in the neighborhood and…"

"Yeah, like he's gonna buy that," she muttered. Heck, Meg hadn't believed her lame excuse when Ellie had asked about Liam's work schedule. Curiosity had been evident in Meg's expression, but for once she didn't meddle. Not that it mattered, because Ellie wouldn't be able to hold Loon Lake gossip off for very much longer.

She could tell the people she worked with were already getting suspicious by the looks they gave her.

She sighed and rested her forehead on her knees. Short of abandoning her family, friends, job, future plans and everything she held dear in Loon Lake, swallowing her pride to confront Liam was inevitable. Of course, showing up with no prior notice might not be the best way to begin this particular conversation. Lately her head had been elsewhere, but she needed to do this in person. This wasn't something that could be handled in a text or even a phone call.

The low rumble of a truck engine alerted her and she sat up and braced her shoulders as a late-model gray pickup turned onto the street and slowed. *Liam.* And he was alone. Thanking whatever lucky stars she had left, she stood and shook her legs to straighten her jeans.

Liam maneuvered his truck into a parallel spot two houses away. She swallowed hard as he shut off the engine. The door slammed shut.

"Here goes nothing," she whispered, and stepped away from the front stoop.

He walked around the back of the truck and she drank in all six feet two inches. Still dressed in his uniform of navy blue pants and matching shirt with the red and bright yellow Boston Fire Department patch, he looked as though he'd just stepped off a beefcake charity calendar. The only things missing were his turnout pants with those sexy red suspenders. Her mouth watered at that seductive image. At least something other than nausea was making her mouth—

"Ellie?"

"It's me," she said with forced brightness and a fake smile.

He frowned. "Is something wrong? Meg, the kids… or you? You haven't—"

"No. No." She waved her hands in quick, jerky movements. *Scare the poor man, why don't you?* Yeah, she should've warned him of her visit but what would she have said if he'd asked why she was coming? For all she knew, he'd moved on from this summer. Unlike her. "Everyone is fine. Sorry. I should have called ahead but…"

He lifted his arms and embraced her in a welcoming hug. She threw her arms around him, gathering strength from his solid warmth. Wait…was he sniffing her hair? His arms dropped away before she could decide and she let go, despite the desire to hold tight. No clinging. She was an adult and could take care of herself. This trip was to deliver news. That's all.

She glanced back at the front door. No outraged woman bursting out demanding an explanation. One less thing to fret about. A small victory but she'd take it. "I, uh… I hope I'm not interrupting anything."

He draped an arm over her shoulder, gave her a quick shoulder hug and let go. "Nah, I just got off work."

"I know. I mean… I checked with Meg before I came." She scuffed the toe of one red Converse sneaker against the concrete. Doing this on his front porch was not an option. She sighed and motioned with her head toward the house. "You gonna invite me in, McBride?"

He pulled out his cell phone. "Sure, Harding, just let me tell the Playboy bunnies inside to exit through the back."

She rolled her eyes. "Yeah, right. Getting them to hide your porn stash is more like it."

"Ouch." He pocketed his phone with a devastating

grin, then motioned for her to go onto the porch ahead of him.

"I won't take up too much of your time." *Just long enough to change your whole life.*

On the porch, she stood to the side so he could unlock the door. He smelled faintly of garlic and tomato sauce. "You on kitchen duty?"

"Why? Do I smell like an Italian restaurant?" He lifted his arm, sniffed his sleeve and laughed, his eyes crinkling in the corners, the wide grin deepening those adorable grooves on either side of his mouth.

Ellie's toes curled. Score one for her newly heightened sense of smell. Except she didn't need to go where his sexy laugh and her rioting hormones wanted to take her. This trip wasn't about that. And once she told him why she'd come, he wouldn't be interested, either. "You never did bring me any cannoli from that Italian bakery you told me about."

"Mike's?" His light blue eyes flashed with mischief. "Sorry, Harding, but even if I'd gotten some, believe me, they would not have made it all the way to Vermont in the same truck as me."

God, but she'd missed him. She was such a sucker for that teasing glint in his eyes, but nevertheless she made a disparaging noise with her tongue. "McBride, it's a three-hour drive."

"Exactly," he said with a firm nod and a wink. "Sorry, but you'll have to make do with frozen."

She gave him a playful shoulder punch before following him into the inner hallway. A stairway led to the upper units on the left and the entrance to the ground floor unit was on the right. Liam unlocked his door and pushed it open, lifting his arm so she could scoot under.

No sexy heels today to add an extra three inches to her five feet three inches.

Flooded with morning sunlight from the large bay windows, the living room was standard, no-frills bachelor fare, with a brown distressed leather couch and matching recliner facing a giant flat-screen television with an elaborate sound system. Two empty beer bottles, a pizza box and wadded-up napkins littered the coffee table along with an array of remote controls. A sneaker peeked out from under the couch. The sunny room, even the clutter, was like a comforting arm around her shoulder and it warmed her. She could do this.

He cleared his throat. "Sorry about the mess."

"It's a wonderful space. I love these windows. They give you so much natural light." She set her purse on the couch.

"Thanks. Meg says if I had some taste, this place could be great." He tossed his keys on the coffee table and glanced around. "She calls my decorating style the 'under arrest' method…everything lined up against the walls as if waiting to be frisked and handcuffed."

Ellie laughed, picturing Meg chastising him. "Sisters."

A new and unfamiliar awkwardness rushed in to fill the silence. Had sex messed with their friendship? Had he moved on? It was not like they'd made any promises to each other or anything. Ellie rubbed the pad of her thumb over her fingers and swallowed another, more urgent, wave of nausea.

"I guess you're—"

"Would you like—"

Bitterness coated her tongue, making it curl in warning. If she didn't get to a bathroom—stat—she was going to throw up all over Liam's glossy wood floor. She covered her mouth with her hand, barely managing to gag the word, "Bathroom?"

His brow furrowed as he turned and pointed. "Down the hall. First door on the left."

She stumbled into the bathroom, slammed the door and dropped to her knees in front of the toilet. Hugging the bowl, she threw up the breakfast she'd convinced herself to eat before driving to Boston. Yuck. It would be a long time before she could eat oatmeal again…if ever.

Well, there was one bright spot to this whole debacle. At least he hadn't had a woman with him.

Pacing the hall outside the bathroom, Liam calculated ambulance response times against how quickly he could drive her to Brigham and Women's Hospital in midmorning traffic. Listening to Ellie being sick brought back memories of his ma spending hours puking in the bathroom after endless rounds of chemo. The word *cancer* blocked his field of vision like flashing neon. No, that was silly, Ellie had been in perfect health eight weeks ago. God forbid, but what if she was in Boston for an appointment at the Dana-Farber Cancer Institute? No, Meg would have said—

He flung the door open with such force it banged against the wall and bounced back, hitting his arm.

Ellie sat hunched over the bowl and he knelt down beside her. "My God, Ellie, what's wrong? Should I call paramedics? Or I could—"

She held up her hand and croaked out, "No," before the retching began again.

He pulled her hair away from the porcelain with one

hand and rubbed her back with the other. Things he could've—should've—done for his ma but hadn't because he was busy burying his head in the sand, convinced she would beat the cancer. His chest tightened, but with the ease born of practice, he shoved unwelcome emotions aside. He refused to fall apart. If he could run into a smoke-choked inferno, he could handle this. Right? "Tell me what's wrong."

She flushed the toilet, sat back and wiped her mouth with the back of her hand.

He reached up and grabbed a towel off the sink. "Here."

"Thanks." She wiped her mouth and hands before giving the towel back. "I'm okay now."

A chill ran through him and he searched her face as if he would find an answer there. "Are you sure?"

She nodded vigorously and began to rise. He tossed the towel aside, put his hand under her elbow and helped her up.

"May I?" She motioned toward the sink.

He sidestepped to give her a little more room to maneuver, but she was pale and sweating so he was going to be a jerk and stay close, even if he had to crowd her personal space. He didn't want her passing out on him. She turned on the faucet, captured water in her cupped hand and rinsed her mouth. He leaned past her for the discarded towel and mentally kicked himself for not going to Vermont to visit her. Why had he fought his own instincts to call or text her on a daily basis? Yeah, that wouldn't have made him look needy or anything.

She splashed water on her face and he handed her the towel. After she dried her face, he offered his bottle of mouthwash. She glanced from the uncapped plastic bottle in his hand and back to him, a frown creasing her brow.

He shrugged. "What? I lost the cap. Swig it."

"You're such a guy," she muttered.

"And I'm sure you meant that in the kindest possible way." He grinned, relaxing because the bantering was familiar, comfortable, easy to handle. That was his Ellie and— Wait. What was this "his Ellie" stuff about?

She rolled her eyes but raised the bottle to her lips.

Folding his arms across his chest, he watched while she rinsed her mouth and spit into the sink. Now that her skin had lost its previous pallor, she looked more like the Ellie he'd left in Vermont, the healthy one. His friend. The one he just happened to—

He shifted his stance and turned his thoughts away from Ellie's eyes and upturned nose with the light smattering of freckles. He'd put himself back out there in the dating world soon and life would return to normal. That's what he wanted, wasn't it?

"Do you mind?" She bumped him with her hip. "A little privacy, please."

She also had freckles on that hip. *What are you doing?* Thinking about Ellie's skin was not the first step in getting back to normal. "Can I get you something to eat?"

Those honey eyes widened. "Really? You're talking food after my little display?"

Damn she was right, but he needed something to do. Standing around feeling helpless was not something he enjoyed. He needed to be productive. "Hmph, coffee then."

She shuddered.

What the heck? Ellie loved her morning coffee. Now

she was scaring him. "Since when don't you like coffee?"

She glared at him. "Oh, I don't know, maybe since I just threw up what I had this morning."

Yeah, that was a lame question, but he hated not knowing what was wrong. "Fair enough. What would you like?"

"Got any decaf tea?"

Unfolding his arms, he stepped away. "I think I still have some from…"

"From who?"

"From Meg. The last time she was here she wanted decaf, so she bought a box." He frowned at her sharp tone. From the moment he'd seen her sitting on his front steps, she'd thrown him off-balance. "What, Ellie, do you think there's a woman in the closet waiting for you to leave?"

Her eyes narrowed but she didn't say anything. He ground his teeth. Damn, why couldn't he just keep his big mouth shut? Because she was hiding something from him. He just knew it and he didn't like it. Nor did he like the way he wanted to pull her into his embrace, bury his face in her soft hair and let her sweetness take his mind off the restlessness that had plagued him these past two months.

He sighed into the strained silence, regretting his remark. Maybe if he had visited her since their time in Loon Lake, he'd know what was going on with her and there wouldn't be this weird vibe between them. "I'll go check and see if I have any tea bags."

"Thanks. I'll be out in a minute." She shut the door behind him with a soft *snick*.

He found the tea in a cupboard and put some water on

to heat. While he waited for the water to boil, he stuck a pod in his coffee maker. Sleep was probably out of the question so he might as well enjoy some caffeine. Why she had come was a mystery, but something told him Ellie wasn't there to renew their friends-with-benefits arrangement. A morning filled with fantastic sex was looking less and less likely.

Ellie appeared in the doorway as he poured boiling water into a mug with her tea bag. As always when he saw her, his heartbeat sped up. It would appear her red sneakers had a similar effect on his libido as those sexy bright blue heels from the wedding. Like that wasn't messed up or anything.

His gaze rose to her face to take in the pink nose and shiny eyes. His stomach tumbled. Oh, Christ, had his tough-as-nails ER nurse Ellie been crying? Had he caused that with his thoughtless comment? What the hell was wrong with him saying stupid stuff like that, to Ellie of all people? She was the last person he wanted to hurt with a careless remark.

"Your tea." He handed her the hot mug, but what he really wanted was to shake her and demand she tell him what was going on. Or to grab her close and never let her go. Keep her safe forever. But keeping her safe was impossible because cancer didn't respect how much or how many people cared.

She wrapped her hands around the chipped ceramic as if warming them. "Thanks."

"I'm…uh…" What was wrong with *him*? This was Ellie and they'd talked endlessly for hours when they weren't—*hey, remember, we're not going there.* "I hope you like that kind. Meg bought it."

"This is fine." She jiggled the bag up and down. "Got any milk?"

"Let me check." He pulled the milk out of the refrigerator and sniffed the open carton. "Yeah, I do."

Her sudden laughter sent a tingle along his spine. He'd missed that laugh, her unique view of the world, her friendship. Okay, that's what was wrong with him. Ellie hadn't been just a sexual partner like others but a true friend. Relieved to find a reasonable explanation for the way he'd been feeling, he grinned. "We can go in the living room and sit."

"Yeah, that furniture looks more…comfortable."

His gaze landed on the wicked ugly collapsible card table and metal folding chairs from his dad's basement that doubled as a dining set. Not that he ever once dined on it. Eating takeout in front of the TV was more his style. Cooking for the guys while on shift was different from preparing something just for himself. "I haven't gotten around to doing much in here yet."

Her golden eyes sparkled. "Why? Did the couch or recliner resist arrest?"

"Took me a while to read them their rights." His mood was buoyed by the shared moment. Yeah, he'd missed that wacky humor of hers.

"You should get Meg to help with the decorating." She dropped her used tea bag into the wastebasket in the corner. "She's done a fantastic job with her kitchen and the new addition. The entire place really."

"I think she's got her hands full at the moment with being pregnant again. They didn't waste much time after James was born." He was happy for his sister, but seeing Meg so settled had him looking more closely at his own situation. And he didn't always like what he saw. But that was crazy, because as he'd told Nick, he was doing exactly what he pleased. He had a full life.

Ellie clucked her tongue. "She's happier than I've ever seen her. I hope you didn't say anything stupid like that to her face."

He picked up his coffee and followed her into the living room. "It wouldn't do any good if I did. As she's been telling me since she was five I'm not the boss of her."

"No, but she respects your opinion." She sat back on the couch but scooted forward when her feet dangled above the floor. "Besides, you like Riley."

He plopped down in the recliner. "I do as long as I don't have to think about what he and my sister get up to."

"Or your dad and Doris?"

He groaned and shook his head. "At least they're not popping out kids as proof."

She took a sip of her tea and set it on the table next to the couch. The sunshine streaming in through his uncovered windows made the highlights in her shiny hair glow, and he itched to run his fingers through all those dark and reddish strands. He tried to think of a word to describe it and couldn't. *Brown* was too plain a term to describe all that lustrous silk.

"What color is your hair?" Oh, man, had he actually asked that out loud? What was wrong with him?

"What?" She gave him a quizzical look.

He shrugged and hoped his face wasn't as flushed as it felt. "Meg has a thing about people calling her hair red and I, uh, just wondered if you had a name for your color like she does."

She ran a hand over her hair. "It's chestnut. Why?"

He nodded, but didn't answer her question. He'd embarrassed himself enough for one day. "Are you planning on telling me why you're here?"

She rubbed her hands on her thighs and drew in a deep breath. "I know we decided this summer was no strings attached, but—"

"About that, Ellie, I—"

"I'm pregnant."

Chapter Eight

Ellie winced. She hadn't meant to blurt it out like that, but he'd been acting strangely. Not that she could blame him, considering her showing up unannounced and then madly dashing to the bathroom. She could imagine him thinking the worst but that question about her hair color... What was that about? She shifted in her seat and glanced over at him. "Liam?"

He stared at her, his eyes wide, his mouth open, his breathing shallow. She'd imagined all sorts of scenarios during the drive to Boston, including him being stunned and angry, surprised and excited. The latter one was the one she preferred but not the most reasonable. *You left out the one where he declares his undying love and proposes.* Yeah, pregnancy hormones might be messing with her, but she was still tethered to reality. She'd been flummoxed to learn she was pregnant. Imagine poor Liam.

At least she knew now the cancer treatments hadn't rendered her sterile. Of course this wasn't the way she would've planned starting her family. Did wanting to be happily married first make her a prude?

"Are you going to say anything?" she asked, unable to stand the silence a moment longer.

He sprang from his chair as if galvanized by the sound of her voice, and came to sit next to her on the couch, crowding her space. He took her hand in his and rubbed his free one over his face. "Are you sure? Did you take a test? See a doctor?"

She tilted her head, lowered her chin and gave him the *are you kidding me* look. "Hello? Nurse Ellie here."

"Oh. Right." He closed his eyes and pinched the bridge of his nose. "This is… I mean… We… I… You…"

"Yeah, we did, but nothing is one hundred percent. Not even glow-in-the-dark condoms." Maybe Liam was as fertile as his sister. Of course now might not be the best time to point out that observation. Maybe someday they'd be able to get a chuckle or two out of it.

"Have you been to a doctor yet?" he asked.

"Not yet. I wanted to tell you before I went. In case you wanted to…to be involved…" Her voice trailed off.

Then she drew in a breath and plunged in with her prepared speech. "Look, I get that this is a lot to take in, but I want you to know I'm not going to force you to do anything you don't want. I have a good job and a great support system with family and friends in Loon Lake and—"

"Have you told anyone yet?"

"What? Why? Tell me why you would ask me something like…like… Liam?" Her voice had risen with each word; blood rushed in her ears.

He lifted their entwined hands and pressed them close to his chest. "Christ, Ellie, don't look at me like that. I figure you must've already come to a decision or you wouldn't even be here now telling me about the baby." He pulled her closer so she was practically on his lap. "Besides, you know me better than that. I know the ability to have children has been a concern of yours, and knowing how much you love kids, I'm sure you want them."

Relief washed through her and she nodded against his chest, the faint garlic aroma making her empty stomach rumble. Really? Food at a time like this? *You'd rather be thinking about sex?* "So why did you ask if I'd told anyone?"

He rubbed his thumb over her palm. "I was there when it happened, so I should be there when you tell your parents. At least I assume you're planning to tell them."

For the first time since coming to Boston, she was able to take a deep breath and released it with a laugh. Relief, or maybe it was oxygen, making her giddy. "I know it's early to be telling people but what happened in your bathroom is only a part of what's been happening. I either avoid my family for another month or tell them why I'm so tired, dizzy and pale. I don't want my mom thinking the cancer has returned. And it's not something I will be able to hide for very long from my family."

"You'd be surprised. I remember Meg hid it for as long as she could." He squeezed her shoulder.

"Your sister's situation was different. Meg was nineteen, still living at home, and Riley had left town, possibly forever. I'm twenty-seven, employed and, if that's not enough, I happen to know where you live." Why in heaven's name was she arguing with him? She should be ecstatic and yet she was…what? Disappointed because he hadn't pledged his love? This was Liam. Over the summer he had become not just a lover but also a friend. Still, he wasn't the most emotionally available guy she knew. Supportive was good. Supportive worked.

"I don't know about your parents, but my dad has this tone of voice…" He leaned against the couch cushions, drawing her back with him. "Makes me feel twelve all over again when he uses it."

"My mom…she gets this look." She blinked. Damn, but she'd never been a crier. She was smart, practical Ellie, a cancer survivor. A survivor who decided she wanted a fling with the deliciously sexy fireman who also happened to be a friend. She'd wanted to experience something a little wild, maybe even a little wicked. Of course she should have known better than to fall for her temporary fling. "I guess I'm a total failure at this fling business. Not getting pregnant must be like, what, number one on the no-no list?"

"A rookie mistake." He brushed his knuckles across her back.

She blew the hair off her forehead. "A big one."

He gently tucked those stray hairs behind her ear. "I'm sure your dad will be more likely to lay the blame on me."

She sat up straighter and pulled away so she could look at him. "I'll talk to my dad, make him understand that forcing someone into ma—into something they don't want isn't a solution."

He untangled himself and stood up, looking at her with that little half grin. "Wanna explain that to Mac, too?"

"I'm sure your dad will be fine." She huffed out a mirthless laugh. "He dotes on Fiona and James. He loves being Grampa Mac. And he has to know at your age that you're, uh, sexually active."

"Did you want to tell Mac while I'm here in Boston?"

"My dad and Doris are on another one of their jaunts in their motor home and not due back until next week." He stopped pacing and perched his butt against the windowsill. "I do need to tell Meg. If she finds out before I tell her, she'll never let me hear the end of it. What about you?"

"I'll tell my parents and since we'll be telling Meg, I'd like to tell Mary before she hears it from someone else. We've become good friends since she's moved to town. I can call her or stop by the farm."

Liam chuckled. "Meg likes to complain about Loon Lake gossip reaching me down here, but she's usually the one to call and tell me stuff. She claims that she's doing it before the chatter reaches me."

"You can still change your mind about coming with me to talk to my parents." She was giving him an out but prayed he wouldn't take it.

"No, I want them to know I'm not some random guy that got you—"

"Gee, McBride, thanks a lot." She wasn't about to confess to Liam how few guys she'd been intimate with… ever. And this wasn't how she'd imagined she'd feel when having a baby. Instead of celebrating with the man she loved, this was beginning to feel more like triage. She scooted off the sofa to go and stand in front of him.

"What? I only meant—"

"I know what you meant." She sighed but couldn't help leaning into his warmth. "That's the problem."

"I know you don't sleep around. What I'm saying is I need to face your dad. Apologize and—"

Her gaze clashed with his. "Liam? Zip it."

"Right."

"So, we need to break the news to my parents and Meg. Is…" She cleared her throat and took a step back, needing space before asking this next question. Correction, she needed space before receiving his answer. "Is there anyone else you might need to tell?"

"Like? Oh, you mean…" He straightened up and away from the windowsill and took a step, closing the distance she'd put between them. "There hasn't been another woman since…there's no other woman."

She released the breath she'd been holding. That tidbit warmed her more than she would've imagined. "Me, either."

"That's because I'm irreplaceable." He flashed her one of his devilish, intensely sexy smiles.

She gave him a backhanded slap on the arm, but she couldn't wipe the silly grin off her face. Or the relief from her heart.

Liam scrubbed his scalp vigorously as he lathered the shampoo and tried not to think, but Ellie's *I'm pregnant* was stuck on an endless loop in his head. No question he needed to step up and be there for Ellie and their child. He ducked his head under the shower spray and rinsed. Ellie would be a great mom. Exhibit one: she wasn't hiding in the bathroom using taking a quick shower as an excuse to build up much-needed defenses.

On a scale from an unplanned pregnancy to Ellie's cancer returning, the pregnancy was less scary every time, but that didn't mean he wasn't scared. Being a dad had been a nebulous idea for the future. Not on today's to-do list.

When he'd seen Ellie waiting for him on his steps, it had taken all his willpower to remain casual, to not confess how much he'd missed her, to not tell her how many times he'd thought about her. The hug he'd given her had been meant as platonic, two friends greeting each other, but the moment she'd been in his arms, he'd wanted her with an intense ache. And it hadn't been all physical. He could handle simple lust but this felt like more. More than he wanted to admit or accept.

Angry with himself for dwelling, he snapped the faucet off, grimacing when the building's ancient pipes rattled and groaned at his careless treatment. He stepped out of the shower, snatched a towel from the rack and dried off, dressing in jeans and a long-sleeve pullover shirt.

He grabbed a pair of socks and went back in his living room, where he found Ellie seated on the couch, watching television and looking relaxed. But the trash was gone from the coffee table, the remotes were lined up like soldiers, except for the one in her hand, and both of his sneakers sat by his recliner. Yeah, Ellie liked organization and structure.

"You didn't have to clean." He scooped up his sneakers and sank into the chair.

"I'd hardly call throwing a pizza box away cleaning." She waved her free hand in a dismissive gesture, but she was white-knuckling the remote in the other.

Before he could think of something to say, she prattled on. "Did you know that there's a nonprofit organization that studies and ranks tall buildings? Evidently they give out awards or something. Who would have thought to give awards to skyscrapers?"

She continued her one-sided discussion while he pulled the socks on.

"Isn't that interesting?" She peered at him, an expectant expression on her beautiful face.

"Uh-huh." He stuffed his feet into his beat-up running shoes, all the while trying to figure out where she was going with all this skyscraper talk.

She thrust out her lower lip. "You're not even listening."

He met her accusing glare and tried not to smile at her being indignant on behalf of inanimate objects. He longed to take that plump lower lip between his teeth and nip it so he could then soothe it with his tongue and then— Whoa. What happened to not going there?

"Liam?"

"I'm listening…honest…nonprofit…tall buildings… awards. See? But I fail to understand why you're sounding like the Discovery Channel all of a sudden." Where was all this going? Had he missed something?

"Would you prefer I sit here and cry?" She set the remote on the table and sniffed.

"God, no. Tell me more about these awards. They sound fascinating." He crowded beside her on the couch. When he put his arm around her, she leaned into his side and he rested his cheek on her hair. Her chestnut hair. Now he needed the name of the flowers it smelled like, but he damn sure wasn't going to ask her—at least not today. Her subtle scent surrounded him like whirling smoke. "I told you, I'm not going anywhere and I'm gainfully employed. That has to count for something."

She sniffed. "But you only wanted a short fling."

He tightened his embrace. Ellie would demand, and deserved, more than what he could give to this relationship, but he had to try if they were going to be parents. "But we're friends. We'll be friends having a baby."

"Have you forgotten you live here in Boston, and I live in Vermont?" She sighed, a sound filled with frustration.

Ellie wasn't a quitter and neither was he. It would take some adjusting, but they could work this out. "Now that you've mentioned it, there's plenty of room in—"

She pulled away. "Forget it. I'm not moving in with you."

Huh, that stung. Way more than he would've thought. And definitely more than he liked. Especially since that wasn't what he'd been suggesting. "I wasn't asking. My second-floor tenant is—"

"No, thanks. I wouldn't like the commute to work or the high city rents." She shot him a sour look.

"I haven't said anything about charging you rent."

"And I don't want to be responsible for putting you in a financial bind. Don't you need both rents to make the mortgage?"

Yeah, losing a rent would make it tough, but he wasn't about to admit that to her. "You let me worry about that."

How were they supposed to work things out if she kept throwing up roadblocks? He tried to pull her back against him, but she resisted. Was she upset because he hadn't asked her to move in with him? "In case you hadn't noticed, Boston has hospitals."

"Why do I have to be the one to move?" she sputtered. "Vermont has fire departments."

In Vermont, he wasn't in line for a promotion. In Vermont, he wasn't a fourth-generation firefighter. Loon Lake was a part-time house. He needed full time with benefits.

And the smaller the battalion, the longer it took to rise in the ranks. "They're not the Boston Fire Department."

"Oh, excuse me." She scowled. "Vermont might not have the honor of having the first fire department in the nation, but they know how to fight fires in Vermont. Last I heard they'd traded in their horses for shiny red trucks."

"I'm a fourth-generation Boston firefighter. It's a tradition that might continue with…" He glanced at her still-flat stomach. Would there be a fifth generation?

She placed a hand over her abdomen as if protecting it from him. "And maybe she won't want to be a firefighter."

"She?" All thoughts of their argument flew out of his head. He swallowed hard. How could a simple pronoun make his stomach cramp? "You already know it's a girl?"

"No, but I couldn't continue to say 'it,' so I started saying she. I figure I have a fifty-fifty shot at being right." She leaned back against the cushions, her expression smug.

"I see." By next year at this time, there'd be a new little person in his life, one he'd be responsible for and— He pushed those thoughts aside. One problem at a time. "So, you'll think about moving here?"

"Nope," she said.

Argh. Why was she being so stubborn? That would be the perfect solution. *You mean perfect for you.* He blocked out the accusing voice in his head. "Why not? Your skills would transfer to any of the emergency rooms here and you could probably earn more, too."

"But I wouldn't be happy. I like living in Loon Lake.

I like where I am, the people I work with." She crossed her arms over her chest.

"But didn't you say you were looking for a new job?" He seized on what he could to convince her while trying to ignore the way her crossed arms pushed up her chest.

"Those plans are up in the air for now." She patted her stomach. "It may take me a bit longer to finish the degree."

Guilt jabbed him. Here he was, trying to get her to do what he wanted to make life easier for him, without giving any thought to how this affected her plans. Was he that selfish? "Is there anything I can do?"

"Not unless you want to carry this baby for a while." She raised her eyebrows at him.

"Would that I could." His gaze went to her stomach. "But if you were upstairs, I could feed you, help you study."

She shook her head. "And don't you think having us living right upstairs would cramp your style? It might be hard to explain to your dates."

"There won't be any dates. I already told you there hasn't been anyone since…well, there hasn't been anyone else." He hated admitting his self-imposed drought, but maybe the reassurance would help change her mind. *That's mighty big of you, McBride. When did you get to be such an—*

"But that doesn't mean there won't be. You're not planning on being celibate the rest of your life, are you?" She raised her eyebrows at him.

Hell no. Huh, might be best to keep that to himself for now. He had better survival instincts than to continue any talk about sex, even if that's what he'd been hoping for when he'd spotted her on his front steps.

And how had this conversation deteriorated into a discussion of his sex life? Ellie had an uncanny ability to know what he was thinking and…yeah, best not dwell on that. She might be ignoring their chemistry, but it still sparked, at least for him. Although this might not be the best time to point that out. "How about we just get through telling the necessary people our news for now?"

"Sounds like a plan. I drank the rest of your milk."

"Oh-*kaay*…" The abrupt change of topic was enough to give him whiplash, but he'd take it. "We can go to the corner store and get more."

Her face brightened. "How far is it? This looks like a nice neighborhood to take a walk."

She wanted to take a walk? Hey, it was better than sitting here, *not* talking about sex. "Speaking of walking, where's your car? I didn't notice it out front."

Her gaze bounced away. "That's because it's not exactly out front."

"Oh? There are usually spots this time of the day. For instance, there was the one I took." He knew where this was going and he was going to enjoy taking it there. Teasing Ellie and watching her eyes spark always made him want to lean over and—huh, maybe this wasn't such a good idea.

"Well…there was only one and I thought… I thought—"

"Are you telling me you can't parallel park?" He leaned closer.

She scooted off the couch and went toward the bay windows. "Hey, it's not my fault. It's genetics. I'm missing the parallel parking gene."

"Genetics?" He stood and followed, as if tethered by invisible rope. "So does that mean this deficiency can be passed on? Isn't that something you should have warned me about?"

"Sorry?" She sucked on her bottom lip.

"Eh." He bit the inside of his cheek, trapping a smile. "Too late now. C'mon. Let's go to the corner store for milk." He puffed out his chest. "And while we're at it, I'll pull your car closer if you want, since I'm in possession of this awesome gene."

"Oh, brother." She rolled her eyes. "This corner store wouldn't by any chance have sandwiches or a deli?"

Was she serious? "You're hungry?"

"Starved."

"But I thought…" Liam tried to remember what Meg had been like when she was pregnant with Fiona and James, but his sister had hidden it or he'd been too blind to notice. Yeah, he was good at ignoring the obvious. Like with his ma. "If you say you're hungry, then I'll feed you."

She shook her head. "Yeah, not with what you've got on hand. I checked."

"You rummaged through my cupboards?" Was she really that hungry?

She scrunched up her nose. "Yes, Mother Hubbard, and I hate to break it to you, but they're pretty bare."

Who cared about what his kitchen cabinets did or did not contain when that pert, freckled nose was begging to be kissed?

"McBride?"

"Huh?" He shook his head, trying to get back on topic. He blamed his self-imposed eight-week period of celibacy for his lack of concentration.

She pointed to her mouth. "Food?"

It was his turn to wrinkle his nose. "You're serious about wanting to eat?"

"Oh, you mean because of the…in the bathroom?" She tilted her head toward the hallway and pulled a face.

He needed to proceed with caution if he wanted to avoid an argument or, worse, hurting her feelings. "You snapped at me for even suggesting coffee."

She fiddled with the neck of her sweater. "Yeah, about that… I lied. Sorry. The smell turns my stomach. I haven't been able to drink it or smell it for the past few weeks."

He glanced at the mug he'd set on the floor next to his recliner. "Do you want me to get rid of mine?"

Her eyes widened. "You mean you'd do that for me?"

"Of course." The coffee was probably cold by now, anyway. No great loss. He could make another cup when they got back from the store.

"That's so sweet," she gushed. "I can't tell you how much that would mean…you giving up coffee for the next seven months."

Wait…what? He opened his mouth but was incapable of forming words.

She patted his chest and hooted with laughter. "Sucker."

Yeah, he'd walked right into that one, but Ellie's laugh was worth it. Ellie made a lot of things worth it. He couldn't imagine going through this with anyone but her.

Chapter Nine

Ellie pondered the situation as they made their way to the corner store. His offer to be present when she broke the news to her parents had surprised and pleased her, and yet at the same time disappointed her. Had she expected more or were her hormones messing with her? Regardless, she had to admit she yearned for an admission that he'd missed her as much as she had him and that he regretted the no-strings-attached part of their arrangement. She needed to remember her vow to stay rooted in reality. *Learn to want what you have, not wish for what you don't.* Even if he'd proposed marriage, she wouldn't have accepted. She didn't want to end up like her mother with a kitchen table that had a lazy Susan but no one to use it. No shared meals or lively conversations. Now, her parents sat in front of the TV so they didn't have to talk and slept in separate bedrooms. They were like ghosts rattling around in the same house. Things hadn't been like that before her diagnosis and Ellie carried the burden of guilt. If she hadn't gotten cancer, would her mom and dad still be that loving, demonstrative couple she remembered from her pre-cancer days? The thought of doing something like that to her own child chilled her.

Instead of dwelling on a past she couldn't change, she pushed aside depressing thoughts to admire the differences and similarities in the homes lining the narrow street. Front porches and columns were common, although some had ornate railings and trim while many of the homeowners had boxed in the rococo trim using vinyl siding. She glanced back at Liam's and admired how his had only original details…except one. "How come yours is the only one with an external fire escape?"

"I'm the only fireman on the block."

Before she could comment, an elderly woman wearing a burgundy sweatshirt that said World's Greatest Grandma came toward them, dragging a fully loaded fold-up shopping cart.

Liam approached the woman. "Good morning, Mrs. Sullivan, looks like you could use some help getting that up your steps."

"Morning, Liam. I'm not the doddering old woman you seem to think, but since you're here…" She opened the gate on a chain-link fence surrounding a three-decker painted the same red and cream as Liam's.

"It's not your age but your beauty that attracts me, Mrs. Sullivan." He took the shopping cart from her.

"Oh, you are so full of it today, Liam McBride." She

leaned around him and smiled at Ellie. "Is that because you have this lovely young lady with you?"

"You wound me, Mrs. Sullivan, I assure you I'm totally sincere." He picked up the cart and set it on the wooden porch of the home.

Ellie's stomach tingled at Liam's solicitous behavior toward the older woman. It confirmed what she'd always known about his character.

"Aren't you going to introduce me?" The older woman clucked her tongue.

"Of course. Ellie Harding, this is Mrs. Sullivan." He motioned between the women.

"Fiddle faddle, I told you to call me Barbara." The woman poked him. "A pleasure to meet you, Ellie."

Ellie shook hands with the woman. "Same here."

"I haven't seen you around here before," the older woman said.

Ellie smiled at Barbara Sullivan. "That's because I live in Vermont. Loon Lake."

"Ah, that explains why Liam was gone so much this summer." The woman grinned and poked him again. "And here you were, telling me you were helping your sister."

He raised his hands, palms out. "I was. I helped them add a new master suite and family room."

"Why didn't you say something about Ellie when I tried to set you up with my granddaughter Chloe?"

He wanted her to live upstairs so he could take care of her? Yeah, right. And how would Chloe feel about a third or fourth wheel? Or maybe he wasn't interested in this Chloe because of their summer fling. Realistic? Maybe not, but it helped her to keep smiling at Chloe's grandmother.

"Shame on you for not telling me you already had someone in Vermont," the woman continued.

"That's because I—"

"We're not—"

Mrs. Sullivan looked from one to the other. "Uh-huh. Usually I see him and he's running or jogging or some such thing to keep fit for the ladies. You're not running today, Liam? But I guess if you've already been caught…"

"I'm not running because—" His brow knit and he hooked his thumb in Ellie's direction. "She's crap at keeping up."

"Apparently I'm crap at parallel parking, too," Ellie muttered. She didn't want to think about Liam and other women. And she certainly didn't want someone insinuating that she'd "caught" Liam as if she'd deliberately set a trap by getting pregnant.

"Don't worry about it, dear. I've lived on this street for fifty years and never learned to parallel park." Barbara Sullivan winked at Ellie.

"You don't own a car," Liam pointed out.

The woman shot him an affronted look. "What's that got to do with it?"

Liam heaved an exaggerated sigh. "Apparently nothing. Do you need help getting your shopping inside?"

"No, but thank you. Now you and your Ellie enjoy your walk." The older woman made a shooing motion.

"She seems nice," Ellie said as Liam shut the gate with a clang of metal.

Liam nodded. "Mmm, she is…for the most part."

"Sorry if she assumed that we were…well, that we were together." Good grief, why was she apologizing? This baby wasn't an immaculate conception—even if that's what she'd love to be able tell her dad. Not to mention all the elderly ladies at the church next time she volunteered at the weekly luncheon. *Oh, grow up, those women were all young once.* "But then, we're going to have a baby so I guess you can't get more together than that."

He frowned. "Are you saying—"

"I'm not saying anything. Like I said—huh, well, I guess I am saying *something.*" *Damn hormones.* "But I'm not pressing you for anything."

"For God's sake, Ellie, I'll do my share."

The rational part of her brain, when it still worked, knew that expecting him to move would be as crazy as him expecting her to move. Offering her a place to live might solve the problem of distance for him, but being on the periphery of Liam's life was not what she wanted. She wanted to *be* Liam's life. She wanted what Meg and Riley, or Mary and Brody, had. Yeah, that right there was the problem. "That might be difficult since you'll be here and I'll be in Loon Lake."

"Careful." He placed a hand under her elbow and pointed to the uneven sidewalk.

"I'm pregnant, not blind." She cringed at her own waspish tone and blinked to hold back tears. Since when did she have the power to make people react or feel the way she wanted? If she had that power, she'd have put her parents' in-name-only marriage back together.

"But with my schedule, I can get ninety-six hours off, unless I take extra shifts. That's four days."

"I know how long ninety-six hours is." And she knew how long it took to drive from his place to hers. How involved could she honestly expect him to be? She might have regularly scheduled hours at her job but it wasn't as if she was always able to leave on time. Same for Liam if they got called out before quitting time; she knew he couldn't just leave.

He blew out his breath. "Are you trying to start a fight?"

"No." *Liar.* "Maybe."

He stopped, placed his hands on her shoulders and turned her to face him. His gaze scanned her face, his blue eyes full of concern. "What can I do to get your mind off fighting?"

An image popped into her head. Yeah, like she was going to suggest something like *that*. She chose option two. "You could try feeding me."

Was that disappointment on his face? Hmm, seems his mind had gone there, too. *Join the club.* But now was not a good time to muddle things with sex, her sensible half pointed out. But it could be so much fun, her daring half argued.

At the moment hunger was the deciding factor. Those cookies and milk she'd eaten while Liam was in the shower seemed like ages ago. "Is that pizza I smell?"

"There's a small place around the corner."

Her stomach growled. "Can we go there?"

"It's barely ten and that place is a grease pit." He frowned.

"And your point is?"

"Grease can't be good for…for—" his Adam's apple bobbed "—the baby."

"For your information, grease is a food group." Despite her insistence, a pizza didn't hold the same appeal as it had a few minutes ago. And yet a feeling of dissatisfaction made her persist. "Are you going to feed me or not?"

"Fine. We can go to there if you really want or we can go to the store and get milk, some stuff for sandwiches and maybe some fruit or salad."

She already regretted acting so disagreeable. Why did being with Liam again make her feel so contrary? She was blaming her body's reaction to his touch. "Fruit and salad? Who are you and what have you done with the Liam I know?"

"Smart aleck." He dropped his hands, but not before giving her shoulders a gentle squeeze and dropping a kiss on the end of her nose.

She fell into step beside him. "Actually, sandwiches sound better than pizza."

He draped an arm around her shoulders. "If you insist on empty calories after sandwiches, I have some snickerdoodles from Meg and—"

"Had," she interrupted.

"Huh?"

"Had, as in past tense. I…uh, found them while I was tidying up. Why do you think I drank the rest of your milk?"

"Huh." He rubbed his chin. "I guess my cupboards weren't as bare as you claimed."

"Don't push it, McBride."

"I wouldn't dream of it, Harding."

A bell dinged and a cashier greeted them when they entered the neighborhood store, reminding Ellie of the Whatleys' Loon Lake General Store; Liam's offer of an apartment in his building flashed through her mind, but she just as quickly discarded it. They'd muddle through somehow, especially since their work schedules gave them both stretches with days off.

The cashier who'd greeted Liam by name as they entered immediately engaged him in a discussion of the baseball playoffs. Listening to the two debate a controversial ruling at second base, Ellie wandered to the rear of the store and a well-stocked deli.

"Morning." A woman with short dark hair and a Red Sox baseball cap stood behind the deli counter. She hitched her chin toward the front of the store. "You a friend of Liam's?"

"Something like that." *Friends who just happen to be having a baby.* Being friends with Liam was easy; resisting his crooked smile and quick wit was a different matter. Sleeping with him again would only complicate things. *But it sure would be fun.*

"What can I get you?" the clerk prompted, tightening the ties on her bibbed apron.

"Hmm…" Ellie's gaze traveled up and down the display case. She never knew what her stomach was going to accept. One minute she craved something, the next it made her gag. Her appetite was as mercurial as her moods.

"Liam's partial to the honey ham," the clerk suggested.

"Okay, that sounds good." At least he could eat it if her stomach revolted. "And some provolone."

Liam approached carrying a loaf of white bread and Ellie shook her head. "I'm not eating that."

He held the package up and eyed it. "What? You don't like bread now?"

She liked bread but was trying to eat healthy, or at least healthier. She was going to be someone's mom and needed to set a good example. "Don't they have whole wheat or twelve grain? Did you learn nothing from me this summer?"

"Yeah, I learned to hide my junk food," he said, and rolled his eyes.

A suspicious snickering sound came from the other side of the counter and Ellie glanced over. The woman's back was to them but her shoulders were shaking.

"Glad you find my being forced to eat healthier funny, Mrs. O'Brien," Liam said in a dry tone.

The woman turned around. "It's about time you settled down with a woman who is interested in taking good care of you, Liam."

"We're not—"

"Oh, we're just—"

The woman winked as she handed over two packages wrapped in white butcher paper. "I sliced it the way you like."

Liam was still stuffing his wallet into his back pocket after paying when Ellie poked into the bag and pulled out a package of chocolate-covered graham crackers. What the hell? He shook his head. She'd given him grief over some stupid bread and she was chowing down on more cookies. He made a mental note to ask Riley if pregnancy made women unreasonable.

Ellie stuck the package of cookies under her arm and held out her hands. "I can carry some of that."

He lifted the bags out of reach as they exited the store. "I got it."

She glanced back as they turned the corner onto his street. "See? That's why I could never move in upstairs."

He turned his head. What was she seeing that he wasn't? The street looked the same as it had when they'd arrived. "I don't follow what you're getting at."

"They assumed we were together."

"Umm…we were."

She shook her head vigorously. "I mean *together* together."

Maybe he was the one losing his mind. He chose silence.

"Once my pregnancy starts showing, people would be asking all sorts of questions and making assumptions."

"Assumptions? Like that we'd had sex?" Damn his big mouth. "C'mon, they'll do all that in Loon Lake."

"Yes, but, judgment or not, they'll also be there for me if I ever need help." Her lower lip came out in a pout.

Ooh, what he wanted to do with that sexy lower lip. Even in a pout, that mouth called to him. "This is Dorchester today, not in the 1950s. No one is going to judge you."

"That's what you think. How come you never went out with Mrs. Sullivan's granddaughter?" she asked as they passed Barbara Sullivan's three-decker.

"Because I have to live on this street." Evidently they were done talking about moving. He'd bide his time, but he wasn't giving up. Huh…he should be relieved she wasn't demanding all sorts of concessions from him, but the idea of her being so far away from him, in Vermont, annoyed him.

"But you said you always part on friendly terms with women you date. No harm, no foul," Ellie said.

"You wanna try explaining that to Grandmother Sullivan?"

She nodded. "Good point."

"And for your information, I'm not some sort of serial dater." However, he'd had enough relationships to understand the signals leading to the point where women began uttering accusations like "emotionally unavailable" and ended things before that happened. He liked to end on good terms. If the relationship progressed to the point of using those phrases, the inevitable parting could become acrimonious. He never wanted anything like that for himself and Ellie. Is that why he'd hesitated getting involved with her in the past? Of course the no-strings-attached thing hadn't exactly worked in his favor. He glanced at Ellie. Or had it? Could a child keep them together?

"You have to admit, you've dated a lot of women," she was saying.

"True, but they've been spread out over sixteen years. Never two at once and I never poached." Why did he feel the need to defend his dating history? He never had in the past.

They were back at his house and he shifted the bags so he could reach his keys.

Ellie reached over and grabbed a bag. "Here, let me take one of those."

Their fingers brushed and there was that spark he'd remembered but had tried to deny for the past two months. He needed to ignore it if he was going to put Ellie back into the friend zone. That was where she needed to be if they were going to work on a partnership for the sake of their child.

After lunch in the living room, Ellie brought her empty plate into the kitchen and paused in the doorway. Liam's hair had flopped over his forehead as he bent over to load the dishwasher and her fingers twitched with the need to brush it back. Their summer fling was over, and pregnant or not, she didn't have the right to touch him with such tenderness, as much as she ached to do so.

"I should leave soon to beat the traffic." She handed him her plate and grabbed another chocolate-covered graham cracker from the bag on the counter.

"Leave? Already?" He glanced up and frowned. "Why don't you stay tonight? You look beat."

"I'll be fine. I didn't plan to stay, so I didn't bring anything with me." She contemplated her cookie before taking a bite. The thought of packing an overnight bag had occurred to her, but she didn't like the message that would send. Whether to Liam or to herself, she wasn't sure. Maybe both.

"We can go and get you whatever you need. Boston happens to be a very cosmopolitan city. Stores, restaurants, hospitals—"

"Don't start with me." While she believed in co-parenting, living in such proximity to him without sharing his life would be impossible. She wanted it all. She was sick of being in the friend zone with guys. Was it too much to want one who saw her as a friend and a lover, a life partner, a guy whose heart sped up at the sight of her? Someone who was interested in something other than her bowling score or batting average? One who wouldn't bury himself in work when life got tough?

Her father used work to bury his emotions brought on by the uncertainty of her cancer. But blocking out his emotions meant he couldn't deal with his wife's, either. Ellie couldn't blame it all on her dad. She understood not everyone could handle all those emotions surrounding such a diagnosis. Of course, she also understood her mother feeling abandoned by the man who was supposed to be there for her in sickness as well as health. Trying not to take sides meant her own relationship with her parents was strained and not as close as it had once been.

He slammed the dishwasher door shut. "If you insist on going back this afternoon, I'm driving. I don't want you falling asleep at the wheel."

"Hello? I'm an ER nurse. I know better than that." If a brisk walk around the block didn't work, she would think of something that made her spitting mad. Angry people tended to be more alert. If that failed, she'd pull into the first rest area.

He leaned against the counter, his arms folded over his chest, his feet crossed at the ankles. "Either stay here with me tonight or I drive you back to Vermont. That's the deal."

She grabbed another cookie. She could argue with him, but what would that accomplish? And she really was dead on her feet and not looking forward to the drive to Loon Lake. Now that she'd delivered her news the nervous energy was gone, replaced with the usual afternoon fatigue. "But how will you get back?"

"One of the guys can drive my truck to pick me up."

"Were you able to get enough sleep on your shift?"

He nodded. "Yeah, a couple callouts but not bad."

"Okay, you can drive me back." Spending more time together was important if they were going to co-parent.

His head jerked back as he studied her. That devilishly sexy grin appeared, the one that deepened the grooves bracketing his mouth. The one that threatened her resolve to not throw herself at him. The one she was powerless to resist.

When he opened his mouth, she pointed her cookie at him. "Don't crow. It's not attractive."

"Says you." He straightened up and pulled away from the counter, his light blue eyes gleaming with mischief. "Let me get some things so *I* won't get caught short spending the night."

"Fine, but if you stay at my place, you'll be sleeping on the couch," she called to his retreating back.

He turned and began walking backward. His low chuckle said he was remembering the things they'd done on her couch. Damn. Now she had all those images in her head.

Those pesky snippets were still playing like movie trailers in her head as they drove through the narrow, winding streets of Boston.

"What can I say to convince you to move here?" he asked.

Tell me you love me and can't live without me. Tell me I'm the most important person in your life. Tell me you're in this for the good times and *the tough ones.* "Nothing. It ain't gonna happen."

He glanced over at her as he took the on-ramp to the interstate and sped up to blend into traffic. "The upstairs apartments are just as nice as mine. You said you liked it and you could decorate any way you wanted."

"I'm sure it's very nice, but I want to stay in Loon Lake." There, she wouldn't have to watch Liam living his life with her on the periphery. In Boston, she'd be cut off from friends. If she were truly already a part of Liam's life, giving up Loon Lake wouldn't be that hard. But she wasn't and it mattered. "You said Meg picked Loon Lake to live in to raise Fiona. I want the same things for my child. I have nothing against where you live. Your street is very nice and if Mrs. Sullivan is anything to go by, the people are nice, too. But I enjoy small-town living for all its inherent problems."

"Okay, I won't press."

"Thanks," she said, but she had a feeling the subject wasn't dead, just dormant. But she'd enjoy the respite. "I love the idea of our child growing up close to Meg's kids."

He nodded and sighed. "There is that."

"Just think, another seven or eight years and Fiona will be able to babysit." Family ties were another reason to stay in Loon Lake. Her child would have ties to the town and its people the same way she did.

"Fiona babysitting. Lord help us all." He chuckled.

Ellie laughed and yawned. She settled back against the seat. It seemed like she ran out of steam every afternoon, no matter how much sleep she'd gotten the night before. And due to her pending trip, she hadn't gotten a whole lot last night.

Despite her pregnancy fatigue, her mind wouldn't turn off. Yes, she wanted to do what was best for her child and she was convinced Liam would be a wonderful father. Not to mention, the rest of the McBrides would surround her child with family and love.

Was it selfish to want some of that for herself, too?

Chapter Ten

Liam had meant what he said. He wouldn't keep pressing her about moving, but he hated having two hundred miles between them. What was he supposed to do in an emergency? What if Ellie or his child needed him? He didn't want to be so far away from either of them.

He spared a quick glance over at his sleeping passenger and grinned. As much as he enjoyed Ellie's company, he was glad she was getting the rest she so obviously needed, judging by the circles under her eyes.

Yep, not letting her drive was the right decision. She'd make a great mother, and surely Ellie could undo anything he might inadvertently screw up. The enormity of the situation was sinking in and he must be getting used to the idea of being a father because he didn't panic each time the thought ran through his head. Well, that whole not-panicking thing was relative.

Before they'd left, he'd decided telling his sister right away made sense and Ellie had agreed. He'd hate for Meg to hear the news from someone else. Slowing Ellie's car, he turned onto the driveway to his sister's house.

The driveway leading to Meg and Riley's began as a shared driveway, then it forked off into two. Her home was set back about one hundred yards from the main road. The house was surrounded by towering trees on three sides, and if not for the other home across the front yard from theirs, Meg and Riley would be all alone in the woods. On the other side of the trees, the lake was visible only during winter.

A swing set, sandbox and bicycle leaning against the open porch announced this was a family home. At one time, Liam had urged Meg to go in with him to purchase the Boston three-decker, but she'd been adamant about wanting a real yard for Fiona and his wasn't much more than a postage stamp. He saw now that she'd made the right choice. Even before Riley returned to claim his small family, Meg had done the best thing for her and Fiona by moving here. Was that how Ellie felt?

He parked next to his sister's car and shut off the engine. Reaching over, he shook Ellie's shoulder. "Hey, sleepyhead, we're here."

Ellie blinked and sat up straight. She wiped a hand across her mouth and groaned. "Was I drooling?"

"Only the last hour or so." He took the key from the ignition.

"Why didn't you wake me?"

"Because then I couldn't razz you about drooling."

"Brat." She unbuckled her seat belt and scrambled out of the car. "Let's get this over with."

He got out and followed her onto the porch. Leaning down, he squeezed her hand and whispered, "Think of this as a practice run before we tell your parents."

Ellie had barely knocked when the front door was flung open and Meg, dressed in jeans and an oversize sweatshirt, greeted them.

"I thought I heard a car pull in." Meg gave Liam a questioning look as he hugged her and kissed her cheek. "This is a surprise."

"I hope we didn't come at a bad time," Ellie said. She was chewing her bottom lip.

"No, no. Come in." Meg waved them in and led them through the original cozy living room to the kitchen. "I hope you don't mind, but I have cookies in the oven and don't want them to burn."

Liam glanced around, surprised by the silence. With two kids and a dog, Meg and Riley's home was usually a lot more boisterous. "Where is everyone?"

"James is taking a nap and Riley had the day off, so he did the school run to get Fiona, and the dog jumped in the truck with him. He texted that they were going to stop at the lake to let Mangy and Fiona blow off some steam before coming home." Meg pulled out a cookie tin and set it on the table. "Sit."

Liam reached for the tin. "Snickerdoodles?"

"Manners much?" Meg swatted his arm. "Let Ellie have some first. These cookies are Riley and Fiona's favorites. They already gave me grief for taking half the batch to you last time I made them."

"I didn't forget, but *someone* got into my stash and ate the rest." He scowled at Ellie, doing his best to hide a grin.

Ellie glared back and pulled out a chair. "Hey, there weren't that many."

"Want some coffee to go with the cookies?" Meg asked, giving them quizzical looks.

"No," Liam practically shouted, remembering Ellie's aversion to the smell. Clearing his throat, he searched for a calmer tone. "No, thanks. Milk is fine."

Meg frowned but pulled a gallon of milk out of the refrigerator and reached into the cabinet for glasses.

Ellie sat down and grabbed a cookie while Liam poured milk for everyone.

Meg leaned toward Ellie. "I knew you were going to Boston, but you didn't tell me you were bringing trouble back with you."

Ellie broke a cookie in half and dipped it into her milk. "I didn't know he was coming. He insisted. You know how bossy he can get."

"You know I can hear you two," he grumbled before shoving a cookie in his mouth. Meg's body language told him she suspected something was up and they weren't going to be able to hold her off for much longer.

He swallowed his cookie and made eye contact with Ellie, checking to make sure she was ready. "We, uh, have something we need to tell you."

Meg did a fist pump. "What's up? I know how you clicked over the summer. You two getting married?"

Liam nearly choked on his milk. "No!"

"Ass." Meg punched his arm, sending milk sloshing over the top of his glass and onto his hand.

"Language?" Liam used a napkin to wipe off his hand and wet sleeve. He tried to act affronted but he regretted his knee-jerk answer. Looking at Ellie's face, he knew he shouldn't have said anything, even if that was his first reaction.

"You deserved it and the kids can't hear me." Meg turned to Ellie and shook her head. "I apologize for my—"

"It's okay," Ellie interrupted. "We don't have any plans like that."

Liam felt like the ass his sister had called him. Ellie was smiling, but her eyes were overly bright. Damn, he'd made her cry twice in one day. He reached across the table and touched Ellie's hand. "I didn't mean it the way it sounded."

"I know." Ellie cleared her throat. "I'm… That is, we're having a baby."

"A baby?" Meg's eyes grew wide. "Wow… Uh, I mean congratulations. That's…serious."

"Oh, we're not—"

"We aren't—"

"Uh, guys." Meg's gaze bounced from one to the other, shaking her head. "Having a baby together is pretty serious."

Seeing Ellie's flushed face, Liam sent his sister a nonverbal warning, hoping their sibling connection would say what he wasn't, even if he didn't know exactly what he was trying to say. "Yes, it's serious, but we're friends who will also happen to be parents together."

Meg nodded, but her expression screamed skepticism. "Does Dad know?"

Liam squeezed his eyes shut. "Not yet."

"At least you're in a better situation than I was when I had to confess," Meg said.

Liam groaned. "It's not like I can use my age as an excuse."

"He'll get over it. Doris has been a good influence on him and she'll be thrilled. She loves babies," Meg said, and turned her attention to Ellie. "I'm happy for both of you and excited to be an aunt. I never thought I'd have that honor. Riley's an only child and, well, Liam, he's—"

"Sitting right here, sister dear," he interrupted, raising his eyebrows.

Meg rolled her eyes. "I'm excited to be an aunt and for Fiona and James and this new baby to have a cousin."

Before Ellie could respond, Meg rushed on, "Too bad you won't be here in Loon Lake. We could be like pregnant sisters."

Ellie shook her head. "Oh, but I have no plans to move anywhere."

Liam ground his molars. Ellie's pregnancy wasn't planned but it was a reality and he didn't appreciate being shut out of major decisions, which might happen if Ellie stayed in Loon Lake. What other explanation was there for his caveman behavior around her?

Meg glanced at him with a *help me out here* look. He responded with a quick shake of his head.

"That's even better," Meg said. "We can be pregnant together. I think Mary and Brody are starting to think about giving Elliott a brother or sister. Wouldn't that be fun? Our kids could form their own play group."

Ellie pulled her hand free of Liam's. She leaned over and gave Meg a hug. "I'd love that. Our kids are going to be family and I want them to be close."

"Yeah, you're getting to be an old pro at this, sis," Liam said.

"Liam!" Ellie poked him with her elbow.

Meg laughed. "What can I say? Riley and I—"

"Riley and I what?" another voice came from the doorway to the kitchen.

Riley greeted Liam and Ellie as he walked over to Meg and leaned down to give her a kiss.

Meg put her arm around her husband's waist. "Where's Fiona?"

"Dang, I knew I forgot something." He leaned in for another kiss. When he finally pulled away, he said, "She's outside with the dog. Mangy's paws got all dirty and I didn't think you'd want muddy prints all over your floors."

"Mmm. Good call." Meg gave him a dreamy look.

Liam brought his hand up and covered his eyes. "Guys, company here."

Despite his joking complaints, something sharp poked him when he saw how happy his little sister was in her marriage. He was glad, he truly was, but seeing it made him realize what he was lacking. Could he and Ellie build that sort of life together? Whenever he imagined his future, Ellie was front and center.

"Oh, yes." Meg patted Riley's chest. "Wait until you hear Liam and Ellie's news. They're having a baby."

"Really? Congratulations." Riley clapped Liam on the back. "When's the big day?"

"Uh, we don't know yet… Ellie hasn't gone to the doctor." Liam looked to Ellie.

Riley shook his head. "I didn't mean the baby due date, I meant— Oomph."

Meg's jab to the ribs effectively silenced Riley, and she turned to explain. "Ellie and my brother are going to be…" She glanced at Liam but didn't wait for confirmation before saying, "They're going to be friends who have a baby together."

Before anyone could say anything else, Fiona burst into the kitchen. "Mommy, I taught Mangy to catch the Frisbee. 'Cept he won't bring it back to me."

"That can be lesson two," Meg said. "Did you tie him to the outdoor run before coming in?"

"Uh-huh, I tied him so he can't run away or run into the woods and get lost. Uncle Liam, I didn't know you were here. Where's your truck?" The redheaded dynamo, a mini Meg, barreled over to Liam and hugged him.

"I came with Nurse Ellie." He gave his niece a bear hug.

"Are you sick?" She tilted her head back and looked up at him.

He chucked her under her chin. "No, Ellie and I are friends, just like she and your mom are friends. We came in her car to visit you."

"How come you came to visit me?" she asked.

Liam laughed. "I meant—"

A baby's cry came from somewhere in the house.

"I'll go get him," Riley said.

"Thanks." Meg pulled him back with a hand on his shirt and gave him another kiss.

Fiona pointed at her parents. "Uh-oh, Mommy, you better be careful. Uncle Liam said all that kissing stuff is what leads to all our babies."

Liam groaned and rolled his eyes. The little blabbermouth. He just couldn't catch a break today.

"Oh, he did, did he?" Meg gave him a stern look. "Fiona, why don't you take Ellie outside and show her how you taught Mangy to catch the Frisbee. Maybe Auntie Ellie knows how to make Mangy bring the Frisbee back."

Fiona scrunched up her face. "Aren't you and Uncle Liam coming?"

"Yes, we'll be out in just a minute."

Riley chuckled and clapped Liam on the shoulder before leaving the kitchen. "Good luck."

Liam watched Fiona take Ellie's hand as they went outside and wished like heck he was going with them.

Once the door shut behind them, he turned to his sister. "You gonna rip me a new one now?"

"Nope." Meg shook her head. "But I will say that how many kids Riley and I have is none of your business, just like whether or not you marry Ellie for the sake of *your* child is none of mine."

"Maybe we shouldn't have stayed for supper with my parents," Ellie said when Liam yawned as they drove to her apartment later that evening. He hadn't had the benefit of a nap as she had and he'd spent the better part of the afternoon chasing the dog to retrieve the Frisbee for Fiona to throw again. "I forgot you just came off a shift this morning."

After leaving Riley and Meg's, they'd stopped at her parents' home to break the news. Liam had suggested it, likening it to ripping off a bandage. Faster was better, he'd suggested. She would have preferred maybe another day to gather her courage but didn't want to take a chance they'd hear it from someone else.

But if she were honest, having to tell her parents she was pregnant hadn't been what bothered her the most about going to her childhood home. When they'd arrived, her father had been in his basement workshop, where he spent most of his time. As if he wasn't a part of what went on above those stairs. Her mom was in the stark white living room, where footprints didn't mar the carpet. Ellie could remember when the house was full of noise and clutter. No, it was the memories being dredged up. She could remember the laughter, the loving glances and tender touches between her parents before she'd gotten sick. She'd taken all of that for granted when she'd had it, thinking it would last forever. Now they were more like polite strangers. They'd remained married because her mother believed that's what you did. The marriage was in place but their relationship had withered and died.

"It's okay. Your mom's a good cook and I slept some last night. Plus, I have time to sleep before the extra shift I mentioned at supper." He glanced over at her and grinned. "Besides, I wasn't about to argue with your dad when he extended the invitation."

She picked at a hangnail. Despite her mom's initial concern over the fact that they had no marriage plans, she was looking forward to being a grandmother. Her dad had started to say something about the risk to her health but her mother shut him up with a stern look and a muttered "It's not our decision." When her dad had suggested Liam join him in the den while she helped her mom load the dishwasher she'd wanted to throw herself into the doorway to block their exit. And her objection wasn't solely because of her dad's sexist attitude toward chores. If she wanted to know something, she needed to ask. "What did my father say to you when you two went into the den?"

"Oh, you know…" He shrugged. "The usual guy talk."

She rubbed her chest. Had he already put her back into the *one of the guys* category? "You forget, I'm a woman." She managed a small laugh. "What's the usual guy talk?"

He took his eyes off the road to give her an assessing glance. "Whether or not the Patriots can go all the way again this year. You okay?"

"Fine." She glanced at the passing scenery as they drove across town. They might not be in any sort of committed relationship, but having a baby together was pretty important. Important enough to share things. "So you're going to tell me that you and my dad went into the den to talk about football?"

He blew out his breath. "It's all in the subtext."

Okay, so maybe they did talk sports. "So my dad didn't come right out and threaten your manhood?"

"Don't go there. Please." Liam winced and glanced down at his lap.

"Sorry," she said, and bit the inside of her cheek to keep from laughing.

"No, you're not." He huffed out his breath. "Your dad was subtle. He didn't drag out a shotgun to polish or anything like that. He did, however, stress that it was important for me to be an involved father and that included financial support. I assured him I'd do my share."

"My mother said maybe we should have started out a little slower, like maybe getting a dog first…see how that worked out." Her mother had been torn between rejoicing at having a grandchild and being concerned over her still-single status.

Liam chuckled. "There's still time…to get a dog, that is. I could check with Riley. I know he researched the one he got for Fiona so it wouldn't aggravate Meg's asthma."

"Yeah, Meg said he was careful before getting it."

"And then he went and spoiled it by letting Fiona name it Mangy."

She choked out a sob of half laughter. "How would we take care of it? With both our jobs, we—" She shifted in her seat. "Oh, God, Liam, how can we be parents if we can't even take care of a dog?"

He pulled into the driveway that led to her rental apartment, but didn't go all the way up to the place. Putting the car into Park, he grabbed her hand and gave it a supportive squeeze. "First of all, we don't have a dog, so quit worrying about a hypothetical situation. You're going to be a great mom. And we have plenty of time to work out the logistics."

"I'm going to be a single mother. Who knows if I'm going to be able to finish everything for my NP certification? That means I can't give up my current job." She hated that she sounded as if she were whining. Her job, while sometimes stressful, was something she enjoyed and it paid enough to support her and a baby; she had it a lot better than most. Plus Liam said he would be stepping up and she knew he was a man of his word. Poor Meg had had to do the single-mother thing for years before Riley came back into her life. Ellie knew Liam had done what he could to help Meg, but she'd still been alone at the end of the day.

"No one is asking you to give up your career goals. We'll work out our schedules."

She opened her mouth to ask how he could be so cavalier, but shut it without saying anything. He was being supportive and didn't need her finding fault. "You're right."

"What did you say?"

She huffed out a sigh. "I said you're right."

"Can I get that in writing?"

"Don't push it."

He laughed and squeezed her hand once more before letting go and driving the rest of the way to her place.

The motion-sensitive lights came on as they approached the three-car garage.

"Do you park in the garage?" Liam asked.

"I haven't been, because there's no inside access to the apartment. Of course, I may rethink that in the middle of winter if the owner of the main house still hasn't moved in."

Liam parked her Subaru and she led the way up the exterior stairs located on one side of the garage and unlocked the door. Her place was perfect for a single woman. But where would she put all the paraphernalia needed for a baby? Even a high chair would be a tight fit for the kitchen.

The *thump* of a duffel bag hitting the floor interrupted her thoughts, and hands came to rest on her shoulders as if he'd been able to follow her silent thoughts. She leaned back into Liam's warmth and strength.

"It's going to be okay," he said as his fingers massaged the kinks caused by the day's tension.

She tilted her head back and stared up at him. He had the beginnings of a five o'clock shadow. He'd let his facial hair grow out a bit on his four-day rotation, but he would have to be clean-shaven when he went back on duty to allow the secure suction his respirator needed. She knew so many things about him and yet they now felt like mere details. "How come I'm the one freaking out and you're the voice of reason?"

His arms went around her and he leaned down and kissed the tip of her nose. "Just abiding by the rules."

"Rules?" She turned in the shelter of his arms. It felt so good to be there, to lean her head against his chest and listen to his steady heartbeat.

"I've decided only one of us is allowed to freak out at a time. I'm counting on you to be the voice of reason when I panic." He gave her a quick squeeze. "Whaddaya say? Deal?"

She hugged him but quickly stepped back, making sure the contact didn't last too long. Like ripping off a bandage. She didn't want him to think she was throwing herself at him—even if that was what she wanted to do. "Deal."

Chapter Eleven

Liam stooped to pick up his duffel from the kitchen floor. Ellie's message was clear that she'd put him back in the no-sex friend zone. But that was good…wasn't it? Friendship was what he'd been telling himself he wanted. Anything more than that meant opening up, making himself vulnerable, which he was pretty sure Ellie would demand, and he was just as sure he would refuse. How could he tell her his concerns about the threat of being left a single parent if the cancer returned? He'd look like a selfish chump saying something like that. Shaking his head at the thoughts dancing around in his head, he followed her into her living area.

Her apartment, around six hundred square feet, was half the size of his place. He remembered all the stuff his sister had needed for Fiona; there'd been baby gear everywhere in the traditional Cape Cod–style house he'd been sharing with his dad and sister. After his ma had been diagnosed, he'd moved back to his childhood home, ostensibly to help, but frankly he'd welcomed being closer to his family during that time. He'd bought his three-decker after his mother's death, hoping Meg would join him, but she'd insisted on moving to the family's vacation home in Loon Lake.

He glanced around. Where would Ellie put all the baby stuff? Ellie was compulsively neat and organized, even keeping her possessions to a minimum in the apartment to avoid clutter.

"Are you going to have enough room here?" If she intended to move, he and Riley could help, maybe even scrounge up a few other guys. She didn't need to be lifting things in her condition.

"You've stayed over before. It was never a—"

"No, I meant after the…" He swallowed. "After the baby comes."

"I told you already, I'm not moving into your upstairs apartment." She opened the linen closet next to the bathroom in the short hall leading to the bedroom.

"That's not why I said it." That was still his idea of the best scenario but he wasn't going to argue with her tonight. She looked tired and his conscience pricked him. Rest was what she needed. "If you decide to move to somewhere else in Loon Lake, Riley and I can help. I'm sure we can find plenty of people willing to do the heavy lifting for you."

She stepped back from the open closet, a stack of sheets and a blanket in her arms. "Right now, I'm not sure I have the energy to pack and move."

He lifted the bedding from her arms. Would the fact that she'd had cancer make a difference to the pregnancy? Could all that she'd gone through have an impact on her ability carry the baby safely to term? "Is that normal? Should we go to the doctor to be sure?"

"Fatigue is perfectly normal in the beginning."

"Like the throwing up?" He crushed the sheets in his grip.

"Yeah, I'm afraid that is, too." She frowned and snatched one of the sheets from his grasp. "Hopefully, both will improve in about a month. I understand the second trimester is actually rather pleasant. Don't you remember any of this from your sister?"

"Like I said, she was good at hiding it the first time and I didn't live with her the second time around." Or he was just that good at ignoring the obvious.

"Given the circumstances for her first pregnancy, I guess that makes sense." She reached for the sheet in his arms and began to put it on the couch. He set the rest of the bedding on the coffee table and began to help her.

"So you were serious when you said I had to sleep on the couch." He raised his eyebrows as he tucked the sheet between the cushions and the back of the couch.

"You can always sleep at your sister's, if she'll have you." Ellie slipped a pillowcase over the pillow.

Okay, she put him in his place. But hey, a guy could try. "I think it would get a little crowded."

"Crowded? I thought that's what the new addition was for." She punched the pillow.

He winced as he watched her treatment of his pillow. "I was thinking crowded more in terms of people and dog, rather than space."

Sighing, she fluffed the pillow out. "What do you think this place is gonna be like once we have a baby?"

"Why do you think I suggested moving into my upstairs apartment?" He regretted the words as soon as they found air. Pressing his point right now was counterproductive.

"Give it a rest, Liam." Ellie smoothed out a blanket over the sheet and arranged the pillow at one end of the sofa. "Well, good night. I hope you get a good night's sleep."

"So you're not going to take pity on me?" he called to her retreating back.

"That puppy-dog face of yours won't get you anywhere, McBride."

"Hey, you weren't even looking."

After she had shut the bedroom door, Liam stripped down to his boxer briefs and got between the covers on the sofa.

A short time later, he jackknifed into a sitting position and glanced around. He sat and listened to see what had awakened him up from a sound sleep. He was accustomed to sleeping around a dozen other guys during shifts at the fire station, so noises in the night didn't usually bother him.

"Are you okay?" he asked Ellie as she came down the short hall from her bedroom.

She nodded. "I got up to use the bathroom and decided to get a drink of water. I'm sorry if I woke you, but I'm not used to having someone here with me."

"It's okay. I just wanted to be sure you weren't sick again." And he wanted to say stuff, but he wasn't even sure what it was he wanted to say, let alone how to say it. And, man, wasn't that messed up?

She shook her head. "No. That's mostly in the mornings but that's not hard and fast."

He nodded. "That's good."

"Glad you think so." Her tone was dry.

Aw, man, could he not catch a break? "I didn't mean... I only meant—"

"You're making this way too easy." She thumped him on the shoulder and grinned.

"And yet you keep doing it," he grumbled, and rubbed his shoulder, but his actions were for effect. She wasn't angry and he was grateful. He certainly hadn't meant to piss her off. "I'm trying to be supportive."

"And I appreciate it, but you don't need to hover."

"I don't hover." And even if he did, who could blame him? Ellie was pregnant with his child. He was doing his best to hold it all together and not let his panic show.

"Well...good night. And sorry for waking you."

"Don't worry about it."

She went back into the bedroom and he sank down on the couch and punched the pillow. He had just stretched out when a noise had him opening his eyes. Ellie was standing next to the couch.

He sat up. "What's the matter?"

She chewed on her bottom lip. "Umm...that couch isn't very comfortable."

"I've had worse."

She reached out her hand toward him and he grabbed it. Still unsure of what was happening, he frowned. "Ellie?"

"I don't want to send the wrong signal but..." She tugged on his hand. She waved her free hand toward the bedroom. "We can share, right? I'm talking platonic."

Relief swept through him as he grabbed his pillow with his free hand and let her lead him to the bedroom. Spending the night in the same bed with Ellie, even in a platonic sense, was important. He couldn't pinpoint why. Too much had happened today to make sense of the jumble of emotions. He just knew he wanted to be as close as possible to her.

Ellie's first thought upon awakening was Liam. She lay in his arms and it wasn't a dream. Oh, yeah, she'd invited him to sleep in the bed. At the time she'd fallen asleep he'd been way over on his side of the bed and she on hers. Now they were huddled together in the middle as if their bodies had taken over while they slept.

Sighing, she burrowed closer, intent on enjoying the moment. This time of year, the mornings could be cool, so waking to warmth was unusual.

"Ellie?" he murmured near her ear.

"Mmm?" She huddled closer.

He cleared his throat. "Could you not do that?"

She moved again, shimmying closer, then scolding herself. What was she doing? She shouldn't tease unless she intended to follow through. Maybe sex wouldn't be a total disaster. After all, she couldn't get pregnant again. She shifted.

"Yeah, that," he groaned, his voice tight.

"Sorry." She scooted away and turned to face him. Did she want to do this? "Truly, I am sorry. That wasn't nice."

"Not unless you plan to—" His cell phone rang before he could finish. He heaved an exasperated sigh. "That's my dad's ringtone."

Ellie was already scooting to the other side of the bed. Interrupted or saved? She couldn't decide. "Then you'd better get it."

"Wait." Liam stopped her retreat to the other side of the bed with a hand on her arm.

She turned back to face him and he gave her a quick kiss. The mattress bounced a little as he got up. She got a good look at his broad back and fine butt encased in black cotton boxer briefs as he hurried into the living area.

Grabbing her robe and pulling it on, she followed him into the other room.

"Hey, Dad. What's up?" He listened and winced. "I should have known this would happen. We had planned to tell you when you got back. So we could do it in person."

Ellie couldn't hear the other end of the conversation but she imagined Mac being more hurt than angry if he'd heard the news from someone else.

Liam rolled his eyes when their gazes met and she smiled.

"Yeah, you did and I was but—" Liam nodded. "I will and yes, I was with her when we told her parents. Thanks. Talk to you soon."

He placed the phone back on the counter. Blowing out his breath, he rubbed a hand over his face.

"I take it your dad found out?"

He nodded and rubbed a hand across his face.

"Meg?"

"Fiona. Dad said at first he thought she was talking about Meg's pregnancy but Fiona clarified before Meg could get the phone away from her."

"Was he angry?" She felt bad that Mac had found out through someone else, but at least it was a family member.

Liam rubbed the back of his neck. "Not about us

not telling him. He understood the situation with them being out of town."

Yeah, Mac was a pretty reasonable guy. "Let me guess, he doesn't understand the friends-having-a-baby part."

Liam stabbed a finger in the air. "That would be the one."

She put her arms around his waist and gave him a loose hug. "Once the baby is here, he'll be thrilled."

"Yeah, I could hear Doris in the background saying congratulations." He hooked his arm around her waist, pulling her closer and kissing the top of her head.

His phone rang again. He dropped his arm and stepped away. "And that'll be my sister."

He picked up the phone and pointed the screen at her. "Told ya."

"Uh-oh." Ellie laughed.

Liam swiped his thumb and answered. "Well, if it isn't my blabbermouth sister."

Ellie was close enough to hear Meg apologizing on the other end.

"When has Fiona ever been able to keep a secret? She takes after someone else I know." He quirked a smile. "Yeah, you. As I've said before, it's like growing up with you all over again."

While he was talking with Meg, she pulled out ingredients to make breakfast. Most mornings she ate cereal but the thought didn't appeal, and since Liam was here, she decided on scrambled eggs and sausages.

Liam set his phone back down. "Do I have time for a quick shower before breakfast?"

"Sure."

After breakfast, he helped her clean up the kitchen.

"I noticed your tire pressure light was on so I thought I'd take your car to get some air in the tires and fill you up your gas tank."

"Okay." She found her purse and pulled out her wallet to reimburse him.

"Ellie." He shook his head. "Put that away."

"But…"

"No buts." He leaned over and kissed her forehead. "We're in this together."

Ellie stayed home to catch up on some studying for an upcoming exam. She wasn't sure if she'd be able to finish her degree requirements in time for her plans for getting a job at the proposed assisted living and nursing facility, but she still needed to keep up with the classes she was taking.

The money she'd been spending on school might be better spent on a bigger apartment. This one would be crowded with a baby. *There's always Liam's offer of one of his rentals*, an inner voice reminded her.

She frowned and rubbed her stomach, sending a silent apology to the new life growing inside. Was being stubborn going to mean her baby would ultimately suffer for her decisions? Or would getting involved with someone who coped with emotions by pulling away and burying himself in work be worse?

The apartment door opened and she slammed her book shut, realizing she hadn't really studied. "That took a while."

Liam closed the door behind him. "I got your oil changed, too."

"You didn't have to do that."

"Ogle insisted. Said it was time." Liam shrugged. "Who am I to argue?"

"Well, if Ogle wanted to do it."

"He's got some kid working for him that he said needed the experience."

"A kid? You and Ogle let a kid change my oil?" She frowned. Her tone carried a bit of annoyance, but she was touched by his actions on her behalf. It was the type of thing her dad did for her mom, even after the break-down of their relationship; she suspected Mac had done it for Liam's mom and now for Doris. Ellie realized it was nice to have someone who had your back.

"Yeah, Kevin says hi." Liam chuckled and held up his hands in a self-protection stance.

She made a moue with her lips. "You shouldn't tease me when I'm hungry."

"Oh, no, do I have a hangry diva on my hands?" He put his arm around her shoulders and squeezed.

"Yes, you do. I slathered peanut butter on a banana for lunch, but it's worn off."

"Don't worry about it. I'm taking you out for..." Liam said and grinned. "An early supper."

"You are?" Her heart skipped a beat. *As in a date?* Here they were, having a baby and never actually been on a real date. That strange quasi-date at Hennen's when they'd run into Mike and Colton didn't count.

"I'm here, so we may as well hang out together."

Oh, but she yearned for more than hanging out. She wanted them to be a couple—a family—a real family. Maybe she should come right out and tell him what she wanted. How could you get something if you didn't ask for it? "Liam, I—"

"Maybe if we'd gone out more, we might not be in this situation," he interrupted.

Maybe now wasn't the time for confessions. She managed a little laugh. "You think?"

His blue eyes twinkled as he regarded her. "Nah, not really. I think it's payback from the universe for all the comments I make about Meg and Riley."

"I think it was a little more than that."

"Really?" He raised his eyebrows. "Maybe you need to show me…just so I'll know better in the future."

"Nice try, but you promised to take me out to supper and I'm starving." Not that she didn't want to explore that chemistry again, but hunger took precedence.

He sighed. "If I feed you, maybe we can revisit this discussion?"

She tilted her head from side to side as if sizing him up. "Perhaps."

"There's nothing more appealing than a decisive woman." He draped an arm around her shoulders and laughed. "So, when you're not tossing your cookies, you're hungry. Have I got that right?"

"It's not funny. Sometimes I feel as though I'm all over the map. One minute happy, the next crying. And food I used to love makes me sick just to think about it."

"I hate to disagree…especially with a pregnant woman but…" He gently rubbed his knuckles across the top of her head. "It's a bit funny from where I'm standing, but I will take you out to eat."

"Ha, you weren't exactly Mr. Calm-and-Collected when I was losing it in your bathroom."

He sighed. "You had me scared to death."

She knew he was probably thinking of his mother, so she didn't tease. "Sorry."

He gave her a smile that melted her heart. "Let's get some food in you before you become unbearable."

Scooting out from under his arm—even though it felt heavenly—she said, "Sounds like a plan."

He reached behind him and scooped up her car keys from the kitchen counter. "Ready?"

"You're driving?"

He jangled her keys and tilted his head. "No?"

"Fine, but quit messing with the presets on my radio."

"If you had decent music, I wouldn't be forced to listen to the radio." He shook his head, looking at her as if he pitied her.

She pushed him toward the door. "We won't listen to anything then. I'll serenade you."

"Oh, good Lord." He stopped dead in his tracks.

She plowed into him and swatted his freaking broad shoulders. "Hey!"

He chuckled and captured her hand and threaded his fingers through hers. "C'mon, let's go."

Chapter Twelve

Ellie hummed to herself the next morning as she pulled out a carton of eggs from the refrigerator. Liam had gotten out of bed and brought her saltine crackers to settle her stomach before jumping into the shower.

Having breakfast ready for him was a good way to repay the favor. She was dicing peppers and onions when her cell phone rang. She wiped her hands on the kitchen towel hanging over the oven handle before answering.

"Ellie, so glad I caught you." Meg sounded a little breathless.

"What's up?" Ellie frowned.

"I really hate to bother you on your day off, but do you think you could watch James for a couple hours today? Riley got called in to work and I'd already promised to help chaperone Fiona's class trip to the pumpkin patch."

"Sure." Ellie glanced at the clock on the stove. "Do I have time to shower and get dressed?"

"Of course. Thanks, I really appreciate this."

"No problem. I'll be there as soon as I can."

Liam appeared in the in the living area, his jeans unbuttoned and riding low on his hips, the band from his boxer briefs visible. He was shirtless, a towel thrown over his shoulder. "Did you get called in to work or something?"

"No. That was Meg. She asked if I could help her out." She swallowed as her gaze took in his gloriously bare chest, remembering how those muscles reacted to her touch.

"What does Meg need help with?"

Of course if he was on one of those calendars, then all women would be drooling over the six-pack abs and the dusting of hair that formed a V and disappeared under the waistband of his jeans. His dark hair was more disheveled than normal.

"Ellie? My sister?"

She forced her gaze upward and her thoughts on the conversation, but it wasn't easy. Liam wasn't musclebound like a weight lifter, but he was fit. Oh, boy, was he ever.

Clearing her throat, she explained, "Meg asked if I could watch James while she helps chaperone Fiona's class trip to the pumpkin patch."

He tossed the towel over the back of the chair and picked up a gray waffle-weave henley draped over the back of the couch. "What time does she need you?"

"As soon as I shower and dress." She checked her watch.

"Do you want some breakfast before we head over?" he said and pulled the shirt over his head.

Her heart rate kicked up. "Oh, you're coming with me?"

"Is that okay with you?" He grabbed his sneakers and sat on the sofa.

"Sure. I had already started on breakfast but I'd better jump in the shower instead."

He stuffed his feet into his sneakers. "What were you making?"

"The ingredients for omelets are on the counter."

He finished tying his laces and came to stand next to her. "Go get in the shower. I can handle omelets."

Liam drank a quick cup of coffee while Ellie was in the shower and rinsed the cup in the sink. He finished chopping the peppers and onions and set about making omelets. He was putting the plates on the breakfast bar when she came back from her shower. They ate quickly and Liam stacked the plates in the sink before they left.

Meg met them at the door, holding James on her hip, the dog at her side. The baby had a piece of a banana clutched in his fist. "Ooh, two for the price of one."

Liam bumped shoulders with Ellie. "You didn't say you were getting paid. Trying to get out of sharing with me?"

Meg led them through the small original living room into the new, expansive family room with large windows and patio doors looking into the woods at the back of the house. They didn't have a deck or patio yet, but Riley hoped to put one in soon.

"Yeah, good luck getting to those snickerdoodles before me," Ellie said, and smiled at James and gave him a kiss on the top of his head. "Hello there, little man."

He waved the banana around and showed her a toothy grin. The dog, an Aussiedoodle with reddish-brown curls, whined, his intent gaze on the fruit.

Meg wiped a piece of banana off his cheek. "He was just finishing his morning snack. I haven't had a chance to get him washed yet."

The baby thrust the smashed banana toward Liam. "Meem."

"Thanks, buddy, but I just ate."

"I can get him cleaned up." Ellie reached out and took James in her arms. "Looks like you're enjoying that nanner, bud."

Meg nodded. "Bananas are his new favorite snack."

He offered it to Ellie, but she shook her head, her lips clamped firmly together. James, imitating her by vigorously shaking his head, opened his fist and let the banana piece fall, but Mangy scooped it up in midair.

Meg laughed. "You guys might want to consider getting a dog."

Remembering how upset Ellie had gotten over the thought of taking care of a pet, Liam winced. He glared at his sister, shaking his head, but Meg threw him a puzzled look. His gaze went to Ellie, but evidently she was too busy talking to James to be upset.

Meg kissed James before Ellie took him to wash his hands and face. She turned to Liam. "What was that all about? Ellie likes dogs. So do you."

He swiped a hand over his face. "It's a long story."

"And I'm in a hurry. Any questions before I leave?"

Liam glanced at the flat screen he and Riley had

mounted to the wall. "As a matter of fact I do. Tell me again the channel number for ESPN on your television."

"I don't know." Meg picked up her purse and keys.

"How can you not know something that important?"

"Yeah, like I have time to watch television. By the time I get Fiona and James down for the night, I'm ready to crawl into bed myself, especially with Riley on nights." Meg patted her still-flat stomach. "At least by the time this one comes, he'll have enough seniority to get a day shift when one becomes available."

"Okay. Jeez. Sorry I asked." He threw up his hands in a defensive gesture but laughed when Meg held up a fist. "I'm sure I can find it."

Meg lowered her arm. "You'll have to find the remote first. It's James's new favorite thing now that he can lift up against the coffee table."

"Not exactly running a tight ship, are we, sis?" As soon as he said it, he realized his mistake. Meg would have plenty of opportunities to point out parenting errors to him in the near future.

She gave him a big, evil smile. "Oh, I am so going to enjoy picking on you when you have one running around."

"Ellie and I will have it all under control." *Nothing like compounding your mistakes.*

"Ha! I love it." Meg laughed and rubbed her palms together. "You are so clueless. I'd help you look for the remote, but I'm already running late."

"So much for sitting around watching sports highlights in my underwear," he muttered as he lifted couch cushions in his search for the remote. Each time he lifted a cushion Mangy stuck his shaggy head under it. He patted the dog's head as he pushed it out of the way so he could replace the cushion. "What you looking for, boy?"

The dog whined and stuck his nose in the space between the arm and the cushion, grabbing something.

Liam latched onto the dog's collar before he could scamper off with his treasure. He pried a set of plastic keys from the animal's mouth.

"What are you two doing?" Ellie stood in the doorway to the large family room, James perched on her hip. The baby spotted the dog and grunted and lunged, but Ellie managed to hang on.

"Mangy and I were looking for the remote and he found these." The dog sat and whined as his gaze followed Liam's hand. "Sorry, boy, I doubt these are yours."

"Here, you take James and I'll wash those keys off."

He shook his head. "If I set them down, the dog is going to run off with them."

She leaned down and put James on the floor. "You stay here with Uncle Meem while I take care of this."

"Don't start with that Meem stuff. I just got Fiona to say it correctly."

"Meem... Meem... Meem," James babbled as he crawled to the coffee table and pulled himself up. One hand rested on the table and the other stretched toward Liam.

Liam tossed the keys to Ellie and reached down to ruffle his nephew's hair. "Hey, buddy, not sure what you're talking about. Can you say 'Liam'?"

"Sorry, but I think you're going to be Uncle Leem or Meem for the foreseeable future. At least you won't have to worry about that with ours."

Liam looked up from his search for the remote. "Why not?"

Ellie clicked her teeth. "Because she will be calling you Daddy."

"Oh, yeah." He scratched his scalp and frowned. "What?"

"That's a scary thought, but I guess if my baby sister and Riley can do it, so can we." Had his dad gotten a mini panic attack thinking about being a parent before Liam was born?

"Can we?"

"You certainly can, you're an ER nurse. Of course you're qualified." Ellie was going to be great. He wished he had as much confidence in himself as he did her.

"Bet they wouldn't let me take home a baby if they knew how scattered I've been lately."

"I find that hard to believe." He jammed his fingers in the back of the couch. That damn remote had to be here somewhere.

She sank down next to James as he slapped his palm on the coffee table. "Believe it. I poured orange juice on my cornflakes last week."

"Run out of milk?" His searching fingers found something and he pulled out a tiny pink plastic hard-hat. What the…?

"No, I didn't run out of milk. I pulled out the OJ by mistake."

"What did you do?" He started to set the tiny toy on the coffee table but looked at James and decided against it.

"I threw them out and started over, but what's that got to do with it?"

"It proves you're good at problem solving, because I would have eaten them."

"You are such a guy."

He wiggled his eyebrows. "Glad you finally noticed. Aha, here's the remote."

Ellie rolled her eyes. "Give that hat to me and I'll put it in Fiona's room. It belongs to her Barbie Builder set."

"How do you know these things?" He put the cushions back on the sofa.

"It's a girl thing."

"Hey, James, how about we watch some sports? Make sure that father of yours is teaching you the right teams to root for." He scooped his nephew off the floor and sat down on the sofa with him.

"I think he's wet. Let me go get a fresh diaper."

Liam held James up in the air. "Now she tells me. Are you wet?"

The boy let out a string of baby giggles.

Ellie came back with a diaper and tub of wipes. "Want me to take him?"

"It's okay. I've changed Fiona's. May as well get some more practice in." He truly did want to be involved.

He put James on the blanket on the floor and unsnapped the baby's pants to get at the diaper. At least he remembered how to do that much from when Fiona was a baby. He removed the soggy diaper.

"Liam, wait! Put this over..."

He glanced up as Ellie launched what looked like a washcloth at him.

What the heck was she on about? He knew how to— Something wet and warm squirted all over the front of his shirt.

He glanced down at his giggling nephew. "Why did he do that?"

Ellie had her fist pressed against her mouth and her shoulders were shaking. She cleared her throat. "It's something baby boys do."

"Why didn't you warn me?" After getting over being grossed out, he could appreciate the humor in it. And he couldn't be angry with an innocent—he glanced down at his giggling nephew. Huh, maybe not quite so innocent.

"I thought you knew. You said you'd changed diapers before," Ellie said.

"I changed Fiona's diaper a time or two and nothing like this ever happened." He shook his head.

"Girls are different but it can still happen."

"So, is there a trick to not getting wet?"

"I think the trick is to keep something over him like the old diaper or a cloth."

"Why would I know something like this?"

"You've never changed James's diaper before?" He shook his head and she continued, "Well, now you know. Look on the bright side, at least your face wasn't in the line of fire."

James began laughing and Liam put his palm over the baby's belly and tickled him. "You think that's funny? Now I'm going to have to wear one of your daddy's shirts and I'll make your mommy wash mine."

The baby giggled. "Meem."

He shook his head at James. There was so much he didn't know about babies and kids despite having spent a lot of time around his niece and nephew. Had his dad been nervous and clueless in the beginning? Maybe by the time his child was old enough to form memories of his or her childhood, he'd have a better handle on the whole parenting thing.

* * *

Once again, Ellie awoke to a cold, empty bed. She'd been doing that ever since Liam's friend Nick had picked him up three days earlier. She rolled over and rubbed her hand over the cool sheets. Liam had only slept over for a few nights, but she'd gotten used to having him here.

She had no idea when she'd see him again. He'd told her that during his time off he was taking an extra shift at one of the part-time stations. He apologized and explained that this had been planned for a while.

Sighing, she got up and pulled on her pink fleece robe against the apartment's early-morning chill. She paused to see if this was a morning sickness day. It wasn't. At least not yet. Of course her nausea didn't just strike first thing; sometimes it lasted all day or hit unexpectedly. Smells could trigger it, too.

The nausea had been getting worse but she knew the extra hormones that caused it kicked in around the eight-week mark, so it wasn't surprising.

Today was her first appointment with the obstetrician. She'd be going alone and part of that was her fault. She'd assured Liam that the checkup was just routine and it was, but now that she was faced with going alone, it felt…sad. It was still early in the pregnancy for the doctor to want an ultrasound. At least Liam wasn't missing out on something like that.

Buck up, Ellie, and quit your whining.

Liam had stepped up, but the fact that they lived three hours apart wasn't going to change unless she moved to Boston. Pulling up stakes, leaving everything she knew and had worked for to move so she could live on the periphery of Liam's life, held no appeal.

"But I'm reserving the right to revisit this decision," she told her reflection as she brushed her hair before dashing out the door.

At the doctor's office, Ellie flipped through old magazines, kicking herself for not remembering to bring a book. Not that it mattered since she doubted she'd be able to concentrate any better on the latest spy thriller than she could this three-month-old *People* magazine. Too many things running through her head. Being in the medical profession at times like this was not helpful.

The blood tests scheduled for today might be routine, but this was *her* baby they were running tests on. That changed everything. She was doing this so she could be prepared, not because she suspected something was wrong. Intellectually she knew her chances of a successful pregnancy were the same as anyone else's, but emotions didn't always operate on facts. But the situation gave her some perspective on what her parents must've gone through when her cancer was diagnosed.

Would she be faced one day with her child having a life-threatening illness? Her hand covered her still flat stomach as sympathy for her parents filled her.

She glanced around the waiting room at the other women in various stages of pregnancy, some with partners, others alone like her.

Heaving a sigh, she tossed the magazine aside just as the inner door opened and the nurse called her name.

Ellie jumped up. At least doing something would be better than just sitting and waiting.

The nurse smiled. "Ellie, it's so good to see you again."

Ellie recognized the woman from hospital rotations during nursing school. "Kim Smith, right?"

"It's Dawson now." The nurse led her down a hallway.

"Mine's still Harding, but I guess you could see that from the chart." Ellie hated the warmth in her cheeks. Plenty of single women had babies these days. Even in Loon Lake.

"It's been a while." Kim stopped in front of a balance beam scale. "How have you been?"

"Is that a professional question or making conversation?"

"Both, I guess." Kim laughed. "Okay, hop up on the scale."

"I hate this part." Ellie sighed and glanced at her red sneakers. "Can I take these off first?"

"Really? At your first appointment." Kim clicked her tongue but grinned. "This is only the beginning."

Ellie glanced at her feet and debated, but giggled and toed her shoes off.

Kim marked her weight on the chart. "Okay, take a seat and we'll get blood pressure next."

"You should've done that *before* you weighed me." Ellie motioned toward the scale. "Having to get on that thing probably raised it."

Kim chuckled. "So you're feeling okay? No complaints?"

"I'm doing good, if you don't count the morning sickness that pops up at all hours and crying over the stupidest things." Ellie sat in the chair and rolled up her sleeve.

"I hear that. I carried sandwich bags and tissues in my purse." Kim set the chart on the table. "Take a seat and we'll get your pressure, then some labs, but I guess you know the drill."

Ellie nodded. "Yeah, I know all this stuff like getting a patient's blood pressure is standard procedure, but when it's being done to you, it doesn't feel routine at all."

So far there was no need for Liam to be here for these mundane things. So why did she feel so bereft?

"Yeah, we don't always make the best patients, do we?" Kim adjusted the blood pressure cuff on her upper left arm. "You still like working in the ER?"

"I do, but I've been thinking of a change." Ellie laid her other hand over her stomach. "Especially now. Do you like this kind of nursing?"

"I'm sure it's not as exciting or interesting as the ER but the hours are easier. Plus, holidays and weekends off is nice for family life." Kim made notes on the chart as the Dinamap displayed her blood pressure.

Ellie nodded. From now on, she'd have someone else to take into consideration. Working twelve-hour shifts might not be feasible. She put out her arm but cringed when Kim came at her with the needle. Being a nurse didn't make getting stuck any easier.

"We should have the results back in one to two weeks." Kim marked the vials of blood. "And we'll just take a quick look today to verify the pregnancy and check for iron and vitamin levels. We'll need to get you started on prenatal vitamins."

After a week of denying her suspicions, Ellie had decided she needed to be proactive. "Yeah, I took some over-the-counter ones, but they don't have the same folic acid levels."

"I've got everything I need. It was good seeing you again." Kim opened the door and dropped the chart in the holder on the door. "The doctor should be in shortly."

Ten minutes felt like an eternity and Ellie was starting to get antsy when the door opened and Kim popped her head in. "The doctor has decided he'd like you to have an ultrasound. Fortunately, we can do one on-site. The tech will be in in just a minute to escort you back there."

Ellie's stomach twisted into knots. Not since being diagnosed with cancer had she felt so helpless. "Tell me what's wrong. Why do they want to do an ultrasound now? What can't wait?"

"Ellie, you of all people know I can't say anything." Kim shook her head. "Let's keep the imagination reined in," she added with a smile before closing the door.

Ellie glared at the closed door Kim had escaped through and wrung her hands. Was she overreacting? The way she saw it, she was allowed to do so. This was *her* baby, maybe her only chance to be a mom.

She should have said yes when her mother had offered to come. But she would've had to take off work and Ellie hated for her to use her PTO to come to a routine first exam. She had assumed the most exciting part would be to hear the baby's heartbeat. Except being alone with only her thoughts for company wasn't a good idea. She sat on her hands trying to keep them warm and swung her legs.

There was a quick rap on the door.

"Finally," she muttered. At least they'd be getting this show on the road. Despite Kim's advice, she'd let her imagination run roughshod over her rational self.

The door opened but instead of the ultrasound tech or the doctor, the receptionist stood in the doorway. "Someone is insisting on seeing you, but we can't let anyone back here without your permission."

Had her mother come, anyway? Who else could it

be? The receptionist cleared her throat and Ellie nodded. "Yes, that's fine."

Before she could react, Liam loomed in the doorway, still in his dark blue BFD uniform. She blinked,
but he didn't disappear. Liam was here! Oh, God, the
news was so bad they called him. No wait, that was
crazy. They hadn't done anything yet and he couldn't
have gotten here in such a short time even if he'd been
in town. Nothing had been wrong ten minutes ago...
but was it now?

Chapter Thirteen

She straightened and pulled her hands from under her thighs. "What are you doing here? How did you get here? How did you find me?"

He shut the door and crossed the small room in two strides. "I'm here because I was serious when I said wanted to be involved. I hit the road as soon as I got off shift this morning and I called Meg to ask where you'd be," he said, ticking off his answers by holding up his fingers. "I think that covers all your questions."

"You don't know how glad I am to see you." Ellie swallowed several times, trying to keep it together, fiercely holding back the tears burning at the back of her eyes. "Something isn't right."

He stood directly in front of her, then nudged himself between her legs until his thighs rested against the table. "What is it? What's wrong?"

"I don't know. It was supposed to be just a routine exam and labs but then…then…" She waved her hands in front of her, fumbling for words.

Without a word, he pulled her into the shelter of his arms and held her close. *She loved him.* She was in love with Liam. Not a schoolgirl crush. Not lust for a sexy-as-sin fireman. But soul-deep, forever love.

She snuffled against his chest. "Oh, Liam, what if something's wrong with our baby?"

His arms tightened into a bear hug. "Then we'll deal with it."

"Did…" He cleared his throat and loosened his hold. "Did they say what could be wrong?"

She shook her head and eased away from him enough so she could speak. "No, but they test for Down syndrome. But they won't have those results for at least a week. I don't know what this means."

He rubbed her back. "The receptionist didn't act like anything was wrong."

"She probably doesn't know and even if she did, they're not allowed to say anything." Next time she was faced with an angry relative demanding answers, she'd have a lot more sympathy.

"Ellie?" Kim opened the door. Her eyes widened when she spotted Liam, her gaze taking in his uniform. "Oh, I didn't know anyone had come with you."

Liam stepped away from Ellie and held out his hand. "Liam McBride. I arrived a bit late. I came after getting off shift this morning."

"Off shift?" She glanced at the Boston patch on his shirt and lifted an eyebrow. "As in Boston off shift?"

Liam nodded. "That's the one."

Ellie leaned to the side so she could see around Liam. "Liam's the…uh, baby daddy."

What a silly thing to call him, but it was the easiest explanation.

"Nice meeting you, Liam. I'm Kim. Ellie and I went through nursing school at the same time." Kim shook his hand. "They've got the ultrasound ready for you. It's just down the hall. Ellie, you can leave your things in here."

Kim glanced at Liam. "Umm…if you'll—"

"I want him with me," Ellie said, and reached for his hand.

Kim nodded. "Of course, I just thought he might want to wait here while we get you ready."

Liam paced the small room, waiting for the nurse to come and get him. His gut churned with every step. Was something wrong with Ellie? Or the baby?

Every time the word *cancer* tried to invade his brain, he shoved it aside and slammed the door. *One worry at a time, McBride.*

"Wait until they tell us," he muttered, and glared at the closed door.

He wanted to fling it open and demand they tell them something. He wanted to run to Ellie and hold her and make everything okay.

Thank goodness he'd listened to his gut, not to mention his conscience, when it told him he should be with Ellie. She had needed him. How could he have thought she didn't? Her assertion that it was just a routine exam had rung false because this was *their* baby. Nothing would be just routine for either of them. But this…

He couldn't imagine leaving her to go through this

uncertainty alone. He remembered his promise to be strong when she needed him to be. It looked like it would be his turn to be the strong one today.

The door opened and he resisted the urge to pounce on Kim and demand answers.

"We're ready for you," she announced cheerfully.

He followed the nurse to a room with complicated-looking equipment and a monitor on a rolling stand. Ellie lay on her back on an exam table with her knees up and a sheet draped over the bottom half of her body.

"This is Liam," Kim said to a technician.

The technician looked up. "Hi, I'm Sherrie."

"I'll leave you to it," Kim said. "Sherrie will take good care of you."

Sherrie smiled as she got her equipment ready. "You know we won't be able to determine the baby's sex yet."

"Yeah, that's not why we're here," Ellie told her.

The other woman nodded. "I wanted to get that out of the way so you won't be disappointed."

Liam went to stand next to Ellie and she reached for his hand.

The technician got out what looked like a wand and rolled a rubber sheath on it. Ellie squeezed his hand. He winked at her and she grinned, some of the tension melting away. He leaned close to her ear.

"I think it's a little too late to give me pointers now," he whispered.

She choked on a laugh.

"Okay, if you could relax for me now, Ellie," the technician said, and scooted the stool to the end of the exam table.

He laced his fingers through Ellie's and pulled her hand against his chest. Watching the monitor, he tried to make sense of what he was seeing. The technician's face gave nothing away. He'd bet they were trained to not reveal anything.

"I'm just going to call the doctor in." Sherrie stood and scooted out the door.

"Liam?" Ellie looked from the closed door and back to him. "I thought I saw—but her face was blank."

"Hey, hey, calm down." Brushing the hair back from her cheek, he tucked it behind her ear and cupped his palm against her jaw. He pressed his lips against her forehead. "You know yourself, technicians aren't allowed to tell you anything."

"They tell you good stuff like 'Oh, look, there's your perfectly healthy baby.'" Ellie sniffed. "If she went to get the doctor, that means something is wrong. Oh, Liam, I'm scared."

"Look at me." He leaned over so his face was directly in front of hers. "Whatever it is, we'll handle it together. I'm not going anywhere."

Tough talk from a guy who'd rather be feeling his way through thick smoke in an unfamiliar structure in danger of collapsing than to be here right now. Ellie's fear gutted him and his belly clenched.

A man with a thick thatch of gray hair hustled in and introduced himself. Liam shook hands but he couldn't hear the man's name above the roaring in his ears.

"Let's take a look and see what we have." Dr. Stanley put on a pair of glasses and settled on a stool in front of the screen.

"What is it?" Ellie asked in a hoarse voice.

The doctor slid his glasses onto the top of his head. "It appears there are two embryos."

Liam cleared his throat. "T-two?"

Dr. Stanley nodded. "Congratulations. You're having twins."

The man's words caused all the air to swoosh out of Liam's lungs. Wait…what? Twins? Was that even possible? *Of course it's possible, dumbass.*

"Thank you… I don't know what to say. I'm so relieved. Thank you," Ellie was saying to Dr. What's-His-Name. "Isn't wonderful, Liam? Liam?"

The doctor jumped up and pushed the rolling stool toward Liam. "Son, I think you need this more than I do."

Liam sank down, still trying to digest the information. Of course he was ecstatic that nothing was wrong…but two babies? At the same time? "You're sure?"

"Most definitely. It's too early to determine the sex yet, but I can tell you they're fraternal." The doctor slipped his glasses back down onto his nose to look at the monitor again. "Everything looks normal for twins. Of course with multiples, we'll want to monitor you a bit more closely, especially toward the end, but I see no reason for concern."

"With fraternal, we could have one of each," Ellie said. "Meg will claim we're trying to keep up with her."

Dr. Stanley glanced between them. "Well, if you don't have any questions, I'll have Kim give you some pamphlets on multiples and a prescription for prenatal vitamins."

"Thank you, Doctor, I'm just relieved everything is okay," Ellie said.

"Sorry if you had some anxious moments, but rest assured, everything appears normal." With a quick nod of his head, he stuck out his hand to Liam. "Congratulations again, son."

Liam shook hands with the other man, but if asked to describe him after he left the room, he wouldn't have a clue. It was as if he was experiencing the world through his respirator…his breathing loud in his ears while everything else was muffled.

"You look a little shell-shocked," Kim observed as she led him to the previous exam room while Ellie got cleaned up and dressed.

"I was just wrapping my head around one and now it's two…at once." His voice cracked on the last part.

Kim patted him on the shoulder. "Believe me, this isn't the first time I've seen that look. Before you leave, I'll put you in touch with the local support group for multiples."

"Support group for multiples…" Liam shook his head. "That's a thing?"

She chuckled. "Yup. Your reaction to the news is quite typical."

"Ellie should be back in a moment," Kim added and left.

He needed to hold it together for Ellie. Today's news was unexpected but he could handle it and keep everything under control. Sitting hunched forward with his elbows on his thighs, his mind raced at the thought of two babies. Would having twins put more of a strain on Ellie's body? Having her move to Boston seemed even more urgent now, but he knew better than to confront her. Ellie could be stubborn. He stared at his boots as if they could supply him with answers. Maybe he'd talk to Meg. This was a role reversal…asking his little sister for advice.

* * *

Standing next to Liam on Meg and Riley's porch, Ellie knocked on the door. Meg had insisted they come to supper while Liam was in Loon Lake. Ellie wasn't quite sure how she felt about Meg treating them as a couple. It wouldn't be long before the whole town was doing that, especially with Liam showing up in time for the ultrasound. The medical personnel couldn't say anything but that privacy didn't extend to the people in the waiting room. Liam showing up in his uniform hadn't gone unnoticed.

Waiting for Meg or Riley to answer, Ellie turned to Liam. "This feels like déjà vu."

He wiggled his eyebrows. "Yup. Déjà vu all over again."

She rolled her eyes but was glad he could joke. His face had drained of color when the doctor had told them she was expecting twins. He'd recovered quickly, but she could see he'd been putting on a happy face. Once the relief that nothing was wrong passed, the truth of her situation had started to sink in. She was going to be a single mother to twins. She wiped her clammy hands on the front of her jeans. Her initial relief that nothing was wrong had started to wear off and it was sinking in that the situation she thought she'd had under control this morning had done a one-eighty.

The door swung open and Riley greeted them with a sobbing James in his arms. "C'mon in. Sorry about this."

"Oh, no. What's wrong?" Ellie's heart ached for a now-hiccuping James. And for herself. She was going to have this, times two!

"He's crying because he's not allowed to play with Fiona's toys." Riley stood aside so they could enter.

"Worried about his masculinity?" Liam chuckled as he stepped into the living room.

Meg appeared and clucked her tongue at her brother. "It's a choking hazard. All those little pieces go in his mouth."

Liam glanced around. "Where is Fiona?"

"She had a half day of school and she went out to Brody and Mary's farm. She spent the afternoon entertaining Elliott so Mary could catch up on some paperwork. They'll bring her home later tonight."

James threw his arms toward Meg. "Mommy."

Riley ruffled his son's hair before handing him over to Meg. Turning his attention to his guests, he motioned with his head. "C'mon in and sit, you two. Supper isn't ready yet. We got a little behind with all the ruckus."

Ellie draped her jacket over the back of the sofa. "Can I help with anything?"

"Thanks, but I have it under control...for the moment." Meg laughed and tickled James's tummy and the baby burst into giggles. "But Riley can take my brother with him to help get the grill ready."

"Maybe we should give them our news first," Ellie said, and glanced at Liam.

Meg looked from one to the other. "More news? Does this mean you two are—"

"The news was from the doctor," Ellie interrupted. She didn't want Meg getting the wrong idea and starting a discussion she had no intention of engaging in.

"Is there something wrong?" Meg adjusted James on her hip. "Guys, you're scaring me."

"No, it's okay." Ellie put a hand over her stomach. "They said the babies are fine."

"Oh, well that's— Wait! Did you say *babies*? As in plural?" Eyes wide, Meg pointed to Ellie's stomach. "You mean…"

"Twins." Ellie couldn't help grinning. She was still riding high, grateful that nothing was wrong. At one point in her life she hadn't been sure she'd be able to have kids at all because of the cancer treatments. At the time of her treatment, being able to get pregnant didn't mean a whole lot but as she got older, having a baby became more important. Now to have two, while daunting, was a real blessing.

Meg shifted James and gave Ellie a one-armed hug. "I'm so happy for you. I know… Well, I just want you to know how happy I am."

When Meg pulled away, Riley gave Ellie a hug. "Congratulations."

"And you, too, bro." Meg gave Liam a quick hug. "Leave it to Liam to try to outdo me."

"I told you she would say that!" Liam scowled at his sister.

Meg sniffed and stuck her nose in the air. "Of course you'd have to be having triplets to catch up, or quad—"

"Bite your tongue," Liam grumbled.

Ellie raised her hand and waved it about. "Let's not forget I'm the one carrying these babies."

"Sorry." Meg laughed. "I'll settle for being an auntie twice over."

"Are there any twins in either of your families?" Riley asked.

"None that we know of. I asked my mom when I called to tell her the news," Ellie said.

"I'll bet she's excited," Meg said.

Ellie nodded. "She's already trying to decide what she wants to be called."

Meg laughed. "She may not get a choice. Fiona called Doris 'Mrs. Grampa Mac' for the longest time."

James pointed a finger at Liam. "Meem."

Everyone laughed and James bounced on Meg's hip, as if proud of having made everyone laugh.

Ellie's throat closed up and threatened to choke her. If, in the future, she and Liam weren't a couple, would he bring the children to McBride family gatherings without her? Would her kids come home and tell her how much fun they'd had? She blinked against the sudden burning in her eyes.

"Yeah, your kids seem to have a problem with names," Liam said, but the look he gave James made Ellie's insides feel all squishy. He might not believe it yet, but he was going to make a great dad.

"And I suppose yours won't?" Meg shot back. "You can call him anything you want, sweetie," she told James in a stage whisper. "Maybe when you get older, I can teach you a few other names."

Riley chuckled and clapped a hand over Liam's shoulder. "Maybe you'd better come help me get the steaks on the grill before you dig yourself an even deeper hole."

With the guys outside, Ellie helped Meg get James ready for bed.

"Pretty soon, we'll be doing this together to your kids," Meg remarked as she put pajamas on James.

"I have a feeling I'll be coming to you a lot for advice," Ellie told her.

Meg picked up her sleepy son and cuddled him. "I'll be here for you. You know that, right?"

"Of course, and I know Liam's going to be a great dad." And she did believe it.

"He will," Meg agreed, and gave James a small blanket with satin binding.

"Nigh-nigh." James hugged the ragged blanket to him and stuck his thumb in his mouth.

"Is it always this easy to get him to bed?"

Meg shook her head as she laid him in his crib. "I wish. No, he calls the security blanket his 'night-night.' I put him in his crib a few times when he was actually asking for his blanket."

Ellie went with Meg back to the kitchen to get the rest of the supper ready while the guys finished grilling the steaks.

Ellie was setting the bottles of salad dressing on the table when Liam came back in carrying a plate of foil-wrapped baked potatoes, Riley was behind him carrying a platter of grilled steaks.

"Hope you ladies are hungry," Riley said as he set the platter on the table.

Meg stepped behind Riley and put her arms around his waist. "For you, dear, always."

Liam made gagging sounds. "How are we supposed to eat now?"

"Can't you control him?" Meg asked Ellie.

Ellie shrugged it off with a grin, but her stomach clenched because she longed for what Meg had with Riley. Liam's pallor over having twins was fresh in her mind, along with the way he'd been fake-smiling on the porch. She needed a relationship that could withstand whatever life threw at them. Was that asking too much?

With a scrape of chairs, they all sat down and began dishing out the food.

"Will you be staying in your current apartment once the babies are born?" Meg asked as she passed the bowl of salad.

Ellie was hyperaware of Liam next to her. "For now. But twins changes things a bit. I had thought I could squeeze a crib into my place...but two?"

She was aware of him tensing and she rushed on, "I definitely want to look for a place in Loon Lake. Staying here is important to me."

In her peripheral vision she saw Liam press his lips together but didn't say anything.

Meg snagged a steak and put it on her plate. "Wouldn't it be awesome if you could buy that house next door?"

"But the property isn't for sale," Riley pointed out as he passed the platter of potatoes.

Meg nodded. "I know, but the owner has had trouble keeping it consistently rented. I'm not sure why."

"That's easy," Liam said. "It's because they have to live next to you, sister dear."

Meg pulled a face. "If you think you're safe because you're on the other side of the table, think again."

"Riley, have you no control over your wife?" Liam joked as he opened the foil on his baked potato.

Riley leaned over and kissed his wife. "Happy wife. Happy life. Right, dear?"

"Jeez, you've got him brainwashed," Liam grumbled, but he was grinning.

"Maybe he'd be interested in a long-term rental." Ellie put butter and sour cream on her potato. "Do you have his contact information?"

"I can call the agent. I think I still have her information somewhere from when I used to clean cottages between rentals," Meg told her.

"Thanks. I'd appreciate that." Ellie knew it was a long shot, but it was worth it to get in touch with the owner. Living next to Meg and Riley would be wonderful. Her children could grow up together with their cousins, as she had.

The table fell silent while everyone started eating.

"Are you here for three days now?" Riley looked across the table at Liam.

Liam shook his head. "Nah, I have to head back tonight."

"You do? Why?" Ellie chewed on her lower lip. She'd assumed Liam would be spending his off time with her. Didn't she have a right to expect that, after the news they'd just received? It wasn't every day you found out you were going to be parents to twins. She wanted to talk about it, maybe make some plans or even argue over names, something for him to show her he was in this with her. She blinked back tears. *Hormones*, she told herself.

His gaze searched hers. "Nick worked my part-time shift today and I promised to work his tomorrow."

She met his gaze and forced a smile. "I'm so glad you could come for the appointment today, but I hate that you have to drive back tonight already."

"It's okay. It was totally worth it." He touched her arm.

"Now who is making the googly eyes." Meg *tsk*ed. "But you're forgiven because finding out you're going to be a dad twice over doesn't happen every day."

Liam's knee was bouncing up and down under the table and Ellie gently laid her hand on it. When he looked at her, she whispered, "My turn to be the calm one. Remember we said we wouldn't both freak out at the same time?"

The wink he gave her said he understood what she was doing and he put his hand over hers and squeezed, but it was as if he'd had his hand around her heart.

She blinked to clear her vision. She'd fallen in love with Liam. Sure, she hadn't had far to go, but now it was like a neon sign blinking in her head.

She swallowed, glancing around the table. What would happen to her if she moved to Boston and left behind her support system? And if she stayed in Loon Lake, could her and Liam's tenuous relationship withstand the stress of long distance? What if her cancer returned? Her heart clenched. What would happen to her children? Would another fight for her life cast a pall over this family as it had hers? Or, unlike hers, would they rally around and wrap her and the twins in their warmth?

Chapter Fourteen

Ellie rubbed her back as she left the ER after her shift. Three days had passed since she'd seen Liam and she missed him. Ever since he found out about the babies a few weeks ago, they had been spending more time together. But talking over the phone wasn't the same. She stretched her neck, trying to work out the kinks. If she was this tired and sore now, what was going to happen over the next few months? The exhaustion should ease up in the second trimester but carrying twins had to be tiring, regardless of the month. What did she have at home to make for supper? She had to eat and she had to eat right, but sometimes she was too tired to go home and do much more than make a peanut-butter-and-Marshmallow-Fluff sandwich.

She and Liam had spoken every night since he'd left. They made small talk, and every night she stopped short of admitting her love. If she said the words, put them out there, would he use them to get her to move to Boston? Would he think she said them to wrangle a proposal or him uprooting his life? She didn't know the answer so she bit her tongue and didn't say anything.

In the corridor, she looked up and saw Liam leaning against the nurses' station. Surprise had her halting mid-stride. He was chatting up the nurses, who looked enraptured by whatever story he was telling. Before she could decide if she should be jealous, he glanced over and a huge grin split his face when he spotted her. The smile, the glint in his eyes, were for her and that knowledge filled her. She felt lighter in spite of her exhaustion.

"Sorry, ladies, but it looks like my date has arrived," he said, and stepped toward her.

Ellie said goodbye to the nurses and fell into step beside Liam as they left the hospital.

"What's this about me being your date?" She asked, torn between the prospect of going out with Liam or putting her feet up in front of the television. At this time of year it was dark when she left the ER, and going home suited her.

"I was talking about feeding you," he said, and stopped under a humming sodium vapor lamp near her car.

She looked up at him in the yellowish glow from the lights. "That sounds lovely but I confess I was looking forward to going home and not moving for at least twenty-four hours."

Would he take that as a rejection? She shivered and pulled her light jacket closer around her. The temperature had dropped along with the sun.

He put his arm around her shoulders and pulled her

against his chest. "No problem. I brought things with me. We can go to your place and I'll cook while you put your feet up."

"I can't tell you how amazing that sounds." She burrowed closer to his warmth and rubbed her cheek against the soft cotton of his sweatshirt. He smelled like clean laundry.

"What were you planning on having if I hadn't shown up?" he asked, his voice rumbling in his chest.

"My old standby. A Fluffernutter," she said, referring to her craving for a peanut-butter-and-marshmallow sandwich. She pulled away enough to look up at him.

He quirked an eyebrow and his lips twitched. "On the appropriate whole-grain bread?"

"Um…" She stared at her feet.

He clicked his tongue against his teeth. "Shame on you, Ellie Harding. After all that grief you gave me."

She shrugged. "I know, but it's not the same if it's not on white bread."

"Well, if you can see your way clear to eat healthy, I brought stuff to make a stir-fry."

"That sounds wonderful. Thank you."

"Don't thank me until you taste it." He cleared his throat. "And I brought something special but you gotta eat the healthier stuff first."

"What? Are you practicing saying dad stuff?"

He laughed. "I have to start somewhere."

"About this dessert. Did you buy it or—"

He held up a finger. "I'm not saying anything except maybe a certain bakery might be involved."

She cuffed him on the shoulder. "Don't tease if you can't deliver."

"Wouldn't dream of it." He kissed the top of her head. "And believe me when I say I can deliver."

She rubbed her slightly rounded stomach. "I know you can."

"C'mon. Let's get you home so you can relax while I make supper."

"You must be tired, too, if you just came off shift."

"Yeah, but I wasn't on my feet the entire time like you and I'm not carrying around two extra people."

"But at the moment your turnout gear weighs more than these two." She pointed to her stomach.

"True, but I get to take it off at some point."

"You got me there." She laughed and rubbed her belly. "If they're wearing me out now, I can't imagine what it'll be like once they're born. I watch Mary's Elliott running around and I can't imagine two doing that at the same time."

"Just remember, you're not in this alone." He met her gaze. "You know that right?"

"Yes, I know that." She did, but part of the time he'd be nearly two hundred miles away. She didn't voice her thoughts. A lot of women had it worse. Meg had been alone until Riley returned from Afghanistan, and Mary had been a single mother with no help until she'd met Brody and they fell in love. Unlike Riley, who hadn't even known about his daughter for years, or Roger, who had rejected Mary and his son, Liam was willing to be involved. Sure, she'd vowed to live her life out loud, but there was that sticky thing called pride. Their children would tie her to Liam for a lifetime, regardless of whether or not they were a couple. If she admitted her feelings and he didn't return them, he might pity her.

She'd had enough of being pitied to last her a lifetime. It was one of those things that eroded self-esteem.

"Okay, let's get you home, warmed up and fed."

Liam followed Ellie to her place, the bags from the Pic-N-Save on the passenger seat. Before going to the hospital, he'd stopped at the local supermarket for ingredients. He wasn't much of a cook but he could do a simple stir-fry and rice. Glancing at the white bakery box with its bright blue lettering on the passenger-side floor, he grinned.

He pulled in behind Ellie's car and cut the engine. Scooping up the box, he stuck it in one of the bags and got out. His chest tightened as he followed her up the stairs. Being back in Loon Lake with her felt comforting, secure. But that was crazy. Why would he need comforting?

Following her into her kitchen, he set the bags on the counter. "Before I forget, someone named Lorena at the Pic-N-Save said to say hi."

Ellie laughed. "Did you tell her you were cooking supper for me?"

"She gave me the third degree as she rang up the stuff. I got the feeling if I said I was cooking for someone else, I was going to be in trouble."

"Small-town life," she said as she took off her jacket. "Let me go change and I'll help."

"Take your time. I got this." He began pulling things out of the bags.

"There's beer in the fridge if you want. Help yourself, I can't drink it," she said, and disappeared down the hallway.

He pulled the rice cooker off the shelf and dumped in

rice and water before plugging it in. Sipping on a long-neck, he began chopping the vegetables. He was slicing the beef when she came back into the kitchen area; when he looked up, his breath hitched in his chest. A strange combination of feelings, a confusing mixture of lust and fierce protectiveness, filled him. He'd experienced both before but never at the same time. This was like a punch to the gut.

"Liam?"

He blinked. "Huh?"

"What can I do?" she asked, frowning when he didn't respond.

"Just stand there and look beautiful." He winced when the casual, teasing tone he was going for fell short.

She sighed and shook her head. "That's hardly productive."

"Then tell me about your day." He poured oil in a pan and adjusted the burner.

She got dishes down and utensils from the drawer, telling him how the EMTs brought in a man having a psychotic episode. "Luckily, Riley and another deputy came in with him."

"Damn." He paused in the middle of adding the vegetables to the pan. He'd heard stories from EMTs about how volatile those situations could get. The thought of Ellie—his Ellie and their babies—caught in the middle of something like that chilled him. "Do you think the ER is the best place for you?"

She set the plates and utensils on the counter with a clatter. "What's that supposed to mean?"

"I know how these situations can go bad. You could've been hurt trying to defuse it." He stirred the vegetables and removed them from the pan once they'd started to soften.

She put her hand over her stomach. "These babies are very well protected at the moment."

"I wasn't talking about them. I was talking about you. You, Ellie, *you*." He pointed at her to emphasize his point, adding the thinly sliced meat to the pan to brown.

"I'm an adult. I don't need someone hovering."

"Since when is being concerned about your safety hovering?" He recalled the time Meg told him how Ellie had gotten beaned by a foul ball during a game to raise money for new water and ice rescue equipment for the EMTs. He took a sip of his beer and put the vegetables back in the pan with the meat. "And should you be playing softball?"

"Softball? It's October. What are you on about it?" She planted her hands on her hips and glared at him. "Oh, wait, I get it. We wouldn't even be having this conversation if I wasn't pregnant, would we?"

The rice cooker clicked from Cook to Warm. He shook his head. "I can't answer that because you are pregnant."

"I assure you, pregnant or not, I can and do take care of myself. I don't need you—"

He turned the burner off and put the meat and vegetables on a platter. "Your supper is ready. We should eat before it gets cold."

She opened her mouth and closed it again. He set the hot pan in the sink where it sizzled when the faucet dripped. With a strangled sound she went to him and put her arms around his waist, pressing her front to his back.

He grabbed her hands in his and turned around, putting her hands back at his waist, and held them there.

She looked up at him. "Why are we arguing?"

He shook his head. "I'm sorry if I worry about you. And I mean *you*. I'm not saying I'm not concerned over the babies, but it's you I think about, Ellie."

"That's good because I think about you, too, Liam." She gave him a squeeze. "And I appreciate you making me a healthy supper."

"Better than a peanut-butter sandwich?"

"Much."

"You haven't tried it yet." He wasn't much of a cook, but stir-fry was pretty easy and healthy.

After eating seated side by side at the breakfast bar, Ellie insisted on cleaning up while he found them something to watch on TV. He decided not to argue with her. Since he didn't do much of the cooking at the firehouse, the guys usually put him on cleanup.

Taking a seat on the couch, he picked up Ellie's pregnancy book from the cushion next to him. He opened the book to the place she had bookmarked.

"Ellie?" His voice sounded strained to his own ears.

She had a bookmark on the chapter about engaging in sex during the different stages of pregnancy. Well, well, well. So, did Ellie have this on her mind? Or was she simply reading the book cover to cover and happened to stop there?

"Ellie?"

"Hold your horses. I'm coming." She came into the living area carrying the bakery box and napkins. Her gaze went to the book in his hand and she stopped short, eyes wide, cheeks pink.

He held up the book. "Interesting reading."

She put the box of cannoli on the coffee table and sat down next to him on the sofa. "I'll take that."

"But I'm not done reading this fascinating chapter yet," he said, and winked.

She tried to pry the book out of his hands, but he was holding on tight.

"I think it's important we read this together. You know, share *all* aspects."

"That's because you're reading the chapter about sex."

"We could read it together," he offered.

She narrowed her eyes. "Just this one? Or all of it?"

"I guess if I was there for the good stuff, I should be there for the…uh, other stuff. Huh?" Leaving Ellie alone to handle all of this would be unforgivable and he liked to think he was better than that.

"Well…" She canted her head to one side as she studied him. "We could start with this particular chapter and then move on to some of the others."

He tossed the book onto the coffee table and jumped up.

She lifted an eyebrow. "No book? Does this mean you're going to wing it?"

His gaze bounced between her and the book. "Is there something special I should know?"

"Not really. I'm not that far along."

That was all he needed to know, as he placed his arm behind her knees and swept her high up into his arms.

"Liam! You're going to hurt yourself."

He grunted and staggered but kept her close in a firm grip. "Now that you mention it…"

"Hey, I haven't gained that much weight, especially with all the nausea."

"If you say so," he teased. He was enjoying the way her eyes sparkled.

"Brat. Put me down," she said, then looped her arms around his neck.

He shook his head as he headed toward the bedroom. "Momentum is on my side."

"Why are you even doing this?" She tightened her hold on him.

"What? You saying you aren't impressed?"

"Maybe if you weren't grunting so much."

He stepped into the bedroom and set her down gently. Straightening up, he put his hands on his back and made an exaggerated groaning sound.

She studied him with a sly smile. "I guess this means you won't be able to—"

He put his hands around her waist to fit her snugly against him. "Does that seem like I'm incapacitated in any way?"

She put her arms around him and nuzzled his neck. "Hmm… I might need further convincing." She kissed him. "Just to be sure."

"Mmm." He nibbled on her earlobe. "Should we get some of these clothes off?"

"Sounds like a plan," she said and pulled her sweatshirt over her head.

His gaze went to the small swell of her stomach. His babies were in there. Without conscious thought, he dropped to his knees and pressed his cheek against the taut skin.

Her hands were in his hair, her nails grazing his scalp as he put his arms around her. The moment might have started as sexy teasing but this was suddenly something more. He searched for words, but the tangle of emotions inside him prevented them from forming.

Her fingers tightened in his hair. "Liam?"

He might not have the words but he could show her what she meant to him.

Rising, he took her hand and led her to the bed, where he quickly disposed of the rest of her clothing.

He caressed her breasts and the areas around her nipples. "Have these gotten darker?"

"Yeah, it's increased pigmentation from…" She swallowed audibly. "Sorry, TMI?"

"You know I'm a sucker for nurse speak." He grinned, then sobered. "You're beautiful, Ellie."

She looked up at him. "And you have too many clothes on."

He reached around her and pulled the covers back. "Get in and I'll take care of that."

He left his clothes in a pile and slipped into bed, taking her into his arms.

Unlike the first time, when they'd both been so eager, he took this slow to demonstrate how much she meant to him. Even if he hadn't said the words.

Afterward, Liam settled her against him and rested his cheek against her silky hair. They worked as a couple and he dared to think about their future. Together.

Chapter Fifteen

Ellie stepped out of the shower the next morning still glowing from the previous night's lovemaking. Dared she hope they had a future together? She smiled to herself as she grabbed a towel from the rack. He might not have come out with the words she longed to hear, but then neither had she.

Liam was taking her to Aunt Polly's, a local restaurant known for its pancakes. Maybe after that she'd—

All thoughts scattered as she felt a slight swelling under her left arm. She shook her head and swallowed back nausea. A swelling where the axillary lymph node was located wasn't good.

Of course there could be any number of non-lethal explanations but her mind insisted on taunting her with cancer. Fighting the urge to curl up in the fetal position on the floor, she wrapped herself in her ER nurse persona and called to Liam.

He popped his head in the doorway and his eyes widened and a grin spread across his face. His smile was her undoing and she choked back a sob.

"Ellie, my God, what is it? What's wrong?" He stepped inside her small bathroom.

"It's here." She lifted her left arm.

"What? What's there?" He stood in front of her.

"A lump...the axillary lymph node is enlarged," she whispered.

His gaze met hers. "Are you sure?"

"Of course I'm sure," she snapped.

He pulled her into his arms. "I only meant that we shouldn't panic. Maybe you bumped yourself."

"Don't you think I've been through all those excuses already? I think I would have remembered bumping myself under my arm. It's not sore or black and blue like a bruise." She buried her head in his chest while he rubbed her back.

They stood locked in the embrace, the only sound was that of a sports show coming from the television in the other room.

Sighing, she pulled away. "I'll need to get a biopsy."

Liam sucked in his breath. "Okay. Where and when do we get one?"

If only it was that easy... Well, it was, but those were the mechanics. The emotions that went along with it weren't. Especially now with her pregnancy. And Liam. Whatever they had was just beginning. She shook her head. Maybe her parents were right not to want— No! She refused to give in to defeatism. "You make it sound like ordering something off the internet."

His fingers were shaking when he reached out. Using

his thumbs, he wiped the moisture from her cheeks. "I'm sorry. I only meant—"

"No, I'm sorry. I shouldn't take my anger out on you." She sighed. "Let me get dressed and I'll make some calls."

Sometimes being an ER nurse, not to mention a resident of a small town like Loon Lake, paid off. Ellie was able to get a biopsy scheduled for that afternoon with her oncologist.

Liam insisted on taking her to breakfast as planned, telling her sitting around and brooding wasn't doing either one of them any good. She appreciated his attempts at proceeding as normal. At the same time they annoyed her. But she had to eat for the sake of the babies so she agreed.

After the restaurant, Liam drove them to the doctor's office. He was by her side and yet...

She clung to his hand in the waiting room, but thoughts of her parents clamored in her mind. Was this how it started for them?

The oncologist, a kindly man in his fifties, carefully examined a cut on her forearm. "This could be our culprit."

"But it doesn't appear to be infected," Ellie told him.

"And maybe your immune system is doing its job and fighting it off." The doctor pushed his glasses on top of his head as he looked at her. "We'll do some tests just to be certain, but I don't want you to worry. We'll have the official results early next week."

Back at home, Ellie tried to take the doctor's advice and remain optimistic. She pretended to read her textbook while Liam fixed her toilet that kept running.

She'd told him she'd put in a work order with the management company but he'd insisted. Not that she could blame him. Doing busywork was probably his coping strategy.

She heard him on his phone and soon he came out of the bedroom with his duffel bag: the one he used when going back and forth to Boston.

"What's going on?"

He looked up from his phone, a flush rising in his face. "I was asked to take an extra shift."

She'd heard him on the phone, though she hadn't heard it ring. Had he called looking for an excuse to escape? She immediately felt guilty for even thinking he'd do something like that.

He ran his hand through his hair, a muscle ticking in his cheek. "It's my job. Something I will need to support these babies."

"Are you sure you're not taking it to escape?" She hadn't meant to challenge him like that, but it hurt that he'd chosen work over her.

"Escape?" He scowled at her. "What the heck does that mean?"

She scuffed the toe of her sneaker on the rug. "Maybe it means that going to work is preferable to being trapped here with Cancer Girl?"

"Why would you even say something like that?"

"You see how my parents are. My dad used work to escape and look what it did to them."

"We're not your parents."

No, her parents were in a committed relationship.

When she didn't respond, he made an impatient motion with his hand. "The doctor said you won't have test results for three days at least. I'll be back once the shift is done. You make it sound like I'm deserting you."

You are! She swallowed and tried to remain calm but it was getting harder. Was this how her mom felt when her dad buried himself in work? Like he deserted her when she needed him? She resisted the urge to act childish by stamping her feet or using emotional blackmail by crying and carrying on. "You're absolutely right, Liam, but I also can't help feeling abandoned. I'm sorry and it might not be fair, but that's how I'm feeling right now. You didn't even consult me."

"I didn't realize I had to." He rubbed the back of his neck. "I'm going to work, not out partying, for crying out loud."

"I know it's irrational but feelings just are…they don't always subscribe to what's rational." It hurt to have him point out that they didn't even have enough of a relationship that he would consult her.

He heaved a deep sigh. "We're in this together."

She glanced at his duffel sitting by the door. "If you say so."

His gaze followed hers and he frowned.

"Could you have refused?"

"It's my job." He shook his head, his face a blank mask.

"My father had a job, too. I saw what my cancer did to my parents, to their relationship. For a while I blamed myself. I was convinced it was all my fault but now I know better. Cancer happened *to* me. I'm not my disease. And I'm sorry if you can't handle it, but that's not my fault."

"I'm not deserting you, Ellie," he said, and shook his head. "I need a little time and space to process all this."

"And that's fine. I understand that." She stuck out her

chin. "I can give you time and space, but I refuse to be in a relationship with a ghost."

Three hours later, Liam walked into the station with Ellie's words echoing in his head. Leaving Ellie alone while she waited for the biopsy results was a cowardly move. But the emotions he'd been trying to deny had threatened to overcome him, so he'd run. He wouldn't blame Ellie if she hated him. He hated himself. By rules, the department couldn't force him to come back early but he hadn't said no. He hadn't said no because he'd panicked. From the moment he'd walked in on Ellie in the bathroom, he'd been unable to take a deep breath. His insides were a tangled black mass threatening to choke him. It was his ma, and to a lesser degree his friend and mentor Sean, all over again. He was going to lose Ellie and it was going to hurt more than the other two combined.

He went about his duties at the house by rote, his mind refusing to be calmed by the familiar routines.

Had he honestly believed being away from Ellie would make his black mass of emotions hurt less, make the panic disappear? Instead, being away increased the pain a thousand times over. He called to check in and they engaged in what could only be described as a stilted conversation.

Had he made the biggest mistake of his life by leaving?

He shook his head and threw the chamois cloth over his shoulder and stood back to check the shine on the engine he'd been polishing instead of watching a movie with the other guys.

"Chief wants to see you, McBride."

Liam nodded and tossed the chamois to the probie. "Have at it, Gilman."

What could the chief want? He hovered in the doorway to the office. "You wanted to see me?"

Al Harris stood up and held out his hand across the desk. "Let me be the first to congratulate you, Captain McBride."

It took a minute for the words to penetrate. Captain? Him? He'd done it. He made captain at a younger age than his dad.

He shook Chief Harris's hand and tried to feel something other than numb.

"You don't look like someone who has just accomplished a lifelong goal."

Yeah, why didn't he feel more? Sure, he was proud, but even that was fleeting.

"Okay, now, sit your ass down, McBride, and tell me what the hell is wrong."

The next morning, after his shift, Liam went straight to the white, Cape Cod–style home where he'd grown up and his dad still lived with Doris. He always had mixed feelings returning here. In the beginning, it was comforting because he felt his ma's presence. But that had faded and this was now as much Doris's home as it had been Bridget McBride's.

He rang the bell and waited. The rhododendrons his ma had loved so much needed trimming, but it was too late in the season to do it now. She had taught him they needed pruning immediately after they finished blossoming or you'd be cutting off next year's flower buds. Helping her trim them one day had actually been punishment for a transgression he no longer remembered.

He rubbed his chest, recalling how, that same day, she'd bought him a treat from the ice-cream truck and let him eat it before supper. She'd winked and laughed as they sat on the front steps eating their ice cream.

Doris answered the door, surprise and pleasure evident in her expression. "Liam, it's good to see you. C'mon in."

"Hi, Doris, is my dad here?" He gave Doris a quick hug and she kissed his cheek.

"Yeah, he's out back if you want to go on through the house." She stepped aside. "Can I get you anything? We've already had breakfast but I can get you coffee or a muffin."

"I'm good. Thanks. I can't stay long."

"How's Ellie doing?" Doris asked as they went through the kitchen to the back deck.

"She's doing good." Other than a cancer scare and being left to face it alone, but he wasn't about to get into all that right now. "She's looking forward to the second trimester which is supposedly much easier."

"Normally, yes, it is but I've never been pregnant with twins."

"That makes two of us."

She laughed and opened the door. "Tim? Liam's here to see you."

His dad paused in the middle of raking leaves and waved. Liam went across the deck and down the steps.

"So glad you're here. I wanted to congratulate you myself, Captain." His dad stuck out his hand and pulled him in for an awkward shoulder hug.

"You knew?" Liam asked when they pulled apart.

"I may have heard something." Mac said and grinned.

"I haven't been gone from the department for that long. I still know a few people."

"Thanks." Liam cleared his throat.

Mac frowned. "What's wrong? You don't look like a man who has just gotten what he's been working toward for years."

Liam swallowed. How was he supposed to explain how hollow he felt? Sure, he was proud of making captain but after running out on Ellie the way he had, all he could think about was how much he'd hurt her. *Selfish much, McBride?* Why was he thinking about his own pain? He should be there comforting Ellie, helping her deal with her pain. Had he thought that, if he wasn't there, he'd be able to better handle the fear?

"What's on your mind, son?" His dad leaned against the rake.

Liam explained what had happened. He hated admitting his cowardice but he couldn't hide from it any longer. "Ellie found a lump and I shut down. I'm not sure I have the kind of courage you had to open myself again to love someone I might lose."

"It's not courage." Mac shook his head.

"Then what is it?"

"It's finding something that's more important to you than your fear." Mac met Liam's gaze. "Is Ellie that important thing for you, son?"

Ellie retrieved her jacket and closed her locker with a sigh. Liam had barely been gone twenty-four hours and the pain of missing him still throbbed, an ache that wouldn't go away. He'd texted earlier in the day but had been vague when she'd asked if he was coming back today, saying he would try but had some business to take care of first.

Had she pushed him too hard? Demanded too much? She pulled the jacket on and grabbed her purse. Maybe she wanted more than Liam could give. That wasn't his fault, nor was it hers. It was just…sad.

She stretched her neck, trying to muster up some energy as she dug around in her purse for her keys. Trudging out to her car, she glanced up and stopped in her tracks. Liam was leaning against her car, arms crossed, head bowed.

"Liam?" She continued walking toward him.

His head snapped up and he blinked, searching her face. "Hey."

She stopped when she was right in front of him. "Is everything okay?"

He reached out and rested his hands on her shoulders, gently massaging them. "It is now. Have you had any news yet?"

She shook her head, not trusting her voice. The look shining in his eyes was making something inside her spring to life, something that resembled hope. Hope was dangerous. Hope made you do things, say things. Hope could be devastating, even if you were careful.

He squeezed her shoulders. "We need to talk."

Talk. Yeah, they needed to talk, but for the moment she was relieved to see him. She did her best to tamp down the hope clamoring for freedom. He might want to talk about logistics or shared custody once the babies were born.

He was peering at her expectantly. Right. She hadn't answered him. "Okay. Come back to my place?"

"I have something I want to show you first, if that's okay."

She nodded, still trying to figure out his mood.

He took her hand in his. "Let's take my truck. We can come back for your car."

"W-what did you want to show me?"

"Our future," he said as he opened the passenger door.

Her mouth dropped open and she stared at him. He put his thumb under her chin and closed her mouth before giving her a chaste kiss.

"Liam, what in the world is this all about?" She still couldn't figure out his mood. He seemed a combination of excited and apprehensive. Or maybe she was crazy. Pregnancy hormones—times two!—were making her giddy.

"I need your opinion on something." He slipped behind the wheel but turned toward her instead of starting the engine. "I need to apologize for taking off on you. I shouldn't have done that."

"And I shouldn't have accused you of abandoning me." She sucked in a breath. "I may have overreacted."

He took her hand and brought it to his lips. "I should have explained myself better. I regret how I handled things with my mom, and yet I was doing the same thing with you."

"I know of a good support group for grieving families, if you're interested." She squeezed his hand. "Maybe we could both benefit from it, but first, I have to see what you want to show me."

He dropped her hand and started the truck. Although he didn't say anything else, he glanced at her several times as he drove across town. Clearing his throat, he made the turn into the Coopers' long driveway.

"Why are you taking me to your sister's house?"

"Meg's isn't the only house here." Liam pulled his truck up to the cottage-style home across the yard from his sister's house. Putting his truck in Park, he shut off the engine. Jumping out of the pickup, he hustled around to her side.

"Careful," he said as he helped her out. "This would have been better in the daylight but I couldn't wait until tomorrow."

She stared up at him, puzzled. "I don't understand what we're doing here."

He ran his finger under the collar of his jacket. "Like I said... I was picturing our future."

Her heart stuttered, then pounded so hard she was surprised it didn't jump out of her chest. She glanced down, expecting to see it flopping like a fish on the ground.

He made a sweeping motion with his hand to encompass the large, open yard between this house and his sister's. "I see kids—our kids and their cousins—running around this yard. Maybe even a dog of our own chasing after them. Baseball games, touch football, along with some hot dogs and burgers on the grill in the summer."

He turned so he was standing in front of her and took both her hands in his and cleared his throat. "I love you, Ellie Harding. No matter what. Now and forever. In sickness and in health. Will you marry me and live here with me?"

Her mouth opened and closed like that fish she'd been imagining a few moments ago. "But...but what about your job? Your house in Boston?"

"When Chief Harris called me in to tell me I'd made captain, we—"

"Wait…what?" She took her hand out of his and jabbed him in the shoulder. "You made captain and are just now telling me?"

He shrugged. "It wasn't important."

"How can you say that? Of course that's important."

"Not as important to me as you and our babies. This right here, with you, is what I want. Chief Harris is always asking me when I was going to sell him my three-decker and yesterday I told him to make me an offer. I tracked down the owner of this one and he's willing to sell. So whaddaya say, should we make an offer on this place?"

Overcome with emotion that her dreams were coming true, all she could do was shake her head and choke back a sob. All the color drained from Liam's face and she realized he'd misunderstood. She threw herself at him and began blubbering incoherently.

He held her and rubbed her back. Finally she raised her head. "I love you, too," she choked out.

He grinned, his eyes suspiciously shiny. "So, that's a yes?"

She nodded vigorously.

"Wait…" He set her away from him. "I was supposed to do this first."

He reached into his pocket and pulled out a ring. "It was my mother's. My dad gave it to me today. Will you marry me?"

"Yes."

He slipped the ring on her finger and kissed her. She pulled away first.

"I haven't gotten the all clear yet on the biopsy," she warned.

"And I don't have another job yet," He brushed the hair back from her face and dried her damp cheeks. "We'll work out all the details."

"McBride, are you telling me I just accepted a proposal of marriage from someone who is unemployed?"

"You're not going to let a little thing like that stop you, are you?" He frowned, then laughed. "I'm still employed and will have to divide my time for now. While I was waiting for you to get off work, my dad called to let me know the state fire investigator's office here in Vermont was looking for someone."

"Would that kind of work make you happy?"

He pressed his hand against her stomach. "I have all I need right here with you and these guys to make me happy."

"What if I don't get good news from the biopsy?"

"Then we'd deal with it together. I'm not going anywhere. Ellie. You've got the entire McBride clan with you, for whatever comes along."

Epilogue

Six months later

"Hey, bud, you didn't have to make this a competition to see if you could get here before your sister or your cousin," Liam whispered to his newborn son, Sean, who was staring up at him. He turned to the similar bundle cradled close on his other side. "And you, Miss Bridget, you'll be keeping all the boys in line, won't you?"

His newborn daughter twitched in her sleep and Liam leaned down to press a kiss to the top of her head. He glanced up at Ellie, his precious wife, who, despite the mad dash to the hospital several weeks early, lay smiling at him.

"You done good, Harding," he said, blinking back a sudden burning in the back of his eyes. "Or should I say 'McBride'? You're one of us now, Ellie."

"You didn't do so bad yourself, McBride," she whispered and sniffled, her lips quivering.

He swallowed and his smile faltered as he adjusted his precious bundles in his arms. "I hope both of you heard that, because it might be the last time she says something like that."

Ellie wiggled her feet under the covers. "Meg is going to be so jealous I can finally see my feet."

Liam shook his head and glanced down at his son. "Looks like the women in this family are just as competitive."

"At least now I can put on my own shoes." Ellie yawned and lay back against the covers. "Good thing you and Riley finished the nursery."

Liam nodded in agreement. The last few months had been hectic, what with a wedding, selling one house and buying another, and starting his new job as a state fire investigator. But he wouldn't have traded one minute of it for anything. Even having to wait for Ellie's biopsy results had been worth the nerves. And the celebration when the all clear came back had been—he grinned at the babies in his arms—best kept private.

"What are you grinning about over there?"

He shifted the babies and stood up. "I was thinking how lucky I am and how I can't wait to start this phase of our lives."

She lifted an eyebrow. "This phase?"

Coming to stand next to the bed, he gently lowered their son into Ellie's waiting arms. "Changing diapers, chasing rug rats around the yard, drying tears and retrieving Barbies from toilets."

Ellie yawned again as she cuddled her son. "I guess I better rest up. Sounds like I'm going to be busy."

Liam leaned over and kissed his wife. "I was talking about us. Ellie, we're in this together. For today and always. No matter what the future brings it's you and me together, sharing everything. Partners."

"Intimate partners," she said and laughed.

As always, her laughter drew him close and filled his heart and world with love.

* * * * *